WHISPERS ACROSS A SEA

WHISPERS ACROSS A SEA

A Novel of Victorian Ireland

Christina Holloway

Published by CAH Publishing, Stanford, California
www.christinahollowayauthor.com

Edited and designed by Girl Friday Productions
www.girlfridayproductions.com

Cover design: Sunny Scott
Project management: Reshma Kooner
Editorial production: Janice Lee
Image credits: Christina Holloway family photo
(front cover), Sunny Scott (back cover)

ISBN (paperback): 979-8-9898260-0-1
ISBN (ebook): 979-8-9898260-1-8

Library of Congress Control Number: 2024901491

First edition

I dedicate this story to my family. Those who lit the path to where we are today, through many generations, and those who will follow.

And to my husband, children, and grandchildren, for the joy of shared love, wisdom, and strength that comes from a family growing, changing, and learning from one another and the world that surrounds us.

WHERE IT ALL BEGAN

In a way the past is woven into the present—
not just lined up with it but braided in.

Nathan Englander

It was a rare rainy day in California, one that dampened, rinsed, and greened everything and got Granny to thinking of her home in Ireland. "Christina, get me a cloth from the cupboard, will you, dear?" she asked. My grandmother sat in a very low prayer chair, meant for kneeling, she had purposely selected to put her closer to the ground to spare her back as she stooped over a dust-covered carton. We had just wrestled the box from the small attic in her duplex in Westwood Village, dust flying in the air as we awkwardly placed it with an uneven thump on the thin Oriental rug in the living room. Granny Lucie shifted uncomfortably on her chair, trying to find a good position; her knees were too high and her dress was tautly stretched over them. I handed her the cloth.

"I am such an Irish housekeeper," she said, wiping the box. "Dust everywhere and I don't really mind. Dear, did you know dust is what we are made of? Ashes to ashes and dust to dust. They always say that at church burials, so it must be true." I had no idea what she was talking about. She blew the last bits of dust off and opened the box. On top were yellowed linen napkins and an embroidered tablecloth with some dark, odd-shaped stains. Underneath that layer, we uncovered a jumble of eyeglasses, passports, quill pens, inkwells, letters on fragile onion-skin paper that looked like they would crumble if we touched them, tiny leather-bound books with "Thoughts for the Day" embossed on each cover, photos, sketches, and paint boxes. Granny let me touch anything I wanted, paying no attention to me as she put her glasses on and began to read the fragile letters of her relatives, the Youngs. She smiled, making soft murmuring sounds and saying, "Ah yes, my dear aunts and my grandfather Thomas. Oh God, they were so good to me."

On this wet, blustery day in October of 1944, I was six years old and living with my seventy-year-old grandmother, Lucie Mary Franz. My mother was in the tuberculosis sanitarium, and my brother and I had been "farmed out" to family. In those days, people with TB languished in special sanitariums for years of bed rest, the only presumed cure. My mother had left when I was three. Our father had taken a job in Northern California at the University of California, Berkeley, and could not take us with him, so my mother's family stepped in.

Delving into the dusty old box was Granny Lucie's idea of a grand adventure into the past, something to keep me occupied while stuck in the house. I loved every minute of it. That is the day when my fascination began with the story of her life and her mother's Irish family, who had loved and raised her.

Some of the stories she told me that day I'd heard before, stories she'd told time and again while she showed the paintings and other pieces in her home to whoever was lucky enough to be her current company. Her home was chock-full of furniture, art, silver, dishes, and boxes of memorabilia that kept coming out of the attic. When asked "Where did all this come from?" she would lean back in her chair and sigh. "It's such a long story but a good one, with a good ending. Suffice it to say these people gave me a home and safety when I needed it. I was a little girl and this new home, my mother's family home, was in Ireland, far away from where I was born in Canada."

That rainy day when I asked her the same question, she waved her hand and said, "Let's just look at what's in here now. When I write my family story, or *you* write my story, I do think it should begin with my beloved grandfather Thomas, though. They were all special, but he was in a category all his own."

She never got to the writing. She died five years later, in 1949. So I have written her story, and instead of beginning with her grandfather Thomas, I began it with my beloved grandmother Lucie. It is a family story and an Irish story, inspired by Lucie's retold memories and the many, many letters, diaries, photos, and paintings I have from the Young family. I further built the retelling of their story around what was happening in their world in the late 1800s. It is fair to say I've written a novel based on history rather than a true piece of my family history. The family members are real: my grandmother Lucie; her grandfather Thomas; her aunts, Elfie and Frances; her mother, Lily, and father, James; as well as Lucie's brothers, Hugh and Knox; and her grandmother Eliza, but I have only discerned and imagined their attitudes and thoughts. Other characters, both Irish and Anglo-Irish, I brought in to enrich and deepen their story and give it a societal context. I blended all their stories to reflect what I've learned of the broader and dynamic environment of Ireland as the nineteenth century was waning and the twentieth dawning.

For me, though, *Whispers Across a Sea* is my grandmother's story, Lucie Mary's story, more than anyone else's. She is the one who brought the rich trove of family possessions from Ireland to America and wove for her descendants the story of her youth and her Irish heritage, using these trea-sured pieces as touchstones. She held our attention with the tragedy of her mother's death when she was just nine years old and her voyage at almost eleven across the Atlantic to be taken in by her mother's family in Dublin. It was dramatic and sad no matter how many times we heard it. Yet as we listened, we knew that in spite of her youthful trauma, she had received from this family what she needed: a safe home where she found love, wisdom, and a place to mature into a healthy woman. She so often said, "It's so true, they saved my life." Lucie Mary em-bodied the importance of family loyalty and support to per-sonal resilience and survival, because she had lived it. These qualities she passed on to us by example as she cared for us. She understood how difficult it was for us to be separated from our mother but that it also could be the making of us. How many times did she stand with her hands on my shoulders, look me straight in the eye, and say, "Christina, stand on your own two feet!"?

As I walk through my home every day, my grandmother and my Anglo-Irish ancestors speak to me through their pos-sessions, and now, with *Whispers*, I hope I have spoken for them.

Christina Ahlm Holloway
Stanford, California
2023

PART ONE

THE RETURN

CHAPTER 1

THE LAST TRIP HOME

Ireland
1920
Lucie

Lucie stepped off the gangplank at Cork Harbor, tucking her head protectively against what might lie ahead. Her husband had cautioned her to be careful when she landed—not about pickpockets or getting lost but about the political situation in Ireland.

"But, Shepherd," she had said, "there's always been a political situation in Ireland, and I've always been fine. We all were."

"It's different now, my dear," he'd persisted. "The British have instated emergency military powers to tamp down all conflicts supporting Irish independence. The point is, Lucie, the Ireland you left as a young woman is not the same Ireland you are returning to now. It's 1920, not 1894."

Lucie made her way slowly through the mix of passengers

and their welcoming families toward the street where a porter waited for her with her luggage and a carriage that brought her to Kent Station just in time for the next train to Dublin's Knightsbridge Station. Shepherd's warning about uprisings and the presence of the military came back to her as she stepped into a cab that would make its way through Dublin toward Rathmines. To her relief, Lucie saw only a more crowded version of the city she loved and no sign of unrest.

When she arrived at Rathmines, the suburb seemed as safe and calm as she remembered. Weariness came over her as she watched the driver carry her bags up the stairs to the porch and then disappear with his cab back down the road toward the city. "Up you go, Lucie," she said with false enthusiasm. This would be her final visit to the home that had been her whole world for nine important years. When this chapter was complete, the book on the Young family in Ireland would close. There would be no reason to return.

At the top of the stairs, Lucie hesitated. She peered through the window by the door, but the house was dark inside. "Of course it's dark," she chided herself. "No one lives here anymore." The thought of what lay ahead sat like an enormous weight holding her in place.

Her fingers burrowed through her crowded purse until they touched silk threads. Aunt Frances had purchased the green tassel on a trip to Italy as a fob for the house keys, a bygone symbol of authority. Well before Grandfather Thomas passed, Aunt Frances had become the *chatelaine*, the mistress of the house. Lucie could still see the wispy strands dangling from the lower corner of her aunt's skirt pocket as she went about her duties. Aunt Elfie had held the keys briefly after Frances passed. Now they were Lucie's, along with the deed to the house and its contents. She freed the keys from her purse and brushed the soft tassel against her cheek, then looked up. Before her was the massive oak front door. A rap of its solid brass lion-head knocker would echo all the way to the third floor. But there was no one left to hear it, and the formerly polished lion was dull with tarnish.

Lucie wondered what other tasks her aunt, in her dotage, had let go by the wayside. *Life turns quickly when you aren't watching,* she thought. Two months earlier, her connection to Ireland had felt steadfast. Her Irish past was something she'd felt would always be with her and so not in need of tending, until one morning when, through the kitchen window of her home in Washington, DC, she saw a young man in a baggy inmate's uniform run across the wide expanse of lawn between the house and the hospital. *What can it be now?* she'd worried. Occasionally one of the more stable patients delivered messages, one of the many quirks of living in the superintendent's house on the grounds of St. Elizabeths Hospital. *Honestly,* she thought, *who but us would live next door to an insane asylum?*

Seeing the man approach had made Lucie anxious. Their daughters were at school and she was alone in the house, but she'd opened the door concerned only about the news she was about to receive. The young man stood breathless in front of her, his head oddly shaped, fair hair spiking in unruly directions, and with one meandering eye. "Mrs. Franz," he said in a hushed voice, "the doctor, your husband, ma'am, he told me to bring this to you as quick as possible."

Lucie sat on the bench in the foyer. She couldn't remember accepting the envelope or closing the door after the man left. The telegram from her aunt's solicitor in Ireland remained in her hands a long time as she read and reread the message:

REGRET TO INFORM STOP ALFREDA
SOPHIA YOUNG DIED APRIL 25 STOP
NIECE LUCIE MARY NIVEN FRANZ NEXT
OF KIN AND SOLE HEIR STOP

"Aunt Elfie's gone?" she said at last. The familiar yew wood bench, worn from use by over two generations of Youngs, cradled her as she wept. It had been the family pew at the Holy Trinity Church in Rathmines, sent to her just two years earlier by her aunts when the church interior was being refurbished. Frances had died soon after it arrived. Now Elfie . . . How strange it had felt to read that telegram where she'd once sat between her two aunts as a young girl. With Elfie's death, there was only herself to remember RockView and the family who had lived there.

Now that she was standing in front of the old house, she couldn't bring herself to go in. She turned from the door and took a deep breath. The air smelled fresh with the earth's moisture released by the afternoon sun. *It must have rained earlier in the day*, she thought. Lucie took in the sight of the surrounding field and outcroppings of rock, each exactly as she remembered, rising out of the high grass.

Her grandfather had particularly loved this time of day. "Note the crisp definition, the soft-filtered light through the trees," he would say, hoping to pass on his artist's eye to his granddaughter. She had been too young then to appreciate his words, preferring to run into the fields and lean against those big rocks, letting her body absorb their stored heat. RockView had been a perfect name for the house.

Enough, she told herself. Lucie faced the door again, patted the lion, and turned the key in the lock. The fading light behind her softly illuminated the entry as she opened the door. A musty odor hit her nose, and it wrinkled in response. Directly in front of Lucie, her great-grandfather, unconcerned by the stale air, stared at her across time from his portrait on the wall. "Hello, again," she said. "I hope you haven't been too lonely. Though I suppose you have," she added, looking at the large empty coatrack next to the painting. Forty-seven years ago, in 1873, her aunts had turned the first and second floors of the house into the Misses Young School for Girls. A bold move for two young and unmarried Victorian women.

Grandfather Thomas, Lucie had learned, would have preferred his peace and quiet, but Aunts Frances and Elfie had been determined. Lucie was eleven when she had become one of those girls. *What would have happened to me if they hadn't taken their future into their own hands, if the Misses Young School had never existed?* she thought, not for the first time.

Lucie gazed up the staircase to the third floor. *A lot of living has taken place in this big old house,* she thought. As a child, Lucie had once counted all the rooms, including the wide second-floor hallway, a large butler's pantry, and the china closet. Three floors, an attic, and a basement, twenty rooms. *Twenty rooms?* Lucie sighed. *Oh my, how will I sort this all out?*

She began by opening windows on the first floor, beginning with the drawing room, pleased to discover she could still locate the light switches without effort. She climbed the stairs and took a tour of the next two floors, surveying each room briefly, becoming increasingly misty-eyed as she went. Everything was there just as she remembered it, the house a tableau of her family's lives, frozen in time and dust. Lucie was about to dissolve in tears when a familiar Irish lilt came from below her.

"How long have you been here, Lucie girl? I brought dinner for us and a bottle of Bordeaux to ease the pain."

CHAPTER 2

FULL OF THE UNEXPECTED

"Norah! God bless you," Lucie exclaimed, hurrying down the stairs to meet her old friend.

"The door was unlocked. I hope you don't mind me letting myself in."

The two embraced, and Lucie felt her strength return.

In the drawing room, Lucie poured the wine while Norah made a fire. Sitting together on the settee, they sipped the Bordeaux with their feet up on a shared footstool. "Norah," Lucie said, "do you remember Frances and Elfie sitting just like this at the end of the school day?"

Norah lifted her glass and smiled. "And now it is our turn as ladies of the house."

"I brought something for you," Lucie said, reaching inside her purse. She held up the black velvet pouch she'd kept safe all the way across the Atlantic and poured the contents on the table.

"Thomas's good luck piece!" Norah picked up the old coin and placed it flat on the palm of her hand. "It's brought you back to me. It *is* good luck!"

Lucie glanced around the room full of books and furniture, stacks of unsorted papers, and paintings—most of the art by her grandfather. "Maybe I should keep it a while longer, then. I'm going to need all the luck I can get while I'm here," she said. "This is just one of twenty rooms." Lucie swept her hand in an arc at all that surrounded them. "Any chance you're planning on staying awhile?"

"Twenty rooms? Is that all?" Norah asked with a laugh. "Not to worry. Seamus and I agreed I will be here most nights to provide food and fuel." She held up the bottle of wine. "Besides, I am curious. What on earth could your family have hidden in the nooks and crannies of this grand old house?"

— • —

Norah kept her promise and returned to RockView most evenings, often staying overnight and heading off early the next morning. They talked about their husbands and children, but Lucie noticed her friend shared little about her own days at her flower shop in the city, waving questions off with "just the usual" and insisting she was much more interested in catching up with Lucie while "getting on to the packing up." Lucie recalled that Norah stood firm when pushed, so she didn't press her to reveal more. Still, she couldn't help wondering what Norah meant by "just the usual."

With Norah's help, Lucie stacked boxes of bed linens, dishes, and sundries by the front door to be picked up by Holy Trinity Church across the street. After they spent an evening emptying out the old dormitory, the dustbins were overflowing, but the women had salvaged two large boxes of Christmas decorations from the deep dormitory closet to add to the charity pile.

By the third week, Lucie at last opened the door of her Aunt Frances's bedroom. She unlocked her armoire, and the scent of Jean Marie Farina Eau de Cologne wafted over her. *Frances's perfume!* Inside, a neat row of finely tailored clothes filled the wardrobe end to end as if they'd been waiting for her selection. Lucie's fingertips released more of the lemon and rosemary scent as they skimmed across the sleeves and shoulders of fine wools, silks, and cottons. They stopped on an especially soft material. Lucie carefully removed her aunt's silk and cashmere shawl and wrapped the taupe weave around her shoulders like a gentle hug.

Out of the corner of her eye, she spotted a familiar book on the bedside table. "Frances's *Book of Common Prayer*," she said. "I'd forgotten about you." She placed her palm on the hard cover of ivory. *It seems anything but common to me,* Lucie thought, enjoying her own joke. She picked it up and walked to the bookcase. Lifting a photograph off the shelf, she smiled at the image of her parents, their wedding party, and their guests in front of the Holy Trinity vicarage. In her mother's hands was Frances's book, with a spray of jasmine cascading from it. *Not common at all,* Lucie thought again. *This is a family heirloom.* Lucie made a mental note to pack both the book and the photo in her suitcase rather than in a shipping box.

As pleased as she was by these treasures, it wasn't until she opened her aunt's desk that she found her first surprise. "Letters!" she exclaimed. Bundles of letters in neat stacks tied with colored ribbons filled the drawer. The ones bound in yellow ribbon had a London, Ontario, return address printed on the back of the envelopes and the RockView address on the front. Both were written in her mother's handwriting. Untying the bundle, Lucie opened the top letter. The thin, translucent paper made for tough reading, with every fraction of an inch covered in her mother's spidery brown-ink handwriting on both sides and up and down the margins. The date was hard to decipher, but Lucie could see it had been written before she'd been born.

> *After I read him the poem, James teased me,*
> *saying, "You will teach me much but I will*
> *teach you too."*

Lucie pressed the letter to her bosom, imagining her parents as young and playful. Straightening her back, she released some of the gathering tension. So many emotions arose from opening the long-closed doors to her family's lives. She could have happily spent all day reading through the letters, but her sense of practicality told her she should wait until she had more time.

She carefully removed the letters and placed all of them on top of the desk. One heavy cream-colored paper stuck out from the tissue-thin envelopes. She gave it a slight tug, releasing it from the pile. Its crisp folds resisted the reveal. What she saw when she ironed it open with her hand was large, masculine handwriting, bold strokes from a broad-nib pen beneath an important-looking engraved family crest.

> *Headmistress Miss Frances Young*

Lucie laughed as she read. Frances had received a drubbing from an irate father over the girls sketching a nude model!

> *Miss Young, you must know that this "cultural*
> *activity," as you call it, is hardly a suitable*
> *exposure for girls so young.*

Lucie couldn't wait to show the letter to Norah. "A nude model?" They would have a good laugh guessing how the proper Victorian Frances had handled that one. "What is it Grandfather used to say? 'Life is never what you expect . . . and full of the unexpected.'" Lucie refolded the stiff sheet of paper and pocketed it in her apron for her evening show-and-tell. *The model must have been Grandfather's idea,* she told herself. *He was the artist, after all*—though she was beginning to wonder how well she'd known her family.

— ◆ —

When the house became too much for her, Lucie took day trips into Dublin by cab, always alert for signs of protest or violence but never seeing any. On one evening, Norah appeared with a skinned knee. She brushed it off to clumsiness at work when Lucie expressed concern. Relieved it was nothing more, Lucie showed off her own bruises that she'd collected since she arrived.

"Can you imagine what your aunties would think of us?" Norah asked, making them both laugh. "Hardly ladylike!"

Lucie had intended to go through the family bedrooms right at the start. But when she'd peeked inside Aunt Elfie's room, she felt discouraged by what her aunt used to call her "creative mess." Lucie hadn't known where to begin. She left the room alone for weeks until Norah suggested Elfie's letters. "She'd have kept some from your mother as well." Lucie sighed in response, but Norah would not be put off. "You might start there, at least."

Fortified by her friend's encouragement, Lucie went straight to Elfie's bedroom the next morning and opened the door. *Mess it is,* she told herself. Inside the top desk drawer, she found the expected, sharpened half pencils, scraps of paper, and a dip pen and well, its ink long since dried. Lucie caught sight of her aunt's signet ring behind the inkwell, along with remnants of red wax. She picked up the etched gold ring, recognizing the delicate ASY design from the tidily opened envelopes in her mother's letter collection back home. Like Frances, Lucie's mother, Lily, had kept each sender's missives in their own orderly stack wrapped with a specific ribbon color. Lucie opened the lower desk drawer. There were Elfie's letters from Lily and others. No sorting or order was apparent. Instead, her aunt had tied them all in one large bundle with grosgrain in blue, Elfie's favorite color. Lucie placed the bundle, unexamined, in the large basket she brought to each room.

She would save every letter she found at RockView. There were certain to be more stories within them that she'd never heard. Not just amusing tales of nude models but intimate secrets between the sisters that had traveled like whispers across a sea, unknown to anyone but them.

There was a lot more to sort through in Elfie's room—she hadn't even opened the wardrobe—but Lucie was expecting a visitor in the afternoon and needed time to straighten the downstairs and prepare the tea. She was starting to close the bedroom door when she spied a familiar object on her aunt's dresser. "Elfie's hair comb!" The Victorian comb her aunt had worn in her thick upswept hair was decorated with inlaid mother-of-pearl—a gift from a man who had planned to marry Elfie. As a child, Lucie had thought a story of lost love incredibly sad and romantic. It had all taken place before she'd first arrived at RockView, and now Lucie wasn't sure she had ever known the details of what went wrong. She slipped the comb into her apron pocket, thinking she might wear it for a social event before she left Ireland, one that called for her to get out of her boring workday housedress. Then she went downstairs.

Lucie recalled Maggie Barrett very well. She had attended the Misses Young School for Girls with Lucie and, if Lucie remembered rightly, was from a highly protected, rather snobbish Anglo-Irish family. When Maggie heard her school chum was in town, she had invited herself over for a "catch-up and a last look at the old place." Not Lucie's favorite, but she was grateful for the company as well as the break from her sorting and clearing. Maggie had barely greeted Lucie at the door before regaling her with harrowing tales of "our Dublin." "Lucie, you're wise to stay right here in Rathmines, especially at night. Unless you're with someone who knows the city, of course. Oh, are we sitting in the drawing room?" she asked, peering into the room off the foyer where Lucie had unpacked and set up the tea service for the occasion. "We were hardly allowed in there when we were girls. How lovely!" She slipped her arm in Lucie's to be led into the room.

"The city is not like when we were girls," Maggie continued once she settled onto the settee. "There are armed paramilitary ruffians. British Black and Tans swaggering all about the city these days."

Lucie handed Maggie a cup of tea and sat down across from her. "I've been to the city on my own, Maggie, and I've seen none of what you describe."

"Then you've been lucky," Maggie answered, putting down her cup and picking up a fork and a plate with a slice of chocolate cake. "To be honest Lucie, I have most things brought to me at the house now. Black and Tans are not choirboys. They are here to crush the Irish who are still hoping for Home Rule, or to rule themselves, I guess. I can never keep these things straight. And the Irish don't seem to care who might get in their way."

Lucie was unable to hide her surprise. "Norah has never mentioned street violence."

"Well, Norah, being Irish, may be clever about how she goes and where she goes," Maggie said. She placed her hand on Lucie's knee to emphasize her concern. "Trust me, Lucie. Do not go into Dublin, and never after dark. The Irish are under strict curfew, and it is not safe for us either."

Is that why Norah stays with me at night rather than make her way home when Seamus isn't able to pick her up? Lucie wondered. And her skinned knee . . . Had that really been from clumsiness? Lucie shuddered. Shepherd's warnings seemed more accurate than she'd wanted to believe. She was as cocooned in RockView as she had been as a child, with no idea of what was happening around her.

Lucie changed the subject before she could be queried further about Norah. Maggie Barrett did not need to know Norah's business or that she had spent most nights at RockView since Lucie arrived or how much that meant to Lucie. They spent the next hour discussing family and fashion and by late afternoon Lucie was back upstairs in Elfie's room, feeling satisfied she hadn't betrayed Norah in any way. Still, Lucie continued to be bothered by how little she understood of Norah's life. They had been close when they were younger, but Norah had always made it clear, in her own way, that she intended to keep parts of her life to herself. She seemed happiest chatting about their school memories that popped up while she helped Lucie sort through RockView. Lucie would never push her friend, but she was curious. By dinnertime, she found herself listening for the welcome sound of Norah opening the front door. It was a blessing for Lucie, the signal for "time to stop for friendship and refreshment." What was RockView to Norah then? Was it a place of refuge, or was her friend putting herself at risk just by traveling out to Rathmines instead of going straight to her own home? Norah might tell her in her own time but wasn't likely to if Lucie asked.

Despite the nine years between them, their friendship had blossomed as young girls when Norah joined the school as a helper. Outside that cushioned realm, their worlds had been sharply divided, but within RockView they'd come to understand each other, beginning with shared feelings of loss and finding their way through new lives. Norah was Irish, and Lucie's heritage was Anglo-Irish. As a young girl, Lucie hadn't really known what that meant, but Norah had.

Disheartened by the thought of sorting through the rest of Elfie's room on her own, Lucie asked for Norah's help when she arrived that afternoon. Norah disappeared without a word into the kitchen and came out with an opened bottle of wine and two glasses. "Lead on," she said. Lucie laughed and kissed her friend's cheek. Over the course of two long evenings, the two women finished the bedroom, with all but the furniture either packed up or amassed in the foyer ready for the church. That left Thomas's "nest." If there was something important to be found about the Young family, Lucie was certain it would be there.

Their morning tea and oatmeal done, Norah slipped out the kitchen door to head to work, and Lucie grabbed her gathering basket. Breathing heavily by the time she reached the third-floor landing, Lucie announced to no one but herself, "Thirty-two stairs and two landings! No wonder they lived so long." She smiled at the memory of her grandfather, cane in hand, working his way down the stairs, his arthritic knees making for slow progress toward his goal: a much-needed morning cup of tea and his newspaper. Opening the door to Thomas's once-cozy lair, she saw her mother's portrait, her soft hazel eyes and youthful beauty still intact. Lily had been nineteen when Thomas commissioned the painting, but she looked just as Lucie remembered her. "Hello, Mother," she said, wondering if she was going to start talking to every portrait in the house. "You are still very lovely," she whispered. "Soon you will travel with me across the sea to be part of my home again. I want my children to meet you."

Lucie plunked herself in the low chair by the cold coal grate. She felt a reverence regarding her grandfather's belongings:

the soft blue wool afghan he used for naps folded neatly at the foot of the bed, his three pairs of reading glasses and a monogrammed handkerchief on the bedside table, and his books. So many books!

Lucie kicked off her shoes and dragged the desk chair over to the bookcase. "No injuries, Lucie," she warned herself, testing the steadiness of the chair's spindle legs. Finding her balance, she reached to the top shelf. As she did, she heard a soft thump as if something had fallen off the top of the bookcase. Back on firm ground, she slipped her hand between the wall and the heavy piece of furniture until her fingers discovered a small book. Carefully, she pulled it out into the light. A diary. A piece of paper had been glued over the rough, worn leather cover, with Thomas's writing across it. "Notes Relating to Family History." Inside the cover was another handwritten inscription:

T U Young, 14 Belgrave Road, Rathmines.

Lucie sat on the edge of Thomas's bed and flipped through her grandfather's journal. On its pages, he had registered lists of family heirlooms and brief observations and significant events. His children's birthdates, his wife's death, a birthday party . . . Lucie stopped midway through. "A fire?" She held the scratchy writing up to the light but could only make out two other words in the entry: *child* and *ashamed.* Whose shame? Lucie put the book carefully in her apron pocket and buttoned it closed. She had found something precious—not just a record of her family, but something written through her grandfather's eyes and heart. As with her aunts' letters, if she started reading each page, she would not move for hours.

That evening, Lucie held out the family diary to Norah, who looked at it curiously. "Oh, wait," Lucie said, pulling the book back to her lap. "I hadn't noticed this before." Gently, she

pried the book to the page marked by a tattered piece of ribbon. It was the final entry in the book. The pages beyond it
were blank. Lucie ran her finger along the faded ink message.
"Oh my," she said. "It's about me."

> *January 5, 1902*
> *Engagement of Lucie Mary Niven to Shepherd*
> *Ivory Franz*
> *November 11, 1901, London, Ontario.*
> *Blessings to my dear Lucie*
> *T. Urry Young*

"Your grandfather died just two months later," Norah said.
"He was almost ninety, wasn't he? Ah, now." She put her arm
around her teary friend and suggested they drink a toast to
Thomas.

Later that night, Lucie lay in bed, the covers pulled up
under her chin. In her hands was her grandfather's diary. She
turned the book up to the bedside light to read the faded ink
meanderings.

Each entry was like a signpost, with the way in between
mostly obscured. She filled in what empty spaces she could
with the family stories she had heard from her mother and
during her own childhood at RockView, but there was so much
more to learn. Her grandfather was right. "Life is never what
you expect and full of the unexpected."

Lucie had thought she'd known the Victorian Youngs well.
Just like she had thought she had known Norah well. She had
been wrong on both counts. This was her last trip to her childhood home, but it seemed her journey to understanding her
Anglo-Irish roots was only beginning.

Lucie's eyes grew tired from deciphering Thomas's handwriting. When she returned to the States, she intended to
write it all down: Thomas's observations, her memories, the

secrets revealed in her mother's and aunts' letters. Before putting her grandfather's diary aside, she turned again to the last entry and imagined her grandfather, his life a thin thread, writing about her and then, soon after, closing his eyes, giving himself permission to dream of his life, unfolding chapter by chapter. . .

PART TWO

THE BEGINNING

CHAPTER 3

MUDDLED THOUGHTS

Dublin, Ireland
September 1873
Thomas

From the depths of sleep, anxiety surfaced. Had Thomas Young fully understood the unrest rumbling beyond the walls of his home, he might have bolted awake. But the painful and personal events that pressed on the sixty-one-year-old Anglo-Irish man that chilly fall morning of 1873 prevented him from seeing the wave of change in his adopted country, coming in on a strong tide. He turned his face deep into his pillow as usual, allowing his muddled thoughts to be insulated a few minutes longer from the unwelcome changes in his life.

Thomas's world had most recently been shaken by a host of upsets beginning with the marriage of his eldest daughter, Lily, followed by her departure from not only his home but Ireland itself! And finally by the anticipation of the loss of his home as he knew it. His two younger, unmarried daughters—with only a cursory acknowledgment of the disruption it would bring him—had turned RockView into a school for girls. Nine boarders from far-flung corners of the country were set to invade in less than a month, establishing territory in his home with their giggles and whispers and constant activity. In preparation for their arrival, he had been packed up and moved to the third floor, into Lily's old room. "Sorry, Father," Frances had said when he protested being thrown out of the biggest bedroom. "To make this school succeed, we need the room." She hadn't sounded sorry.

His daughters were nearly finished converting the entire second floor of the house into a dormitory, classroom, and study room for their little intruders. His option, Frances pointed out, was to remain in his bedroom on the same floor the girls occupied night and day. At least his Elfie had shown some understanding of what it meant to be ousted from his private sanctuary. She'd sat with him to select and pack all that he wanted to have in his new room, but really . . . such dislocation! *Doesn't anyone think about me anymore?* he thought pitifully. He disliked being a grumpy old man, but he felt like one.

Thomas rolled over on his side, rousing the ache in his joints. He could not deny that Elfie and Frances were only thinking of their future. They desired a source of income that he would not always be able to provide—a discomforting thought that did nothing to temper his annoyance. *I'm not that old after all. I still work at the academy. And the house, last I heard, is still mine. I've cared for this family very well for many years. My daughters are too impatient,* he thought. Once married, they would be well cared for. If they chose well. The sadness he had awakened to returned. Lily had chosen well and left.

Thomas forced himself to sit up, pulling the covers to his

shoulders. He glanced to the empty side of his bed and an image of his sweet, fragile Sarah on their wedding day swam before him. December 20, 1837, St. Mary's Anglican church in Cheltenham, England. The date and place were forever ingrained in his mind. *Not yesterday, but surely not thirty-six years ago,* Thomas thought. He felt again their excitement at leaving England as newlyweds for a life across the Irish Sea. Sarah had wanted to teach children, so they set out on the promise of an act of the British Parliament that supported early childhood education in Ireland. Thomas had secured a position at the Royal Hibernian Academy's National School of Art in Dublin. "How many artists are able to make a living from their work?" he'd reassured Sarah and her parents. He'd been fortunate. *They'd* been fortunate. Ireland was their chance for a fresh start. It was also true, though he didn't like to think of it, that they could live better in Ireland, where affordable help was plentiful. *Sarah and I may have been young and idealistic,* he'd told himself and others over the years, *but we've always treated Biddy and Mary well.*

As blessed as he and Sarah had been to find well-paying work and a nice home, they couldn't help but be aware of the many Irish who were hungry and poor. And then the potato blight arrived, wiping out or pushing out the poor Irish for seven long years. As British citizens living near Dublin, the couple had been mostly insulated from the devastating effects of the Great Hunger. They were neither Irish nor dependent on the success of crops to survive. They were Anglo-Irish—part of the Ascendancy, a privileged British social class—and got along quite well, though not as well as the wealthier plantation-owning Anglo-Irish in the west, where the famine was at its worst. *Their* lives seemed barely touched by the misery surrounding them.

The couple's own time of suffering came with the loss of six children, all in infancy. "Poor sweet Sarah," Thomas whispered.

He missed the comfort of her warm body close to his in the night. "My Sarah." He sighed again. Thirteen years she'd been gone, and now their eldest, Lily, had married and moved to Canada, and his two youngest daughters seemed to read the change as a reason to take over the house! Three daughters. He and Sarah had treasured each one, but it was only natural to have a favorite. Lily had known his mind better than her younger sisters, and if she had never married and then left, he doubted the school would have happened. Lily had been his confidante. Her leaving felt like the loss of a limb. From the time she was eleven, at her mother's death, she had become his devoted daughter, his buffer from reality. "Coddling him," he had heard Frances say more than once.

How had Lily left him? It was a question he asked himself daily. A thought flashed, as if a mirror had been turned toward his own life—he and Sarah had left England just as James and Lily had left Ireland. Had he thought of his parents, of their happiness when he left? As he did with many questions that made him uncomfortable, he let it go without an answer.

The press of nature required a hasty departure from his down-filled lair. With effort, he forced himself out from the covers and paid homage to the chamber pot, his toes lifting to avoid unnecessary contact with the cold floor. It was only September, but he would soon wear socks to bed. "I feel old," he said. As far as his ears could catch, his daughters Frances and Elfie were still in bed. He should hurry if he wanted a moment's peace to himself. Soon enough his mornings would be jarred by the muffled sounds of doors closing, hurried footsteps, and youthful voices. Whether he liked it or not, his house was destined for a new life.

He had only himself to blame. RockView had begun as a barn in the south of Dublin in the early 1800s, when the district of Rathmines was still a farming area. By the time Thomas bought it, RockView had been turned into a rustic lodge, big, roomy, and informal, surrounded by open fields for hunting and shooting. Thomas was not overly handy, and what his wife envisioned for their new home was beyond simple home repair. That agreed, they carefully saved money to hire help and buy materials to make changes when they could. Hiring men for this kind of work in Ireland was not as expensive as they had thought. The Irish needed work and were good craftsmen. Maybe if it had been left as the barn it was, his daughters wouldn't have the inclination to turn it into a boarding school for girls.

Thomas's tall, slender frame quaked as he gingerly made his way to the window and pushed aside the heavy drapes. The house sat on the edge of open fields beyond the former grounds of Rathmines Castle and across from Holy Trinity Church, which sat right in the middle of Belgrave Road, the street splitting around it. Thomas looked out to his garden and to the park beyond. *I'll admit the view from the third floor is quite spectacular.* He could see much farther across the fields from his new perch.

Overnight the world had changed. An early rain created a sparkling surface across the bushes and small trees. To his artist's eye, the soft predawn light caused the trees to float like pencil drawings on a landscape dominated randomly by harsh dark rock formations. On a warmer morning in happier times, the dramatic scene might fire his imagination and draw him outside with his sketchbook. Thomas felt like a ghost watching and waiting, disengaged from his art and from the new life that swirled around him.

Even so, no one could say he'd shirked his duties. He'd continued with his teaching responsibilities at the academy, hadn't he? Last week, he'd arranged a field trip to the rolling, rock-cropped countryside. His students were young men from wealthy merchant and aristocratic families. They eagerly accompanied him on those days in the "plein air." Thomas found their excitement nearly contagious. Nearly.

There was a time not so long ago, before Lily's shocking announcement of her move to Canada, when Thomas had set about on journeys alone, mostly on foot. His needs for his outings were simple: a supply of well-sharpened pencils, a sketchbook, hard cheese, bread, and, if he was lucky, a cup for water or tea provided by a farm wife as he sat on her humble doorstep. The warm drink would be offered for the opportunity to look at his sketches of the pastoral landscape and its inhabitants, which he would gladly provide. With her permission, he'd then turn to a blank page and, with a few strokes of his charcoal pencil, capture the woman's face and round or angular figure as she watched him work. Once finished with the tea and with no further excuse to take her time, he'd slip the book safely into his pack and return the cup. Their parting exchange—"Thank you, madam," "Good day, sir"—was always the same before he continued on his way.

He suspected that in his absence, each woman he'd visited would have a good chat with her neighbor about the funny man who drew her likeness for no reason. All the while she'd be fingering the ha'penny, nestled in her apron pocket, that she'd found in the otherwise empty teacup left for her on the doorstep.

"Begin again," Thomas told himself and turned from the window. "Like each painting or sketch, the challenge is to begin to fill the blank page. I must journey to the countryside again soon, make my own freedom."

Two floors below, someone would already be in the kitchen heating the stove and putting on the kettle. Only Mary or Biddy if he was lucky; otherwise, he would have the company of one of his daughters at breakfast. Frances, most likely, who would be jabbering on about school business with her large notebook full of long lists, reading off her schedule as if he cared to listen. That was not at all how he wanted to start his morning. Thomas gathered his trousers, knitted vest, and jacket from the desk chair where he'd left them the night before, inadvertently knocking his diary to the floor.

He picked it up, putting his clothes back on the chair, and reached for his glasses on the nightstand. He turned to his last entry: Saturday, August 2, 1873, Lily's wedding day. Thomas marked all the important occasions on the pages of this small book, though he had yet to inscribe the date of his daughter's departure right after the wedding. *Too painful.* He had asked Lily several times why they couldn't remain in Ireland, and she had always given him the same answer: "We want a life unbound by a society locked in by a calcified class system and contentious power struggles. And young doctors like James are needed there, Father." He could not argue. The possibilities for social and financial success for all immigrants in Canada seemed boundless. It was disturbing to think he was being left behind in the old world and, at the same time, all of what he thought of as familiar and comforting was in upheaval. *I'm too old to live in a construction area!* He placed the book back on the desk.

His aging knees resisted any downward movement, and they felt especially stiff this morning, so Thomas leaned against the side of the bed to carefully work one foot and then the other through the legs of trousers, finishing the process with an upward jerk over his long underwear all the way to his waist. He worked his way into the beloved gray vest that Frances repeatedly insisted belonged in the rag box, and he caught his image in the long mirror inside his armoire. Clothing was a blessing. It covered the worst of what time had done to his body and cut close observation to a minimum, thank goodness. His gray hair needed brushing, as did his full beard, which cascaded from a pair of thick muttonchops to his upper chest. A frosted mantle might be a sign of age, he thought, but it should also be a sign of authority. "I'd say authority's hard to come by around this house," he grumbled.

He heard a click and the whine of a hinge that needed oil down the hall. Frances would beat him to the kitchen after all. She could have the first cup of tea. He would sit in his rocking chair and read for a while to give the old knees some time to awaken in peace.

CHAPTER 4

MORNING TEA

Frances

From her third-floor bedroom on the southeast corner of the house, Frances listened to her father's desk chair scrape against the floor followed by the repeated creak, creaking of his bed and finally the snap of his armoire being opened and slamming closed. Two heavy thumps jolted her all the way down the hall. *He's dropped his boots again,* she thought with a sigh. *Why does Father insist on rising at such an early hour?* She tried not to be judgmental but, in truth, he had few early commitments and he detested the cold. *He can afford to rise at a later hour.* She closed her eyes and counted to ten. *Father is old,* she reminded herself. *How does Elfie stand it with her room next to his? He clumps around, drops things, and clears his throat constantly. It would drive me crazy.*

"He can't hear the noise he is making, Frances," Elfie reminded her each time she complained. "It's not his fault."

Frances suspected there was more to it than that. They had forced change upon him, and she was well aware his mood was delicate. It had been that way since Lily announced she was moving away. Then again, the wedding and all the changes to the house and to their routines made her scratchy, too. Her sister Elfie seemed to be happy, even thriving, in the chaos. Frances preferred order. Their father would have preferred that nothing ever change.

Frances's bedroom was her haven, the one place in the large house that she could call her own. In just a few weeks it would become her only refuge from a life of constant observation and example setting. Located on the other end of the hall from her father's, the room was a large, pleasant space with windows on opposite sides that provided cross ventilation in the summer and what sunlight there was the rest of the year. She had her fireside chair and a small settee. To make them cozy, she had chosen soft green fabrics and florals, which complemented the green-and-white arts and crafts tiles on either side of the coal grate. Frances thought again of Elfie, who professed to like her middle room. She said it was "snuggled in," as it had fewer windows and drafts as well as Frances and Thomas as her "insulation on either side."

Frances felt invigorated by the crisp air, and the darkness before dawn was time stolen just for her. Since she was a little girl, once she threw off the covers and stood on the floor, she was ready to meet the day. And this day needed her full attention. They were about to launch the Misses Young School for Girls. Frances was anxious to begin on the right foot. The carefully laid out routines she and Elfie had created would give the girls a sense of security, and her a sense of order. *But first,* she thought, *that cup of tea.*

Turning from the armoire, her gaze rested on the bookcase, which caused her to smile as it always did. The large piece of furniture had once belonged to her mother's father,

Grandfather Wilderspin, and had come upstairs from the master bedroom when they started the conversion. Father had generously offered it to her, saying, "You are a schoolmistress now, Frances, so you will be adding regularly to your collection of books and need the extra shelf space." It wasn't the clever folding bookcase her grandfather had used when he traveled. That one graced her father's new room, though Frances had argued it would be better placed in the common areas where her students could appreciate and be inspired by it. Her own bookcase was elegant, solid, reliable—like herself, she hoped—and filled with information that interested her. Frances was proud of the carefully chosen volumes on history, science, and poetry that she kept on the bottom two shelves. The next shelf held the contemporary plays she enjoyed reading before going to bed and a well-handled collection of small red leather-bound books of Shakespeare's plays, another generous gift from her father. On the top shelf was her sister's wedding photograph.

"Oh, Lily. Between the two of us, we have shaken up this family." A half-finished letter to her elder sister waited for Frances on her desk. *Maybe tonight, Lily darling.* Frances was not one to put off any chore or project, but she had other plans for her morning. If she waited any longer, she would miss any chance for a glimpse at her father's newspaper and a quiet cup of tea before her time was fully consumed with a long, busy day of planning, preparation, checking on painters, and one final and very important interview for a prospective student.

The school needed nine students to be profitable. It had only eight, and neither Frances nor Elfie had sufficient funds of their own to make up the difference. Had Lily's wedding plans not taken up all their summer, Frances was certain she wouldn't have been worrying about completing their roster so close to the start of school. A loud cough from her father's room got her moving again. She peeked into the hall. His door had not opened.

Frances slipped out of her room, pulling a soft beige shawl over her tailored dress, and walked toward the stairs. She was particularly fond of the dress. The design and material she'd chosen herself: a finely woven wool, dyed a dignified taupe, finished with delicate white lace at both the high neckline and the sleeves that covered her wrists. Her father was an artist, her mother had an eye for creating elegant but welcoming rooms, and Frances understood the beauty of clothes. She spent what time she could studying fashions from England and the Continent. Dublin was hardly a fashion center, but she had a good seamstress, Madame Violette, who could copy anything she brought her.

At the mirror on the third-floor landing, Frances paused to see a handsome, well-dressed, slender young woman looking back at her. She smoothed back an errant strand of her long chestnut hair that was otherwise neatly swept up and held in place by a gold comb bearing her initials, F.A.M.Y., Frances Anna Miriam Young. It had been a gift from Lily and James. At twenty-four she was still of marriageable age, yet suitors had not been knocking at her door. Was it her confident "I can take care of myself" manner that put men off? Frances shrugged. She was never going to be the kind of woman who flattered her way into a relationship.

Of course, she hadn't seen Lily acting foolishly around James. But James seemed to be an exception. He didn't demand that kind of thing of Lily. Or maybe it was Lily who was the exception. Whatever the reason, Frances had her school, and its success was now her focus. Without a husband to provide for her, it had to be. *The feeling of independence is its own reward,* she told herself. *Men and marriage can wait.* But would they? *Mama worked all her married years at the school when her health allowed, so perhaps marriage and the school are not mutually exclusive.* The thought was reassuring.

Frances raised her index finger and pressed it to the small

tic at the outer corner of her right eye to calm its annoying activity. The tic had a way of arising with conflicting thoughts. All through the summer plans for Lily's wedding and travels, the twitch by her eye had been relentless. Too many projects for the school had been held up until after the wedding and Lily's departure. Frances had made meticulous plans right down to the last bedsheet. The wait to put them into action had been exhausting, like holding fast to the reins of a team of horses chomping at their bits, ready to bolt. Fortunately, the delivery of the new casement windows from England for the second floor had been delayed, or Frances might have been forced to have them stored in her own bedroom. *Maddening,* she thought again. Her hazel eyes locked with her mirrored image. The strength they projected pleased her more than the flattering reflection. Even so, the tic persisted. "Courage and confidence, Frances," she said. Turning from the mirror, she hurried down the stairs to the kitchen.

On the ground floor, Frances followed the clanging sound of pots sliding onto the stovetop and the smack of Biddy's rolling pin hitting the wooden surface to knock off any extra flour before diving into the biscuit dough. Giving the corner of her eye one last press of her finger, Frances pushed through the door. The kitchen was the warmest and most appealing room in the house on a chilly morning. Two woodstoves belched forth an astounding degree of heat, and the kettle whistled forth its stream of steam. Frances pushed back her sleeves and inhaled the soft, warm air. The kitchen was a cinnamon-laced tropical retreat compared to the rest of the house.

"Good mornin', Miss Frances," Biddy greeted her, barely looking up from her work. Frances watched Biddy force her bulky body forward over her worktable with a mighty thrust to roll out the biscuit dough, then quickly stand straight up and repeat the movement at a different angle. The power she exerted spoke of strength and experience and something else that Frances could not name. At the sink, Mary was washing and drying bowls and measuring cups.

"Good morning, Biddy, Mary," Frances said.

Without raising her head, Biddy said, "There's tea on the side of the stove. I expect your father will be here soon, so I best get these in the oven. He rang for warm water at six, so you know he'll be down before long." Biddy's usual ready smile had been replaced with a tight-lipped scowl.

Trouble at home? Frances wondered. *A fight with Conor or one of the children?* Biddy would never tell her what was bothering her, so Frances didn't ask. There was pressure on all of them with the school coming soon. She looked at Mary to see if she might offer a clue, but Mary kept her eyes on her work. Frances focused instead on pouring herself a cup of tea.

She settled at the end of the long, smooth wooden bench and rested a blue-and-white Staffordshire cup and saucer, her favorites for tea with warm milk and honey, on the kitchen table. Her father's newspaper was neatly folded on the table. Frances turned the paper to face her. She saw a short article on Charles Stewart Parnell, the gist of which was that he had given a speech in Dublin that had worried the British. Parnell was the financial executor for their student Anna Monteforte. Frances hoped the association with the man would not reflect badly on the school.

She had just turned the paper back to its place and walked toward the stove to pour her second cup of tea when her father came through the swinging door, moving with unexpected ease and energy. "Good morning, Father," Frances said while thinking, *Ah well, at least Father hasn't lost his spryness even if his hearing is going.* His lean figure was draped in his old gray knitted vest, which seemed to grow in length every time she saw it. His hands were pushed deeply into the pockets, stretching them ever downward. Inside one would be two sets of eyeglasses and a handkerchief, a good-sized magnifying glass in the other. Frances smiled at the sight. *It is a long way to the third floor if you forget something, so bring it all!* she thought.

"Good morning, Frances," her father said softly. His hands appeared from his pockets to accept the warm cup of tea offered him. "Thank you, Biddy."

Biddy had been on Frances's mind since she and Elfie first thought of turning the house into a school. The housekeeper had just turned thirty-two and had been with the Youngs for most of Frances's life. She was so much more than someone who put hot meals on the table and kept the house tidy. She was part of their family—they always said so—and she would be an integral part of their school. *If I was seven years old when Biddy first arrived, that means when Biddy came to us, she was*—Frances stopped to calculate—*only fifteen!* Biddy had always seemed like an adult to her. Their parents, or more likely their mother, had hired Biddy to help the cook. Biddy had done the washing up, peeling, and chopping, but also laundry and errands, especially when their mother was in poor health. When the cook left, Biddy suggested her cousin Mary could come along to learn how to be "in service." Frances guessed Mary and Biddy were about three years apart, making Mary twelve at the time. They had been so very young, but she had never considered their ages when she was child; they were in charge and so they seemed older. From the family accounting ledgers that she now managed, Frances knew that at first Biddy had been paid a small wage along with her meals, while Mary had only been paid in meals. The Youngs were not a wealthy family, but Frances supposed her parents had paid as fair a wage as they could manage.

Over the rim of her cup, she watched Biddy move about the kitchen, following a morning routine that Frances knew well enough not to interrupt. Her mind was still calculating Biddy's age through the events in the family's life. *When our mother died, Biddy was younger than Elfie and I are now!* she realized. Their mother's health had been so fragile for so long that Biddy had already eased into caring for Lily, Frances, and Elfie by then. Frances appreciated Biddy's take-charge personality even then, and Mary had been at Biddy's side as her helper. The sisters were very fortunate to have both of them in their lives, then and now. Frances thought they'd always made a good team. More than ever, she felt grateful to have them in her life.

Despite the added expense that would come straight out of any profit the sisters might make, the first thing she and Elfie did once they agreed to start a school was increase the wages for Biddy and Mary. Frances stayed awake at night worrying how they would make ends meet if the school wasn't a success, but the school could not be a success without Biddy and Mary. *All the more important to make a good impression at the interview with Elizabeth Fenn's parents today,* she thought. Biddy's job, and therefore Mary's, had already grown immeasurably, and the students hadn't even arrived. They were already planning three meals a day for nine additional people, ordering supplies that filled the pantry, airing the blankets and linens they would use for nine new beds they had to prepare, and making lists for Frances of what additional things were needed so that each girl had her own fresh bed linens and towels.

Frances had felt relieved when the supply of white pinafores, the uniform for the school, arrived the day before. The girls would wear them over their own clothes and get a fresh one each week, which meant the school needed eighteen of them. This morning, the laundry girl, Peggie, was in the basement starching and ironing each of them—which, to begin with, had required Biddy's watchful eye and trips downstairs. There was a lot of extra work for the help. Frances had worried that Biddy and Mary would up and quit despite the better pay, which, truth be told, still wasn't a great sum. She hoped the women felt like part of the family. She had told them both that she thought of them that way and only wished she could offer them more. Biddy and Mary were from Irish Catholic families that went back generations in Ireland. Their loyalty to the Youngs, by comparison latecomers to Ireland with nearly forty years in the country, was not something Frances wanted to test. She needed them.

To her relief, Biddy had responded by telling Frances, "We're quite content being stuck with you and yours, Miss Frances. You have always been fair with us. Mary and I appreciate the raise, knowin' you see the extra work the school is makin' for all of us. It's more for you and Miss Elfie too, Miss Frances."

— ♦ —

Thomas

Thomas, wishing he had brought down the latest issue of the *Dublin University Magazine*, wondered if he dared ask Frances to retrieve it for him. These were changes he had to get used to. Lily would have noticed its absence right away and brought it from his room without bidding. The magazine had been publishing a series urging reacquaintance with the Gaelic tongue and ancient Celtic traditions, which interested him. The Anglo-Irish, in general, seemed to admire Ireland's literature and traditions, but the magazine mentioned that the romantic movement toward the old ways was increasingly viewed as politically, more than culturally, motivated. Thomas enjoyed politics. And because politics was deeply entwined with Irish culture and nationalism, he had become interested in them, too. The man behind many of the articles, the lawyer, poet, and writer Sir Samuel Ferguson, was a champion of this thinking. For Thomas, that meant he was an intellectual and cultural force not to be ignored. Ferguson, he felt, spoke to the soul of Ireland.

Almost as compelling to Thomas, in the absence of his magazine, was the news in the *Times* waiting for him on the table. He sometimes wondered if Biddy ever read the articles or at least skimmed them. And if she did, what did she make of them? He'd never asked, in great part because he suspected her education was limited. *She could read, though, couldn't she?* He would never have asked her that either. What he did know was that Biddy was a bright and levelheaded person, and he didn't wish to embarrass her.

Several articles that morning were about Home Rule. That Charles Parnell in County Wicklow was making his mark on the movement with another fiery speech favoring complete severance of Ireland's ties with England. Parnell was an agitator. Thomas believed in Home Rule—to a point. He was in agreement with giving the Irish a greater degree of self-rule but liked his adopted country remaining part of the United Kingdom. There was too much tension in the movement for his liking, and the issue of separation was at the core of it. *Parnell is* Anglo-*Irish; his roots are in England. Why not cooperate with our powerful mother country?*

Thomas glanced up from the paper at the two women moving about the kitchen, inadvertently catching the eye of Mary, who looked startled and quickly refocused on the dishes she was washing. Thomas wondered what they thought of this Home Rule business or if they even thought of it at all. It wasn't his place to ask nor theirs to tell him, and therein lay the rub of it all.

He put down the paper in frustration. "Just how much more chaos can one man take, and how can any problem be resolved if people can't talk about it?" he asked, addressing his daughter in full expectation that she would know what problem he was referring to. But when he looked around, she was nowhere to be seen. He shook his head. Frances was off with her lists and had left without a word.

CHAPTER 5

IT'S ALL GOING TO WORK OUT BEAUTIFULLY

Elfie

When she heard her father pass her bedroom and head downstairs, Elfie paused her letter writing, taking the opportunity to work the cramps from the fingers and joints of her hand. She picked up the letter carefully so as not to smudge her accomplishment. She wanted to add something about the early-morning magic of the garden below her window but felt the press of time and thought better of it. *Love, Elfie,* she wrote, putting closure to her weekly report to Lily. The translucent paper told of the expected changes in their household once the girls arrived and the successes she and Frances had already had with their new boarding-school endeavor. She'd also expressed again her wish that their father would come out of his melancholy.

During the month before and after "the departure," as they'd come to refer to Lily's leaving, their father had moved beyond her understanding. He seemed to have frozen into a brittle version of his once-cheerful self. His dreary behavior created an unfortunate coolness and a certain amount of stress within the house. *Frances the stern, Father the grumpy ghost, and Biddy the overworked,* she thought and then laughed. *I wonder how they think of me?* She supposed they were all less-than-satisfying company just at this moment. *Our new routine will come soon,* she thought, *and then we will all settle in.*

For herself, Elfie wanted more from life than being mistress of a school. She longed for a husband, children of her own, love. She hadn't shared those thoughts in her letters to Lily. She didn't want to appear self-pitying. Elfie had liked Frances's idea of bringing the girls into their home. Her own interests would come soon enough. Though she couldn't put a finger on exactly why, those common and expected events had not yet shown themselves to her. Until they did, there seemed to be nothing she could do about it. Meanwhile her books and letter writing would keep her company until the girls arrived. *Of course,* she told herself. *The girls will be the highlight in my life this year. And that should be enough for me for now.*

She was grateful that Frances had agreed to take breakfast with the young ladies when school began. This would give Elfie time to write, think, and prepare the lessons she would teach that day. In return, Frances would retire in the evening while Elfie put the finishing touches on the girls' bedtime rituals, each with its own all-important variation. "It's all going to work out beautifully," she told her reflection in the mirror. "Though I expect there will be a few bumps to smooth out." Her sister believed the girls should follow a strict routine right away. Elfie had other ideas. When the girls arrived, she planned to make a special effort to meet with them individually to ask about their homes, mothers, siblings, and nannies. She'd already begun a list of questions: Were there any bedtime rituals they followed that would help them feel comfortable? Were they used to making their beds, dressing themselves, brushing and braiding their own hair? She had explained her thinking to Frances thus: "They are young and need reassurance, small comforts. They have just left home, family, and nanny for the first time." Her sister seemed less than confident in her logic, but Elfie would have none of it. "Over time, attention to these details will become less important," she had assured her. "Leave the soft touches to me, Frances!" And for once, her sister had barely bothered to argue.

Elfie and Frances were different in many ways, beginning with their appearance. Frances had their father's height and svelte body with their mother's long straight hair, whereas Elfie was blessed with a rounded, ample body; curly dark brown hair; and a quick, easy smile that she felt made her the more approachable of the two. She was the youngest in the family, only a year younger than Frances but more accustomed to moving gently past obstacles to get what she wanted. Frances, who Elfie felt was pretty, could appear austere when lost in thought, which was often. Her sister seemed to see life as a challenge to be met head-on with all the energy and intelligence one could summon. The result of her sister's decisiveness was fewer decisions for Elfie regarding the running of the school—and in life. Without the need to be eternally practical, Elfie wore the world and its cares more freely. Lily had once described her youngest sister's imagination-caught life as a "swirling canvas with surprising dimensions, gracious subtleties, and eternal variations," which Elfie took as a compliment.

In her spare time, she had devoured novels and dreamed of a more dashing, romantic life for herself than Frances, who seemed to share none of her creative thinking. As far as Elfie knew, Frances had never even shown an interest in painting, whereas Elfie not only watched her father sketch and paint but also tried her own hand at it. She found the activity helped her to become an acute, aware observer of subtle nuances in nature and human nature. Writing was her natural place of comfort, but she enjoyed the time and attention her father gave her. *Perhaps Frances is jealous of me,* she considered.

As children and even as young adults, the differences between the two sisters were obvious to both of them. When it came to dividing the duties and responsibilities of the school, their differences generally seemed to be working for them. Elfie could only hope the same would be true in practice. There were those moments when she wished she could stand up and march right out the door like the heroines in her novels, slinging epithets, when Frances criticized her—most recently for her thoughts on the girls' bedtime ritual. "We don't want to baby them" is what she had said. What did Frances know about babying? She had never received it, nor had she seemed to have wanted it. Lily had given Elfie the warmth and support she craved, and Father had, too, in his own way. She would give as much to the girls and maybe someday have the nerve to tell Frances what she thought of her nurturing skills!

Elfie addressed her letter and sealed it with the signet ring she had received from Lily and James at their wedding. Red wax dripped into a rich pool below the match flame, and she affixed her mark. There was a sense of relief that accompanied this ritual, a confessional sealed and sent far away. Her thoughts and feelings, joy and pain felt less problematic once rendered on paper. With this weekly communication she gained a perspective she would have been unlikely to have otherwise. Lily had filled the house with laughter and made the most mundane task a source of fun. Elfie sorely missed her. Since she'd left, her absence had been filled with an ongoing tension.

She and Frances *and* their father must push through this time of change to open new doors. Elfie prayed that new sources of comfort and satisfaction lay behind those doors, beginning with the school. So far, though, her father only saw disruption in their house. Elfie worried he might be right.

CHAPTER 6

THE FENNS FROM SLIGO

George

George Fenn did not bring his daughter or his wife with him to the interview with the Misses Young. There'd been resistance at home to the idea of Elizabeth leaving. Wisdom and desire for a calm household dictated that he see the Misses Young School for Girls and the house for himself. What he *did* bring with him was the strong recommendation of the school by his Dublin banker, along with the impression the sisters were middle-aged spinsters, most certainly beyond childbearing age.

When they greeted him at the door of RockView, he didn't know whether to be pleased or concerned that his assumption had been so incorrect. One sister was tall and slender, the other about his wife's height and slightly rounder. Both ladies were simply but fashionably dressed. The shorter one smiled readily, the other more reservedly. A similarity in their eyes showed they were related. He guessed the women to be in their early twenties. Somehow, they managed to hold the glow of youth and health while bearing themselves with a maturity and an appreciation of the world that he hoped Elizabeth would carry someday.

The sisters introduced themselves and invited him to the drawing room. As they passed the dining room, Miss Frances Young paused. "This room, Mr. Fenn," she said, "is where our students will have their first etiquette lesson. The subjects of English, mathematics, science, and history are the mainstays of our curriculum, but my sister and I believe it is equally important that they learn to be ladies."

"We are certain your daughter will come to us with fine manners," Miss Elfie Young said quickly. "My sister had the idea to appeal to the girls' sense of fun by having them take turns at playing the role of the gentleman seating the lady."

Miss Frances Young smiled. "We want them to be comfortable with being treated like ladies as they grow from girlhood to being young women in society," she explained. "Their time here will be useful and academic, while we will make sure there is also time for fun. Shall we go to the drawing room, Mr. Fenn?"

As they entered the room Miss Elfie asked, "Will you take tea with us, Mr. Fenn?" She walked over to a tea service on the library table behind the sofa while George, still standing, looked out the window at the garden and surveyed the framed landscapes on the walls of the drawing room. "Our father's," Miss Elfie Young said. "Milk and sugar or lemon, Mr. Fenn?"

"Nothing, thank you," George responded, and she handed him his cup. George took a closer look at one of the landscapes, and Miss Elfie Young explained that her father was a painter as well as a teacher at the Royal Academy.

"He'll be home soon," she said. "We would like you to meet him." George was certain she was about to say more, but her sister directed him to the settee, and he felt the tone of their meeting was about to change from conversational to interview.

He sat down carefully, balancing his teacup on the saucer. Both sisters sat across from him in chairs at a slightly higher level. Behind them hung the most dramatic of the paintings in the room, very different in style, depicting a stormy ocean with a boat tossing about in the waves as two sailors strained to hold fast to the lines on the sails. The seating arrangement he considered well planned to the sisters' advantage; they were clearly on the high ground and in charge of the direction of the coming conversation. He admired them all the more for their strategy.

"We are interested in hearing about your daughter, Mr. Fenn," said Miss Frances Young, "and why you wish her to attend our school."

George began without hesitation. "My daughter, Elizabeth, is a strikingly beautiful child, and intelligent, of course. She holds great promise. Her eventual marriage should expand opportunities for her as well as for her family."

The sisters nodded. "Our school has been established in part for just that purpose," said Miss Frances Young. "But only in part."

"In part?" George asked.

"The girls of course will be well educated in both academics and the social graces. Learning to be ladies is vital to their prospects. We will also broaden the girls' social and cultural worlds for their own benefit."

This time it was George who nodded in agreement. The Fenns lived on the distant, provincial northwest coast of Ireland, where George ran the family business. Facing the wild Atlantic Ocean, the western edge of Ireland was harsh and rocky though rich in natural resources—crystal-clear lakes, salmon-filled streams, peat bogs, and vast wheat and flax plantations controlled by the British aristocratic class. Plantation land was inherited, originally given by the Crown generations ago. With it came built-in privilege. The aristocracy in Ireland lived as country ladies and gentlemen in fine manor houses, behind high walls and locked gates. The Irish did their work.

The Fenns were neither aristocrats nor Irish. They were of the merchant class. George had inherited a family shipping enterprise based out of Sligo's port. He needed to live in Sligo to run his business despite the necessity of frequent trips to secure contracts and keep his fleet up to date. He was financially successful, but as part of the merchant class in the western provinces, his family was walled off from direct entrance to high society. It was a social fact that he accepted, though after a whiskey or two he was known to lament that in Sligo his family "was sullied by involvement in honest work." He wanted more for his daughter. Elizabeth hadn't been born into aristocracy but in another place, such as Dublin, that might not matter so much. That's why he was willing to send her across the country to where commercial and intellectual activity in the city were creating a strong and well-respected Anglo-Irish merchant class. "My father introduced the first steamship to Sligo's port," he told the Misses Young. "Our business is profitable and Sligo is our home, but the social world available to us, more specifically to my daughter, is limited. Elizabeth is meant to see a broader world."

Again, the sisters nodded politely.

"She requires a more sophisticated education that cannot be found in Sligo," he reiterated. "My wife and I, of course, considered sending her to school in England, but we could not bear to have her so far away." He was certain the sisters had heard something similar from the other parents, but George wanted them to know just how important Elizabeth was to him and Bessie.

"We understand," Miss Elfie Young said gently. Her words and soft voice relaxed George, though until then he hadn't realized he'd been anything but relaxed. The younger sister's manner and tone reminded him of his wife's: kind, sincere, with a clear intelligence behind it. By the completion of the interview, George Fenn had made his decision. His daughter would come to the Misses Young School. Bessie would be pleased, eventually. George stood and slipped his hand inside his jacket pocket, ready to pay the full year's tuition right then in order to assure his daughter's acceptance.

The elder Miss Young spoke before he could withdraw his billfold. "We would welcome Elizabeth if you choose to send her to us."

Once again, George was impressed. He had come to interview the Misses Young, but they had from the very beginning turned the tables and interviewed him. *What remarkable ladies,* he thought again. His daughter would be in good hands with them.

"Would you like to see the rest of the school and dormitory?" Miss Elfie Young asked. Pointing to the staircase, she said, "They are on the second floor. We have made a number of changes to the house for our students, who will all be boarding with us. The first floor is for their dining and leisure." It had been George's intention to ask for a tour, but he had lost track of the idea. The Misses Young had not.

"Yes, thank you," George said, rather enjoying the fact that these women were so pleasant and in charge.

The tour ended back in the foyer, where Miss Elfie Young handed him an envelope with information for new students. George handed them an envelope with the year's payment and thanked them but hesitated at the door. He breathed in deeply. "Ahh, there is a wonderful stew cooking in your kitchen. Could I meet your cook?" The sisters exchanged a glance. "I always like to know who is in the kitchen," he explained.

The women silently led him past the dining room and through the swinging door to the kitchen where the cooks looked up from their work, clearly surprised to see a visitor. Miss Elfie Young led the introductions.

"I just had to tell you, Biddy and Mary," George said with enthusiasm, "that savory aroma wafting from your kitchen caused my mouth to water. It makes me very happy my daughter will be coming to this school." With a wink he added, "I always like to have friends in the kitchen."

Biddy stepped away from the cutting board and wiped her hands on her apron. She lifted her eyes to him almost shyly. George was quick to say, "I do not intend to stop your good work, madam, but I couldn't resist offering my compliments."

Biddy smiled. "You are kind, sir. We do our best."

George Fenn thanked them all and took his leave. Descending the front steps, he saw an elderly gentleman heading straight for him. "Mr. Young?" George asked, stopping to introduce himself. "I have just passed the interview with your lovely daughters and will bring my Elizabeth very soon to join the school."

Thomas Young offered his hand. With a wry smile and a wag of his head, he said, "Congratulations, sir. My daughters are quite the team. Not easy to get by them. I will look forward to seeing more of you. Not many men around here these days."

George, searching for more of a connection, replied, "We met John Yeats recently in Sligo where his wife's family, the Pollexfens, live. I understand he sometimes teaches at your academy."

"Yes indeed," Thomas replied. "Er, not my academy, of course, but yes. Lively fellow. I enjoy his company for a round at the pub."

"Such a small world," said George, who tipped his hat adding, "Good day, sir. We shall have a nice chat when I return."

— • —

Sligo

Traveling back to the west coast took three days, which gave him plenty of time to think. He was relieved to have found a good school for Elizabeth within the country. Presenting his decision to his wife and daughter was something else. Arriving at last in Sligo, he stopped at the local to quench his thirst and get the kinks out from the eighty-mile carriage ride over rutted roads. He further rationalized the delay in going home by telling himself it was important for a man in his position to listen to and chat with the people who lived and worked in the town.

George pulled up a stool beside two men he'd shared a pint with before. Niall and Aeden had sons working hard beside them on the docks, sons who were saving money to leave the country. He had a sense that some of the ways they were "makin' some extra" might not be legal.

George leaned onto the counter and ordered himself an ale and another round for his companions. The two men glanced his way and Niall lifted his glass with a "thank ya, sir," but Aeden was on a rant George had heard before. "Fookin' Brits keeping themselves above 'scum' like us. If I was young like me sons," he slurred, "I'd go too!"

George held his tongue but placed his hands on the two men's shoulders. Shaking his head sadly, he said, "I hate to see your boys leave. Keeping our youth is our only hope for the future. It's a loss for all of us."

George said no more. The men may have appreciated his pints and his ear, but as a local business owner, his political opinions were not welcome. His son did not face the same odds theirs did. The local was their place. He was just a visitor. George ordered another round for the men and took his leave. He walked out into the damp, coastal air, grateful for that hour in the pub before heading home.

Twenty minutes later, George stood before his blazing fireplace with a large glass of his favorite smoky peated single-malt whiskey in hand, venting his frustration to his wife. His view on current politics was not what she was waiting to hear, but he was too fired up to stop, not to mention worried how Bessie would react to his decision about Elizabeth's education. He wasn't keen to have that conversation just yet. George placed his hand on the mantel and spoke into the fire to avoid making eye contact with his wife. "Let those Goddamn aristocrats try an honest day's work and then be robbed blind as their reward. Then they'll know a bit of how they make their bloody money. Hard enough for us, Bessie, but there's no avenue for the poor Irish to win." He glanced over his shoulder. His wife sat still in her rocking chair, holding her hands in her lap and watching him closely, a sign she was waiting for him to finish. George took another sip of whiskey. "They are destroying Ireland, Bessie. Like it or not, we must give Elizabeth a life beyond what we can give in her in Sligo." He turned to his wife, who looked dismayed. Upstairs a door slammed shut.

— • —

Bessie

As soon as he'd walked through the door, Bessie Fenn knew her husband had arrived at a decision about their daughter's future. Just as she knew the door slam upstairs was from Elizabeth, who had been nervously awaiting her father's return. Her husband made no secret that he frequented the local pubs, so she wasn't surprised he'd stopped at one on the way home. She had little interest right then in listening to him go on about a system of entitlement and oppression. It was Elizabeth she was concerned with, but there was no hurrying

George. "It's a tragedy," he told her. "Such arrogance makes me seethe against my own countrymen!"

There was a time when Bessie might have shared her own thoughts on the treatment of the Irish by the British, thoughts that weren't so different from her husband's, but she could no longer summon the energy. Not for a while and especially not recently. She worried George thought less of her because of it. Her husband was a rare man. He valued his wife's opinion when it came to issues beyond cooking and child-rearing. But these days he had so much to say himself, he seemed not to miss her participation. She placed her hand on her belly without thinking. The doctor had warned her against bearing another child, but what could she do? She hadn't said anything to George yet about her condition. Surely he must have guessed. Bessie felt her fragility was the reason she was losing Elizabeth. Whatever faith her husband may have had in himself, and by extension in her, to move their family forward in the world, he was now placing it all in their daughter.

Bessie had only agreed to send Elizabeth to a boarding school if her husband found one suitable and not too far away. And now he had. The Misses Young School was in Dublin. Closer than London. Still, she'd let herself hope something would change to keep her daughter with them.

George finished his speech with an anguished tone that echoed Bessie's own feelings of loss and frustration, though for very different reasons.

"You would approve of the school, Bessie," he said at last. "When you're feeling better, we'll travel there together. I saw the house and met their father, Thomas Young, as I was leaving. He's a painter and instructor at the Royal Academy. The house is full of his work. The sisters are a pleasant surprise, and they have an excellent cook. I was very impressed." Bessie knew that George's appreciation of a good meal had given the final boost to his decision.

He sounded so certain. More than that, her husband spoke as if he believed her own health would improve. How could she not agree to send Elizabeth to Dublin? "Yes, dear," she said. "Of course. Dublin is a much more progressive place than Sligo."

George leaned down and kissed his wife on the cheek. "We are right to give Elizabeth the chance to be part of a new Ireland where there is hope for independence. We don't want her sitting here brooding over injustices as we do." Bessie said nothing but was certain her daughter was not brooding over anything beyond her own world.

When they called Elizabeth to announce their decision, she entered the room, her face sullen and arms crossed over her chest. George had barely spoken before their daughter turned away. "I knew it," she said and ran upstairs in a fit of tears. Bessie wanted to follow but stayed. "Bessie," George said, placing his hand on her arm. "Go and comfort her. Tell her the school is in her best interest."

"George, she cannot see that yet. It will have to come in time. I can barely accept the truth of it myself, though I know the Dublin school will be good for her. Here, she lives more with the servants than with us. I will hold on to the belief that our daughter will return to us a confident young woman. She will miss us, of course."

"Of course, Bessie," George replied. "I meant to tell you, the father, Thomas Young, knows John Yeats. You remember meeting Yeats at the Frazer's dinner last month? The portrait artist who married Susan Pollexfen. So it isn't as if we're handing her off to complete strangers, now, is it?"

Her husband was reaching further than usual to offer her comfort. He'd conveniently forgotten she had found Mr. Yeats far too outspoken and bohemian for her taste. Even George had been put off by his eccentricities. Bessie was too tired and disheartened to argue. It was easier to convince herself they were doing the best for Elizabeth than to convince her husband that

Elizabeth should stay home with them. Then, too, there was the problem with the servants. Their preoccupation with the supernatural was filling her daughter's head with notions of banshees and fairies. Bessie had heard the tales so often she knew their charm. She was also with child again. The doctor had prescribed rest, and Elizabeth was such an active child.

"Yes, George," she said, giving him her final statement on the matter. "Elizabeth needs more. In some ways, I see her going to Dublin like a long visit to another country, a different culture. It will be good for her, but I will miss her terribly."

CHAPTER 7

BIDDY

Walking gave Biddy a feeling of freedom no matter the season. The early fall weather of 1873 brought a stiff breeze off the Irish Sea, but that night the temperature remained mild even as the sun drew closer to the horizon. This was her time, between two busy lives, each with its own work and personalities to navigate. Biddy could almost make the familiar two-mile walk from RockView to her home in the Liberties with her eyes closed. She had made the trek to and from the Youngs' since she had been only fifteen years old and a hired helper to their cook. The route had not changed much. The trees had grown, of course; houses had been built; and the streets were busier though not better cared for. The walking paths and lanes remained muddy, and the shortcuts through open fields stayed the same until the day a fence went up and you had to walk around. The frequent rains made craters, large and small.

Closing her eyes was not really an option, she thought, taking a quick sideways step to avoid a water-filled hole. *I wonder how many miles I have covered,* she mused, *and how many pairs of shoes I have worn through in all those years?* The half-hour-plus walk, depending on the energy she put into it, was her only time to herself and to sort herself out.

Biddy had been a scrawny twelve-year-old when she first arrived in Dublin from Cork. She stayed with her mother's family in the Liberties near the Guinness Brewery. That was all her father needed to know before she left. "If she's living near Guinness, she'll be living in the right part of town. She's old enough for work and there is work aplenty in Dublin town," he'd announced as way of giving his approval.

Her mother had arranged for Biddy to stay with her aunt Deirdre. "You'll be loved and cared for there." Biddy hadn't minded, really. Moving to Dublin was an adventure, and she was bored and too often hungry at home. Aunt Deirdre's home was crowded, yet there was food and, as her mother had promised, love in abundance. She shared a bed with Mary, her younger cousin, and soon found temporary positions working in service in Anglo-Irish homes until she was lucky enough to secure a permanent position with the Youngs.

Biddy and Conor had migrated separately from Cork to the big city for opportunity, and when they reconnected in Dublin, they felt they had found their chance for happiness in one another. Their families had been friends, and they attended the same church as children. She always fancied him because he was boisterous and full of playfulness as they walked the lanes home from services. Sometimes their families shared a meal on Sundays and he would wink at her and make funny faces to amuse her. Conor was memorable.

Three years after her arrival in Dublin, Biddy was on one of her daily walks across an open field in Rathmines when she recognized "that boy, Conor" from Cork. Except he was no longer a boy. It was a young man who walked toward her, head down, watching his step, and she said, "Is it Conor Gossett from Cork, then?" He had looked up, smiled, and immediately stepped in a hole, causing the most unfortunate language to spill forth.

Biddy had chided him. "Is this the boy I used to sit in church with sayin' those devilish things?" She clasped her hands in front of her chest, as if in prayer, and said, "Dear Lord, forgive us our sins."

Conor laughed. "You got me, Biddy. So how are ya, girl? Where ya going?"

"Home," said Biddy and, without a word, Conor wheeled and changed directions, falling in step full of cheerful chat about family and friends as he walked her home. Aunt Deirdre laughed when she saw him at her door. "Always cheers my soul to hear another Munster Irish voice in this home," she said, inviting him inside. From then on, Conor Gossett became a regular visitor, always with a keen eye for Biddy, which everyone including her could see. He tried to be helpful, cleared the plates and stood drying them after Biddy washed them up. When they finished, he would ask, "How 'bout a walk, Bid?" and she would always say yes. It was no surprise to anyone when at age nineteen, with blessings all around, Biddy married Conor and moved out of her aunt and uncle's home.

The Liberties was a mostly Irish community but there were Dutch, French Huguenot, and English tradespeople bringing silverwork, wool and silk weaving, and the smelly tanning industry to the area to join the breweries. She and Conor moved when they could afford to, finding a slightly bigger flat as their family and combined incomes grew. By 1864, they had saved enough to rent a place with two bedrooms, this one closer to RockView, with a bedroom for little Patrick and Jack to share and a room in the back for Biddy, Conor, and the baby when it came. No longer crammed into tiny one-room flats located three floors up, the Gossetts were proud to be living on the ground in a one-story house. They shared a wall on each side with neighbors, but their front door opened into a narrow lane where communal life bustled: chairs were dragged out, rain or shine, and men smoked, ladies knitted, children played ball, small gardens were tended, and neighbors chatted.

Biddy was about to have her third child when they moved in. Conor had a full-time job with a construction company as a bricklayer and Biddy, who had just turned twenty-four, was head housekeeper and cook for the Youngs. When Norah was born, Biddy was given a few precious weeks at home as a new mother and Mary carried the load for her at RockView during her absence.

Aunt Deirdre, God bless her, had lost a baby, a stillborn boy, just before Norah arrived. Her tragedy meant she was able to wet-nurse Norah. Even so, she brought the two boys and the baby to RockView once a day to relieve Biddy's miserably swollen, leaky breasts. Biddy had packed them with nappies, but that didn't keep them from soaking her dress within a few hours of the last feeding. Holding the baby in one arm to suckle and stirring stew with the other arm was Biddy's bliss. Deirdre enjoyed the opportunity to come into the Youngs' home, even if it was just their kitchen. "Quite the setup these people got here," she'd declare, as if it were her first time there. Mary would break a scone in half to hand to the boys before sending them out into the garden to play, while Deirdre sipped her tea and bit into her own scone laden with butter. Only after she'd finished eating would Deirdre offer to stir so Biddy could sit in the chair and cuddle Norah.

As Biddy made her daily pilgrimage home, she often thought how her aunt's cheerful, unquestioning help had made it possible for her and Conor to hold their jobs and have a secure and growing family. They had paid Deirdre, but to Biddy, care from family was beyond price. Now Norah was nine, and

Biddy gave thanks every day for her close, tight-knit family. They had always helped one another. Miss Frances and Miss Elfie were learning, inch by inch, how to work together, a way of cooperating in their new roles while having the school right in their home. That was interesting to watch. Mr. Young was taking a little longer to adjust, but Biddy was certain he would come around.

The Gossetts felt at home in their house. It was similar to the houses they had grown up with in Cork, with its walls of wattle and daub. The main exception had been their home in the Liberties with its metal roof that made Conor lament, "I miss me old thatched roof. Feel like I'm in a war with all that bangin' goin' on and on when it rains." The front door of their home had been a half door, and the top portion had warped to the point of requiring a lot of lifting and joggling to get it to close tightly. The two halves had ceased to meet in the middle since God knew when, making a secure closing all but impossible. The only good thing about it was it let the fresh air in, along with much-appreciated light, and the smoke out from the crooked chimney that did not draw properly. Conor replaced the "lousy door" with a stout one, over which Biddy complained, "It's much too heavy." The new door soon sagged on its hinges and made a terrible scraping sound that was an everyday annoyance for Biddy. Conor said it was like having a door guard. "You always know when anyone is arrivin' or leavin'." Biddy raised her eyebrows and shook her head at his attempt at humor. "Truly, Conor?" she said in her most sarcastic tone. She missed her half door.

During those early years there was always much work for them to do on their home and little time to do it. Conor frequently damned himself in frustration for not "startin' the blinkin' thing over and buildin' himself a fine, sturdy house of bricks." He had neither the time nor the money, so they made do. Over time they refreshed the uneven walls with white paint, added a Welsh dresser for the dishes, straightened the chimney so it reliably drew the smoke up and out, placed a fine cooking stove in the old hearth fireplace, and built shelves in the kitchen.

For all its faults, they had the nicest, most cared-for home on the lane, and Biddy took pride in that. She'd wanted to hang lace curtains in her front window as a signal to any passerby that the people in the house had done well, but Conor refused, saying they didn't need to be signaling thieves. She and Conor had grown up poor, rural Irish and were lucky their families could afford the tax for a single window, so she didn't argue. They were proud of where they came from and even now were not rich, but they had more than most. She had heard the Youngs say exactly that of themselves, and privately she snorted at the comparison.

There was one part of their home that continued to draw Biddy's criticism and Conor's blind eye. "Conor, you can see as well as me those open eaves above the bedroom look like a hayloft. I'll not have people thinking we live in a barn." The space was half-filled with boxes of old blankets, clothes stored for other seasons, and anything else there was no room for downstairs. She had plans for its empty half, plans she thought best to keep to herself or Conor might argue there was no need to cover the loft.

She kept her pleasure to herself when he finally dragged in the lumber and built a proper wall with an opening for a ladder access to the storage. Conor brushed his hands together and admired his work. Biddy gave him a nod of approval and made his tea as a reward. It was only then that she brought up the idea of turning the loft into a bedroom for the boys, who were growing up and who grumbled daily about having to share their room with their little sister.

Conor smiled and shook his head but said nothing. Biddy kissed him on the cheek and said nothing either. There was no need. Before the evening meal, Conor had added a rod for Biddy to hang a quilt for a door and another inside the loft to hang a curtain separating the boxes from the new bedroom space. He also punched a small latched opening into the back wall for air circulation "so the buggers won't suffocate up there." That finished, he placed his clenched fist firmly on the table and announced, "That's it, Bid."

Biddy had slowed her gait with all her thinking. She shook her head to focus on getting home. Life just kept veering off course in directions you didn't see coming. Change was the only constant she could count on. The most recent changes at the Youngs were the hardest yet for Biddy in terms of her workload. Her back ached and her feet hurt at the end of every day. The additional work with the school and nine new residents had expanded Biddy's chores and responsibilities. "That's a lot of chamber pots and coal to carry up and down two flights of stairs," Biddy had told Miss Frances when she first mentioned the idea of the school. "I'll need Mary's help in the kitchen more than ever, too," she added. The newly hired laundress was young and needed a lot of supervision to meet the standards of the house. Mary, too, was doing much more than helping in the kitchen, so the Youngs had engaged a girl to come in once a week to help Mary with the cleaning, dusting, and general housework. Even with the extra help, Biddy now worked at RockView six days a week instead of five. On Saturdays her work had doubled as she prepared and left a cold stew or roast chickens, fresh baked bread, muffins, hard-cooked eggs, and sliced meats ready for their Sunday meals when she had her day off.

The saving grace was that the girls would return to their homes for almost four weeks over the Christmas holiday and then in June for almost four months. In addition, all the Youngs, including Mr. Young, tended to travel over the summer. Biddy was already looking forward to that long break. She was going to need that time to recover. During the summer she would continue to work at RockView to oversee any repairs or changes to the house. Her hours would be her own, and Mary could cover if need be. Crossing the bridge at the canal to enter the Liberties, Biddy thought, "Praise the Lord, I'm almost home."

As she drew closer, a flicker of light caught her eye. *Norah must be home,* she thought. Her daughter had become helpful in reheating or sometimes cooking the dinner Biddy had prepared as well as taking in and folding the laundry. Biddy could not leave RockView until after serving five o'clock dinner to the Youngs and the girls. Mary did the tidy-up, so Biddy was home most nights by half past six. Norah's help was a blessing, and Biddy made sure she knew it was appreciated. Their sons, Patrick and Jack, stayed out with neighborhood boys until Conor got home, sometimes late and a little wobbly, from the pub. When Biddy rang the bell for dinner, it was often after eight at night. That made for a very long day for all of them.

Biddy glanced up again at the candle throwing its tiny light through the kitchen window. She was glad her daughter was in the house and not out with her brothers or worse. Recently Biddy had arrived at home to find a scruffy lad of indeterminate age talking to her daughter out in the lane in front of the house. He walked with a limp and Biddy wondered what had happened to him. *Born that way? A fight with another boy? Who knows?* The cause was often violence in the family. She felt sorry for the lad, if he *was* a lad and not a man. Neighbors were out chatting and sweeping, the men smoking, so she did not think Norah was in danger. Still, she didn't like the looks of this man-boy and told Norah so.

Norah said, "Oh, Mum, Willy is just a strange boy who thinks he likes me. I was only being polite. He has a bum leg, you know."

Alarmed at hearing her daughter call him strange, Biddy

answered sternly, "That's exactly what worries me, Norah. He seems off to me. I don't want him around, do you hear?"

"Yes, Mum. I cannot stop him from coming in our lane, you know."

"No," said Biddy, "but you can go in the house and lock the door." Norah had laughed, but Biddy made her promise to do as she said. There was always someone to worry about.

CHAPTER 8

ADJUSTMENTS

October
Elizabeth

Elizabeth Fenn, nine years old, stood stiffly in the foyer as Miss Frances Young opened the school register and recorded her arrival at the Misses Young School for Girls on October 5, 1873. Elizabeth smiled politely at her teacher and followed her upstairs to the dormitory while holding a single thought. Elizabeth's mother had assured her that if she wanted to come home after one year, she would speak to Elizabeth's father. Elizabeth had her own idea about how long she would stay at the school.

As the days passed, she tried to find something to cheer her up, but everything about being in a boarding school felt unfamiliar, restrictive. At home she was allowed to speak her mind, and her parents trusted her common sense enough to allow her to play outside with her friends without the watchful eye of an adult. RockView was quiet and old-fashioned and smelled unfamiliar. Not bad, just different, and very unlike her lively home by the sea in Sligo. Her mother's friends referred to the Fenn home as a "social hub of the community." RockView was as far from being a social hub as it could be. The school was orderly and boring when she wasn't learning something new. The Misses Young were good teachers. She couldn't argue that.

Several times she'd caught Miss Elfie and Miss Frances watching the girls in unguarded moments. What were they looking for? To see if they were homesick, she bet. Being away from home was hard, and Elizabeth was determined not to be a baby about it. A friend would help. She had yet to find the girl she wanted to make her friend, someone to have fun with before and after school. Most of the girls seemed so protected and babyish. *If something doesn't change soon*, Elizabeth promised herself, *I will not stay at the Misses Young School no matter what my parents have decided for me.* How to execute her escape she would think about later.

On her third Friday evening at the school, Elizabeth lingered in the dormitory after the girls had readied themselves for dinner and were starting downstairs. She should be with them, but she couldn't resist taking a moment to herself. "I'll be there in a minute, umm . . ." she said to the last girl out the door, who had turned to see if she was coming.

"It's Violet," the girl said.

"Of course," Elizabeth answered with a smile. Alone at last, she flopped down on her bed, propped her head on her hands, and closed her eyes.

"Everybody needs a moment's peace," her father frequently reminded his children. Her father had meant *they* should let *him* be, but now she thought she understood the feeling. Very little about RockView felt right to her, and she needed a moment's peace to figure out why. Her home in Sligo had more windows than this house, and it had French doors they kept open during the day to bring in the sea air and sunlight. Her mother liked it that way, and now Elizabeth knew that she did too.

The rooms in RockView were dark: dark wood wainscoting with dim-white walls rising to dark wood moldings around dark wood ceilings. The cheeriest parts of the house were the paintings, though the only ones she had seen so far were of the countryside or the sea. *Are they ever going to let us see some of it for ourselves?* she wondered. There was one exception, and she wasn't sure how she felt about that painting yet. It was a large portrait of a gentleman and hung in the foyer across from the front door. He looked nice enough, but she thought it creepy that his eyes seemed to follow her whenever she passed by.

This may be my new school, but it will never be my home, she thought. *Too gloomy.* She missed having her own bedroom. She missed her mother and father. She even missed her brother, Philip, whom she generally wanted to smother. *They were family and these people were strangers.* Her mother's words came to her, unbidden: "Feelings change, dear. You'll see."

Elizabeth opened her eyes. *I suppose Mother's right.* After all, hadn't Elizabeth once adored her father and thought he could do no wrong? Then he'd brought her all the way across Ireland to a school on the outskirts of Dublin for what he insisted was "her own good."

"You are much like me, Elizabeth," he'd tried to assure her the day they left for Dublin, "a homebody. Once you find your wings, I assure you there will be no containing you." She wanted to believe him. Miss Frances and Miss Elfie were kind, and the girls were nice enough. The school still felt like a borrowed dress that did not fit—uncomfortable. *Why me?* she thought every day. *Let someone else wear it.*

Laughter filtered up from the stairway. Was that Anna

Monteforte? Anna was the only girl whose full name Elizabeth remembered so far. She was different from the other girls. She was friendly in a shy way, but she was also smart, aware of all around her. And there was something else about her. Sometimes, Elizabeth noticed that Anna's eyes would dart back and forth and she would take in a deep breath as if she had a secret she was guarding. That made Anna even more interesting to Elizabeth.

Another rising peal of laughter spurred Elizabeth off the bed and out of the room to see what she was missing. *What could possibly be that funny?* she thought. Miss Elfie stepped out into the hallway, startling Elizabeth.

Before Elizabeth could apologize for not being where she was supposed to be, her teacher placed a hand firmly on her shoulder and smiled. "It just takes time, dear," she said. Elizabeth blushed at being singled out and headed down the staircase, not daring to look back. Her mother and father had told her nearly the same thing. She hoped they were right, because like it or not she was stuck there until the Christmas holidays. She had no escape plan.

— ◆ —

November
Elfie

Every evening Monday through Friday, Elfie and Frances sat in the drawing room to go over their notes on the academic and social growth of the students. Elfie had suggested a weekly check-in, but her sister was determined to keep careful records, and that meant meeting every school night while the girls got ready for bed.

"It will be our only time to sum up the day and be free of

young eyes watching our every move," Frances told Elfie. Elfie couldn't argue with that but did wonder if the girls felt they were constantly being observed. Because they were.

Her sister had created four ledger pages for each girl, giving them enough room to keep track of the students' progress and to write detailed information to use in the letters they would send to families about the girls' progress.

Before the school opened, Elfie and Frances agreed they would send letters after the second week of each month to the students' parents, who would be wondering how their daughters were faring. The sisters had missed the first deadline by one week. There was just too much to do and too many constant adjustments to make. The school was a whole new world for them. When they met in the drawing room on the third Friday of October to discuss the girls, the subject of their overdue letter writing came up again. "Let's agree to forgive ourselves," Elfie said to Frances. Frances nodded. "I don't know about you. *I* am learning every step of the way." Shaking her head, eyes closed, she registered her disappointment. "It is just not in my nature to miss deadlines. Yours either."

"No," Elfie agreed. "Honestly, Frances, I feel we are experiencing instant parenthood of a family of nine." They both laughed, and Elfie added, "We could add Father and make it ten."

Frances sat back looking relaxed. "I suspect, dear sister, we may learn more about ourselves as we evolve in our new roles than we are able to teach these girls in French and geography."

Their father had surprised them by offering to take whatever letters they completed to the General Post Office in Dublin on Monday, his first offer of help with the school. Motivated by his unexpected generosity, the sisters met on Saturday evening and divided the task of writing between them. Elfie opened the ledger and read aloud from the dictated notes that Frances had carefully entered regarding Elizabeth Fenn:

Kind. Attentive to her lessons. Open, confident manner showing unusual maturity and leadership for her age. Appears to be warming to a friendship with Anna Monteforte.

Elfie peered up at her sister. "Does that capture enough?"

Frances nodded. "Even if Elizabeth doesn't see it herself, the other girls naturally follow her. She seems to have found her place here."

"Well said, sister. I'll include that in the letter to the Fenns."

Elfie added her signature to the finished letter and waited while her sister neatly addressed and sealed the envelope. Frances reached for a wet cloth to dampen the back of a Penny Black stamp carrying Queen Victoria's image and placed it on the upper right corner, then placed the letter on the growing pile.

They saved Anna Monteforte's letter for last because they hadn't yet decided who to send it to, her mother or her financial executor, Charles Parnell. "'Anna is doing well,'" Frances read from her notes in the ledger, "'but I feel a curious struggle in her.' I don't think we should put that in the letter," she added quickly before reading on, "'A strong presence; good at her studies; reticent; a loneliness about her.'"

Elfie nodded in agreement. "I too believe she is wrestling with something. I wonder if it could have anything to do with her sponsor."

"Possibly," Frances said. "I've come to a decision on who to send the letter to. I don't want anyone seeing our school posting letters to Mr. Parnell. They might think we are starting a revolutionary cell on Belgrave Road."

Elfie was less concerned and somewhat intrigued by Mr. Parnell. Frances, she felt, was a born worrier, but she didn't argue the point. Instead, she changed the subject. "I think having a friend like our self-assured Elizabeth might be a way for Anna to ease whatever trouble she is carrying." Elfie had learned from her letters to Lily the importance of having a confidante. The act of revealing one's innermost thoughts and concerns could be liberating. *Getting things out of your head makes monsters shrink,* she thought with a smile.

The sisters found their speed and expertise in writing encouraging but honest assessments of their students had improved by mid-November. They even felt confident enough to allow themselves a smidge of sherry while they worked. Lifting her glass as if to propose a toast, Elfie said, "We are getting good at this, don't you think?" Sure their letters would arrive before Visiting Day at the end of the month, Frances concurred. "I hope the parents feel the same, Elfie. I fear our school's reputation may be impugned if even one of the parents changes their mind about retaining their daughter in our care."

— ◆ —

Anna Monteforte

Anna woke early, her mind filled with worrying thoughts just as it had been most mornings since she had arrived at RockView. This morning was worse than usual because today was Visiting Day and that meant Mr. Parnell was coming.

Oh, stop, she told herself. *You are one of the lucky ones.* The fact that she didn't feel lucky at all made her feel worse. She was being ungrateful. "Not every girl who loses her father gets a gentleman—a famous gentleman at that," she whispered, mimicking her mother's voice, "to step in as the financial executor for her family." Anna wasn't certain what that meant. She wasn't even sure what the gentleman looked like. "Of course you know what he looks like," her mother had told her. "You met him when you were a little girl. Mr. Charles Parnell," her mother added, as if his full name would help her remember. "He was a friend of your father's and, despite his busy life, he has offered to visit you at school from time to time." *Does he have to?* she had not dared to ask. Try as she might, Anna could still not recall his face.

What she did know was that Mr. Parnell had a reputation, and for that reason alone she hoped to keep him hidden from the other girls. Her mother *tsked* whenever she read the newspapers calling him a "firebrand." *Firebrand doesn't sound very gentlemanly,* Anna worried again. She sighed and turned onto her back to stare at the ceiling again. The word had stuck in her brain, and she thought it might have stuck in the brains of other people too, people like the families of the girls she went to school with. Why couldn't she have a life like everyone else's? Why had her father died, and why did they have to be friends with Mr. Parnell? She wanted to be the same as everyone else, *not* to be associated with someone who was making trouble for the very people she lived with.

Anna took a deep breath through her nose as Miss Elfie had taught them to do when they had a case of the "worries." The quick rush of cold air almost made her sneeze. She pinched her nose until the feeling passed and then slowly breathed out through her mouth. In the dim light of the dormitory, she glanced at Violet, then Elizabeth, in the beds on either side of her. She hadn't wakened them.

None of the girls knew her father had died, and Anna wanted to keep it that way to appear as normal as possible. *They probably don't even know who Mr. Parnell is,* she told herself. *How nice to be unaware of such things.* The moment he stepped in to help with her mother's financial affairs, Anna had no choice to but to be aware of his political interests; her mother made a point of reading her every article that mentioned his name. "It's important that we show an interest in him, Anna," her mother would often remind her.

Anna sighed. Elizabeth had said that her father hoped to come on Visiting Day. She seemed excited. Anna wished she could be excited too. A soft creaking in the hallway signaled Mary's approach to the dormitory. Time to get up.

— ♦ —

Mr. Charles Parnell arrived before breakfast was served. Anna's stomach dropped as she made her way down the stairs. Maybe, she hoped, she could get him out of the house for a walk and avoid the other girls and their parents. She heard the man before she saw him. He was in a spasm of coughing in the drawing room. When she entered, she noticed how tired he looked. His thin body curled forward toward his handkerchief with each cough. "It's Anna Monteforte, Mr. Parnell," she said shyly.

Biddy rushed into the room behind Anna, carrying a pot of tea. Her speed made for an unbalanced tray clattering with cups and spoons. "Just to settle your throat, Mr. Parnell," she said.

He looked at the housekeeper with a weary smile, his posture straightening, and said, "Thank you. This will pass." To Anna, of whom he at last took notice, he said, "Sit down, my dear. I will be fine soon with this warm tea." He nodded toward Biddy. "Thank you again for the tea. You are very kind."

Anna smiled wanly and waited quietly. He did seem better after the tea. "We could take a stroll in the park. If it's not too cold, I mean," she said.

"Good idea." He smiled and stood to leave with her. Once down the porch stairs, he reached his hand out to hold hers before crossing the street. Anna glanced over her shoulder to see if anyone noticed them. From the dormitory window on the second floor, Elizabeth waved at her. Anna pretended not to notice.

Once inside the park, Anna felt an unexpected happiness in holding Mr. Parnell's hand. He seemed to genuinely care for her. Her hand was small and hot and his was long-fingered and cold, but still they held tight. Neither spoke. They just walked. To her relief, once they were well within the park he began telling her stories of his travels to the United States, where his brother lived; about Alabama being as green as Ireland but instead of bogs there were swamps full of alligators and snakes and brightly colored birds.

"Will you go back to see him soon?" she asked.

"Not right away." Parnell began coughing again and suggested they find a bench in the sun, "where we can rest and continue our conversation." Anna saw a sunny spot to sit and pointed to it.

"Good young eyes, my dear. Let's take it before someone else does."

She walked ahead and brushed leaves off the seat for them.

Settled on the bench, Parnell once again took her hand in his.

"I plan to become a member of Parliament, Anna," he said. "And that's what I've really come to tell you."

Anna nodded but didn't understand why he wanted her to know something like that.

"I'll need to speak to a lot of people in Ireland," he said. "Not just in the cities, in private clubs and public spaces, but in the countryside where the common people congregate . . . gather. . . such as the crossroads outside the villages."

Her face must have given away her surprise that he would stop somewhere like that, in places her mother had warned were "full of criminals and danger," because he laughed again and told her he would be perfectly safe. "You want to be with the people who are moving their crops and animals from farms to the market?" she asked.

"Yes, that's exactly right, Anna. I want to give these common people, who work tirelessly on the land with small reward, my message of hope for Irish Home Rule."

"Oh. Home Rule," Anna said, as if she knew what the words meant. She had heard them often enough when her father had read the newspaper to her, labelling the term in her head as "something grownups talk about."

Anna didn't have anything to say about farmers and Home Rule, yet she felt she was supposed to say something because he had stopped talking.

"Well, I don't know you very well," she said. "I do think you are a very good storyteller, Mr. Parnell," she said earnestly. "People like stories, and I like listening to your voice, so other people will too."

He laughed kindly and said, "I hope so, Anna. Thank you for your encouragement."

Anna waited for him to say more. When he didn't, she searched for something to fill in the silence. "I hope you've received my letters telling you about my schoolwork, Mr. Parnell. I'm not a very good writer yet. I do like to draw and paint. I haven't asked yet, but I hope to learn about drawing and painting with Mr. Young. He is a well-known watercolorist, you know." Anna blushed at her rush of enthusiasm. In case he thought her too forward, she added, "I have one person I think will stand with me in asking for this honor. Her name is Elizabeth Fenn."

Parnell lifted his head after a brief coughing fit and patted her knee. "I am so glad to have this time with you, Anna. I find you charming and intelligent and, of course, very pretty too. You should do very well at the Misses Young School for Girls."

Anna started to say, "Thank you," but he didn't pause to let her speak. "It's my pleasure to continue to make certain that your schooling here is not interrupted unnecessarily. You should know I may not be visiting you soon, however. Once I begin campaigning, I won't be able to visit as often as I had hoped, and maybe not at all for the next year."

Anna finally understood why he had come to see her, and now she truly didn't know what to say. She'd wanted to keep him a secret from the other girls, but now that she'd gotten to know him better, she didn't want him to disappear altogether. To her surprise she started to cry.

Mr. Parnell patted her hand awkwardly. "A British MP from Ireland would be a big and new step for our country. Of course, Parliament has no intention of hearing what Ireland has to say. I must try, Anna. You understand that, don't you?"

She supposed she did. "British MP" and "Parliament" were just words to her, like "Home Rule." But instead of feeling bored with them, she felt proud that he wanted her to understand them.

Anna and Mr. Parnell walked back to the school and said their goodbyes at the bottom of RockView's steps just as Elizabeth and her father appeared at the front door. Anna froze. There was nothing she could do to stop them from seeing her with Mr. Parnell, and sure enough, Elizabeth's father hurried down the steps toward them. "I am very glad to meet you, Mr. Parnell," he said, offering his hand. "I am an admirer. This is my daughter, Elizabeth," he said, summoning her to his side. "She attends the school with your daughter."

Anna blushed and stared at the ground.

"No, sir," Mr. Parnell corrected him, "Anna is not my daughter, though that would be most pleasant. Her father, who recently passed, was my friend."

In less than a minute, Mr. Parnell had revealed all of Anna's secrets. Her ears throbbed in her embarrassment, and she heard only bits of their conversation: "Sligo town." "Family business." "Western Steam and Navigation." Words that meant something to Mr. Parnell, because he ended the conversation with "We must talk another time, Fenn."

Mr. Parnell then gave Anna a pat on her shoulder and disappeared into the cab that had been waiting for him.

"Well, that was something, girls!" Mr. Fenn exclaimed. "Charles Parnell right here. You are a very fortunate young lady to be so well acquainted with a man who intends to bring great changes to Ireland." Anna, stunned by all that had occurred during the past few minutes, managed a weak nod. "I must be off," Mr. Fenn said. "Elizabeth, I will see you when I return from London."

The girls stood side by side watching Mr. Fenn turn on Church Avenue toward Rathmines Road Upper, where he could find a hackney ride. When he was out of hearing distance, Anna turned to Elizabeth. "Will you keep my secret? About my father and about Mr. Parnell coming to see me and about his being a friend of my family. Please. He has a reputation"—Elizabeth looked at her with interest—"as a firebrand," Anna said beneath her hand.

"Oh," Elizabeth said. Anna thought she looked disappointed, but she said that of course she'd keep Anna's secret.

Anna put out her hand. "Shake hands on it?"

Elizabeth took Anna's hand. "Of course," she said. "We're friends, aren't we?"

CHAPTER 9

MARY'S MORNING

Mary entered the dormitory struggling with a large pitcher nearly full with cooling hot water for morning face washing. Each day it was her early morning challenge to make the trip out of the kitchen—minding the infernal swinging door—cross the entry, and climb the fifteen stairs to the second floor without spilling her cargo.

The girls were still under their quilts when she arrived, except for Violet, who had tossed hers off and sat on the edge of her bed at the sound of Mary's approach. Toes stretched stiffly upward to avoid the cold floor, the girl leaned forward to retrieve a pair of clean socks from her drawer. Mary poured water into the bowl on her dresser, smiling at the girl's get-out-of-bed strategy. "Good morning, Mary," Violet whispered.

"Good morning, Miss Violet." In a few minutes the rest of the girls would be awake. Mary thought how angelic they looked as they lay in their beds. Married five years, she held a deep sadness over her own three babies, all lost to miscarriages. Still, she continued to pray for a child of her own to watch over, like these sweet girls sleeping snug in their beds. *Not yet, but God willin',* she thought. Anna stirred and Mary filled her bowl next. The girl lifted her covers above her head as far as her arms could reach, then let them drop dramatically over her face. "Your water is getting cold, Anna," Violet informed her.

Anna giggled and exposed her head to the chilly air. "Violet, you always beat me and get the hot water."

Violet returned the giggle. "Too bad, sleepyhead." With that, Anna sat up, and Mary moved on to the other bowls in the room, grateful as the pitcher lightened with each pour.

Morning duty had been Mary's job from the start of the Misses Young School: get the girls up and out of bed, washed, dressed, hair combed and pinned back. Miss Frances wanted them to make their own beds. Mary wholeheartedly agreed.

The room gradually became a sea of motion: covers tossed, squeals as feet hit the frigid floor, and water sloshing. The porcelain's thick, cool surface quickly negated what little heat remained in the water, so she didn't reprimand the girls for splashing their faces rapidly and following that with a brief-as-possible encounter with a cold towel.

Mary was glad to see Anna in good humor at last, smiling and talking with Violet as they combed their hair in front of the two tilted mirrors in the far corner of the room. The visit from that Mr. Parnell seemed to have done her some good. Biddy had said he was an important gentleman, someone wanting to help the Irish. Mary didn't know about that, but he had done right by the girl and that was enough for her.

A few of the girls were still in their nightdresses and socks, taking their turns at the mirror, considering, as Anna and Violet had, how they would wear their hair that day. *Seems like a lot of fuss to me,* she thought. *'Course, they'll grow up to be fine ladies, not a maid like me. Just push our hair into a clean lacy cap and that's that.* Miss Frances had been clear and businesslike with her instructions to the girls: "No untamed, in-your-eyes hair. We need clear vision for our work." They made great effort in choosing their hairstyles each day but always settled on braids or a simple ribbon to tie back their hair. *Quite the luxury,* thought Mary. She wished they would hurry on with the ritual and get down to breakfast.

In a bid for their attention, Mary raised her voice. "It's cold this morning, so a few layers of wool to go under your pinafores is a good idea. Don't forget to make your beds." Mary had spent plenty of time caring for children as she grew up, and she was still good at it. She hadn't been certain when she was first given the morning responsibility, but she eventually grew comfortable with being in charge of young British girls for that brief part of the day. *They aren't so different from the Irish girls at that age,* she thought. Even so, her cousin Biddy took the lead downstairs, and Mary was content to remain quiet and keep her place. As her mother liked to say, "Smart women keep their heads down so they won't get them shot off."

The pinafores were the school uniform, and Mary stood at the door making certain each one was securely tied around a girl's waist before they headed down to breakfast.

Mary followed the girls as far as the landing, where she smelled Biddy's freshly baked scones. Her young charges smelled it too and descended briskly on the wide staircase, calling out an excited "Good morning" to Mr. Young, who was attempting to walk up the stairs as they passed. Anna was the only girl who stopped to greet Mr. Young with the respect Mary felt he deserved.

"Good morning to you, Anna," replied Mr. Young. He was leaning back against the banister, and Mary worried that he'd stopped to catch his breath. She hadn't meant to eavesdrop, yet there it was.

"Just taking a moment to mind the view. I'm an artist, you know," he told Anna. "I like to take time to observe."

"Yes, sir. I know," Anna said. "I'd like to become an artist too, Mr. Young."

"Wonderful to hear. Why not start by looking out the windows?" Mr. Young turned to start up the stairs again, then looked back at the girl. "Only on your own time, eh? We wouldn't want your teachers thinking you were daydreaming during class."

Elizabeth, the last to leave the dormitory as usual, slid by Mary and greeted Mr. Young on the landing, nodding when Mary told her not to run. Mary *tsked* her frustration. *Of course, she has stopped to talk with Anna.* Instead of moving on with the others, Anna had remained rooted to the spot where she had conversed with Mr. Young. *Some mornings take longer to get going than others,* Mary reminded herself, but if they didn't get a move on in the next few seconds, she'd remind *them* that scones disappeared quickly and she had other work to do, thank you.

Anna pointed to the garden. "Mr. Young just told me to look out the windows," she said.

"Why?" Elizabeth asked.

"Because it's what artists do—and I have an idea." Elizabeth raised her eyes and grinned, but Anna put her finger to her lips. "I'll tell you tonight."

Mary was only slightly curious about what the girls were discussing. She was more interested in moving on with her day. Just as she was about to say something, Anna took Elizabeth's hand and they headed down to breakfast. Mary watched them until they entered the dining room. *Done,* she thought, then walked back to the dormitory to make sure all was in order before returning to her downstairs role as kitchen helper.

CHAPTER 10

THE NIVENS

London, Ontario, Canada
January 1874
Lily

James gave Lily a lingering kiss at the door. With one arm still around her, he stepped back to retrieve his coat from the rack with his other hand, kissing her one more time before letting her go. Lily laughed and slipped away to help her husband with the heavy sheepskin coat that covered him from neck to boot. The coat was a recent purchase, one he assured her he needed for the wintery rides to work and home visits at all hours. He playfully showed off the garment's practicality by lifting his boot flap to open the long vent at the back and said, "See, it's practical, warm, easier for walking and riding."

"Yes, James, practical and warm," she said, grinning. "And it goes with your new hat." He took the shearling earflap cap from his wife's hand and put it on. As a final touch, he wrapped around his neck the red wool muffler that Lily had knit him for Christmas and looked in the mirror.

"Oh my, I do look a little like Saint Nicholas." He pulled her to him again. "Darling Lily, be good while I'm gone," he teased.

Lily laughed, pressing herself as close to him as the coat allowed. "Father Christmas, you are my gift every day." She continued to be amazed at the pleasures of marriage, their intimacy bringing them close in a way she had never imagined. *I wish you didn't have to go,* she thought but knew better than to say. Her husband had his work. He had to leave, no matter how long the days stretched out for her.

She wouldn't be truly alone. There was young Jim, their groom and handyman, who arrived each morning with an armful of firewood before mucking out the stall and attending to whatever task might be needed. He usually had Count ready for James each morning, but James said he had sent him on an errand in town and he would not be at the house until the afternoon. The next few hours would be hers to fill before the inscrutable Mrs. Bennet arrived. James had hired the woman to help around the house in the afternoons. Unfortunately, her presence made Lily uncomfortable. She was an apparition, appearing and disappearing without a word while she worked. Lily missed Biddy and Mary's cheerful chatter. *I will choose the next domestic,* she promised herself. *Someone with more personality and less quiet.*

Lily watched her husband through the living room window. She couldn't help smiling as he strode through a light dusting of snow to the barn. *Lily, you've chosen a very athletic-looking husband.*

— ◆ —

James

James looked up as he led Count out of the barn and waved at Lily in the window. If only he could go back inside to their bedroom instead of going to work. James patted Count's flank. "There, boy." He placed his foot in the stirrup and swung the other over the saddle. "At least one of us is anxious to get going."

On the long road into town, they cantered past deep-green conifers sparsely decorated with the overnight snow, and the puddles in the fields caught the rising sun. The cold air felt refreshing on his face and in his lungs. *This is what I came here for. This is what I want for Lily and myself.* The open spaces held a freedom and possibility that a troubled Ireland had lost.

Too soon the snow-covered road became mud, and he slowed Count to a trot, then a walk before entering the well-graveled streets of the town. The clip-clopping of Count's hooves hitting the rock reminded him of when he was a boy growing up in Lisburn, Ireland, the crackle of gravel on the driveway a signal that someone was arriving or leaving.

James sighed. His mother became too easily lodged in his thoughts and once there was hard to shake off. Eliza meant well, but James found her needy and exhausting. Only the previous day he had received word that yet another package from Lisburn was awaiting Mr. and Mr. James Niven at the train station. He had dispatched Jim that morning to retrieve it. *What has Mother sent now?* He understood it had been difficult for her to see them leave Ireland. Watching her only child sail away with his bride was a blow. The loss of control over her boy and the distance placed between them, a double blow.

Their mother-son history had been complicated by the death of his father when James was twelve. James had become the sole focus of her feverish affection. He pushed away the memory and walked Count into the blacksmith's barn, where he dismounted and handed the reins to the smithy's helper. "See you this evening, old boy." He patted his horse on the neck, then walked the block to the surgery to begin his day.

— ♦ —

Lily

With nothing pressing her into activity that morning, Lily lingered by the living room fireplace, lifting her skirt slightly to warm her legs. She envied the freedom of her husband's ride through the countryside. While James had Count and interacted with people every day in town, Lily was limited to solitary walks when the weather permitted and amusing herself within the walls of their house.

Looking around the large living room, she scolded herself. *Here I am, warm and comfortable in my very own beautiful home. I have nothing to complain about.* She sat in one of the two wingback chairs that faced the fireplace, each with a cushioned footstool. The round table between them was eternally strewn with papers and books. *Baskets,* she reminded herself. *He might even use them.* Within their first week of marriage, she'd discovered she had married a gentleman used to others tidying up for him. Her father had been much the same. She straightened up the tabletop and sat back down to consider her next project. There were always letters to write, of course, but there wasn't always something new to put in them. Lily could not remember being unoccupied in Ireland. If she had been there now, she would have been arranging her father's birthday party. *No, that was my old life,* she scolded herself. She was making a new one.

Lily reached into the table drawer next to her and pulled out her knitting needles and yarn. The success of the red muffler had inspired her. She would surprise James next with a pair of fine blue wool socks.

Jim arrived at the house after lunch with a heavy, long package from Ireland. Lily read the accompanying note:

> *Why bother with a small amount when you are sending it so far?*
> *Love, Eliza*

Oh dear, Lily thought, then laughed when she and Jim uncovered an enormous bolt of flower-strewn fabric. Her mother-in-law had a point, but large quantities were better suited to Eliza's flamboyant more-is-better personality. Lily tended toward the conservative and tailored and, in truth, was just developing her own taste and style. *At least its contents will give me something new to do.* By the time James returned home that evening, the living room chairs were draped in floral chintz, compliments of Eliza.

"Just like my mother!" James hooted.

CHAPTER 11

A TURNING POINT

Dublin, Ireland
Elfie and Frances

All of the girls returned to the Misses Young School for Girls just after the new year. Both Elfie and Frances were relieved, even more so when they saw their students settle easily into the school after their Christmas holidays. The routines they'd set for the girls at the beginning of the school year had paid off. "I feel pleased with us Elfie," Frances said. "Now, let's see what we can do about the weather."

While the residents of RockView were used to the Irish weather that forced them to stay inside, they were not yet used to being forced to stay inside together.

Elfie said she had a grand idea for breaking the indoor tedium. "How about taking them on a walk to St. Patrick's Cathedral?" Before Frances could disagree, she added, "They often have concerts in that great space. It would be the perfect way to use some of the energy cooped up in this house while taking in a little culture in Dublin town. These rainy, cold days will soon have us on top of one another!"

To Elfie's surprise, Frances answered enthusiastically. "Elfie, that is a wonderful idea. With the proper attire, a walk in the rain won't hurt any of us. I will look in the newspaper for the schedule. But first," she added, "let's celebrate the girls' progress and ours." Frances left the dining room and returned with two glasses and a nearly full bottle of sherry. "I guess I am the butler tonight," she said, pouring a glass for each of them. Smiling, she placed her chair on the other side of an ottoman and rested her feet toe to toe with her sister's. "My back aches. Can't wait to take off my corset."

Elfie closed her eyes and rested her head on her chair. "Wouldn't Mother be proud of us for starting our own school?" she said. "I begin to more fully understand now why she was so often tired and unavailable to us. Can you imagine, Frances, having children of our own, a husband, less than robust health, and a household to cope with after a day of teaching?"

Frances shook her head. "The school is much more work than I thought it would be. Mother's standards were high. Ours are too. *I* am proud of that."

Elfie raised her glass in silent agreement.

"I think of her when I open the ledger to make notes on the girls," Frances said thoughtfully. "That is exactly what Mother did, you know. Father showed me her ledgers when we proposed the school. He warned me about the long hours and dedication required. I'm not sure I believed him."

"We were determined," Elfie said. "I mean we *are* determined!" She opened her eyes and sat up straighter in her chair as a tingle moved gently through her body. The sherry was traveling, loosening her composure, and she liked the feeling.

She wondered if her tightly composed sister had the same reaction.

"When Father says, 'You girls are so like your mother,'" Frances continued, "I am quite sure he is talking about the dedicated teacher in us and not our manner or grace." She put her feet on the floor and sat up. She closed the ledger. "Time for bed," she announced. "We can make notes tomorrow." Elfie kissed her sister lightly on the cheek, and they both went up the stairs, turning off the gas lamps behind them.

"It wouldn't hurt Father to join us on the outing," Frances suggested. She automatically put her finger to the corner of her eye, but there was no need. In fact, Frances realized that her eye had not twitched all day. Things were looking up.

On the second floor, Elfie turned toward the dormitory to make sure the girls were in bed and to read them the next chapter of *The King of the Golden River*. Frances thought the book old-fashioned, but it had been one of Elfie's favorites when she was young. "There's nothing old-fashioned about love winning out over selfishness and greed," Elfie had stated matter-of-factly. "And besides, I am in charge of the girls' bedtime." Elfie smiled, marveling again how quickly the dynamics of their household had expanded since the school began. There were new roles for everyone at RockView. She and Frances were in charge of the school and therefore had more of a say about the house and its residents. That felt right, if still a little uncomfortable. *We have our new roles. I'm certain Father will figure out what his will be.* Frances was right. He should come with them to the cathedral. With so many people to consider, being a sister, mother, teacher, *and* daughter was a big order. "We shall see how the plan for the outing sorts out," she said wearily. "We shall see."

— • —

Thomas

The following week, the front hall came alive at ten minutes before two o'clock, with young girls locating their hats, gloves, coats, and scarves and tugging on knee-high walking boots that to this point had been cleaned and oiled for them by grooms at home. Fortunately, Biddy had found a man who would come to the school to maintain the boots' supple leather after a splashing outing like the one the girls were about to take. The light overnight snowfall had melted, and the sky was making a hopeful gesture, lightening to a brilliant overcast. Clear roads and a brightening sky—not much more could be wished for in Dublin in January.

Thomas stood on the landing above the first floor, observing the wiggly mass and wondering at the wisdom of giving up the opportunity for a few hours of peace and quiet in his own home for an afternoon of chaperoning young girls. He had been sullen for too long, and his daughters were losing patience with him. His acquiescence to taking part in the outing seemed to please them. The journey would be slushy and messy but getting outdoors and stretching his legs with a clear destination and activity in focus appealed to him. If he was honest with himself, a walk and a concert offered a diversion he looked forward to.

Frances emerged from the kitchen hallway in a long charcoal-gray coat carefully buttoned from the neck to below the knee, where it remained open to the ankle to accommodate her strong walking gait. Her heather-gray felt hat sat at a smart angle on her upswept hair, reminding Thomas of Sarah when she'd been young and healthy and ready to take on the world. Frances's left hand firmly held soft dove-gray leather gloves, and a small basket rested on her right arm. Biddy and Mary had undoubtedly made some wonderful treat that would renew energy before they started the return trip. Frances caught Thomas watching her and smiled.

"Young ladies." Frances's voice was firm as she surveyed the crowd from the first step of the staircase to be sure all were present. The girls quieted and turned to look at their teacher. Thomas noticed they'd already learned that "young ladies" meant more than "pay attention." The term served as a reminder that they were carefully selected young women representing the Misses Young School. Before Frances could further instruct the girls, the front door opened, letting in a rush of cold air accompanied by his youngest daughter bundled in a brown wool coat, her neck wrapped in a red paisley scarf and a round felt hat precariously perched on top of her brown curls.

"Girls, I've just been out to look at the sky. It appears quite promising," Elfie announced. "But the muddy streets will give us a challenge. We will turn up at the cathedral door with a good amount of Dublin's earth on our shoes, I'm afraid."

Thomas looked ruefully at his beautifully polished boots. *Biddy's young man will have quite a job on his hands when we return,* he thought. To feel part of the parade, he called out from his perch on the landing, "Nothing wrong with collecting some of Dublin's finest mud on a good walk!" His voice seemed to stun his daughters and the girls into a quiet amazement. *I should speak more often,* he thought.

"No indeed, Father," Elfie agreed, smiling broadly. Her words broke the spell, restarting a ripple of movement and giggles through the foyer.

"Choose a partner and we will be on our way," Frances instructed. They took hands but waited for The Rules that even Thomas knew would be forthcoming. "The rules for today's outing will be as follows," Frances said. "First, everyone must keep apace, or we will be late for the concert. Dawdling and silliness do not become young ladies of your breeding. But neither does running. The roads are muddy, and you are to watch for wagons and carriages that might splash us and, of course any stray cattle that may want to join our march to the cathedral." The girls smiled, as did Frances and Elfie.

Thomas wondered if his daughters had considered the possibility of running into political demonstrations along the way, another reason he had decided to come along. The near-daily rallies calling for Irish independence were creating tension in the city, where the revolutionary idea was not universally welcomed. He'd mentioned his concern at breakfast, but Frances replied that pickpockets were more likely. "As always, I will keep alert," she reassured him. "I hope we all will." It was close to a dismissal of his concerns, but she had given a tiny nodded acknowledgment of them by cleverly making him share the responsibility for keeping a lookout.

The brisk air and bright silvery sky put a spring in their steps, and the group made good time walking up Mount Pleasant Road to the Grand Canal. They passed a small skiff with three men fishing in the murky water as the group followed the embankment toward the bridge at Harold's Cross Road. On the banks below, a cow grazed, small boys threw stones into the water, and a young man, pipe in his mouth, held the reins of his horse as it took its fill from the slow-moving canal water heading sluggishly toward the River Liffey and Dublin Bay. There was no missing the rank smells rising from the canal and the number of people and animals living in the city.

Thomas paused on the bridge, letting the girls pass him. He wanted a moment to himself. Behind him was Mount Jerome cemetery where his wife, Sarah, lay with six of their children. He missed her company. Frances was too preoccupied with the "troops" to notice he'd stopped. Over the past few years, his youngest daughters had lost interest in his life and opinions. *They have their new school and charges on their minds, of course,* he conceded. Elfie, bringing up the rear, looked up at him. He waved her on and she frowned as she walked by. *They just want me to behave. Like the children,* he thought. *Whether I like it or not.*

After the last of the red-cheeked girls made their way across the bridge, Thomas followed at a distance. He knew a few of their names. Elizabeth Fenn, for one. Her father sometimes visited the school on his way to London for business and liked to talk about nationalist politics with Thomas. Thomas watched, with interest, the Fenn girl positioning herself next to Anna Monteforte, whose name he remembered only because of her benefactor. A bit of a hush-hush, Frances had told him, as the man was a well-known politician. Elizabeth reached for Anna's hand, but the other girl pulled hers away. *Good for her,* Thomas thought. *She knows her own mind.* Then he noticed Anna looking at Elizabeth as if she had only just realized who was next to her and offering her hand back. The girls giggled, and Thomas felt suddenly alone.

To his dismay, there hadn't been one protest or sign of unrest as they walked, nor had their pockets been picked, as far as he knew. His daughters probably thought him overly cautious and hadn't paid attention to his earlier warning anyway. *Of course, there's always the walk home,* he thought.

At the corner of St. Patrick's Close, the small group gathered and took in the sight of the cathedral surrounded by an open park. The enormous length of the building and its imposing tower made St. Patrick's arguably the grandest church in Ireland. The nearby Guinness Brewery sent a steady perfume of stout into the air. If he closed his eyes, he might be sliding into a booth at Harold's Cross Pub, anticipating the taste of malt and hops hitting his tongue. Thomas smiled thinking of the men heading to church on Sundays imagining the same thing when they slid into the pews and closed their eyes to pray.

The scale of the monumental stone building hushed the girls as they followed Frances and Elfie down the long central aisle to file into pews close to the front. The girls seemed mesmerized by the jewel-like light of the stained-glass windows that spread like wings on either side of them, transforming the interior into the cruciform shape of the holy cross. He was pleased by the girls' silence and sense of awe. His daughters were teaching them well.

— • —

Elfie

To Elfie's pleasure, her father joined them in their pew. He'd made clear to both his daughters the previous night that he preferred to sit at the back where, he judged, the acoustics would be best. Elfie assumed "where he was away from the girls" was closer to the truth. Elfie was even more delighted at what happened next. Just as her father sat down, Elizabeth Fenn and Anna Monteforte unexpectedly changed pews and sat on either side of him. Elfie and Frances exchanged glances. The first bright chords from the enormous pipe organ reverberated throughout the chamber, causing Elizabeth to reach out and take Thomas's hand. He seemed as surprised as Elfie, but he didn't disengage. He smiled! Elfie nudged her sister's arm and nodded toward their father.

"Well," Frances whispered, "that's heartening."

Elfie was thrilled. A thaw might be beginning, after all. Their father's sixty-second birthday was only a few weeks away. *He might be more agreeable to celebrating it,* she thought excitedly. *Isn't it wonderful how one inspiration can lead to another? First the field trip comes to mind, and now a birthday party for Father. I can only wonder what might come to me next!*

Elfie returned her gaze to the choir, but her thoughts floated toward the birthday party. Her father's lack of interest in anything beyond his loneliness and politics had taken its toll on their Christmas and New Year's celebrations. All through the holidays, he'd stood by the windows, looking out toward the street in hopes of a letter or package from Canada. *Well,* she thought, *this time will be different. He can't possibly refuse to participate in a celebration that's all about him.*

During the rest of the concert, Elfie prepared her arguments in case her sister objected to the party, finally settling on the assertion that celebrations and things to look forward to were important for both the young and the old. Frances, if she agreed to it, would likely prefer a quiet, staid affair, but Elfie had something more joyful in mind. During the walk home after the concert, her mind buzzed with ideas. She was so preoccupied, she almost missed seeing Elizabeth and Anna on either side of her father, each one holding his hand. *This outing is just what we needed. I'm so glad we brought the girls here.* She pursed her lips in a private smile and thought, *I'll take credit for that idea too. Frances and Lily aren't the only Young sisters who can make things happen.*

CHAPTER 12

PREPARATIONS

Elfie

"She's coming!" Elfie walked into the drawing room, holding an opened letter in her hand. "Eliza, I mean." She handed the reply to Frances and then settled into her chair. "I've been wanting to tell you all day; there just was never a good time. Read it aloud if you would. I haven't read all the way through yet."

Her sister frowned but did as Elfie asked without scolding her for inserting personal news before their school planning meeting.

"With James and Lily abroad," Frances read, "I have been hungering for an excuse to come to Dublin and visit my cousin Geoffrey Touth and his wife, Alexis. The additional pleasures I desire, other than your good company, are finding a decent dressmaker, seeing a play, and sitting for an hour or two in the Trinity College library to enjoy the beauty of its warm woods and the smell of books, and to surround myself with elegant architecture. . ."

Frances paused to look up at her sister. "Yes, of course," they said at the same time. "The library!" The two immediately agreed to make the library a future outing for their students. Frances picked up the letter and read aloud Eliza's description of "the leather-bound miracle" of the library's book collection and the ancient *Book of Armagh*, which was reason enough for a visit. "Food for the soul," Eliza had added. Elfie made a mental note of both phrases to share with the girls.

"I'm curious to learn Eliza's idea of a 'decent dressmaker,'" Frances said with what Elfie thought sounded like envy. Her sister preferred being fashionably dressed and took pains to ensure her clothes flattered her figure. For herself, Elfie preferred comfort, but she was proud of her sister's choice of restrained stylishness in clothes.

"Eliza does have a certain flair for clothes," Elfie said. "To each their own, I suppose," she added for Frances's benefit, and was rewarded with a smile.

Eliza ended her letter stating that she had a wonderful idea for a gift for Thomas, and of course did not mention what it was. "What did I say about the fun of anticipation?" Elfie reminded her sister.

Frances nodded in agreement and handed the letter back to Elfie. "Speaking of anticipation," she said, opening the school ledger on her lap, "shall we begin?"

— ◆ —

Frances

Once their meeting was over, Elfie went upstairs to check on the girls in bed, and Frances let her mind shift from the school to the upcoming party. Party planning had been Lily's domain, with her and Elfie acting as support. Frances was excited to at last take the lead. *We'll need to close the door to the entry hall once the guests arrive, to keep the draft from making the candles drip on the table,* she thought. *Biddy and Mary should wait until the day before the party to buff the table, but the tall silver candelabra polishing can be done two days before if needed.* Frances thought they hardly needed to be told to replace the everyday blue-and-white Staffordshire pottery and utilitarian glassware with the blue-and-white Spode and the French crystal glasses. She would find a casual way to mention it, just in case. *And why would Elfie assume I would object to the celebration? I've been just as disappointed as she with Father's dismal mood souring our holidays. Did she think I'd given up trying? Elfie is right about one thing. Father's birthday is a wonderful reason for a celebration. Things are looking up!*

Frances walked around the house before heading upstairs to her bedroom. The improvements made in anticipation of Lily's wedding had initially irked her as a waste of money. Lily was so easy to love and spoil because she was pretty and light-hearted. Frances loved her elder sister, but her role as their father's "pet" had been difficult to tolerate. Every pound their father spent on Lily's wedding festivities had seemed a direct affront to Frances. Her own requests for house repairs for the school had been ignored while precious pounds were spent on Lily's trousseau, gifts for the wedding party, the bridal bouquet, flowers for the church, and linens, flowers, luncheon food, and service for the reception, plus refurbishments to the house that seemed, at the time, frivolous. She'd been furious and had not contained it well. Her father had sat quietly while she blew off steam, which irritated her all the more. When he *had* finally spoken to her, she'd felt more childish than relieved. Keeping his voice low, he'd answered with what for him was a stern tone. "Frances, as soon as the newlyweds are off, we will deal with your list. The workmen have your meticulous instructions and the materials are ordered. We cannot do it all at one time. There is too much confusion in this house already." As much as his reply had galled her, every one of her desired changes for the school had been made in time.

Well, that, she told herself, *is all in the past now. I never said I was perfect.*

Her father had been right about the level of chaos they had all endured. The moving plans alone for Lily and her soon-to-be-husband, James, had taken on the dimensions of provisioning for an encampment in a wild, uncivilized place. Lily selected pieces of furniture from her room to take with them, and Thomas presented four of his paintings to be shipped to her for their new home. James repeatedly assured them of the comfort and civilized society that awaited them, but the trunks in the foyer continued to multiply. Every day the contents of the trunks grew to meet each newly imagined challenge of the Canadian outback. The new world beckoned—James worried and enthralled them with stories of open land and a growing population with a frontier mindset.

Did Lily realize that her leaving would create an opportunity for Elfie and me to become more important to Father? She must have known her exit would be hard on him. Frances shook her head. *Who knows what Lily was thinking while dealing with wedding plans and packing up for her new life across the Atlantic with James? She may have shared her thoughts with Elfie, but she didn't share them with me.* Frances caught herself feeling impatient and critical again and changed course. *Detaching herself from the only home she'd known in anticipation of a daring life adventure must have been difficult for her,* she told herself. Frances admired her sister's courage and resolve. Frances and Elfie were resolved, too. Just because they hadn't been successful so far didn't mean she and Elfie hadn't made concerted efforts to lift their father's spirits, hoping he in turn would come to appreciate their value to his life. *The party is a good next step,* she thought, *and there certainly is a lot to do. Thank goodness for Elfie.*

Over the next two days, the Youngs received brief notes of acceptance from the Yeatses, the Dunnes, and the Touths, whom they'd only met during Lily's wedding festivities. "Of course, Eliza will be staying with her cousins if she comes," Frances had told Elfie as they made their list of invitations. "We can't very well not invite them."

On Sunday, their father's longtime friends the Winfields, out for a carriage ride after church, stopped by to personally give their reply and to make a proposal. "How I miss all those wonderful occasions when dear Lily and I performed together on the piano," Mrs. Winfield said. "She was wonderful at so many things, don't you agree? In her absence, my gift to your father, and of course to all in attendance, will be to play Chopin at the party. The one Lily so often played for him," she added, gazing at the piano. Elfie suspected Mrs. Winfield had truly stopped by for the express purpose of learning if the instrument had lost its tuning in Lily's absence.

"How kind of you," Frances said, politely. "Fortunately, Elfie plays the piano daily for us. We keep the instrument in good tune."

The sisters maintained their smiles as the woman seated herself at the piano, played several measures from half a dozen classical pieces, and announced her approval.

"Between Eliza and Mrs. Winfield," Elfie said, after closing the front door behind their unexpected guests, "the evening should be very . . ." She paused, trying to think of the right word.

"Entertaining," Frances interjected.

— ◆ —

On the day of Thomas Young's birthday, the Misses Young sent the girls upstairs at five o'clock to change their clothes for the evening's activities. Frances used the free moment to make a last sweep of the first floor to be sure nothing had been missed. Their charges were notorious for leaving a stray book, glove, or stocking in the entryway. Everything inside appeared in good order. Outside, however, the skies were opening and rain began to tap and drip on every window. A typical January evening, and there was nothing to be done about it. When the girls returned for an early supper of soup and bread in the study hall, they were in high excitement, able to move about, talk, and joke in a way they never could in the dining room. It was like a holiday. Elfie kept an eye on them from the hall while Frances went to check on Biddy and Mary.

In the kitchen, she found both Biddy and Mary in high spirits—a relief, as Biddy had seemed a bit down of late. Frances wasn't going to worry about that, not tonight. After all, there was nothing like a party to cheer people up, and Biddy and Mary would do their best for Thomas no matter what was tugging at them from their own lives.

A yeasty aroma rose from the oven—fresh rolls in their last minutes of baking. A leg of lamb rested on the counter. Potatoes were peeled and ready to go on to boil. Biddy was in full command of the intricate timing involved in making all the food ready at the right time. She was the bread baker, her specialty. The finished rolls would soon rest under a linen towel atop the stove, and then she would reheat them before serving by popping them in the oven briefly at the last minute.

Mary was the cake baker, a skill she had learned from her grandmother and was very proud of. With Frances and Elfie's approval, she'd chosen her gran's recipe for thin layers of a light sponge with whipped cream filling and a final frosting of butter and sugar laced with cocoa from Holland that she'd hoarded for the occasion. Mary assured Frances that the cake had turned out perfectly and that it sat carefully hidden from view in the icebox to keep it a surprise and to avoid the kitchen heat. "I wish Gran could see it!" Mary said in her excitement. "The cake looks ever so lovely on your family's crystal cake plate." Mary continued peeling and cutting the carrots into small pieces "on the angle" as her cousin Agnes had shown her. "Just like the hoity-toity hotels serve 'um," she told Frances. "Pull out all the stops. Everything the best for Mr. Young," she said—clearly the motto for the evening. Frances gave full approval and slipped into the dining room to check the table and seating arrangements.

Elfie had left name cards for her on the dining room table, and she began the important task of arranging the seating. Frances started with the easiest one, their father, followed by Mrs. Yeats on his left, Eliza Niven to his right. Mr. Touth she placed next to Mrs. Yeats, because he had cousins in Sligo, her hometown. "Elfie will sit on the other side of Mr. Touth, with Mr. Winfield on her left," she said as she set down their name cards. Men on either side would please her sister. Frances sighed as she put the next two cards on the table. *Mr. Winfield might be a little dull,* she thought, *but Mr. Touth is an attorney and was a witty conversationalist at Lily's wedding reception.* She placed Mrs. Dunne next to Mrs. Winfield, to whom she gave the honor of the end of the table, opposite Thomas. Mrs. Tessa Dunne was a rather stiff but well-meaning woman, a suitable match for the attention-seeking Mrs. Winfield, who would hardly notice her. Frances chuckled at that pairing, then seated herself across from Elfie, between Mr. Yeats and Mr. Dunne. *Two men for me too,* she thought, smiling to herself.

For the centerpiece, Frances had chosen the yellow Sèvres bowl Lily had brought home from Paris. Frances had initially hesitated to use her sister's gift to their parents, and she hesitated again now. Would it remind her father of Lily's absence or of her presence? *An impossible question to answer,* Frances answered herself. He seemed so much better of late, and the centerpiece was so lovely, She decided it would stay. From there, the rest of the table arrangements fell easily into place. *Why do I waste my time worrying about such things?* she wondered. On either side of the yellow bowl she placed two silver candlesticks to lend soft light. Frances admired the room once more and then left to help Elfie with the girls, whom she could hear giggling all the way from the first floor. *Father will at least be pleased with the dining arrangements,* she thought.

By quarter after six, the sisters had successfully moved the girls to the drawing room, where they clustered around the piano. Elfie played the Irish tune the girls would be performing that evening. Most of the young choir hummed along. Some silently mouthed the lyrics about fairies blessing the day by shining the stars and calming the waters so the moon could find the one you love and bring him luck. They'd practiced so often, Frances was certain they could sing it in their sleep. *She* certainly could. Frances left the room to retrieve the guest of honor. When she and her father returned to the drawing room, the girls were still in practice, nervously bumping one another, pulling up on loose socks and down on tight frocks, tugging at tight braids, and giggling. Frances stole a glance at her father. Without a word, he moved to the table that held the liquor and glasses, all the while keeping an eye on the tumult as if to be certain the girls did not, in their zeal, topple this valuable cargo. *Father is still Father,* she thought. *The calm and control he once felt in his home exist no more. Not easy at his age.* There was nothing she could do about that now.

CHAPTER 13

THE BIRTHDAY PARTY

The wind and rain picked up just as the first three guests arrived. Mr. and Mrs. Touth managed to enter the foyer barely damp in their elegant attire, but they nearly faded into the walls when their houseguest, Eliza Niven, removed her cloak. Lily's mother-in-law had come dressed for the evening in shimmering taffeta that swept the floor. The color was such a deep blue it flickered to black as she moved. Sizable pearl buttons swung pendulously from large cuffs that folded up nearly to her elbows. Matching pearls decorated the gown's high neck. That would have been more than enough for Frances or Elfie, but Eliza had further accessorized with a grand display of gold jewelry—earrings, necklaces, and bracelets. She was all jingle and glitter and quite spectacular. Frances wondered incredulously if Eliza was wearing the new look she had come to the Dublin dressmaker for. The woman's theatrical voice and full body filled the entryway. She offered her umbrella and cloak to an amused Mary, then sent the poor woman into the rain to bring in a gift for Thomas from the coach.

Eliza liked to arrive exactly on time and especially so that night, as she wanted to meet the "young ladies" before the other guests came. "What a band of angels we have here!" she declared as she swept into the drawing room where the girls were waiting. In her hands she carried two gifts, a box of sweets and a book. Elfie whispered to Elizabeth to step forward and accept the gifts for the girls. Eliza handed Elizabeth the candy and, holding the book to her bosom, said with some drama, "*This* is Ballantyne's *The Gorilla Hunters*. It is a story of three boys and their adventure in the wilds of Africa. You girls can imagine yourselves as the adventurers. Girls should have adventures, too."

"Thank you, Mrs. Niven," said Elizabeth. Both Frances and Elfie were pleased to see her confidence and poise as she addressed this larger-than-life, gift-bearing woman. "Your gifts remind me of home. My father is a great one for winning our hearts with sweets, and, on very special occasions, a book. Mr. Ballantyne's sounds very exciting!" She turned to look at the knot of silent girls behind her, then back to Mrs. Niven. "Thank you again. My new sisters and I will enjoy your presents." Wiggles and giggles followed as Elizabeth rejoined the group.

Eliza beamed her delight on Thomas, who responded with clear amusement in his voice, "I see I have competition for your affection, Eliza."

"That you do, Thomas," Eliza said, returning his warmth. She took a colorfully wrapped package from a rain-spattered Mary, who had just appeared in the doorway, and handed it to Thomas. "But tonight is your night. Happy birthday, dear Thomas! I know you remember the Touths, my cousin Geoffrey and his wife, Alexis," she said, turning to the couple who had followed her into the drawing room. Geoffrey shook

Thomas's hand and gave the hands of Frances and Elfie polite kisses. Alexis, a dour-faced woman, waited for Thomas to greet her, showing little enthusiasm for this reunion with James's in-laws.

A knock on the door caused Thomas to step back into the foyer as the Yeatses stepped inside with a flurry of wet overcoats, umbrellas, hats, and scarves. *Eliza's entrance was so smooth,* Thomas thought, *and she came in from the same bloody weather.*

"For God's sake, Thomas," John Yeats said, "the devil himself must have decided to attend this celebration. And here I am!" Susan Yeats gave Thomas a warm smile and a kiss on the cheek. "Happy birthday, Thomas. It is an honor to celebrate with you," she said, and then added with a sly grin, "I brought John to liven up the party." Thomas laughed appreciatively and ushered his friends into the drawing room while Elfie waited for the remaining guests to arrive.

She soon appeared, escorting in the Dunnes, who would have entered the drawing room quietly enough to go unnoticed if Elfie hadn't announced them. Not surprising to Elfie or Frances, Margaret Winfield arrived last, dressed in black for her piano recital, with her husband, Edward, in tow. "Frances," Elfie whispered, pulling her sister aside, eyebrows raised. "This is quite a range of personalities. Was it a mistake to include the Dunnes?" Peter Dunne was the rector of the Holy Trinity Church. Of the couple, it was Peter who was cheerful and "grateful for God's blessings," while Tessa was stiff in her overstarched piety. Her support of her husband's service to God and community were present in her ramrod carriage and pursed lips, which implied a prim judgment of all but herself. *Not much fun,* Elfie thought, but they could not very well invite one Dunne without the other.

"Nonsense," Frances whispered back. "At the very least Tessa Dunne and Alexis Touth should have a lot in common."

She pursed her lips to mimic the women, and Elfie stifled a giggle.

Gifts for Thomas were placed on a round mahogany table near the window. He took in the colorful wrappings and thought giddily, *I still like presents. I suppose I am not dead yet.*

Mary served sherry and whiskey, and the guests settled into conversation. With a chord struck softly on the piano, Elfie signaled it was time for the girls to perform for the guests. Louisa Buckle, a gangly nine-year old, introduced the program. "Mr. Young, we want to offer you our best wishes on your birthday." She turned to Elfie, who lifted her hand for the girl to continue. "We will sing a song for you that Miss Elfie wrote, and we have for you a poem and a gift we made ourselves. The song is titled 'We Polished the Stars for You,' and the poem was written by Elizabeth Fenn. She will read it herself." Even Mrs. Dunne and Mrs. Touth smiled in relief for Louisa and in appreciation for her effort. The song was loudly and sincerely rendered, followed by even louder applause from the audience. Frances motioned for Elizabeth to step forward to read her poem, and the room quieted down.

Elizabeth stood in front of her audience, clasped her hands, looked directly at Thomas Young, and began her well-practiced recitation.

> *"A Birthday Wish" by Elizabeth Fenn*
> *Papa Young, this is your day.*
> *For you, we wish to sing and play*
> *With our happiest and freshest voice*
> *Your special day we do rejoice.*
> *Happy Birthday!*

The guests burst into applause, including Thomas, who rose and approached Elizabeth. "Thank you, my dear," he said quietly, taking her hand.

Frances and Elfie glanced at one another. "Papa?" Frances mouthed to her sister, who also looked surprised. Yet Elizabeth seemed to have struck the right chord with their father. The party was off to a good start.

Patricia Farwell, their smallest, youngest student, brought forward the girls' gift and handed it to Thomas. "Every one of us made stitches on it," she said. "The laurel leaves in the ribbon are for peace, which we know you do not have with us in your house." The adults burst into laughter, this time with the girls joining them. Frances laughed too, wondering if she had ever dared to be so direct and honest as a child. Thomas opened the box and removed a framed piece of ivory linen cross-stitched in blue and red. He read the message aloud.

> *For Papa Young*
> *May God Bless You on Your Birthday*
> *The Misses Young School for Girls*
> *January 1874*

Thomas patted Patricia's shoulder. "Thank you all . . . my daughters." Frances and Elfie could hardly believe their ears.

"Time for these young ladies to retire," Elfie said. "Please say goodnight to our guests and follow Mary upstairs. You were marvelous."

"Such fine children," Mrs. Touth said as they left the room.

"What could be nicer or less economical than having twelve daughters at the age of sixty-two!" John Yeats exclaimed, making Thomas laugh again.

Biddy entered the room and rang a silver bell. "Dinner will be served in the dining room, Mr. Young."

Frances helped the guests find their places while Thomas's favorite foods appeared on the table: leg of lamb with fresh mint sauce, boiled potatoes with butter and chives, and gingered carrots. Thomas lifted a decanter, and Biddy took it from his hand to serve the wine. "A toast to friends and family," Thomas said, lifting his glass. "Thank you for coming out on this stormy night to celebrate with my daughters and me. It appears their preparations and this fine food will make your journey worthwhile. I am honored by your presence. Thank you, Frances and Alfreda, for making this fine evening in my honor." Their raised crystal glasses sparkled in the glow of the candle flame.

Geoffrey Touth got the conversation started by addressing John Yeats. "What keeps you here in Dublin, sir?" It wasn't the pithy question he had hoped to come up with; still, not a bad start.

"Fortunately," Yeats replied, "I have a temporary position teaching portraiture at the academy where Thomas and I are colleagues. My wife and I live in London the rest of the year." Gesturing toward his wife, Susan, he said, "We have a rambunctious nine-year-old son, William, and daughters too. A steady job at any time of year for this former lawyer is most welcome. Keeps me out of the pubs, where I have a tendency to linger!"

Touth then turned to his host. "Thomas, do you have an opinion on how Mr. Gladstone's government will fare in the election next month?"

Frances and Elfie watched as the table grew silent. Politics already? They were not at all certain of their guests' leanings and hoped the question would not create an uncomfortable exchange.

Thomas opened his mouth to reply, but Mr. Winfield surprised them by speaking before his host. "I'll spare Thomas that answer. What's the difference?" His face flushed with emotion. "The English Parliament is bent on one thing: sacking the Irish, along with all the British colonies."

Thomas replied diplomatically, "In my opinion, there will be a new Tory majority and Gladstone will fall. But I agree with you, Edward. It will matter little to the cause of the Irish."

Yeats wore a mischievous expression as he leaned forward toward Thomas and said, "Speaking of politics, Thomas, I hear you have a student under your roof associated with the delightfully outspoken Parnell." Both Elfie and Frances held their breath. The Dunnes exchanged glances, and Biddy, who was refreshing the water glasses, tried to appear as if she weren't listening. Mrs. Winfield cooed, "Oh, how very exciting."

Thomas hesitated. He had not yet sorted out his own feelings on Parnell, but he was clear about defending his house. "The girl you refer to is a fine student and not related to him. As I understand it, her father was a school chum of Parnell's. His affiliations are not hers but his own. She is an innocent child, and we are happy to have her with us." He looked to Frances and Elfie for confirmation, and they were so relieved at their father's cleverly stated support, all they could do was nod in agreement. Silk, wool, and satin fabric rustled under the table as the guests repositioned themselves in their unease, and Biddy left the room.

Eliza, never one to miss an opening, jumped in. "The fact is, Britain continues to pour large sums into this country. I see it in shipbuilding in Belfast. The return in their favor is *e*-normous." She looked around to judge her audience's response, which seemed to be agreeable and curious. "But the Brits always extract much more than they bring to Ireland. The balance in their favor is *e-nor-mous*." She dragged the word out for effect. Frances laughed to herself, thinking that Eliza was never short on drama when she had a captive audience. "Ireland," Eliza finished, "loses to the British, every time."

Biddy had been standing in the pantry listening to Eliza Niven when Mary beckoned her back in the kitchen, whispering, "Work to do. They're just blatherin', Bid." But Biddy, who had never heard such political views expressed at RockView before, stayed put.

Frances was quietly impressed with Eliza's honesty and self-assurance. She and Elfie were less inclined to express their thoughts on politics outside the family, where a woman's opinion wasn't often sought or valued. *Eliza's experience in a man's world, gained from being involved with Richard's linen mill after his untimely death, must give some weight to her position,* Frances thought. *At least it appears so with the people around our table. Or she's stunned them into appreciation.* Frances smiled to herself and looked to Elfie for help with a less controversial turn for the conversation.

"I have been seeking," Elfie began slowly, "my own way to ease this struggle. The Gaelic revival, for example. A mutual appreciation of Celtic culture and history appears to be a way to unify the Irish and Anglo-Irish." Her statement was greeted by silence, and she blushed.

Once again, Frances tried to think of something to say, this time to save her sister from embarrassment. She needn't have worried.

"I believe you have an interest in that area, Mr. Yeats. Am I correct?" Elfie asked.

Yeats smiled grandly. "Yes, but for me, it is support for the inherent qualities of the Irish and less about their history. I am interested to hear what you are learning, Miss Elfie."

Frances marveled at her sister. Leave it to her to find a cultural road through a political discussion. Elfie's hands rose from her lap, gently emphasizing her words as she talked about the growing revival in literary circles regarding the rebirth and retelling of Celtic myths and stories. "Interestingly enough," she said, looking at each person in the room, "the leaders in this literary movement are actors, poets, and writers."

"Brava!" Mrs. Winfield exclaimed, bringing charitable murmurs and head bobs all around—except for the Dunnes, who looked perplexed.

"Our son, Willy, is obsessed with fairies and mystics," Yeats said. "He speaks of them with great reverence as we walk along the track, as if they were real and hiding behind or under every rock."

Susan Yeats furrowed her brow and tried to catch his eye. Her husband tended to take over and dominate a conversation. Paying no attention to his wife, the artist continued, "And he does so at his teacher's encouragement! Well, of course I had a talk with the man, and do you know what he said?" John Yeats now had the full attention of the table, and he paused for effect before answering. "Exactly what you've told us tonight, Miss Elfie Young. 'Anglo-Irish children should respect the culture, myth, and language of Ireland to live their lives comfortably and honorably with the people of this country.'"

Elfie grinned with delight. She opened her mouth to speak, but Reverend Dunne chimed in. "I am reminded of the sermon in Ephesians 2:14. 'For He is our peace.'" The reverend pointed his finger in the air for emphasis as he continued, "His presence destroyed barriers dividing the wall of hostility."

Mrs. Dunne smiled brightly and nodded to Mrs. Touth, who smiled politely in return but remained lost as to why they were discussing the Irish at all. Elfie thanked the reverend for his contribution and continued with her own thoughts before he had the chance to interrupt again. "I admit I do wonder if the movement will change things, but it is a beginning. Perhaps young William and his generation will be the ones to lead the way."

Frances nearly clapped at her sister's smooth conclusion. Susan Yeats smiled, and Jack lifted his glass, bowing his head in deference to Elfie. "Well said, Miss Young. It will take many paths and minds to bring unity to this country, but we cannot forget the Irish people need their freedom."

Elfie bowed her head and raised her glass. "We agree, Mr. Yeats."

Edward Winfield cleared his throat and raised his glass to gain their attention. "I would like to toast Miss Elfie and Miss Frances for planning this lovely evening in Thomas's honor and inviting us to share in it." Everyone at the table raised their glasses to the sisters with a "hear, hear!" and Winfield saw his moment to continue. "And a toast to a better future for Ireland and to keeping our children home."

Eliza sighed audibly. "It's true," she said, "the best are leaving." Waving her hand toward the front door, she continued, "My only son, James, and Thomas's daughter are lost to the wilds of Canada." Heads shook sympathetically around the table. Jack asked for "a touch more wine," ignoring his wife, who was once more shaking her head. All glasses were refilled by Thomas and then again when Jack raised his hand once more with Thomas stifling a sigh as he watched the last drops of his favorite Burgundy disappear.

Outside the dining room, Biddy and Mary waited for a pause in the conversation so they could clear the dishes. "These people have no idea how right they are," Biddy whispered to Mary. "My boys talk of following others to America when they're older, and of the sacks of money arriving here from our people over there to put guns in the hands of the Irish."

"Biddy, hush!" Mary warned.

The conversation in the dining room had riled Biddy and brought up her deepest fears. "I have half a mind to share a thing or two with these folks that would scare them silly." Mary nodded in agreement but pulled her cousin back into the kitchen. "It's Mr. Young's birthday party, Biddy," she said. "Not a soapbox."

Mary had heard her own share of frightening talk on the street and in the pub. Tonight she worked for the Youngs, and they were counting on her and Biddy. That was enough for her to keep her place.

Biddy sat at the kitchen table and sighed. "They *talk* about our problems," she said. "Blatherin' is not going to keep my boys home."

Mary stood by the door, half worried she would miss their cue to clear the dining room, half worried the guests would hear Biddy's complaints. Mary put her finger to her lips and continued nodding in agreement to appease her cousin.

"Even the Youngs can barely see the truth of what's really happening in our lives," Biddy whispered. "It's as if there's a sea," she explained, gesturing with her hands to emphasize her point, "that's separating the Anglos and us instead of just a pantry door."

"Biddy, calm down." Mary's sudden display of authority caught Biddy off guard. "We must go into the dining room now and clear," she announced and walked out of the kitchen to do her job.

Fifteen minutes later, Biddy still hadn't left the kitchen, but the cake, blazing with candles, made its entrance on a cut-glass pedestal with the aid of Mary. Frances, Elfie, and Mary led the singing of a round of "For He's a Jolly Good Fellow."

Thomas smiled broadly. "Mary, you have outdone yourself," he said. "Do we dare touch it with a knife, let alone devour it?"

"If you don't, I will cry all night, sir," responded the proud cook.

The cake and tea disappeared even faster than the wine. The meal concluded, Frances rose from her seat. "We have some entertainment to lighten our evening thanks to Margaret Winfield," she announced. "Shall we adjourn to the drawing room?"

Thomas stood and waved his hand toward the doorway. "Please join us."

Yeats was last to rise. He stood, taking the back of his chair to steady himself, while Thomas waited at the door. When Yeats reached Thomas at the doorway, he lowered his voice and whispered conspiratorially, "I've something to show you, Thomas."

Thomas chuckled and suggested they first join the other guests, but Yeats held fast to his shoulder. "No, No," he said. "This isn't for prying eyes." With his free hand he awkwardly dug two fingers into his vest pocket, finally pulling out an old coin.

"A copper coin?" Thomas asked.

"A good luck copper coin," Yeats clarified.

Thomas wasn't sure what his friend was getting at. He heard the slur in his speech and thought that maybe Yeats wasn't sure either.

"Won it in a wager in the pub."

Thomas grinned. "Maybe we can find a good horse race at the downs, and when I pick the winner, I will walk away with your luck!"

Frances swept back from the drawing room. "Father, your guests are waiting."

"Come, come, Frances," he replied. "Yeats is sharing the secret of his luck with me."

Frances sighed and kissed his cheek. "Yes, it is your party, Father. But the celebration has moved across the hall."

— ◆ —

As soon as Thomas entered the drawing room, Margaret Winfield walked over to the piano, flounced her black taffeta dress over the bench, and placed her hands on the keys.

"One more thought," Touth whispered to Thomas when

they settled into their chairs. "Are we part of the problem? With the Irish, I mean."

Thomas sighed. "You are likely correct, Geoff, and from the day we decided to live our lives in Ireland." Aware of the watchful eyes of his daughters, Thomas quickly pivoted the conversation. "Margaret, you are lovely tonight. Are you ready to play?"

Margaret had been waiting for his attention. With a dramatic nod, she informed her audience in her high-pitched, nasal voice that she was going to perform Piano Sonata no. 14. "Also known as *Moonlight Sonata*," she added. She waved her hand in a grand gesture toward the ceiling. "You might imagine some of those shining stars the girls sang about as I play." Frances felt Margaret's suggestion ridiculous, but she closed her eyes and was soon transported by rich sound. When the piece ended, Margaret stood up and took a bow to enthusiastic applause. Thomas thanked her, and she received a robust "Brava, Margaret!" from John Yeats. She beamed, bringing the entertainment part of the evening to a close.

The men stood and gathered around the library table pouring themselves whiskey, leaving the women to sit and chat. Eliza leaned forward as if to share a confidence. "Men and their whiskey," she said in a loud whisper that carried across the room. "They think they are the only ones with interesting things to talk about. Personally, I am betting a good number of Home Rulers will return to Parliament in next month's election. Any thoughts about that?" Her question was met with silence from the group, followed by a rattle of the windows from a strong gust of wind. "It seems the weather has some thoughts," Elfie said, causing the women to laugh.

"Actually, Eliza, I've been admiring your dress. Did you travel to Paris?" Frances asked, successfully changing the conversation from politics to seamstresses, fashion, and travel, topics that carried on through the next hour.

The rumble of distant thunder brought the evening to an early end. "I thank you all for coming out on such a night," Thomas announced, "but I think it's time to let you go home while it's still safe to do so!"

The minister and his wife, who had added little to the women's conversation, were the first to leave. With smiles and words of appreciation for a wonderful evening, the remaining guests soon followed suit, exiting into the rain-swept night and their waiting carriages. Eliza and the Touths, along with the Yeatses, were the last to leave. "I do hope you will enjoy the gift I selected for you, Thomas," Eliza added, clearly disappointed that he had not chosen to open it in front of his guests.

"I am not unappreciative," Thomas responded. "For now, I am still enjoying the present of everyone's presence."

"You are a true host," said Yeats, who had been listening in as he helped his wife with her coat, "and a clever man!"

Geoffrey turned to Thomas before following the Yeatses out the door. "Be wary," he said. "Reasonable men, such as ourselves, may be caught up in violence before this is over."

Thomas placed his hand on his friend's shoulder. "Geoff, I hope it does not come to that," he said. And then suddenly the foyer was empty and quiet.

Thomas faced his daughters. "No one could have done better," he said.

Elfie and Frances moved forward and gave their father a hug. "It was a grand celebration," Frances said, "and we had fun too."

The sisters disappeared to the kitchen to thank Biddy and Mary, and Thomas climbed to his lair, patting the vest pocket where he kept his final prize of the evening: an unopened letter from Lily and James. Their gift, a painting of a bustling street in their new city, had arrived along with the letter and sat in his bookcase. He would savor both the painting and the letter in the quiet of his room. The other gifts could wait until morning.

Geoff Touth had warned him earlier about Eliza's present. "A yellow silk smoking jacket. With red trim. Not quite your style, I think." Thomas laughed, imagining Frances's expression if he wore it to breakfast the next morning. *She might prefer it to my old gray vest.*

Once in bed, he opened the envelope and found not one but two letters enclosed, one from Lily and one from James. As he started to read, the rain whipping at the windows took him instead back to the evening's conversation. *The political climate in Ireland is becoming as stormy as the night outside,* he thought. He shuddered involuntarily at the idea of violence. Again, he hoped Touth's prediction was wrong. Thomas looked to the letters in his hand. *Let's hope for some good news from the other side of the ocean.*

CHAPTER 14

BIDDY'S CROCK

Biddy

The birthday celebration had been a success. *And why not?* Biddy thought, closing the RockView kitchen door behind her. Her upset earlier that night had cooled by the time the guests left. *Poor Mary!* she thought with a smile. *Probably thought I was going to take us both down with my over-loud complaining.*

Biddy's quick-fire anger had surprised her as well. *My, my,* she thought, but forgave herself quickly. *Lord knows, putting on a fancy party like that can make a body tired and a bit cross.* It was ten-thirty at night, a time she was usually fast asleep. She should make it home by quarter past eleven. The storm had broken, making it a perfect time for a walk, except for the mud and puddles. Her lantern would help her make her way safely.

Biddy pulled her coat close at the neck as she moved toward the street, stepping onto Belgrave Road. She stood for a moment and took a deep breath. The air smelled fresh after the steamy kitchen. The worst of the evening's storm appeared to have blown through and left. A few stars peeked out, a slice of moon hung above, and only a light rain was falling. She walked carefully, holding the lantern in front of her.

"How Miss Frances and Miss Elfie got Mr. Thomas in the mood for a celebration, I'll never know," she clucked. Throughout the day and again at the close of the evening, both she and Mary had received genuine appreciation from the family. Miss Frances had placed nice tips for each of them in crisp envelopes with their names written in her beautiful handwriting and placed them on the kitchen table before the guests left. *Now, that was real appreciation,* she thought with a smile. Pulling her new bright red knitted scarf up over her nose, she thought how the tip would pay for the scarf and then some. Biddy had bought it the week prior on impulse from a woman who sold her knitting on the street. "Knit it meself with these poor hands," the woman had said. The woman hadn't appeared much older than Biddy until she lifted the scarf to show it off. Her gnarled fingers looked painful and swollen at every joint. For Biddy, those hands were a reminder of the realities of hard work and the cruel conditions that were this poor Irish woman's life. Biddy counted herself fortunate.

The tip money from the Youngs lay deep in her pocket, soon to be secreted in her crock at home. Knowing her wee stash of coin was there allowed Biddy to dream some. Little luxuries were rare. *Maybe new stockings for me and the* faiscre grotha *cheese Conor is so fond of with my soda bread?*

Home at last, she shook the rain from her coat and hung it and the damp scarf on a peg by the door before peering into Norah's bedroom. Her youngest reminded her of a cat balled into herself in the middle of the bed. Biddy crept up the ladder to the loft to check on Pat and Jack. There was a sense of relief to know all three of hers were accounted for and asleep, as they should be at this hour. She had not known when she would get home and was relieved her boys had not decided to slip out and leave Norah alone. The boys were almost teens, easily tempted to be out in the streets after dark. *Children safe and sound,* she thought, closing her eyes in gratitude.

Her and Conor's bedroom was empty, but no mind, she thought. Conor was likely at the pub and would come weaving in after taking a piss out back.

In the kitchen, the stove's warmth relaxed her weary body. She added some peat to make it hotter, pulled up her chair, and sat down. Biddy glanced over at the shelves Conor had built on each side of the sink and above the window. They held her earthenware crockery, neatly stacked and waiting. No dishes in the sink. Norah had thought of her mother's long night at work and cleaned up after their meal. *Good girl.*

Her crock of coins rested on a small shelf above the stove, a place of honor in her mind. Conor had bought it for her from a rummage dealer when they were in Cork on holiday. That was a long time ago, before the children came. She hadn't thought much of the crock at the time, but Conor had fancied its crude feel. "Hey Bid, feels like me face with a good stubble," he said playfully, rubbing his hand over the simple sailing ship image an artist had scratched into the dark glazed surface. It was not *fine,* like things in the Youngs' butler pantry, but for her it had become a prized possession, a reminder of love and a light-hearted time. She stood up, dug into her pocket and, rising on her toes, dropped her evening's tip, still in its envelope, inside the secure spot.

She hoped Conor would come home with an easy temper and not too tipsy. Too full of drink, he tended to argue. At the pub he wove grand stories and cast himself as the hero or the high-minded one, but at home he felt free to release his frustrations. He took slights as imagined challenges to his place as head of the family or his ability to provide. Less food in his bowl than in the boys', he'd say to Biddy, edgy and annoyed, "Am I not the man of this house? Do I not deserve as much as a wee lad? I worked a long day to buy this food while they were messing about and ditching school." Biddy kept quiet at these times but thought, *I work too, Conor, and then cook your bloody food after my long day.*

She shook her head to clear the unpleasant thoughts and smiled at the friendly crock. It had the power to bring good memories of a simpler time when everything seemed possible. She and Conor had survived the famine, married young, and built a life by their own hard work. Unlike the Youngs, they did not have life stacked in their favor, but Biddy and Conor generally refused to focus on what they didn't have and remained optimistic despite the odds. "Why not?" she'd say when her sons questioned her outlook. "Landing a job with the Youngs was a blessing, and your da has steady work as a mason. Dublin is still building its city." They had a good life, a reliable, if small, income, and three healthy children now proving to be a new sort of handful growing up in the bustle of Dublin city.

Biddy started to sit down again, but something pulled at her. She closed her eyes and took a deep, quieting breath. *The party,* she thought. The political conversations she and Mary overheard from the pantry still stirred her mind. Biddy opened her eyes and frowned. She moved the stockpot of soup she had prepared that morning onto the warm side of the stove to let it come up to a simmer in case Conor was hungry when he came home. Then she plopped back down in her chair, letting her gaze settle on the soothing crock. "I wish the Youngs and their guests had asked me what I think," she told it. "I'd have given 'um an earful." She almost laughed to herself, knowing she was safe enough with that thought because they never would ask her, of course. *But if they had . . .*

Frustration rose again in her throat. This time she did not swallow it back. She drew herself up in her chair. "If I'm honest about it, Mr. Crock," she said in a low voice so as not to wake her children, "I am frightened. Who wouldn't be in my position? I watch strangers come around our street to lure my young boys to their gangs. Fighting in the streets for independence with God only knows what besides their small fists. Whose independence are they wantin' anyway, Ireland's or their own? My Conor tells me he sees young men outside the pub smoking and tellin' big stories. 'Angry, frustrated,' he tells me, 'only wantin' to prove they're ready and brave enough to fight.'" Biddy wiped her brow with her handkerchief.

"My boys see school as nothin' but a dead end," she continued, shaking her head. "I want more for them than fightin'." Too agitated to stay still, Biddy stood up and paced the room. "They ask me, 'Why go to school, Ma, if we have no future?' What a question! Our Norah is only ten, but she hears her brothers swagger on about striking out, leaving Ireland for a better future. I don't want that kind of nonsense in her mind! Patrick talking big about someday moving to the United States or Canada and tellin' Jack they should pack their sacks and go together. What do they know of either of those countries?" Biddy paused to acknowledge that she knew little of those countries too. "The thought of losing 'em makes my heart ache," she said, resuming her one-sided conversation. "But can you blame them? The only choice they see here is livin' under the thumb of the British or fighting against them. Those *Brits* at RockView tonight . . . they don't see it." Biddy looked to the crock and waited. It remained mute. She laughed at herself and sat down.

What do those privileged Anglos, she thought, purposely reverting to the more respectful term, *sitting all proper and pampered at the Youngs' fine table know about the Irish? Those ugly drawings of the Irish I see in Mr. Young's newspaper . . .* Biddy shook her head in disgust. *They paint us as dirty, lazy, and drunk. We are parents raising children, and a parent is a parent.* Biddy knew being an Anglo-Irish parent wasn't like being an Irish one, *but we all love our children just the same, don't we?* She stopped and wondered if that was true. Mr. and Mrs. Young had loved their children as she loved her own. Biddy sat down again in her chair, feeling like she might cry. She rested her hardworking hands on the wooden kitchen table, its edges worn smooth by her family sharing meals, playing games, reading, talking. The feel of it settled her.

She turned her eyes upward, raised a finger, and addressed the crock again. "My children want change. Conor and me, we just want them to be steadfast and go to school and work hard and make a good life. We all want our own to be safe, don't we? Irish lads, they feel no security. They see themselves as livin' under the thumb. They say, 'Ma, I'd rather die than live as their slaves.' God help us. They see no future in Ireland except lifting, serving, carrying heavy loads for others, or cookin' and cleanin' grand homes they can never hope to own."

Biddy stopped talking, blushing at her own frankness. *Forgive me, Mr. Young, Miss Frances, and Miss Elfie too,* she thought. She couldn't really imagine speaking so directly to the Youngs, whom she appreciated and cared for. "Understand," she said to the crock, "Conor and I take it our own way, not the same as our children. They see Ireland as our country, not the Brits'. Or the Anglos'," she added, though she knew to her children they were one and the same.

Strands of her dark brown hair marked with silver had fallen across her sweaty forehead. Biddy pushed them back. She turned Conor's chair toward her own and put her feet up one at a time. Her knees thanked her.

"Even Conor says the British government has one goal," she said, "to keep the Irish down. Says I don't always see it clearly because I spend my days working in a nice tidy Anglo-Irish world." She suspected he was right. The Youngs must know *some* of the Irish realities, but they were not living them.

Biddy heard grinding truths from her neighbors in the lane, while Mr. Young received his packaged neatly in the *Post* as he sat in his warm, safe kitchen. Sometimes he read an article out loud. Did he know she was listening? He never asked her for her opinion, and there were times she wanted to yell out, "Does that paper of yours count my people as human, as worth something? And not just lives to throw away?"

The soup on the stove boiled over, putting an end to her speech. *Might well have lost my good job if I'd said any of that to the Youngs,* she thought, shaking her head wearily. Good thing the crock would keep her secret. Biddy cleaned up the spill that had run onto the floor. Rising with the soppy cloth to the sink, she took a few deep breaths. *You're not as young as you used to be, Biddy girl.*

She made her way to the bedroom after a few chilly minutes outside in the loo. In her room she lit the light, hung her clothes on their pegs, slipped on her nightdress, and sank gratefully into bed. Still her mind would not rest. She and Conor saw themselves as lucky because of the famine, she thought with a start. Such an obvious thing, but it came to her as a revelation. They had dug graves and laid to rest so many who did not make it. Their survival was the reason they were willing to be satisfied with what little security they had been able to gather. Of course her children wanted more than that.

Biddy heard the front door open and close, grazing the floor. *Please, someone fix that damn door,* she thought for the umpteenth time before rolling over on her side. She would welcome her husband's warmth in the bed; still, she closed her eyes and feigned sleep. There was no energy left in her for chat or anything else he might have in mind that evening.

CHAPTER 15

AT THE KITCHEN DOOR

March
Elfie

Dear Lily,

I have but a few minutes before getting the girls to sleep, so this will be a short letter. I promise a longer one, soon. Father and I are making plans for a journey to the west coast and Sligo this summer! I don't think we've been there since we were children, do you remember? Such a beautiful place. Father and I have been invited to stay with the family of one of our students, Elizabeth Fenn. She is a charming girl and has worked her youthful magic on Father. Nothing will ever replace you in his affections, but Elizabeth and her friend Anna have recently

*expressed an interest in his teaching them to
draw, which in turn seems to have rekindled
his desire to explore and record his impressions
with his pencil, pen, and brush.*

Elfie paused to crack open the window to let in some fresh air. Unfamiliar voices rose from the garden, and she looked to see where they were coming from. She saw the shed in the back corner was open. A young boy appeared, walking backward through the door, ducking his head to avoid the low beam. To her delight, she saw a younger boy sitting in a barrow as it came into the light. *Biddy's boys!* Frances had mentioned hiring Patrick and Jack to help with the garden chores. Elfie vaguely remembered they were very close in age. *They must be twelve and thirteen by now. And good-looking, healthy boys, who know how to have fun. I do hope they pull some weeds and cut back the bushes as Frances has asked.* Her father had also wanted them to plant bulbs to brighten the spring garden. Watching their antics, Elfie had doubts they would get to it today.

Her mind shifted back to her letter, and she picked up her pen again.

*Our school year will soon enough be winding
to a close—what a success it has been! I am
checking the rail connections, but they seem
more suited to commerce than personal travel.
If Father agrees, we will go by mail coach,
which is less costly but not uncomfortable and
still allows for small stopovers and detours for
country walks, sketching, and journal writing
along the way. Frances has four girls from the
school she is escorting to the Continent and*

seems happy to be going her own way. We are very much together in the school year so it is a break for all of us.

At the sound of a shout, Elfie paused again to look out the window. The boy in the wheelbarrow was now on the ground, while his brother stood over him laughing. *Boys will be boys,* she thought at first, but then she recalled last week's strange occurrence and wondered if that was true.

The day had begun so nicely, with Elfie in the kitchen enjoying her morning scone in peace before Mary roused the girls. She didn't recall hearing a knock, only that the back door was open and there stood Norah, Biddy's daughter. She was one or two years older than the girls upstairs, yet she seemed older somehow. Her thick auburn hair was pulled back, well off her lovely face, and tied with a ribbon. She wore a shawl the color of her dark-green eyes over a clean dark-blue blouse and a near-matching skirt. Beneath her modest attire, Norah's womanly curves pushed at the limits of her clothes. She was what Elfie's artist father would describe as "young and budding."

"Mum," Norah had said without coming inside, "Da says he's fixed the stove and going to work, so not to worry."

"Where are your manners, girl? Say hello to Miss Elfie."

"I'm sorry, Miss Elfie," Norah said, remaining in the doorway. "Good morning."

Before Elfie could respond, Biddy asked, "Who's this?"

Norah looked uncomfortable. "Just a bloke from the neighborhood." From the shadows of the back porch, a scruffy young man appeared behind her. "He was just walkin' my way, Ma."

The man stepped around Norah and moved into the kitchen uninvited. "I've not a pretty face," he said, removing his cap, "but hello to you, Norah's mum. It's Willy Kelly, Mum. I just walked along with your beautiful daughter to keep her company."

The young man behaved as if he hadn't seen Elfie, which was unusual enough in her own home, but Biddy hadn't pressed him to acknowledge her either. She felt like she was watching a scene in a play.

Biddy grimaced, making no effort to hide her feelings. "It's Mrs. Gossett, not 'Mum,' and this one's too young to be with the likes of you. Be off and don't come near my girl again."

Norah's eyes widened—in embarrassment or fear; Elfie couldn't decide. Her own cheeks had reddened at hearing Biddy speak so brusquely in front of her. She was certain Biddy would rather she not witness the unpleasant scene unfolding in the kitchen, but to leave then would have brought more attention to her presence. Elfie needn't have worried. The young man grinned, then turned and left the kitchen, brushing by Norah. The door banged behind him. Elfie heard him thump unevenly down the back stairs, and as quickly as it had begun, the incident was over.

"Please excuse the intrusion, Miss Elfie," Biddy said. "You shouldn't have to see any of that. I hope you won't mind if my girl stays until he is well away. Then she'll go right home."

Elfie nodded. "Your children are always welcome here, Biddy."

But Biddy had moved on. "Norah, there's work to be done at home and you need no company while doing it. What made you think to bring that fellow with you?"

Norah lifted her chin slightly in defiance. "I told you, he followed me, Ma."

Biddy went back to her work, appearing stern and annoyed. Elfie was unhappy for Biddy and for Norah, who sat sullenly at the kitchen worktable, her body slumped and eyes downcast, waiting for her mother's release. Not wanting to move until things settled, Elfie turned her attention out the window. Willy Kelly was walking slowly up the street. His right leg was shorter than his left and moved unnaturally. *He has a wooden stump,* she thought, surprised. *What horrible thing happened to him? An accident? A fight?* His manner and appearance told her the story, whatever it was, would be unsavory.

Elfie finished her scone and tea and stood to leave, which acted as a signal for Biddy. "Go quickly, Norah, and safely home." Biddy's sharp words chased the girl out the door. Once it closed, Biddy apologized to Elfie again. "I don't know what my Norah is doing with that grimy hooligan. She's old enough to know better. Growin' up too fast, that's what it is. A woman already, and too young. That bloke must be twenty if he's a day. Too old to be hanging around her." She shook her head. "I canna watch her all day, and she's been expelled from school for being cheeky with the nuns. Mr. Gossett and I will have a stiff talk with her tonight, Miss Elfie. This won't happen again."

Elfie had wondered why Norah wasn't in school. Now she had her answer. She couldn't imagine any of her girls being cheeky. Elfie left the kitchen feeling troubled for Biddy and grateful for her students, who were fortunate to have the security and standards of her home and school. A shiver traced her spine. That man, whoever he was, did not belong anywhere near RockView. Their girls had a safe place here while men like Willy Kelly were out there. Elfie was aware there were two worlds in Ireland. That day was the first time a darker realm had appeared at her kitchen door.

Elfie picked up her pen once again to finish her letter, but her worries from that day continued to hold her thoughts. Was her sister experiencing something similar in Canada? If so, Lily had not written of it, and Elfie, who continued to think of London, Ontario, as the wild west, could only hope her sister was safe. *In any case,* she decided, *there is no reason to dwell on unpleasant things and plenty of good news to share.*

> *I haven't told you the best news of all! The girls are preparing to take the British education*

exam. How different our lives would have been if we had been able to attend universities! We do hope some of our girls will go on to more education. At the very least we want them to know it is available in ways it never was for their mothers or us. There is even hope for opportunities to open for both Protestant and Catholic women to join the workforce and, we can hope, professions such as medicine and higher education. It's been men only for too long.

Oh dear, it's getting late and the girls will be waiting for me. I really must go now.

Love, Elfie

CHAPTER 16

MORALITY LAWS AND THE MODEL

Thomas

Thomas quietly left the house for the academy once the girls were all in the dining room for breakfast. He had no reason to sneak about other than wanting the morning to be his without the well-meaning greetings and giggles from his daughters' students. Thomas felt invigorated. He had risen early to be sure he would arrive well before his students. As he walked to the edge of the city through the agricultural lands of Harold's Cross, he thought less and less of his home life. Streaks of light were already finding their way through the morning gloom, catching his eye and striking his imagination until he once again felt like an artist and a teacher, rather than a grandfather figure at a girls' school. *Rather liberating,* he thought. He hailed a carriage as he came to the Grand Canal, which took him across La Touche Bridge into Dublin and to the academy on the other side of the River Liffey.

At the studio, Thomas made sure all was ready before opening the door to his students, who had been eagerly waiting in the hallway since his arrival. Quickly, they arranged their easels at varying angles to capture the subject of a life drawing lesson. Even as they settled in, their attention remained riveted on the rich blue drape covering the live model at the front of the room.

At Thomas's nod, the model let go of the cloth, which fell gracefully to the floor of the classroom. Thomas had requested a female model for his students. "Not an older woman but not a girl," he had explained. "Someone with experience in being a woman." He guessed she was near the age of twenty-five, her body full with soft curves and classic lines. She had a long braid of thick amber hair. Thomas moved toward her to give instructions on the placement of her arms, hands, and head as she lay atop three pillows on the settee. He wanted the pose to render a languid mood and sensual power. Thomas stepped back to assess the image and feeling she portrayed. One of her legs dangled toward the floor; the other was bent with the foot beside the knee. He gestured toward her hair, and she brought her braid quickly over her shoulder so that it covered part of her right breast. *Yes,* he thought, just the charged atmosphere to bring depth and passion to his students' work. He nodded his approval, and her gaze wandered away from him toward the high studio windows, closed that day to make the room comfortably warm for her.

"Gentlemen," he announced, standing in front of their subject to block their view, "today we will work on sketching our model, and in future weeks we will turn our drawings into paintings." Thomas looked purposefully at each of the young men. "Think about the overall design of your work. How will you use perspective? Our reclining figure is on a horizontal plane. How can you add depth and detail that will carry the eye past the figure and add to the experience? Your imagination can place the subject in a harem, on the beach, in a garden, or in the bedroom." At the last suggestion, eyes caught between the students, causing a few suppressed smiles. "You are *artists*. The details will tell the story. I will move around the studio as you work and make suggestions. But remember, this is your painting, not mine. Any questions?"

Thomas moved aside and the model had their full attention. Precisely what he wanted. At the back of the room, he set up his materials and began to consider his own composition.

Queen Victoria's morality codes—frequently referenced by spiritual leaders driven to control "man's low and devilish nature"—allowed an avenue in the art world to express the wonders of the sensual satisfactions of the flesh. *Thank God for that,* Thomas thought, *and for the Royal Hibernian Academy.*

After his beloved Sarah died, Thomas had the occasional relationship that moved from friendship to the bedroom, and alone in the quiet of his room he was able to find some satisfaction from reading the likes of Flaubert's erotic *Madame Bovary* . . . those French! This model made him yearn for those bygone moments of warmth, passion, and intimacy. He recalled an article reporting that the French painter Cézanne purposely chose models who were solid and stocky, as if their physical heft helped him concentrate on form rather than flesh. *Not today, Mr. Cézanne,* thought Thomas. He picked up a soft pencil and put it to the canvas.

Time seemed to dissolve and by noon he had little to show for his efforts. The model stretched, relieving her body from her pose. She pulled the blue drape around her body and slipped toward the screen just behind her where her warm, sheltering clothing awaited, and the class broke for a midday meal. Thomas smiled. The sensual pleasure of a warm meal on a cold day would have to do.

At three o'clock, Thomas dismissed his students and waited on the other side of the door until his model dressed. When she appeared in the hall, he offered to pay her carriage ride home, but she declined. "There is already one waiting for me," she said with a sly smile. Thomas blushed, assuming it had been sent by a "patron," and thanked her again. He closed the studio, leaving enough of a sketch behind to complete from memory at another time.

With the glow of his day still coloring his mood, he walked home through streets filled with hawkers, end-of-day shoppers, and newsboys. When he reached St. Stephen's Green, he saw a gathering around a young gentleman wearing a clerical collar. Thomas couldn't resist. He stepped into the crowd to hear the message. It was one he had heard before and would likely hear again: Irish families thrown off their land, homes ruined, and livestock killed by ruthless hired agents. Thomas took in the faces of the crowd to read their reactions. Frustration, anger, even disgust. Most of the audience, he guessed from the working clothes they wore, were Irish, but there were some in fashionable attire and one or two wearing wool suits similar to his own. Anglo-Irish, he assumed. "For the love of our Lord, we must help these people," cried the priest. Thomas listened for a few minutes longer, then wandered back to the street. He agreed with the man—hard not to—but Thomas was no longer young and carried little sway in society, so he kept quiet. Change was necessary, and yet what could he do? Still, the words of the priest stayed with him, washing away the memory of the morning, and he felt a deep impotence when it came to discovering any possible resolution to either situation.

He continued onward, his thoughts roaming toward the changes in his life as he drew closer to RockView. Schoolgirls underfoot, daughters too busy to attend to their own father. They were moving on with their lives and changing his in the process. The hollering of another stump speaker on a street corner broke into his thoughts. "Discontent is on the rise!" he heard the man say.

Yes, yes, he's right, of course, he agreed. *Terribly unfair. Something should be done.* Though he had no idea what that might be or who should do it.

CHAPTER 17

TRAPPINGS

London, Ontario, Canada
April
James

James patted his coat, feeling for the letters protected in his pocket from the splatter on the cobblestone streets. Spring, his patients had repeatedly told him, was arriving late to the city. "April will be as cold this year as January, Doctor," he'd been warned, as if the weather were of more significance to his patients than their broken arms or hacking coughs. The wind and chilling temperatures on his rides to work told him his patients were right: spring had no intention of arriving anytime soon. He hoped Lily was warm enough at home.

One of the letters in his pocket was from Frances. His wife would read it many times, and the parts Frances gave her permission to share she would read to James. Only when the next correspondence arrived would his wife place the well-read letter in the box by her side of their bed where she kept all her letters, divided into bundles with ribbon—one each for Frances, Elfie, Thomas, and Eliza. With each letter that arrived from Ireland, he wondered if they would ever see their family again. Lily must wonder too, he thought.

The other letter in his pocket was from his mother, addressed to both of them. She wrote several times a month, her letters arriving in bundles of two or more, making James first sort them out according to date if he wanted to make sense of any of their content. His mother had a habit of writing as if their letters to each other were ongoing conversations, touching back and forth on subjects without preamble. He guessed she was lonely, though she was certainly busy enough with running the family business and with her social schedule.

Besides Fiona and the other servants, who quickly came and went, for nearly twenty years it had just been James and his mother living in that large house. His father had died when James was twelve. Eliza became fearful of losing her son, too. For weeks, she refused to let him leave the house. "What if something happens to you?" she'd say from the bed that she never left. "I could not bear it." James could still feel the touch of her fragile fingers wrapped around his hand, trapping him until at last the medicine Fiona had given her took effect and her hand fell softly onto the pile of bed quilts hiding her body.

James had sat in the house bored and alone except for Fiona, who had served him his meals in the dining room while his mother remained sequestered in her bedroom. His only real relief was to go to the stables while she slept. The stable hand was a few years younger than James and shy around him. With time, though, he had allowed James to help with brushing the horses and leading them about for exercise. James's love for horses and the equestrian life began with his first encounter with the earthy smells of horse sweat, urine, damp straw, and dung.

It was their family doctor who had rescued James—in truth, both him and his mother. Dr. Simpson visited Eliza nearly every week, bringing her flowers to lift her spirits and flattering her progress. He prescribed laudanum for rest and also long walks, when she could find the strength, to ease her grief and reconnect her to the living world. Eliza seemed to enjoy having a man to rely upon and relaxed her grip on James enough to allow him to return to St. Ready's.

The dear doctor, thought James. His return to school had felt like a jailbreak. That precious freedom gave him room to breathe and to heal.

With Simpson's encouragement, Eliza eventually rose from both her bed and her stupor to resume her community involvements and her flamboyant manner. The latter was not a trait James was fond of in his mother.

Knowing her bold intelligence, Dr. Simpson had suggested that she consider involving herself with her husband's business, which she did, surprising everyone with her acumen.

The doctor had counseled her to help her son, a task that Eliza embraced all at once, telling her friends she had to be strong "for the sake of my son." Always the drama. He didn't know which version of his mother had been worse.

God bless James Simpson, he thought. The doctor had died in 1870. He had never met James's beloved Lily, but James was certain he would have loved her and, unlike his father-in-law, been happy for James and cheered his Canadian adventure with his new bride.

James kept the reins taut as he and Count Lisburn moved from the city into the countryside. He was anxious to get home, and he could feel the young dapple gray's desire to move faster across the snow-packed road, but James would not risk the letters. They were his wife's link to the family and home she missed. How lucky he had been to find Lily. He wanted her always to feel the same of him.

If he was honest with himself, he too missed many of the attractions of life in Ireland. In Dublin he had lectures, libraries, theatres, pubs, and a broad assortment of acquaintances. With Lily it was love from the first time he heard her erupt in ill-timed laughter during an event at Trinity College and saw her profile, elegant and intense as she focused on the speaker. The lecture was on the work of William Makepeace Thackeray, the satirist and parodist. The cover of the program showed a hilarious cartoon caricature, a self-portrait of the author making fun of himself, that set the tenor of the evening. The lecturer read from a collection of Thackeray's serialized articles entitled *The Book of Snobs*. Though nearly thirty years old, the satire still rang true in its humorous and biting portrayal of exaggerated British snobbery. The younger members of the Anglo-Irish audience, who must have been keenly aware of the cartoonish British view of the Irish as drunken ruffians, seemed willing to enjoy a good laugh at their own expense. A man seated next to James said under his breath, "Thackeray caught our inbred British sense of superiority spot on!" The mood was light and playful, and the open honesty of the audience's response was for James quite refreshing. He was a little surprised there were no naysayers groaning at this unflattering comedic depiction, but then they would have stayed away from a Thackeray lecture.

After the intermission, James saw a young woman buckle forward in laughter, then cover her face. It was Lily. She later explained she had picked up another level of meaning in one of the lines she had heard, just as others were settling down and the lecturer was about to resume. Her blush and beauty as she worked to stifle her mirth captured James. This was a woman who could fill life with fun and more than a touch of irreverence.

He arranged to make her acquaintance through friends immediately after the lecture. They went to The Shelbourne with friends for a nightcap, and he was entranced. Her ability to find humorous and unintended meanings in the most mundane things was so unusual. Most young women, he'd found, were stifled by propriety, but not Lily. She captivated him, and he never took his sights off marrying her from that day forward. She was twenty-two and he was forty. He had no regrets. "Please, God, let my wife have none as well."

When he reached home, he brushed down Count in the stable and made sure he had oats and water in his trough before heading inside. Lily had repeatedly asked him to enter through the front door. "It isn't seemly for a doctor to sneak into his own house," she'd say. "What will people think of me?" Her happiness aside, some things a man was entitled to at the end of the day. He held fast to his preference for convenience and entered as usual through the nearby kitchen door, shedding his boots on the stoop and walking inside in his socks, his feet happily free after a long day.

Lily's face lit up when she saw him, which pleased James even more than finding the letters at the post office. He reached inside his pocket and offered the protected prize to Lily, holding the letter up for her to see her sister's handwriting.

— ◆ —

Lily

After their dinner, the couple retired to their chairs by the fireplace, Lily with her letter and James his newspaper. "We've done well here, haven't we," he said more than asked. Lily looked up from Frances's news about their father, startled by the interruption. It wasn't like her husband to talk once he had a newspaper in hand.

"Of course, dear," she reassured him.

"It's not as if we've left Ireland entirely behind," he said. Lily understood then what was bothering her husband: his worry they had come to this somewhat untamed place by his choice alone. Did he suppose she would take up and leave him? She watched her husband surveying the room, taking measure of each piece of furniture they'd brought with them to Canada. Their new home was furnished with a blend of items from Chrome Hill, his childhood home in the north of Ireland, and from RockView, including four of her father's paintings. "These trappings from our old world in Ireland bring us both comfort," he said. "Trappings from our old world" had become an oft-used phrase by her husband, referring to something they probably should but couldn't quite let go of.

Lily was pleased that James hadn't completely let go of his old life. Ireland was something they had in common. *And now Canada, of course,* she reminded herself. When she first met James, his desire to escape from Ireland and create a new life had nearly frightened her off, until she realized that she too wanted to escape. Not so much from Ireland, but a life of taking care of her father, whom she adored, would have destined her to spinsterhood. Lily had no intention of letting go of their tangible reminders of Ireland, and her husband knew it. "I treasure our roots in Ireland, and I'm very happy here," she said. "Besides," she added, placing her hand on her growing abdomen, "I'll soon have great company."

She smiled at James and turned back to the letter she had been so anxious to finish. Frances had written of a new spark in their father's step, and Lily had yet to discover her sister's account of it.

CHAPTER 18

A BEDTIME STORY

Dublin, Ireland
Elfie

Frances was not feeling well. "A respiratory weakness," the doctor had said. "Nothing to worry about as long as your sister gets the rest she needs." Frances had insisted she carry on, until her congestion required quick use of every one of her lace-bordered linen handkerchiefs and she at last agreed to stay in bed for at least a day. One day had become two, and listening to the sound of her sister's cough that evening, Elfie suspected it might stretch at least one more. Biddy had generously volunteered to oversee the meals until Frances was back on her feet. Dear Biddy! Upstairs, the girls were readying themselves for bed. Their giggles floated down the stairs. She would be telling the girls a bedtime story soon. But before she did, she needed a quiet sit-down to catch up with herself.

In the drawing room, Elfie saw that Biddy, or possibly

Mary, had left her father's *Post* on the table by her favorite chair. She sat down to read the front page but couldn't get beyond the headlines until she turned to page two. "PM hopeful C. S. Parnell," she read, "is scheduled to speak in the open air at St. Stephen's Green." Elfie perked up.

Oh, how I would like to experience firsthand the passion of his rhetoric rather than just imagine it from distilled summaries in the next day's newspaper. British troops would be on hand to maintain order, she reasoned, and to monitor Parnell's remarks, which were often critical of the Crown. Elfie admired him for standing up for the Irish. *The Gossett Irish, of course, not Irish like Willy Kelly, who likely belongs in prison. I wonder if Father could be persuaded to go with me?* She frowned. Frances would disapprove. "Attendance at a political event is not a good look for the school," she said, mimicking her sister's voice. *Makes me want to go even more. It's a public meeting, not the gathering of a revolutionary cell.* She would convince her father to take her.

The grandfather clock struck nine. Despite the long day, she felt a bounce in her step as she walked up the stairs. She had made it through the teaching day on her own, and now she had a plan to hear Parnell speak.

Inside the dormitory, the gas lamps cast long shadows across the floor and walls from the tall dressers and the girls moving about. The girls had to share the dressers—three drawers each, for undergarments, socks, nightgowns, and toiletries. Shoes were kept under the beds except for three times a week when they were placed atop their personal trunks at the feet of their beds to accommodate Mary's "sweep and a dust." Selected possessions were kept in the trunks, along with each girl's carefully folded dresses to wear beneath their pinafore uniforms.

Elfie stood in the doorway watching her young charges as they sat on the edges of their beds brushing and braiding each other's hair, an activity their nannies had performed for them at home.

Elizabeth and Anna were whispering together on Elizabeth's bed. Elfie opened her mouth to stop them, but the girls giggled and shook hands and whatever they were whispering about came to a quick end on its own.

While Anna carefully worked and reworked her friend's hair into a braid, Elizabeth chatted about her mother's summer parties on the great lawn at their house by the bay. "Mother brings out tables and chairs from the house and furniture from the porch to create an outdoor room under the yew tree," Elizabeth said. "Do you ever have summer parties at your house? I hope you can come to one of ours one day. It is so romantic at night, with all the lamps lit and the stars out." Elfie watched Anna's expression and considered that little in the girl's life had been like Elizabeth's. Little in Elfie's had either. An outdoor summer party sounded wonderful to her. She and her father had been invited to spend the coming summer with the Fenns. *Is Mrs. Fenn planning an outdoor party while we are there?* Elfie thought, losing her focus. Elizabeth turned and saw her teacher. "Oh, good evening, Miss Elfie," she said, which prompted the rest of the girls to look her way. Their greetings brought her back to reality.

"Good evening, to all of you. Another ten minutes, then I'll continue with our story." Elfie listened as Elizabeth talked on about watching the ships' lanterns moving across the bay below their house. "When Papa recognizes one of his Western Steam and Navigation ships, he says, 'Salute that ship. It is paying for this party!'" Elfie hid her laugh behind her hand, wondering at the family life of a merchant, so different from her own. Elizabeth held up her hand mirror to look at the finished braid. "My hair looks lovely! Thank you, Anna."

Elfie sat at the foot of Violet's bed, a signal for the girls to climb into their beds for the story to begin, which they did promptly. She made a point of choosing a different girl's bed each night, showing no favorites. Her voice softened, and her eyes opened wide, shining with anticipation. "Last night," she said, "we left Maeve deep in the forest near Kilkenny Castle. It's the seventeenth century, and Maeve is working her way in the evening's falling light toward her grandparents' cottage that sits just below the castle high up on the hill." Elfie glanced around the room. All eyes were on her. She wanted to smile but kept a serious expression as she continued the story.

"The castle up on the hill was occupied by James Butler, the first Duke of Ormonde. His family had been in Ireland for almost two hundred years, and now the Butlers and many of their relatives lived in a grand castle at the edge of a forest, along with many servants, of course."

"Was he a real person?" Violet asked. "And was he a bad duke or a good duke?"

"Hush, Violet," Elizabeth said. "She already told us he was real. Let Miss Elfie tell the story, and we'll find out if he was good or bad."

Elfie waited for the girls to settle again. "Whether he was a good duke or a bad duke is something you can decide for yourselves at the end of the story," she said. "What I can tell you is that the duke was Briti—Anglo-Irish, like we are, and he was the first duke at that castle to be raised Protestant and not Catholic."

"I thought all Anglo-Irish were Protestant," Anna said.

"Not at first, Anna," Elfie answered. "Remember, this story takes place two hundred years ago. I believe almost all Anglo-Irish were still Catholic until King James the First of England insisted the Butler clan become Protestants because that was the chosen faith in England. Even if you live across the sea in Ireland, it's not easy to go against your king."

"I would never want to go against the king," Violet said.

"Neither did the duke," Elfie said. "So he did what his king commanded and confiscated all the Catholic-owned lands in his duchy, causing great fury among not only the Irish Catholic farmers but also his own family, who did not want to let go of their Catholic faith. The Butlers had been a Catholic family for generations and, as such, supported the very people the duke was wrenching land away from. It made for a big family quarrel."

"I know about family quarrels," Violet said.

Some of the girls started wiggling and giggling, and Elfie sensed she should move on from the history lesson. "Let's find out what Maeve is up to, shall we?"

"Yes, go on!" the girls replied, and Elfie grinned this time.

"Remember, Maeve's grandfather worked as a blacksmith up the hill on the grounds of the castle. She had no idea as she sought refuge with her grandparents that she was walking into the midst of a rebellion! And an armed one at that."

Olivia Whelan, in an unusual display of bravado, called out, "Oh no. A rebellion!" and pulled a pillow over her head with mock drama, acting scared and silly to make the girls laugh.

Elfie quickly continued with the story. "The night was clear and the moon almost full. Maeve ran as fast as she could through the forest to her grandparents' home. She was afraid of the falling light and the dangers the dark might hold. The forest's night calls began to echo from all directions, making her spine tingle with fear. Fortunately, there were watch fires around the castle ahead, tiny points of light leading her forward.

"As she crept closer, she heard horse hooves coming up from behind and the heavy breathing of a large beast at full gallop. Quickly, she hid beside a clump of bushes at the side of the path. The horse stormed past, and she saw a young boy clinging to the horse's neck as if he were one with the beast. He looked terrified. Maeve waited behind the bush until her breath calmed before continuing onward. As she walked, she looked behind herself apprehensively in case whoever—or whatever—came upon her."

"What's *apprehensively*?" Maggie interrupted.

"That means *worried*," Anna answered.

"Maeve's caution turned out to be wise," Elfie continued. "Within minutes, two horsemen rushed toward her, and she hurried again to hide. The poor girl waited for what felt like a long time before continuing. Stepping back onto the path, she could just make out her grandparents' cottage near the bottom of the castle. With fear driving her, she hurried as fast as her legs would go and knocked hard upon their door.

"'Oh my goodness, it's you, Maeve,' her grandmother said, pulling her inside and shutting the door quickly behind her. 'You shouldn't be out by yourself at night. Very strange things are happening in the castle.' Maeve followed her grandmother to the hearth. She sat in a chair and leaned close to the fire to warm herself. Her grandmother brought her food in a rough wooden bowl, and Maeve gratefully breathed in the rich smell of venison stew. 'Your grandfather has been called to the walls of the castle to fill muskets and sharpen spears,' her grandmother told her. Maeve looked up.

"'Does this mean fighting?' she asked. Her grandmother nodded. Maeve suddenly felt exhausted. She put down the stew and curled up on a pallet of straw near the fire, snuggling beneath the quilt her grandmother offered. 'I hope Grandfather will be all right,' she murmured as she fell asleep. 'And that boy I saw . . . I hope he has found a safe place to hide.'

"'What boy?' her grandmother asked, but Maeve had already fallen asleep."

Elfie smiled. "That seems a good place for us to stop for the night," she told her audience.

"I want to know more about the boy," Anna said, bringing on more laughter from the girls.

"Tomorrow night I will tell you about the boy," Elfie said. "And more about the duke, too."

"I think he's a bad duke," Elizabeth said. "He shouldn't take the land from those people."

"Feudal ways are hard to change, Elizabeth," Elfie replied, "but Anna's family steward might agree with you. Land is being confiscated to this day in Ireland." The girls lifted their heads to look at a stunned Anna, and Elfie wondered if she'd made a mistake. If so, it was hers to mop up. "Mr. Charles Parnell is doing his best with the Land League to bring reform to farmers," she explained. She noticed Anna glancing around the room. This time the girls were smiling at her, and Elfie felt pleased. She had made Parnell into a hero. *And,* she thought, *possibly made a few parents unhappy with the school.* She hoped not and decided not to mention his upcoming lecture.

"That's my speech for tonight, girls," Elfie said, standing up and moving to the door. "Maybe the famous Mr. Parnell will want me to join him on the hustings," she said playfully. "I'll have to ask him the next time he visits." She put her hand on Anna's shoulder and Anna grinned appreciatively. The girls giggled, and Elfie turned out the lights.

After she closed the door, she listened to make sure the girls stayed in their beds. Violet's voice piped up, laughter bubbling from deep in her throat: "Can you imagine Miss Elfie on a hay bale making a political speech?" Peals of laughter followed. With the further rise and fall of their laughter, Elfie reopened the door. "Good night again, ladies," she said, setting off another gale of laughter. That was a happy way to end the day.

As Elfie made her way toward her room, she saw a light under her sister's door. She listened for sounds of coughing. Hearing none, she continued to her room instead of knocking on the door. If Frances had heard the uproar from the dormitory, she would want to share some words of wisdom with Elfie regarding appropriate decorum at bedtime. Elfie was too

tired to listen to it. She liked hearing the girls' laughter. It reminded her of life when Lily was still at home. *I should include
something about that in my next letter to Lily,* she told herself.
She closed her door gently, proud that the girls felt they could
make a little fun of her. She would include that in her letter to
Lily too.

CHAPTER 19

ACROSS A SEA

October 1878
Thomas

With hope of news from Canada, Thomas looked out from the drawing room window, searching for the postman's approach. A strong morning wind had cleared the air, leaving a scattering of autumn's leaves on the road in interesting patterns. *I would like to experience the colorful change of seasons in Canada,* Thomas thought, knowing he never would. Lily's letters only occasionally mentioned what occurred outside her home and growing family. A third grandchild on the way, and he hadn't heard from her in several weeks. He had written her two letters in that time and was certain Elfie and Frances had posted at least one each. Should he be worried?

The distance that separated them was real. A letter from Lily, sealed with a dollop of red wax and a press from her signet ring, took up to three days to board a steamship crossing the Atlantic, another ten to twelve days to arrive at the port in Liverpool, England, and up to six days to travel to Holyhead in Wales, cross the Irish Sea, and arrive by train at the General Post Office in Dublin before landing in Harold's Cross. Thomas felt certain one should be arriving today.

The weight of the bag slung over the postman's right shoulder forced him to walk at a strange angle. His glasses seemed permanently perched on the end of his nose, allowing him to read each address carefully to be sure he placed the correct letters in the correct letter boxes. *The man must be nearly as old as I am,* Thomas thought. *How does he do it?* The postman walked up the stairs to the Youngs' letter box on the porch, holding several envelopes fanned out in his hand as if he were choosing cards to play in a game of whist. *Bills or letters?* Thomas wondered. He opened the door, and the man was already at the bottom of the stairs ready to continue his route. "Good day, postman," Thomas called out. The man smiled over his shoulder and waved but didn't stop.

Thomas took the envelopes out of the box and carried them into the house before looking to see what was there. It was a game he played with himself, waiting until he sat comfortably in his chair before going through the mail. Letters were precious. Lily's handwriting rose to greet him, and he ran his finger over the address as if by doing so he could transport himself to her world in Canada. The envelope was addressed to all of them. With a smile, he got out his pocketknife and opened the blade, carefully running the edge beneath the seal. He was pleased to be the first to read the letter. *Maybe this time,* he hoped, *she'll include a snippet of news of Canadian life, not just of the children.*

CHAPTER 20

AN INVITATION

London, Ontario, Canada
Lily

Lily glanced out the second-story window of her bedroom, distracted by the sounds rising from the garden. The children were bundled in their coats against the cool winds sweeping across the peninsula. London, Ontario, sat on a finger of land between two of the Great Lakes, Erie and Huron, making the climate temperate in the summer and a damp penetrating cold in winter. The Irish Sea created a similar northern coastal clime. Lily noted with satisfaction that her children had their hats on. Marian had argued with her against the necessity of the latter, but Lily insisted.

Marian had long ago replaced Mrs. Bennet, and with the arrival of Lucie, followed by Hugh two years later, she had taken on the duties of part-time cook and occasional nanny. By the time Hugh arrived, Lily trusted Marian to care for the baby more often than she had with Lucie. Truth was, she trusted herself now as a mother. With a third child on the way, Lily was grateful that Marian had agreed to work full time, lifting more of the day-to-day burdens of the household and leaving Lily more time to spend reading and playing games with the children. Her own mother had been busy teaching the children of the poor during the day. When she was at home, her poor health and grief for her own lost children created a distance from her daughters they'd been unable to cross.

Lily suspected Marian hadn't needed the extra work but didn't question her good fortune. Marian was forty-five and unlike Lily, in her twenties, was a seasoned wife and mother, having raised her four boys and a girl in the nearby countryside. Her husband, Logan, was a tall, wiry-strong, good-natured man who worked their small dairy farm with their two grown boys. They made cheeses with cow and goat milk and sold their milk locally. Marian and Logan were both from Scottish stock. She had carrot-red hair laced lightly with threads of gray and a strong, erect body that spoke of the hard work she had done raising her family and helping Logan on the farm for many years. Their daughter, Aileen, was not yet married and kept their house so Marian could be away working for the Nivens.

Down in the garden, Marian was sitting on the bench Jim had placed under the spreading canopy of Lily's sycamore maple. With the exception of the windbreak, a line of spruce that James had planted before the house was built, Lily felt the trees were *her* trees. She had selected and placed each of them in the garden, which was a source of pride and accomplishment. As its leaves fell, the sycamore's sturdy skeleton was exposed. *Father would sketch that with just a few easy strokes of his pencil,* she thought each fall. Lily missed him.

Home, children, and garden set the parameters of Lily's daily life, but after five years she hoped for more than that. She was confident she was doing a good job as wife and mother, but a lingering not-quite-satisfied feeling came and went. There was no question her life at RockView had had its limitations. Most of her time in Ireland had been spent caring for her father and managing the household. But she had also found time to be with friends, to play her piano, and to attend lectures and gallery openings. How had she done all that?

Can't look backward, thought Lily. *It's up to me to find satisfying engagements outside our home.* Her sisters rarely wrote about their friends or cultural outings. *I suppose the demands of their school and Father aren't so different from mine. But they must miss that part of their life as I do.* Lily smiled, thinking, *James will do nothing but applaud my desire to move beyond my home.* Pleased with herself, she rested against the back of the chair. *I am the one to choose my path,* she thought. *I will uncork this bottle myself and let the genie out.* The image made her laugh.

The sun started breaking through the clouds, and the laughter below called to her through the closed window. Soon enough another winter would be upon them with snow, bitter temperatures, and brutally cold winds that chilled to the bone. In Ireland, the winters had dragged on, turning RockView dark and gloomy. Lily still could call up the claustrophobia she had felt on damp, rainy days. As a young child, she would break its hold on her by charging down the stairs, flinging open the front door, and running out on the porch, where she breathed in the fresh, moist air, letting the rain splatter her face and pinafore until one of the adults, usually Mary, brought her back inside.

Fortunately, James had understood Lily's desire for a garden. Before they were married, he'd purchased a lot on Dundas Street with more than enough land for both a beautiful home and a large garden. Dundas Street was a road carved in the dirt. It was still not completely graveled but led directly to

London and was central to the city's expansion into the country. The estate agent had convinced her husband of it. "You'll
have the best spot out here, Dr. Niven," he told James. "And
you and your bride will have neighbors before you know it!"

Lily stood up, steadying herself on the back of the chair.
Soon enough, she would be confined by both the weather and
the aftereffects of childbirth. "I don't think we're up for a race
across the lawn with your brother and sister," she told her un-
born child. "But a walk will do us good." She smiled at the familiar words. Her father had uttered them whenever he felt the
need to escape his "house full of women" or take a break from
painting. Lily intended to take advantage of the fall weather
and her mobility while they lasted.

Down on the first floor, she felt her step lighten with a
sense of freedom as she approached the front door. She lifted
her hat off the rack and pulled on her coat, laughing at herself
when she saw her image in the entry mirror. The coat barely
buttoned around her. She left Marian a hasty note on the entry
table so she would not worry, and opened the front door.

Without hesitation, Lily headed south, away from the city
and toward the low hills. She didn't know when it happened,
but the city girl inside her had become eager to encounter and
watch her new companions the hawks and eagles. The birds
flew over the open fields and in and out of the dense stands
of pine forest at their edges, their freedom and grace exciting
to her. *A friend to walk and talk with would be nice too,* she
thought.

Lily flushed at the thought of the invitation from Susanna
Harwood still awaiting her reply. Susanna Harwood was host-
ing a luncheon with the intent of starting a women's literary
club. Friends, books, food, and intellectual discussion. What
was she waiting for? Lily seemed destined to be behind on her
correspondence, but she was looking forward to attending.

Who knows? she thought. *This invitation could lead to my first step beyond family life.*

Lily paused along the road to catch her breath. She felt certain the baby was pressing on her diaphragm, and her chest heaved as she refilled her lungs. "Is it your head or your foot, little one?" She remained where she was until her breathing evened out. The view, so different from RockView's spare, rocky landscape, held the last fading greens of summer as Canada prepared itself for winter. The careful lines of cultivated fields and the wild grasses along the road were taking on fall's golden hues.

Her father had taken many trips on foot in the country to sketch a rural scene either alone or with his students. She had to travel all the way to Canada to understand his enthusiasm. It occurred to her that he might enjoy reading about her walks in the country. *The rest of my letter is going to write itself!* she thought happily. She would also respond to Susanna's invitation the moment she arrived home. Lily pivoted toward home with new purpose.

CHAPTER 21

NUANCE AND OPPORTUNITY

November
Lily

Once she had committed herself to the literary luncheon, Lily considered the nuances of the invitation. The envelope had been addressed to and meant for her, Lily Niven, alone. She was delighted. Something just for her, a ladies' luncheon!

She was as excited at the thought of making new friends as she was at seeing Susanna's house. "It will be interesting to see how she has decorated her home," she told James after they settled by the fireplace after dinner. "Mother often said that a home revealed a lot about the people who lived there. Their décor reflects their personal tastes and even their family history." Lily had hung one of her father's paintings in her entry and another in their dining room. They did give her a chance to talk about her family to the few guests they'd had thus far.

James remained quiet while she talked. Instead of being pleased for her or teasing her by asking what their home said about the Niven family, he appeared thoughtful, off-center, and she couldn't help but wonder if her husband felt she'd taken her excitement too far by accepting the invitation before talking with him. She dismissed the idea as unlikely. *James simply isn't that sort of husband,* she told herself.

Lily did have a concern she thought would amuse James and lighten the atmosphere. "But, James, what will I wear? I look like a circus clown in most of my dresses."

"Lily," he said, looking at her with a disarming gentleness, "you are beautiful, clever, and a good conversationalist. That's what they will see."

What he means, Lily thought, placing her hands on her rounded belly, *is I am worrying over nothing, because in a doctor's view being with child is nothing novel.* There were things men would never understand. How could they?

"I appreciate your compliments, James, but I plan to visit my seamstress soon," she said, straightening and smoothing the voluminous fabric around her. "A new dress will make me feel less like a bouncing ball and more like a fashionable mother." Her husband nodded. "You're right, of course. No amount of clever tucks, folds, and stitching will hide my current state. I had better decide to shine as a clever woman."

"You are always that," he said absently. "More than likely you will not be alone in your condition."

"Yes, James, of course." Lily was becoming impatient with his distracted contributions. "My condition is 'an ongoing epidemic for young women,'" she said, quoting him. In Ireland she might have been "in confinement" during her last few months, as her mother had been. In Canada the custom was different; women were free to go about their lives when they were carrying a child. It was liberating to have left Ireland's Victorian mores behind. Besides, this would be her third child. She was no neophyte.

"Ontario homes seem more open and lighter compared to our families' homes in Ireland, don't you think, James? Ours certainly is," she said, glancing around the large room. "That was a lovely surprise. I've always thought the tall windows facing the garden are the nicest feature of our home. We've both seen how the interior walls of the houses in town are painted neutral or primary colors, and of course the wallpapers have open designs, much like in our bedrooms. But I do prefer our wooden walls in the main living area. This is just what I wanted for our home—some of the old, but overall the light, cheerful feeling of the garden and the forests and fields surrounding her." She looked at James and stopped talking. She wasn't interested in giving a soliloquy.

"James?" she prompted.

He reached over and brushed her cheek with his fingers, his expression serious. "I'm sorry, dear. Of course I am interested in your observations, Lily. They tell me you are appreciating the life we have here in Canada. I admit I've been wrestling with something entirely different."

Lily pushed her thoughts aside and leaned toward him and waited for him to continue.

"I've come to the realization that I have not left Ireland behind as much as I thought I had. I never provided medical care for the Irish before we came to Canada. I only helped the Anglo-Irish, advantaged as we are." James got out of his chair and moved onto the sofa to sit next to her. Taking her hand, he said gently, "The thoughts you shared about your friends' homes make me think about the variety of people I am treating here in Canada. Many of them do not live as you describe. Those are the homes of people like us. To be honest, my practice here in London has given me a jolt and made me more of an egalitarian."

"An egalitarian?" Lily almost repeated with mirth. But now wasn't the time for teasing. Her husband was opening up to her and was quite serious.

"House calls many times take me to humble dwellings. Dirt floors. Rough if any furniture to speak of. Privies out back and a metal tub near the stove for whatever bathing they manage to do. In Ireland, the British have made sure the poor Irish have no chance, but here they are meant to have opportunity and education, and yet real poverty continues to exist. I may sound naïve, but it has been a large dose of reality to come face to face with how unequal life is. My existence was sheltered in Ireland, practicing and living in a world away from poverty. I knew of it but . . . to see it . . . smell it . . ."

Lily lifted his hand to her lips and kissed it. "You are a lovely man, James. We've both lived comfortable lives. I'm sure you've felt shocked by what you've seen." Her husband's open expression of his collision with poverty had dampened her anticipation for the coming event. Since falling in love with James, she had held the dream that she could live anywhere with him and be happy, make a good life. They were doing that, but as life unfolded, she was learning that the journey was more complicated and layered than her youthful, romantic, idyllic plans.

Something her husband said made her conscious of a subtle itch she needed to scratch. *Opportunity,* she thought. *James said, "They are meant to have opportunity." That's what I've been looking for. An opportunity to do something beyond our home that is constructive and interesting.* Her sisters had found theirs. Her mother had purpose outside the family. She must look for hers, because it hadn't come knocking at her door to announce itself. Lily realized her husband was waiting for her to say something, and she took a breath to clear her thoughts.

"James, you are a very caring man. My mother once told me that it is our job to use all we have in a humble manner and make our lives of benefit to others. You do that every day as a doctor. That is part of why I admire you."

He kissed her on the cheek and moved back to his chair, appearing relaxed now. Watching him read the newspaper again, looking so peaceful, her own itch pushed and rearranged within her. But it was late and the enthusiasm she'd felt all day had drained her. She was tired and her body no longer felt like her own. *Someday I will take on the world beyond home,* she thought, *but not until I am good and ready. Meanwhile, I'm going to bed.*

Lily covered her mouth, stifling a yawn. She was exhausted.

— ◆ —

On the day of the luncheon, Lily stood before the mirror, inspecting her image. The dark blue merino wool dress was as becoming as it could be. Her seamstress had done well. She had suggested lace ruffles—"from the neck to the leg. They're becoming quite popular in England"—but Lily stayed with an empire waist. The added lining moved easily over her abdomen, which was easily irritated these days. She picked up a lapis-and-pearl necklace—a gift from James when Lucie was born—opened the clasp, and closed it behind her neck. The necklace curved just below the neckline. She held up the pearl earrings Eliza had given her after the wedding. Appreciating her mirrored image, she thought decidedly, *Yes Eliza, they finish it off beautifully.* She was as ready as she was going to be.

In the entry Marian handed her the mink cape she and James had purchased for her last winter for dress occasions. It always made her feel like she was wrapped in silken elegance. Stepping outside, she also appreciated its warmth.

Sean McBride arrived at 11:15 sharp to take her to the luncheon. James had arranged the transportation for her. "I must be sure you arrive at Susanna's like a lady, Mrs. Niven," he'd assured her with a mock bow. James had called the transport a trap, but what she saw was a sweet little buggy.

"Is this what Dr. Niven travels in when you drive him?" Lily asked Sean.

"No, ma'am, he had me borrow it special from the farrier, Mr. Dougal, who was glad to have you use it. Mr. Dougal bought it for his young wife, Ena, bless her soul. He lost her not long ago to diphtheria. He told me Dr. Niven was kind and helpful to her to the very last. He also said we Irish like to help our fellow Irish."

"How very kind of Mr. Dougal," said Lily. "I must thank him the next time I am in town." She said nothing at the Irishman calling her Irish rather than Anglo-Irish or British as if a breed set apart, but his inclusion of her as one of his own made her happy. She must remember to tell James that he was right. Canada *is* a place for new thinking. Sean gave her a hand and a little upward push to get her into the buggy and onto the black leather seat. After taking his place in the front and untying the reins, he turned and asked, "You all right there, Mrs. Niven?" Lily nodded and they were off.

The buggy had good springs to deal with the uneven road surface, but still she held on tight while enjoying the view as the roof fringe swayed above her. Soon enough they turned onto a road shaded by the long branches of mature chestnut trees. The road became a circular driveway in front of Susanna's Georgian-style house. Lily liked it at first sight. The entrance and exterior details were typically Georgian, painted white, but the walls were of stucco in a pale yellow. Lily had the feeling she'd arrived at a large estate. Sean pulled up the horse and helped Lily descend. He took her arm again to help her ascend the stairs to the porch. "I will return at two o'clock, Mrs. Niven, and wait until you are ready to leave."

"Thank you, Sean," she said, thinking *wish me luck* as she lifted the heavy brass knocker to make her entrance.

Susanna greeted Lily, taking her cape and exclaiming at its beauty as she lifted the fur to her cheek. "This must feel wonderful on these chilly days." Lily had forgotten how forthright Susanna was. Most hostesses would not comment on a fur cape. *Doesn't everyone have one?* Lily worried. *Shame on you, Lily,* she scolded herself. *Susanna is just making you feel at home.* Taking a deep breath, she reminded herself once more that yes, she was very much a mother-in-waiting, but she was in a room with interesting women, with similar circumstances. *It's up to you to get to know them, find your common interests. Look for opportunities, Lily.* She smiled and followed her hostess into the parlor.

CHAPTER 22

THOMAS'S DISTRESS

Outskirts of Dublin, Ireland
Thomas

Thomas felt good to be out in the country again, and with purpose. November rains had held off for over a week, so he chose to follow a dirt track that led outside of Dublin's western limits for a day of sketching and painting with four of his students. Less than two miles beyond the paved streets and Georgian homes, Thomas was surprised to find a cluster of cottages. Dark smoke curled up from the roofs in the cool morning air. It was a picturesque Irish country scene, if not cliché—a good subject to sketch. Alerting his companions, he steered them toward a copse of trees perched on a hill a short distance from the settlement, where they would have an added view of the surrounding landscape. "Those low rolling hills in the background will offer dimension to your subject," he instructed while they walked. "As you sketch, take notice of the ancient oaks, how they are silhouetted against the grassy fields."

"The dirt road we were on recedes into the distance beyond the cottages," one of his students said from the back of the line.

"Yes," Thomas said. "Indeed." He liked the composition. Yet when the small group settled into their vantage point in the trees, they could see they had discovered not a hamlet of charming cottages but four poor shanties, each with a flap of sheepskin for a door and no windows. The smell of animals and humans mingled with the woodsmoke and traveled to where the artists stood. Their presence at this scene, even at a distance of a hundred feet, felt intrusive.

Thomas was deciding whether to continue on their way when one of the young students pointed to horsemen riding toward the settlement from the opposite direction. "I think we should remain here," Thomas cautioned, "and make our presence less obvious." The group sat behind the trees and watched the horsemen approach the hamlet at a gallop. From their hiding spot, Thomas counted five men. They pulled up their horses in front of the first hovel.

A sharp voice called out, "Show your face! Come out of that unholy hole and show yourself." The horsemen laughed, and their mounts moved nervously. Thomas and his students watched silently, their eyes glued to the unfolding scene. There was no response from inside the dwelling that they could ascertain.

A second shout from the leader was followed by the report of a pistol shot into the air. Still the huddled artists heard no response. The leader waved his hand and one of the men dismounted. He removed a stick from the back of his saddle, lit it, and threw the torch onto the roof closest to them. Smoke billowed, followed by screams and cries rising from within the building. The door flap flew open and a young woman burst out, holding a baby, followed by four scraggly children. With her free hand, she waved and pointed back inside the burning home.

Thomas was shocked. He had heard rumors of such incidents but had suspected they were rare and exaggerated in the press. He certainly never thought he would be witness to one.

The horsemen were enforcers, hired by a landowner who gladly distanced himself from the dirty work of eviction. Gruff, indiscernible exchanges drifted up to where they stood, while the woman continued to cry out. She passed the baby to one of the children and ran back inside the burning dwelling. She reappeared pulling the arms of the slack body of a man she dragged along the ground. By now people had come out of the other shanties and stood well away, looking dumbstruck and fearful. No one moved to help the woman. Thomas surprised himself by stepping out of the copse and toward the scene. One of his students reached out and held his sleeve. "Sir, you should be careful. These men are armed."

"Oh my, sir," another student said, haltingly, his eyes growing large with terror. "I believe they are riding straight toward us." Thomas watched as the hooligans left the smoking village and its inhabitants and passed below his small group.

The young man who had counseled Thomas to remain hidden suddenly stepped forward and called out to the riders, his voice quivering with anger. "What right do you have to burn their home?"

The leader drew up his horse and turned. He headed slowly toward the young man, who walked down to meet him beside the road. The horse's nostrils blew warm and moist air toward the young man's face, and his eyes flinched as he took a step backward. Thomas stood up with the rest of the students. The leader, sitting well above them on his mount, slowly rose in his stirrups and examined all of them as if considering their fate.

"We have every right," he spat back at them. "It's our job.

What's your job, boyo?" Thomas wanted to object to his man's rude manner but thought better. "You think you can speak to me when you sissy boys haven't even got hair on your balls yet?" Not waiting for a reply, the man continued, his voice dripping with condescension. "Those Irish there are scum," he said, pointing toward the huts. "Two years no rent, so out they go. We'll burn the rest of 'em if they don't pay. Next time there better be coin to jingle in my purse." He kicked his mount hard and turned to leave. The horse lifted its tail, dropping a steaming, smelly pile right at the young man's feet. "A gift just for you buggery shits," he yelled over his shoulder. His men joined him, laughing as they took their leave.

Thomas and his students stood tongue-tied and frozen to the spot until the men were out of sight. Then they turned their mute attention to the flaming structure and the people trying vainly to put it out with handfuls of dirt.

"What cruel principles rule the thoughts of men who do these things?" The question came from the same young man who had challenged the horsemen. Jonathan Sprague was familiar to Thomas for his candor, not for brave remarks or deeds. Jonathan walked to the settlement, and they all followed. There was little they could do except to offer words of concern and what little money and food they had brought with them. Thomas watched curiously as Jonathan wrote on a piece of paper from his sketchbook and handed it to the woman.

That night Thomas had trouble sleeping. When he closed his eyes he saw the face of the young woman, the man on the ground who was surely dying or dead, and their unkempt children holding on to one another, wide-eyed with fright. The woman's pleading eyes haunted him. *What, dear God, is my obligation in this fight?* he asked himself. He wondered if he should relate the event to Lily and James to caution his daughter not to walk alone in the country. *No. She would only worry about me and tell me that Canada is not like Ireland.*

How many times has she told me there is enough for everyone in Canada to have a decent life? But Thomas knew bullies and men of ill will existed everywhere.

What did it say about his country that a simple ramble outside his own city brought him face to face with this disturbing reality? It was so close by and yet stood like a separate universe from the life he lived between RockView and the academy. Was he so cloistered, so sealed off from such scenes as he witnessed that day? *Biddy and Mary's world is different from my own, but nothing like the one I saw today. Surely they are protected from such upsetting intrusions or they would tell me, wouldn't they?* In either case, he would send Lily a letter in the morning, strongly advising her to only go walking with James or a companion. *Especially in her delicate condition,* he thought. *It's only common sense, after all.* Having made a decision, Thomas felt better, though not enough to fall asleep right away.

CHAPTER 23

LILY THE SUFFRAGETTE

London, Ontario
Lily

The ladies stopped their chatting, and Susanna introduced Lily to those she did not already know.

Emma Manson stood up and took Lily's hand. "I have wanted to get to know you, Lily, for the longest time. Your husband and Dr. Cattermole have been a godsend to this community. The previous doctor, my husband liked to say, was so clumsy he must have gone to a veterinarian school for large animals." Her comment brought laughter from the others.

Lily smiled gratefully at Emma. "James is a good doctor. I am proud of him, and I am happy to hear you appreciate his services. I also hope you have a good vet."

The women laughed again, and Ava Andrews rose to kiss Lily on each cheek. "Good to see you, Lily," she said. "I see we'll soon have another Niven in our city."

"Not soon enough for me," said Lily, creating a few more knowing chuckles.

The last woman Susanna introduced her to nodded without smiling, causing Lily to temper her own. She did feel better about her mink, though, after seeing the amount of jewelry the woman wore. Lila Harrington was clearly wealthy. Even so, Lily thought she wore far more than was appropriate for daytime. *Unless excessive jewelry is something else that's acceptable in Canada.* Lily couldn't imagine it for herself.

"We were to be six today," Susanna said, addressing all of them. "Eloise Chapin sent her regrets. She is under the weather. It's too bad, but for the rest of us the show must go on. Let's go in and have our lunch."

Name cards directed them all where to sit at the table, and the other women continued chatting among themselves as if they'd known each other all their lives. Not finding an easy way to break into a conversation, Lily studied Susanna's dining room. The room was fresh and appealing, like her hostess. Neither carried an ounce of the heavy Victorian style of old Ireland. Even the botanical prints on the walls reflected what was framed in the two large windows that looked out on the garden, bringing the outdoors in. *How clever,* she thought. Lily hoped they would be invited to explore the garden later.

The table quieted and Susanna made light talk about weather and family as their food was served. The young serving girl had bright red hair and a rosy complexion. Lily thought she looked a lot like Marian's daughter, Aileen. *Scottish,* Lily bet herself. White china plates with a light silver pattern circling the edges framed their meal of sliced roasted duck breast, new potatoes covered in a morel sauce and, sliced on an angle as Biddy liked them, minted carrots. Each plate was like a work of art.

"Today we enjoy the fruits of Canada's wilderness," Susanna said. "The duck is compliments of my husband, Raymond; the carrots are from my garden; and the morels were gathered in the local forests." Forks were raised tentatively as the guests waited for the hostess to begin. Yet rather than begin their luncheon, Susanna instead announced (to what Lily could only assume was collective surprise) the topic of discussion. "I know I invited you to start a women's literary club," Susanna said, "but let me explain." All forks were lowered and hands returned to their laps. "My sister in Toronto, whom I visited recently, has joined a group they call the Toronto Women's Literary Club. Let me tell you straight out: their club is not about literature. It's something much more exciting. Much more innovative. Much more advantageous to our well-being as women. It's a society." Susanna paused and looked at each one of them. "A women's suffragette society."

Lily sat wide-eyed. Some of the women looked down at their plates. Susanna continued as if she hadn't noticed. "The women in the club very carefully do not call it a suffrage society. They made the decision to use their time together to promote and educate themselves and others about women's rights."

Susanna, sitting very straight in her chair, continued with a brief history of the movement, then again paused and looked at her guests, this time as if expecting a response. Lily could almost hear the wheels turning in the heads around her. *What to say?* The air was electric with uncertainty. She did not want to embarrass herself with her ignorance on women's rights. She had come to make friends, not to make a fool of herself.

Susanna spoke again. "It is my position that women like us need to work together to get the vote in Canada so we can determine our own lives." The statement resonated with Lily, and she nodded her head. Not knowing what possessed her, she decided to speak. "The same is true in Ireland. Women have no vote and are barred from pursuing nearly all professions of consequence. That hardly seems right. My mother-in-law is in charge of a very successful business, after all, but only because she inherited it from her husband."

Susanna smiled at Lily appreciatively for breaking the tension. In the silence that followed, something else occurred to Lily, something she had not previously thought of as a women's-rights issue.

"My two sisters in Ireland have made a bold move. They have started a boarding school for girls." Lily glanced around the table. "They provide the girls not only with a social and academic education but also with a cosmopolitan education so they can, at the very least, hold their place in conversation with men. My sisters, Frances and Elfie Young, are teaching their students to think about the events of the day, not just repeat what they read in books. Or hear from the men in their lives."

"Hurrah for your sisters, Lily," Susanna said. "They sound like capital women we could use in our cause right here. Has it been successful? We need to find ways to spark change and create opportunities just like that for women right here in London, Ontario."

Lily was about to answer when Lila Harrington, whom Lily now knew was the wife of a local barrister and judge, spoke. Her voice carried an edge as she challenged Susanna and Lily. "I don't feel it is appropriate for women to engage in public issues. It is not dignified and, frankly, my husband, Jeffery, would never allow it. He has my best interests in mind and I am sure represents them well in defending his clients' interests and the public interest in the courts. I don't have to waste my time trying to be part of men's conversations, and this is not the conversation I came here expecting."

Lily felt the intended blow. She supposed Susanna had been aware Lila Harrington might stir up her guests. What would others say? As of yet, nothing. Some of the women picked at their food with empty forks to fill the silence. Lily watched Susanna's expression and considered that Lila might not be at the next luncheon.

What would Frances or Elfie do if they were here? Lily wondered. She stifled a smile. She couldn't wait to write to them about her luncheon. Lily was betting on Ava, who was never shy, to make the next move. She was right.

"I believe, as I am sure you do, Lila, that our husbands love us and protect us." Lila Harrington nodded her agreement. "We must also be realistic," Ava continued. "Your Jeffery is a barrister and my Evan is a grain merchant. I had to listen to Evan the other evening ranting about three temperance ladies who had come to visit his business offices. They insisted on an interview with him. Of course you know grain is used in making alcohol, and they wanted him to cut his supply to the distilleries. But what really seemed to amaze and annoy him was that they also wanted women to have the vote. Well," she said, giving them each a knowing look, "he was not pleased with their visit! Not for the first time, I admonished him about the dangers of drinking for some, and I told him that I hoped he was polite to them."

Lily stole a glance at Lila, who appeared torn between agreement with Ava's stance on alcohol and disapproval at how she had spoken to her husband.

"I am for temperance," Ava clarified, "but I'm not for prohibition. Evan's interests, like all our husbands' interests, are well served by maintaining the status quo. No need to change what gives them power and makes money, even when changing would be the right thing to do. I will be careful how I share this meeting with my husband. I hope over time, as I build my arguments with all of you, I can help him to see his interests are better served when women have the right to vote. Social change is our job."

Ava seemed to have made a definite impression on

everyone, including Lily. She wondered how much controversy their hostess was prepared to hear at their first meeting. *For that matter,* she thought, *how much controversy am I prepared to hear?*

Emma's eyebrows had moved up and down at each turn in Ava's story. As soon as Ava was finished, she spoke up. "From what little I've read in the newspapers, there are divisions in the suffrage movement, just as there are at this table." Her eyebrows lifted again and she looked at each of them. "Voting is not the priority for everyone. Some, like Lily's sisters, are more interested in women gaining access to education and even, for some, employment. Others, it seems, want to vote. Education is the first step and tops my list." With that, her eyebrows furrowed and she looked down at her plate.

"It is also true," Ava said, "we are a favored group of women with many freedoms. Others do not have the same protections we enjoy." With that, Ava apparently was done, too.

Lily had been looking forward to the meal as much as the conversation when she'd arrived, but found what was happening around the table far more engaging than what was on it. "I agree with Emma," she announced. "My family has always known that access to education is important. To answer Susanna's question regarding my sisters' success: they have just graduated their first class of nine. Four of those young women are going to further their education at home with tutors. One of them, Anna Monteforte, was under the financial stewardship of Charles Parnell, champion of Irish nationalism, and Miss Monteforte has shown an interest in politics. Her generation will no doubt demand the vote."

Lila Harrington pursed her lips, and her face carried an edge of defensiveness. Obviously stinging from Ava's remarks, Lila sniffed and took her turn looking at the women around the table. "Do I hear a hint of nepotism, Lily, in using family connections to advance your Miss Monteforte's career?"

Lily was stunned. How had the woman come to that conclusion? It was Anna's connection, not the Youngs', that was "advancing her career." No one responded to Lila's hostile remark, and she sat back, appearing pleased.

"Bravo!" Susanna said, breaking through the stunned silence without in any way recognizing the previous remarks. "Lily, your sisters are moving all women forward with their work. We must do the same. We must always move forward with positive energy. Anyone want to run for city council?" All the women except Lila laughed. The tension was broken. Lily flushed, proud of herself for speaking up and proud of her sisters. She was grateful to Susanna for saving her.

Susanna at last took a bite of her food, and the rest of the women followed. Surveying her guests, she said, "This was a good exchange, and I do apologize for springing this on you the way I have. My sister and her friends told me that it is best to have these discussions with like-minded women and to use the cover of a literary club." She looked at Lila, who sat stony-faced at the table. "Clearly, we have diverse opinions and experiences to bring to the subject. To that end, shall we choose a book to read so your husbands and others will not suspect us? I suggest Jane Austen's *Pride and Prejudice*. The sparring between Elizabeth Bennet and Mr. Darcy seems appropriate to our cause." There was some tittering over Susanna's jest, and she went on. "I hope Eloise can join us with new ideas. Bring your arguments with you and prepare to be challenged! If you do decide to repeat any of these thoughts," she added in a quiet and serious voice, "please do not attach a name to it. We want to be able to speak our minds freely here. Not every husband or friend will understand. For now, let's continue our conversation and enjoy our meal."

On the ride home, Lily recalled discussions at home in Ireland where she and her sisters had voiced their frustration about women not being allowed in the Hibernian Academy or Trinity College. A woman's right to vote had not ever been part of the conversation. Their father appeared to agree quietly with them but, in truth, he had done nothing to change the academy's rules, nor did he encourage his daughters to try to make a change. James did not prevent her from speaking her mind. Rather, he seemed to rather enjoy listening to her opinions. What would he think of her wanting the vote for herself and all women? She would find out.

— • —

After putting the children to bed that night, Lily readied herself to begin a conversation about votes for women. But when they retired to the parlor, James had a concern of his own to share. In a raised voice, and very much on his high horse, he told her there were plans for a countryside steeplechase that coming weekend. Lily couldn't imagine why he was so bothered by a horse race and sat back to find out. She would have to wait for an opening to bring up her own issue.

"The chase," James explained, "is organized by The Orange Order."

Lily raised her eyebrows. "I'd hoped we'd left them behind in Ireland."

"The Orangemen are wanting to raise funds to help settle Protestant Irish in Canada. Helping them goes against my grain. They only wish to use their money to swell their numbers in this country. The Order is no friend of Irish nationalism or independence. It seems it doesn't matter what we want," he lamented. "Nonetheless, I have made a choice." He had Lily's full attention now. Was her husband going to make a stand for Irish independence in Canada? It seemed the day had been ripe for controversial matters.

"I have placed," James said, "a good-sized wager on a young Irish lad whose name I don't even know." Lily raised her eyebrows again, this time in surprise. "I have watched him ride, and the boy is fearless. He attacks the wild country-side course of hurdles, ditches, and streams. He and his horse launch themselves over every barrier. He's more than likely a Catholic, so I can rationalize making a sizable bet to support him. Protestant Orangemen be damned. Let my Irish Catholic win, and my winnings will go to him."

Lily almost laughed at James's convoluted reasoning but left it alone. Her husband liked to make a wager now and again—plunk his money down showing confidence in his choice.

Lily saw her chance to take the floor. "Speaking of rides through the country," she began, and then recounted for her husband Dougal's remark about "the Irish helping the Irish." "Isn't that wonderful? No one ever called us Irish in Ireland!"

James agreed but bemoaned that the old order was still trying to establish itself in this country. "I am against it," he said fervently.

"Then maybe you will be *for* what happened at the luncheon," Lily said, directing the conversation back to her day. Without further preamble, she told James about her afternoon at Susanna's.

When she finished, her husband cocked his head and smiled. "And I thought *I* had an interesting day. No light-hearted, polite lunch conversation for these ladies!" he said. "Maybe Elfie's not going to be the only radical in the family."

Lily was annoyed. He was not taking her seriously, and she responded heatedly. "What's wrong with women having a serious discussion? The point is we have been left out of the conversation for too long, and it is a disservice to all women, not just to me and my friends."

James looked surprised by her quick-hot response to his lighthearted remark. Hoping to rectify the situation, he said, "I see I have missed my mark. I hope you can count it as no harm done. I am interested."

Her husband seemed sincere now, and Lily calmed down enough to recall that she too had been taken aback when Susanna first brought up the subject of suffrage. She would go easy on James. "I think you may be right," she said, beginning with a conversation starter that had worked with her father—with most men she'd known, for that matter. "Elfie is not the only blossoming radical in the Young family. And that isn't a joke."

Lily felt a shift in her own mind, a realization that the changes she and James had sought by running so far from home might be further unfolding. Lily watched her husband watching her, or more accurately her rounding body. He reached toward her and made a gentle circle with his hand on her belly. "Doctor's wife, mother of three strikes out for women's vote!" he said, smiling. "I am not teasing you, Lily. My mother is a very strong and capable woman, but this conversation would never have taken place in her home. She was more about getting her way, not making the way for others."

Lily quietly thanked God that her husband was a confident man who did not cling to the old ways. *Wasn't that why we came to Canada, to experience something new?* Lily was certain neither of them had considered that would mean women having the right to vote. And now that was exactly what she wanted to happen. *It's a new world, Lily,* she told herself. She no longer felt she had to look for others to offer her opportunities. She would make her own.

CHAPTER 24

THOUGHTS OF SLIGO

Dublin, Ireland
May 1881
Elfie

The eighth year of the Misses Young School for Girls had come and gone. Elfie would miss the girls—she always did—yet after each graduation it was thoughts of Elizabeth Fenn and Anna Monteforte that lingered with her. Of all the girls who had come and gone through Misses Young's, Elfie felt closest to Elizabeth and Anna.

They were young women now, recently moved to England. Both wrote occasional letters to the sisters, but it was George Fenn, Elizabeth's father, who kept the Youngs updated on the two "girls" each time he stopped at RockView on his way to London. "Hardly 'girls,'" Frances would say after he left. "His own daughter is nearly engaged to be married!"

Elfie's attention was caught by something else during his visits. In their drawing room, George Fenn regaled the Youngs with stories in a way that showed he was at ease in their company. *He feels at home here,* she thought, something she tried not to take as anything more than a deep compliment to the friendship that had grown through the years. *That's only natural,* she told herself. She and her father had been summer guests of the Fenns many times.

"As you know," George said on his latest visit, "Elizabeth is staying in London with my aunt, who is introducing her to society, but I'm afraid so far Elizabeth is not impressed. She has developed an interest in describing her perspective on the identity of the Anglo-Irish in Ireland, where they are viewed as Monarchists, versus in England, where they are viewed as less than British."

"How anthropological of her," Thomas commented.

"My own fault, I fear. I worry her observations may not go over well with her prospective in-laws if she is not careful in choosing her words. In truth," George added, sotto voce, "I am proud of her. She confided to me that she hopes to have her observations published!"

Elfie and Frances exchanged glances. "That may be our fault," Elfie said. "We do encourage our girls to develop self-confidence and their own opinions."

"And to express them in a way they can be heard, diplomatically," added Frances.

George laughed. "I imagine her suitor and his family, then, are very appreciative. As am I. Of course, I reminded her that newspapers and journals are rarely willing to accept work from a woman, and that's when she told me she plans to use a nom de plume!" George beamed at his daughter's cleverness.

Elfie was thrilled by both Elizabeth's spirit and the thought that one of the school's very own might actually be published, even if anonymously. And their Anna was working as an assistant to a senior clerk in the office of an Irish member of the House of Commons!

"She's quite open about the fact that her guardian had a hand in her procuring the position," George said, when Elfie mentioned Anna's name. "Humble girl, but quite capable, I understand. I'm glad she and my daughter are friends."

Elfie was glad too. Friendships were important. She was especially glad Elizabeth would be home in Sligo for the summer. Elfie knew Elizabeth had made several trips home since her mother died. Elfie's upcoming one-month stay with the Fenns was unearthing some conflicting emotions for her—excited to get away, looking forward to the reunion with Elizabeth, and yet saddened when she thought of Bessie Fenn being gone. She had been a lovely woman, a gracious hostess and friend to Thomas and Elfie during their visits. Sligo would not be the same without her.

There was something else bothering her. What was she concerned about? The answer came quickly: *George.* What would it be like with only George as their host?

When Bessie died, Elfie had assumed the responsibility of writing to George and Elizabeth to extend their sympathy and support. The funeral and burial were in Sligo during the school session, which had meant the Youngs were unable to attend. Elfie sent brief notes to George through the year, hoping the lighthearted content—school anecdotes and reports on her father's work—might lift his spirits. Now she hoped her letters had not seemed "forward" during his time of mourning. She probably should have written more to Elizabeth and not just to George, but she hadn't.

As the day of their trip to Sligo approached, Elfie fretted about the propriety of being a single woman staying in the Fenn household. At the very least her presence would cause curiosity in the local population in Sligo. The worry was exhausting. *I sound like Frances,* she thought, annoyed with herself. *A maiden schoolteacher and her father coming for an extended visit with the widower Fenn. Now is that proper?*

Elfie was having trouble sorting out her feelings. She was also uncomfortably aware that her youthfulness had dimmed, especially over the past year. The school was a lot of work. In the mirror she saw crow's feet, as Frances called them, and frown lines that marked her passing years. *Away from my reflection, I feel young and eager, ready for a holiday.* She smiled slyly at her image. *Maybe a little impropriety will bring out the laugh lines.* Her image smiled back.

Elfie felt the heat rising to her face again. George Fenn had brought a playful and masculine energy into their home. Her father always perked up in his presence. George made the girls laugh, made Elfie laugh, and even drew smiles from Frances. He and Thomas tossed about political speculations and enjoyed their time together. Between visits, her father made a habit of collecting articles on controversial topics for their next conversation.

On one visit, George had herded the Youngs into the kitchen to be with Biddy and Mary. "You, Biddy," he announced, "are why I chose the school for Elizabeth. Nothing but good can come from a house with a good cook! You wouldn't by chance have any wee 'samples' for a weary traveler?" Biddy had laughed and brought him warm scones, along with an offer to taste from a large wooden spoon she dipped in a pot of slow-simmering stew.

George had charmed the entire household with his warmth, kindness, and humor—except for Frances, who cast a cool eye on him whenever he stopped by. "He is too unguarded with his ungentlemanly openness," Frances said to Elfie. "He stirs things up."

Thank goodness, thought Elfie. *We can use a little stirring up around here.* George freely shared juicy tidbits from political notables such as Charles Parnell garnered from his club in England and editorials in the London *Times*. Elfie noted that Frances sat uncomfortably during these conversations. Wagging a finger at Elfie after George had left and their father had retired, Frances would let loose. "Don't you see it is undignified for us as teachers to be too involved in the hurly-burly of national politics?" *And yet you never leave the room when he shares with us, but stay to hear it all,* Elfie thought. Her sister could sound like a stuffy old maid at times. She let both thoughts pass and said nothing. It had occurred to Elfie more recently that it might be something else about George's presence at RockView that bothered her sister. And that stirred up Elfie.

— ◆ —

Thomas

Thomas's letters to Lily and James that spring had been full of plans for their outing to the west coast. His past travels to Sligo had been an artistic, and something of a financial, success, something he hadn't experienced in a long while. This summer would be their third stay with the Fenns, and he was full of anticipation.

In honor of Thomas's seventieth birthday the coming January, the academy was planning an exhibition of his work featuring Sligo's rocky west-coast landscape and the ruins of ancient monasteries on Inishmurray. The merchant class in Dublin had become entranced with paintings of the vast Atlantic Ocean crashing onto Ireland's western doorstep. Fortunately for Thomas, they saw an Irish landscape painting displaying an untamed western seaboard, the beloved green and rocky countryside, or remote monastic settlements as a source of national pride to display in their homes. Unfortunately for Thomas's bank account, aristocrats remained steadfastly interested in displaying their own portraits, along with paintings by famous European artists. He'd heard rumors that those with a sense of daring had begun purchasing the works of the upstart French impressionists. For the wealthy class in Ireland, the land they lived on, and where they earned their living off the backs of the Irish poor, held no other interest. They preferred the grand art of the French Salon to colloquial Irish scenery.

Thomas's work appealed to a more parochial Irish bourgeoisie audience, and that was fine with him. They could afford his art and his profits were reasonable. Commerce in Ireland was growing, and a middle class who could buy his work was growing with it. Many of these urban dwellers had roots in the land of their forebears who tilled their own soil or had others do it for them. There were first- and second-generation city folk who enjoyed being sentimental about the Irish life and countryside. Merchants or professionals no longer tied to the seasons and the land, they found pleasure in the memories and stories his paintings held. Thomas's landscapes were often just what they were looking for.

Frances never joined them in Sligo. She preferred taking her summer holidays on the Continent with a few of their students. By the middle of June each year, she was already in Europe.

Elfie and Thomas were nearly on their way. The morning of their departure, their travel bags were packed with clothing for all weather and in the foyer. Elfie checked her satchel one last time to make sure she had her books, pens, ink, and writing paper. Thomas, taking special care, had wrapped his pens and pencils and placed them in small wooden boxes next to bundled sheaves of paper and sketching books in a large leather case. A second case held his collapsed folding easel and watercolor box. Thomas tested the lid once more to be sure it had closed tightly. "I believe we are ready for anything that may come our way!" he said, hoping to draw a smile from his unusually quiet daughter.

"I believe you are right," she answered. Thomas didn't think she sounded convinced.

CHAPTER 25

ELFIE SEES TOO MUCH

Galway and Sligo Counties, Ireland
July
Thomas and Elfie

From their previous trips to Sligo, Thomas and Elfie had learned to avoid the "charming country experience" of traveling by post coach across the country. Five days of jostling on dusty back roads with small taverns as overnight hostels quickly became tedious. The trip was scenic but slow, and once had been enough. Instead, they took the Midland Great Western Railway, traveling from Kingsbridge Station to Galway in one, albeit long, day. "Worth the extra expense," Thomas said, stashing his bags and settling into his seat, watching the last-minute bustle of activity on the train platform through the window. Elfie agreed. Her body felt the train's forward motion as she sat comfortably observing the outskirts of Dublin fading from view.

They arrived in Galway still fresh but ready for a fine meal and a comfortable bed. From their well-appointed accommodations at Western Railway Hotel on Eyre Square, they could walk to the quay, something Thomas planned to do the following morning. They made a two-night, two-room reservation to give them time to rest before the next leg of the journey by coach.

The next day, Thomas headed for the harbor armed with his sketchpad, collapsible easel, and folding stool, leaving Elfie safely with a couple from the hotel to go on a coach tour of the city. Frances had given her sister a copy of James Hardiman's history of Galway with the additional "A Copious Appendix." Elfie knew what she wanted to explore in the ancient port city, and the couple, who did not, were happy to follow her lead. She handed the coachman her map, instructing him to begin at the Spanish Arch. "The gate," she read aloud from her notes, "sits at the mouth of the River Corrib where it meets Galway Bay." Elfie laughed as she read the next bit. "'From the ferocious O'Flahertys, Good Lord deliver us' is carved in stone over the gate. So many eras, tribes, cultures, and layers have built a rich history here." *Wouldn't it be wonderful if we could bring our girls here,* she thought. The coachman was familiar with the places she wanted to see and took his three passengers on what she would later describe to her sisters as "a delightful four-hour jaunt."

While his daughter was off exploring, Thomas settled himself on the quay, where he had a good view of the ships' cargo being loaded and unloaded. Galway was a colorful port on the edge of the Atlantic, alive with commercial activity moving to and from Spain, France, Portugal, and America. He observed the energetic activity with fascination. There were dockhands and large cargo shipments swinging precariously overhead between the ships' holds and the dock. Men bellowed orders he could not understand to hands on shore and on the ship. As far as Thomas was concerned, this was life!

He unpacked his equipment and began to capture the men at work above the ship's wavering reflections on the water. He was inundated by a cacophony of sounds—the din of wagons, heavy loads dropping in place, shouting, pithy talk of last night's visit with the local whores, laughter, and, he imagined, foul language laced in every declaration. The shifting light, sounds, colors, and activity, so different from his sheltered, safe existence in Dublin, filled his senses and lit his imagination. Hours later, he returned to the hotel hungry, happy, and with several sketches, large and small, to remember the sights and excitement of the day.

He would have to conjure the smells and sounds from memory, the color and light from his notes on each drawing, as was his habit. To further seal his memories, he shared each detail with his daughter that night, taking her occasional yawns as a sign of exhaustion from her coach tour of the city rather than disinterest in the detailed account of his day.

The Youngs left the next morning in a hired coach that would take them over two nights and three days from Galway to Sligo. Two men joined the Youngs on the first part of the journey. Within an hour, the air inside the carriage was heavy with the odor of tobacco and sweat mixed with strong cologne. When they stopped for tea, Thomas informed his daughter that the smell reminded him fondly of his local pub in Rathmines. *Good Lord,* thought Elfie, putting an end to whatever curiosity she had about ever visiting a pub with her father one day.

Back on the road, the portlier gentleman of the two worked to establish himself with Thomas while Elfie tried to avoid listening by focusing on the passing scenery. "My family's lands are in County Mayo, Mr. Young. Granted by the crown over two hundred years ago. One unlucky son of each generation gets picked to move to this wild, uncivilized place to manage the land. As I am the third son . . ." He turned up the palms of his soft, manicured hands and laughed to show his resignation to his fate as a country gentleman in Ireland.

In an offhanded manner, his companion added, "Say there, Malcolm, it's not so bad. We have lots of good whiskey. We live for the hunt and our wives for the occasional ball."

"True, true," the first gentleman acknowledged, and then turned his attention again to Thomas. "Personally, I try to maintain a foothold in far more civilized London where, as we all know, the power and influence resides." Both men informed Thomas they knew of the Hibernian Academy and asked if he painted portraits. Elfie nearly rolled her eyes.

The men complained about grain prices, applauded themselves for every financial success, and blamed poor harvests, blights, and weather on their Irish tenants with their "backward farming methods." Elfie was revolted.

Thomas kept his thoughts to himself. He had long suspected that each social class had its different types. Their companions were aristocrats but of the tattered variety. The ne'er-do-wells of British aristocracy. The type that felt justified sending a group of ruffians to burn down the homes of their poorest tenants. He shuddered and turned his gaze out the window.

To Thomas and Elfie's great relief, their fellow passengers alighted the next day in County Mayo, clearing themselves from the compartment but leaving their attitudes toward the Irish and mix of odors still hanging in the air. "Sour reminders of sour men," Elfie proclaimed to Thomas. "Good riddance."

Thomas nodded at the truth behind her vehemence. "Trips like this are an education for both of us. You have witnessed how ungentlemanly men can be, and I have heard firsthand their harshness toward the Irish."

— ◆ —

Elfie

Their carriage proceeded north to their coastal destination with the windows opened enough to allow in some much-needed fresh air. The town of Knock was their last stop for the night, and they found two reasonably comfortable rooms above a tavern on the main town square.

Grateful to stretch their legs, they surveyed the square while their bags were taken to their rooms. "Do you think you're up for a stroll this evening, Father?" Elfie asked. "I'm feeling the need to be carried by my own two feet." But inside the tavern, the proprietor warned his guests about rumors of a protest in the square that evening. "Best you keep to your rooms. British are not welcome in these gatherings. People are angry and some are looking for a fight. You don't want to be in their way."

Elfie was too antsy to prepare for sleep yet. She caught up her diary, enjoying her own descriptions of their coach companions, then opened a book to read. Elfie had to sit on her lumpy bed, as there was no space for a chair in the tiny loft allotted to her and her few belongings. A small window above the head of her bed faced the square, but each time she stood up without care, her head banged on the sloped ceiling. Within the next hour, though, Elfie was pulled from her reading by the noise of a crowd gathering in the square outside. Curious, she cautiously knelt on the bed to see what was happening.

Elfie had never witnessed a protest before. A crowd of thirty people or so stood in small clumps chatting, with lots of hand-waving for emphasis. The gathering did not seem dangerous to her. People were milling about, some carrying placards she could not make out. Most appeared to be talking calmly and greeting one another. Elfie thought it looked like a community meeting.

The movement of a young man climbing nimbly onto the bed of a cart in the center of the square caught her attention. He stood with his arms raised and then clapped his hands above his head. People turned toward him as he beckoned them closer to the wagon. By this time, Elfie estimated the crowd had doubled in size as people continued to enter from all directions. There were shouts of approval, or possibly frustration, as they moved forward. Then the square quieted down, and all eyes were on the young man standing in the cart.

Elfie felt an impulse to run outside to hear him speak. For two days she had listened in aggravated silence to the offensive bluster of two landowners. She wanted to hear the Irish side of the equation, from the Irish. Going out alone at night in a strange town wasn't sensible; she knew that and she had been warned. *Oh, whenever will I have another chance like this?* she asked herself.

From her vantage point she saw mostly Irish farmers, along with their wives and children. Her clothes were too expensive, tailored, and British to blend in. *In the darkness they might not be noticed,* she reasoned. She grabbed her bonnet and shawl and tiptoed down the narrow stairs. Slipping out the side door of the tavern, she felt unexpectedly thrilled by her success at escaping unseen by the proprietor, who would have given her a scolding or even barred her way.

What had seemed a civil gathering from the safety of her room was agitated and much larger when viewed from the ground. Elfie nearly returned to the tavern, but a wedge opened in the fluid crowd and she stepped determinedly through it. The smell of dung, hay, and sweat was overwhelming as the men and women around her pressed forward. Searching for her handkerchief to hold against her nose, Elfie was jostled, then literally swept off her feet, becoming part of a mass of bodies lurching toward the speaker. She struggled for her footing. She felt her elbow pushing into the ribs of the person nearest her. "Let me go," she called out, and then suddenly there was a small space around her, and she was standing on her own feet again. She had given herself away.

Amid frightening shouts of "Get out of here" and "You *fooking* bitch," Elfie found herself pushed back to the perimeter, or else the mob had moved on without her; she wasn't sure. Either way she was worried, her hair had come undone, and her bonnet was gone. Somewhere in front of her, a woman screamed and a shot rang out. Elfie looked toward the sound in time to see the young speaker pitch forward off his platform into the shadowy forms below. Elfie froze in horror. A girl jumped off the cart to where the man had fallen. Elfie blinked in the eerie silence that followed. *That girl,* she thought. Something about her looked familiar. Her auburn hair and that knitted shawl . . . Elfie thought she recognized it. But she couldn't focus her mind to be sure.

A hand grabbed her elbow and she saw the innkeeper beside her, pulling her back to the tavern just as British soldiers appeared on the square shouting orders while shooting their muskets into the air over the crowd. Once inside, Elfie leaned against the closed door, breathing hard. *Through your nose,* she told herself. How many times had she told the girls to do the same thing to make themselves calm? Now it was her turn.

Outside, the shooting had stopped, but she could hear angry voices yelling, "Ya redcoat bastards!" and "Get out of here before they kill us all!" The innkeeper led Elfie to a chair and shook his head. "What were ya thinkin' goin' out there? Are you bloody crazy?" She nodded and said weakly, "A lapse in judgment, yes." He stayed beside her. *Probably making certain I'm not going to bolt outside again,* she thought. Feeling foolish and embarrassed, she thanked the man for rescuing her, then stood uneasily and walked up the steep stairway to her room. Outside her father's door she hesitated, wondering if he had seen her in the square, knowing he would be furious with her but also glad to see her safe. She wouldn't mind receiving a drubbing right then from someone she loved; she was well aware she had overstepped. A sharp snore came from inside his room, and then another. Her father was asleep, and she was alone with her thoughts. Elfie went to her own room, where she lay in bed breathing in through her nose and pushing the images from that night out of her mind until she fell into a fitful sleep.

CHAPTER 26

HOME AGAIN

Dublin, Ireland
August
Elfie

Elfie arrived at RockView feeling miserable. Between her experience at Knock and a humiliating faux pas with George Fenn, she was left distraught. There had been wonderful moments with the Fenns, and she tried to remind herself of them. Once she'd settled in at the Fenns' home, she was relieved that time spent with George by the sea served as a counterpoint to her earlier unsettling experience. But in quiet moments, both at Sligo and now at RockView, thoughts of the young man who'd been shot haunted her. *Did he die?* she worried. She could only think so. *But* someone *cared for him.* The thought brought her close to tears. *How can life hold such extremes?* The contrast between the violence of that night and the wonderful time she and her father had with the Fenns was nearly too much to bear.

To get herself through those upsetting moments, Elfie reminded herself that there was no point in focusing on unpleasant matters she could do nothing to change. There was plenty to worry about right in front of her. She had fallen in love with George Fenn but was no longer certain he felt the same about her. *What a mess I've made of things!*

On the evening before their departure from Sligo, George had nearly proposed. He had asked Elfie to take a stroll with him down to the beach. It was a bold proposition, as he had not invited her father or his own daughter to accompany them, yet somehow his request felt natural and right. Resting her hand on his arm for balance, Elfie had blushed but had made no move to distance herself from the warmth of his body. The effect on her was electric. *Breathe, Elfie, breathe.* Near the water's edge, he glided her onto a stone bench, and they sat next to each other admiring the lights glimmering on the bay. "Could you imagine living here on the west coast?" he asked. He looked directly at her then, and she found she could not look away from him. Of course she could imagine living on the west coast! That was nearly all she'd been imagining for weeks. There was the Misses Young School to think of. Her sister needed her. "I . . . I have responsibilities in Dublin," she managed to say. "And then, you seem to be in the city more often than in Sligo . . .?" she added hopefully.

George had nodded. "My selfish wish is that you would want to stay here. . . . You are right that I would see more of you if you stayed in Dublin," he said. They walked back to the house and spoke no more about it. Elfie burst into tears that night, certain she had pushed away her only hope at love.

Frances arrived at RockView two days after her sister and father. Elfie said she was anxious to begin with the school planning—"Only six weeks left before the girls arrive in October!"—so the following morning the two sisters took their early-morning tea in the drawing room, its small fireplace ablaze. Elfie was relieved. They had a lot to do and little time for chatting over their summer experiences. She was still not sure how much to say about her summer—about Knock or about George Fenn, however much he was on her mind.

"I have an idea about expanding the girls' Irish history lessons," she said.

Frances frowned. "You mean the bedtime stories you tell the girls," she said.

"This summer, I visited the monastic ruins on Inishmurray off Sligo's coast," Elfie continued.

"Father must have enjoyed that," Frances interrupted.

"Oh," Elfie said. "Father wasn't up to going. It was just George and me."

Frances raised her eyebrows.

"And Elizabeth, of course," Elfie added. "The point is, I believe the girls would be entranced by stories of the hermit monks who lived simple, remote lives in monasteries where they created beautiful, elaborate scrolls to preserve the teachings of their faith." Elfie had worked on her presentation to Frances over the summer and was determined not to lose her ground. "George loaned me some books with drawings of the scrolls to show our girls."

"You want to introduce our girls to Catholicism?" Frances asked, sounding incredulous.

"Hardly, Frances. I wouldn't know where to begin, would you? I want to introduce them to the *history* of Irish people's religion."

Her sister looked unconvinced.

"You've always added flourishes from your travels to the Continent in your lessons," Elfie said defensively. "I believe we've been remiss in not teaching our students about Saint Patrick's introduction of Christianity to Ireland. There is no need for us to take the subject further."

"Except for your monks," Frances said.

"Except for the monks," Elfie agreed.

Frances nodded and turned her attention to the ledgers and long-established lists of divided responsibilities with deadlines delineated. A new class was coming, which meant another round of actions and items to be checked off, including making sure they had an assortment of pinafores starched and ready, reading notes on each new student from tutors and parents, and dealing with scattered arrival times. Plenty to do.

An hour later, they walked to the kitchen to confer with Biddy. She was sitting at the kitchen table, going over her own lists for the household with Mary, when they came in.

"Morning, Miss Frances, Miss Elfie," Mary said.

"Can I make you breakfast?" Biddy asked from the table.

"Yes, you can, Biddy, thank you," Frances answered, "and we would like you to join us. We have a lot to talk about to get the school year underway."

Without looking at the sisters, Biddy said, "I'm not hungry, thank you. I have work to do. I can join you when I get my work done." Elfie frowned and looked at Frances, who shrugged. Over soft-boiled eggs, toast, and jam, Elfie and Frances continued to observe Biddy, who moved about the kitchen as if she was unsettled or annoyed. When she pulled onions from a sack and chopped them with a fierce intensity, Elfie spoke up.

"Biddy, is there something troubling you?"

With her free hand Biddy used the corner of her apron to dab at tears on her cheeks and then dismissed Elfie with a wave of her hand, as she had when the sisters were children asking too many personal questions. Both Elfie and Frances looked to Mary for an answer, but she turned away, busying herself at the sink.

"Biddy," Frances said, unwilling to be put off. "What is the matter?"

Biddy stopped her chopping. She dropped the knife on the

table and slowly turned around. "The truth of it is, Conor and I . . . and our boys . . . are feeling desperate about Norah. Against our will, she went off to the west coast with a young man."

Frances and Elfie exchanged sideways glances.

"No, no. Nothing like that," Biddy said. "Norah just got all caught up in his standin' up for Irish independence. She claimed she was doin' her bit for Ireland, and that if we cared anything about being Irish, we'd be joinin' her!" Biddy put her hands in her apron pockets and shook her head. "That was over a *month* ago," she said, looking to the floor. She wiped her cheeks with the back of her hand. "We haven't a word from her since. Patrick and Jack heard something about how she was taken by the British somewhere up in County Mayo. But I'll tell you, that bit came from that good-for-nothing Willy. I don't trust him to be tellin' us the truth. Why would the Brits want our Norah?"

Elfie's eyes grew wide. The town of Knock was in County Mayo.

"Lord save me," Biddy said, wiping her cheeks again. "Conor is drinking and in his cups every night. Thank God he still gets up and goes to work, though it's not a pretty sight." She brought the edge of her apron to her face and blew her nose.

Frances stood up to escort Biddy to the table, offering her words of encouragement, while Mary brought her a fresh cup of tea. "Oh, Mary," Biddy sniffed, looking at her cousin, "what has come of my girl?"

Elfie's mind raced. The young woman she'd seen at the protest, hovering over the man who had been shot . . . Could that have been Norah? It didn't seem possible. A coincidence, more likely. Elfie's presence there had been a mistake, and she didn't want to recall anything of that night. "Biddy, I'm so sorry!" she said. "How can we help?"

Once Biddy calmed down, she shooed the sisters out of the kitchen, telling them the best way to help was to let her get back to her work. "It calms me."

Elfie went upstairs to her bedroom, closing the door to be alone with her thoughts. *You're not a silly girl,* she scolded herself. *You* were *at a protest. You* did *see a young woman taken away by British soldiers. Stop pretending otherwise.* What else had she seen that night? There was a shiver of recognition, not just of the girl but of the man with the limp who moved the body of the man on the ground. *Oh my,* she thought as the pieces started to come together for her. *Willy . . . Wasn't that the name of the strange young man who followed Norah to our kitchen years ago?* Elfie had been repulsed by him and felt relieved when Biddy had chased him out of the house. She had only noticed his limp when she watched him walking away from RockView.

She sat down heavily in her chair. *Norah is in trouble, but what has gotten into me? Sneaking out at night? Attending a political protest? Refusing to believe it happened? And holding hands with a recently widowed man!* Elfie flushed at the lines of propriety she had crossed that summer.

In the foyer below, she heard Frances greet their father on his way out. Elfie opened her door and hurried down the stairs to talk to her sister. Frances may judge her, but Elfie couldn't keep her secrets to herself any longer. She might have lost her chance at love. She was not going to miss her chance to help save Norah.

— ◆ —

Thomas

Thomas was glad to be home, especially because everything

seemed to be just as he'd left it. Biddy was out of sorts, but that wasn't unusual before the start of a school year. She had a lot to do with the school opening. *I would be out of sorts too, if I were her,* he reasoned. He did his best to be helpful and kind and to stay out of her way whenever possible, which was probably the most helpful and kind thing he could do. Frances and Elfie were fussing about this and that in anticipation of the girls' arrival. He was happy to stay out of their way too.

When the house was most full of female busyness, as it was that day, Thomas took refuge outside with a brisk walk followed by a rest on the porch, where his thoughts often lingered over his summer travels. George had been a wonderful host. Thomas grinned thinking of the probable reason for it. George had asked his permission to marry Elfie. *That was quite something to observe,* he thought. *George doting on Elfie.* Watching them, he'd been reminded of when he and Sarah began their courtship and of the excitement and anticipation of early love. A nice feeling to recall; almost made him feel young again. He was sure Elfie thought he was too old and self-focused to notice their attraction. *Why do people think that because you are old you lack brains?*

From his perch on the porch, he could hear the mumbles of Biddy and Mary chattering while at their chores inside and of Frances and Elfie deep in talk in the drawing room. The pleasant sounds lulled him into a nap on the lumpy porch chair, where he slept until a thick cloud of humidity escaped through the open windows of the basement and woke him up again. *The laundress must be here,* he thought, yawning. Thomas took out his pocket watch. He'd skipped breakfast just to be out of the house and now was feeling hungry. In thirty minutes, Biddy would serve his noon meal. That gave him a little time to slip inside uninterrupted and consider where to place at least one of his Sligo paintings when it was finished and framed and also to begin another project that had been nagging at him.

During the school year, the sentimental family heirlooms that gave his home meaning became a mere backdrop to the seemingly endless hubbub. Rarely could he interest anyone in the house in stopping to notice them, let alone learn about their history. *Who will remember any of it when I'm gone?* he worried. The question had increasingly bothered him. The enormous task of recording the objects and artwork passed down from the family seemed his only option. Thomas sighed and stood up. *Best get started then.* He entered the house and removed a small leather-bound book from his jacket pocket.

The scattering of the Young family had begun when Thomas's father left the Isle of Wight, his family's home since the fifteenth century, for Cheltenham, England. "And then Sarah and I married and came to Ireland . . . ," he said, checking the front pages of the book to make sure he had written down those dates. "Then dear Lily left . . ." He had naively assumed his family would all stay near him, and eventually they would lie together for eternity in Mount Jerome cemetery. *I suppose Grandfather thought the same thing about the All Saints on the Isle of Wight!*

The first floor continued to be the center of activity in the house, so Thomas walked up to the second. Lily's portrait hung in the gallery, along the wide hall between the landing and the classroom. Thomas dragged a chair from the classroom and sat in front of the image of his eldest daughter. "Lily's portrait" he wrote at the top of a blank page in his book. He'd had it painted by a visiting colleague at the academy who wanted to make a trade for some of Thomas's watercolor Irish land-scapes. The fellow specialized in portraits and Thomas did not. Lily had been nineteen, just the age to capture the delicate bloom of womanhood. Why hadn't he commissioned portraits of Frances and Elfie? He couldn't remember. Surely something he'd meant to do. Lily's portrait was rather formal, but he was comforted by the softness of her beautiful eyes gazing at him.

And now Lily was carrying her third child! How he wished he could meet little Lucie. From Lily's descriptions, Lucie was exactly like her joyful, full-of-life mother. Just as Thomas's mind turned toward imagining their life in Canada, Biddy called him to lunch. "Thank you, Biddy," he called back. Hurriedly he jotted a few more notes about the painting, then headed downstairs. *If I daydream each time I open this notebook, I'll be eighty before I've catalogued it all,* he scolded himself.

Thomas ate alone in the dining room, something he had once enjoyed. Despite initial misgivings, he found that the schoolgirls in his house added a mix of amusement and engagement, if not occasional irritation, and he missed their company. His visit with the Fenns had reminded him of the long-term potential of these relationships. Thomas had realized that Elizabeth Fenn was once a student, and now, if Elfie married George, her family would become part of the Youngs'. He also hoped he would live long enough to meet his granddaughter and her younger siblings. Neither of the boys had his name, but of course James had named them for his family. . . *Still, they carry my blood.* Thomas smiled. He liked babies and young children. *Not all men do,* he thought. *Yet my grandchildren are so far away.*

His daughters appeared in the dining room as he finished his meal, bringing an end to his quiet reflections. Before they could involve him in one of their projects, Thomas stood up to excuse himself, but something in their manner caused him to sit down again.

"Father," Frances said. "Elfie and I need to speak with you. It's about Biddy and her daughter, Norah."

"And me," Elfie said.

CHAPTER 27

GALWAY GAOL

Galway, Ireland
October
Norah

The young woman next to Norah lay on a filthy straw pallet. She moaned and coughed, a horrible rasp that continued until she retched, though there was not much to throw up. Three other women sat directly on the small cell's floor, across from Norah and the ill woman, their faces blank, their voices a whisper if they spoke at all.

Norah squatted and leaned against the wall for as long as she could, feeling more secure off the ground. She put her head in her hands and closed her eyes. There was plenty of time to spin dark thoughts, and no answers had revealed themselves, yet. Her romantic dream of protest and progress with Gavin had become a nightmare. She had seen him fall and knew he was dead.

Hungry and depressed, Norah willed herself back to childhood, to some good memory to remove her mind from the present. She recalled vaguely the feeling of teetering at the summit of a carefully stacked cut-and-rolled pile of turf. *Grandma Aine and Grandpa Finn always brought nice memories.* The pile she was on had been drying in the summer sun behind their cottage. Norah smiled weakly at the memory. At five years old, she'd known she was in a place she should not be. Grandpa Finn told her again that this fine pile she had just scrambled atop was precious. "'Tis next winter's warmth for your grandmother Aine and me. Our old bones need it." This was, for her grandparents, the invaluable reserve of heat to take them through Cork's bitter winter months. Through the years her father would say, "This peat is the closest thing Finn has to money in the bank, and he surely ain't got that." He was looking for a laugh and almost always got one. Norah had understood that money and heat were important; she just hadn't been able to resist the climb. Now she wondered why she had done it. As she stood on top, her small feet and hands slippery with sweat, the overpowering smell of decomposing plant material had made her want to pinch her nose, which she did. Wobbling back and forth on her increasingly unstable platform, she'd tried to wave her arms for balance. Uncle Garrett spied her from the back door and came rushing, his arms outstretched and hands ready to lift her to safety. Setting her gently on the ground, he said, with a kind look and a caring smile, "Little Miss Norah, you are a chancy girl." The title stuck.

She had been a chancy girl and then a chancy young woman. The latest risk she'd taken had landed her in a hellhole far from her family. Did they know where she was?

Outside the cell door the jailer rattled his keys, and Norah looked up. A mistake. The lock turned with a heavy clank and the deadbolt slid noisily away. "You'll do," he said, grinning at Norah. Too late, she tried to move to the rear. He caught her arm with a greasy hand and pulled her roughly out of the cell.

CHAPTER 28

HOLIDAY PLANS

London, Ontario, Canada
Lily

Two weeks into October, Lily looked out the window, grateful to see the spires of the spruce and pungent pine keeping a steady green on the landscape. Fall was rushing toward winter. Almost as soon as the maple leaves had snapped into brilliant colors, strong winds from the north sent them flying off in a race to unknown destinations. Temperatures had plummeted and seemed intent on remaining so. Lily pulled around her shoulders the light blue cashmere shawl her family had given her last Christmas and stepped back from the chill radiating through the windowpanes. "I hate seeing this season slip away," she grumbled. "The cold lasts too long without a real fall." Her father had also complained in his letters that the floors were already frigid under his bare feet at night. "Being close to the same latitude," she had replied, "often makes for shared seasonal joys and grievances between the Youngs and Nivens." A strange comfort when so little else was the same.

Her sisters' life was the bustling girls' school, with several weeks to themselves between school years, while hers was a family and deepening friendships. Hugh and Knox were noisy, playful boys, and Lucie was becoming quite a young lady by comparison. "No time off to travel each summer, but then I do not have to eat daily meals at a table set for twelve, endlessly prepare and teach lessons, and then tuck nine girls into bed each night." Her family of five was enough, thank you.

Lucie and Hugh were off at school and Knox was in the second-floor nursery with Marian and his wooden blocks. Lily heard them crash down, followed by an excited "Let's do it again!" She laughed and almost went upstairs to join them, then, remembering her responsibilities, stayed put. From the secretary, Lily pulled out a sheet of paper and began writing the list of things she wanted to do for the coming holidays. "Photography appointment for Christmas," she wrote. *When we are all old and gray, having a record of the children each year will be as important for our families in Ireland as for James and me.*

Lily had already ticked off her list for celebrating the Canadian Thanksgiving, but she took it out of the desk and reviewed it again. The newish holiday was almost upon them—three more weeks, in fact. Lily was excited. *Eleven people at our table! Just like when I was at RockView.* Her children were excited, too. James's partner, William, and his wife, Molly, were bringing their two children. Hugh and Knox asked if they could show them their toys after dinner, which James thought an excellent idea. "If you do so in your bedrooms," he told them and then turned to Lily with a smile. "I'm sure Molly and William will appreciate some quiet time, too." Lily thought again how fortunate James was to work with William. Especially having found him through a newspaper advertisement.

Lily considered adverts in the paper both risky and uncouth. "How else do you suggest I find work in Canada all the way from Ireland?" James had reasoned with her all those years ago. "This is the *Irish Times*, Lily," he'd added. "Perfectly respectable." James had to look at a map to find London, Ontario, and after measuring distances, he assured her the city was not far from Toronto, a city she'd at least heard of. He wrote to Dr. William Cattermole of his interest. The response James received was honest and lively. The doctor was only a few years older than James, and had lived in Canada for the past two years with his new bride, Molly, and a child on the way. "The growing population coming from many parts of Europe," he wrote, "means there are more patients than I can handle. London is just the place for young families—a growing economy and a good community. If you hunt, we've got plenty of duck, grouse, quail, and elk. Fish too." James had responded immediately.

Lily marveled at her husband's good sense. Or was it good luck? She smiled. *Either way, here we are eight years later, well settled, with three children and an active life.*

Lily had also invited the Nilssons for Thanksgiving, which meant pie for eleven people, half of them hungry children. Lily recalculated and doubled the recipe. She would serve two sweet-potato pies. Lotta and Pers lived nearby on Dundas Street—their first neighbors! Lily had begun to think their estate agent had sold them a bill of goods about having neighbors "before you know it." She was relieved when they finally arrived. Thoughts of living next door to another Lila Harrison had worried her. Fortunately, Lotta Nilsson was bright and interesting, and Pers was quiet but taught physiology at the new University of Western Ontario and so had something in common with James. They were good company, as were the Cattermoles, and they all planned to contribute dishes to the meal! Lily still felt odd not providing all the food.

The covered-plate idea had been Lotta's. She'd been so keen about it that Lily felt it would have been rude to insist otherwise. It didn't take her long to work out the wisdom of not having to prepare for a formal evening. There would be less work for her to do, and Marian could leave earlier in the day to be at home with her own family. "A more casual family gathering will be fun," she told a frowning James. "How many times have you told me that Canada is a frontier where formalities can be more easily set aside? We will be formal at Christmas, and that's just around the corner."

"Hardly just around the corner," James had protested. "It's only October." Lily closed her eyes and smiled. Ordering items unavailable in their city was a chore, and packing and shipping gifts to Ireland had to be done at least two months ahead of time. That meant the children's photograph appointment could not be delayed. She asked James to make the appointment for the coming Saturday.

Each year the Nivens sent framed photos as gifts for her family and James's mother. *And* this *year, I'm also going to have them made into holiday postcards for my friends in Ireland,* she decided. She was fortunate Edy Brothers Photography was right in town. Lily had been told by more than one friend that the most prominent people in London used their services for family and professional images: "The backgrounds for their photographs are painted by an artist in New York, and the results are always fashionable and in classic good taste." Personally, Lily was delighted by their closet full of props. In the past, she had chosen a snowy background with her children in woolen Christmas hats and a sled, varying only who sat and who "pulled" the sled. *Maybe it's time for a change this year,* she wondered.

Even James had used their services. Two years ago, he had required a portrait of himself for a talk at the McGill University Faculty of Medicine. Lily thought the photograph made her husband look very distinguished. "Even without props and a painted background," she'd teased him.

"I hope my audience will be less taken with my photograph and more interested in my speech," he replied nervously. "It's on improving public health by preventing the spread of disease in less advantaged populations through teaching sanitation, you know."

"Yes, I know, dear," she said. "But it is a *very* good photograph."

Lily had copies made, along with the medical school's article about his talk. She sent one to Eliza and another to her father and sisters to reassure them of James's success. *They can't possibly think of us living in an untamed country now,* she'd thought with satisfaction.

The day before the children's Saturday appointment, Lily had Marian lay out their clothes, bought for both this occasion and the holidays. When they came downstairs the next day in their outfits, James declared, "Well, my handsome children, I hope you will cooperate with your mother and the photographer. They need you to sit very still, and that will be a challenge for you boys."

"Oh, Papa, we can sit still," said Hugh, clasping his hands and withholding a giggle. Lucie, looking on and knowing her brothers well, said, "Yes, they can, Papa. Mama has bribed us with an ice cream treat afterward."

"It's not a bribe, Lucie. It's a treat for being good," said Hugh, pushing out his lower lip and attempting a sour face.

"What I really like," Knox said, "is when the man puts his head under the black cloth and holds his hand up with the stick that explodes and makes smoke." Hugh giggled and put a napkin over his head and a hand in the air. "OK, children," he said, "look at the birdy!"

Lily laughed. These children of hers were so much freer than she had been as a child. When Lily and her sisters were growing up, their mother had insisted upon stiff dresses and formal portraits. The photographer had even threatened to use head clamps to hold their heads if they did not stay still and assess extra charges if additional plates had to be used.

It's not that Lily never scolded her children; she tried to keep her admonishments playful when she could. *Mother was so serious by nature,* she remembered. *I don't think she even considered playful discipline as an option.* Lily felt slightly ashamed by her criticism; her mother's health had often been compromised, and a scolding from her was rare. *Because we never wanted to be responsible for her "taking a turn for the worse,"* Lily reasoned. After her mother's death, the exhaustive rules of Victorian etiquette began to loosen at RockView without her watchful eye to guide them. Even her father became more relaxed. *Nothing wrong with a little change in routine,* she thought.

Lily gathered her children in the foyer while they waited for Jim to arrive. She rebuttoned the top of Hugh's jacket, smoothed down Knox's hair, then stood back to assess her children. "You all look quite smart. Let's keep it that way until after the photos." Hugh looked through the long window beside the door and exclaimed, "He's here! Let's go!" He grabbed Knox's hand and ran out the door. Lily and Lucie followed, showing a bit more decorum and smiling at one another over the boys' exuberant behavior.

Once in town, Lily directed Jim to the market first and asked if he wouldn't mind staying with the children while she picked up a few things. The sweet potatoes were out in front with the onions and other root vegetables. She chose four and went in to charge them to her account. Emma Manson from their faux women's literary club stood in line two people in front of her. They smiled and nodded their heads knowingly at one another in a way that spoke to a bond. Lily had good friends now, women who discussed important subjects and shared their innermost feelings about being women and their desire to have a stronger role in society. This bond had added a dimension of confidence and satisfaction she could feel right now while standing in the store. She walked out carrying her purchase and looked at her children, waiting for her in the trap, thinking, *Lily, you are a very fortunate woman.*

"Children," she said, as Jim drove them toward the studio, "I heard the Edy brothers have a real Christmas tree this year. What do you say we use it in your photograph?"

CHAPTER 29

A WELCOME CHANGE

Dublin, Ireland

Elfie

The day after Frances and Elfie told their father about Norah's plight, George Fenn appeared unexpectedly at their doorstep, delighting Thomas and nearly causing Elfie to swoon with happiness. Later, Elfie would say that her entire life began anew that day: "There was a soft glow to everything."

From that point on, George Fenn became a frequent visitor to RockView.

Biddy was especially thrilled. George had agreed to look into Norah's disappearance and to do his best for her. Only Frances was perturbed by the change and found new ways to express her unhappiness. "Father," Frances said when she found him checking his supply of whiskey after an evening with George, "be careful you're not drinking too much."

"My dear," Thomas answered, "I find it excellent for my health; you might try some."

Her latest complaint was that George talked too much. "Doesn't he believe that women have something to add to a conversation?" she asked Elfie, who closed her eyes and paused. To be fair, Elfie understood that her sister was less agitated with George than with what his presence meant, not just for Elfie but for herself and the school.

Elfie did agree with her sister about one thing: George was a talker. While in Sligo, she had listened to him with interest, trying not to allow herself to read too much into their time together. At the time, she told herself that George needed friends to listen to his rambling sorting of his life. Still, she had written to Lily for her thoughts on the matter. "Nothing close to this kind of interaction with a man has ever presented itself," Elfie explained. "How did you know about James?" Lily had since written back that George would make his intentions clear soon enough either way.

Any remaining doubts Elfie had disappeared the evening George announced that he had leased a flat in Kingstown, near the harbor—a signal that he was settling into Dublin rather than passing through. Elfie was thrilled until she saw Frances's back straighten at the news. Her sister had been cool about George's visits up until then. Now the tic by Frances's eye jumped.

Annoyed, Elfie turned to her father. "Wouldn't it be nice if George and his family joined us for the holidays?" she asked.

Thomas beamed and so did George. "Lovely invitation, thank you," he said. "Elizabeth and Philip seem to be occupied for the holidays. Elizabeth will remain in London this year. Romance, of course. Philip and I have been invited to spend Christmas with Bessie's family on Lough Corrib. Have you been there? Beautiful spot. Philip and his cousin Charles will have a fabulous time trout fishing. They're great friends. Went to Clongowes Wood College together." George dropped his head. "This is our second Christmas without Bessie. . . . It's important my children be happy, especially at the holidays. I admit Lough Corrib would not be a happy place for me." He straightened himself in his chair and smiled. "Your invitation is most welcome, especially this year."

Frances's eyes closed and Elfie thought, *For heaven's sake, Frances. It's Christmas.*

After supper that evening, the two men sat before the fire in the drawing room, sipping and raising their glasses of whiskey to one another.

Frances and Elfie were taking turns eating with the girls at five and taking dinner at seven with the men. One evening after her turn with the girls, Frances caught Elfie on the second-floor landing. "Father is down there carrying on with George about articles in the *Nation.* You would think the two of them had invented humanist philosophy!" Frances's face was flushed with irritation, and Elfie tried her best to be patient.

"Of course not, Frances. It is only natural for George to be excited about a newspaper he just invested in. Don't you agree? And it is relaxing for Father to have a male companion to carry on with. We are so occupied by the school that we are not very good company. If George has an enlightened attitude toward the Irish situation and father is open to learning about it, then so be it."

The truth was, Elfie didn't know what to make of George's growing involvement in politics. When he was in town, he spent much of his time lunching with nationalist politicians at Stephen's Green Club, his Anglo-Irish men's club. If his conversations with her father were anything to judge by, the Irish Parliamentary Party and Home Rule were the club's favored subjects. Elfie was happy George had her father to share in those interests. Her own interests, being more cultural and historical in nature, were far more appropriate for a school-teacher. *And safer,* she reminded herself.

Her work as a teacher seemed to fly by. She was almost surprised when December ninth arrived and the girls left for the holiday. *Only two weeks until Christmas!* she thought as she waved goodbye to the last family to pick up their daughter. She came to breakfast the next morning with pen and paper. Frances and Thomas were already enjoying their tea and reading quietly.

"Mornin', Miss Elfie," Biddy greeted her. Her sister and father didn't lift their eyes. It was the first day of their monthlong break from the school, and they appeared happy to quietly inhabit their individual worlds, but Elfie was full of energy, excited as a ten-year-old about Christmas.

She decided to engage Biddy regarding the holiday meals to see if she could spark any interest from Frances and Thomas. "Biddy, shall we order a goose for Christmas Day and have a fine roast beef on Christmas Eve before we go to midnight services?"

"I will place the orders well in advance with the grocer," Biddy replied. "Unless there is any objection?" she asked the others. "Apparently not," she said, sharing a smile and a shrug with Elfie. Elfie was pleased to see a lightness in Biddy again. *Christmas plans do tend to bring out the best in us,* she thought, which reminded her. . .

"How would you and Mary prefer to work the Christmas holidays at RockView?" she asked. The women usually took turns, but it was always left up to them to decide.

"Mary and I talked and, if it is all right by all of you, I will work Christmas Eve at RockView and she will work Christmas Day," Biddy answered. "We will prepare our specialties well in advance."

Elfie turned to Frances. "What do you think, Frances? Do you like Biddy's plan?"

Frances glanced away from the newspaper their father was reading and to Elfie's surprise said cheerfully, "It sounds splendid, Elfie. Good of you to get the organizing started. We should sit down together after breakfast and make our plans. We need gifts for our delivery people and . . ."—she looked over at Biddy—"some other very special people too."

Elfie reached out to Frances, placing her hand on top of her sister's. "Let's work together to make this a special Christmas, Frances."

Frances looked at her lap. "I admit," she said, raising her eyes to meet Elfie's, "I was taken aback by your inviting George without consulting Father and me. That was silly of me."

Elfie squeezed her hand. "Thank you, Frances."

Elfie felt something release inside her. With Frances now willing to accept George in their lives, Elfie could too. She felt a wave of affection for her sister.

"I will have Father to escort me to midnight services," Frances said, "and you will have George."

"Would someone get this old man, who is gratified to know he still qualifies as an escort, another cup of tea?" Thomas asked. Frances laughed and reached for the teapot.

Elfie felt truly happy. Her thoughts drifted to a delicious topic. *I must think carefully about what to give to George*—followed by the question *I wonder what he might give me?* She reached for her pen and began to make notes to avoid revealing the color rising in her cheeks.

FAITH AND SORROW

December
Biddy

Every day seemed long to Biddy. She used to enjoy her morning ritual of rising early to have an hour before her family stirred. Since Norah had been arrested, the ritual became a mere habit, her one pleasure sipping tea through a sugar cube held in her teeth as she stirred the oats in a big pot of boiling water. The absentminded rhythm of the spoon was comforting and sent her mind drifting to the days ahead. The meals for the Youngs and their school were always planned well in advance, but there were the meals for her family to plan for and to either prepare the ingredients for in the morning or do it all when she returned home. Biddy didn't have the energy she used to. Even on a day off like today, it was an effort just to get out of bed. She looked up at the stubby little crock sitting comfortably on the shelf, and she thought, *Don't just sit there.*

You know how tired I am; help me. She shook her head wearily. "You're just like everyone else. 'Don't worry, Ma'll do it.' Well, one of these days I might not do it just to see how that sits. 'What, Ma, no meal?'" she said, mimicking her sons. "Norah used to help some, bless her."

Biddy's energy shrank in proportion to her hope for her daughter's release. The thought of her girl in some terrible place crying for them to help pulled at her day and night. For a long time, the Gossetts hadn't even been sure where she was. Then Elfie's Mr. Fenn had learned that after a night in the local jail, Norah had been moved to Galway Gaol. He assured Biddy he was working for her release. "I cannot promise you nor want to give you false hope for clemency," he said. *Clemency.* Biddy was not stupid, but the unfamiliar word made her uncomfortable and uncertain. It was Miss Elfie who clarified its meaning for her: "You are right, George; Norah deserves the mercy of the court. She did not commit a crime. But, Biddy," she added, placing her hand on Biddy's arm, "I'm afraid Mr. Fenn is correct in not making you any promises. We just don't know yet." *Mercy. Clemency.* Biddy could only pray. Was there a God to pray to? She hadn't been to Mass in years. "Might as well try God," she told the crock. "The legal system wasn't made to help people like us." She'd understood what Mr. Fenn and Miss Elfie had told her about Norah's chances being limited. Should she pray for Mr. Fenn? For all she knew, the Anglo-Irish had a more direct way to reach both God and the legal system.

Biddy's sons, Patrick and Jack, had tried to convince her the Galway Gaol was one of the good ones. "I heard some of the Irish up there are breakin' the law just to get in, the food is so good and the place is so clean," Patrick told her. Jack had nodded eagerly in agreement. Biddy knew better, having already learned from a neighbor whose son swept and cleaned slop in a Dublin jail that parts of Galway Gaol were grim, crammed with women and even young girls considered traitors, with child out of wedlock, or "repeaters," meaning thieves and prostitutes. They were all thrown together with little food or sanitation. The thought of it made Biddy shudder. Her Norah was none of those things. She was determined that Conor should go to Galway and demand her release. "It's what a father should do," she told her crock. To be honest, Mr. Fenn was working at a level beyond her understanding. How could she trust him? "You know they're all Brits at heart, even the Youngs. Not a one of them a true Irish." The crock didn't disagree.

After supper, she sat down at the table, dropped her head toward her chest, and said, "Conor, you must bring our Norah home." Conor shook his head, wearily. "I feel the same, Bid. You know I canna leave. They'll fill my spot with one of them younger men waitin' for work at the gate each mornin'. I'll never get it back."

Pat stood up. "I can go, Ma."

Conor and Biddy looked up at their eldest son. He towered above them, a big man at twenty-one.

"Whadaya think, Bid?" Conor said.

"No! Not the boys," she said. *It's a father's job,* she thought, but when she glanced up at Pat, his determination was clear. Biddy stared at her son and sighed. "Can you be off from your job?" she asked.

"Yes, Ma. They hired another wagon man. He'll like the extra work . . . for a while."

Biddy stood and lifted the crock from its place of honor, reached inside, and brought out a small cloth bag. Conor stared at the bag. "So, you been saltin' away, have ya, Bid?"

She stood proudly. "There should be enough here," she said. "I've been puttin' away for something special. It should pay for the train."

Pat took the bag, weighing it in his palm. "If there's enough coin, can I take Jack with me?"

"Sure enough," Conor answered for his wife. "You'll be

safer together too." There was relief in the room, and resignation. Biddy wiped away a tear and then another, proud of her family, proud of the money she had to give, worried about sending her boys out, and feeling guilty about the money she'd spent on herself for her beloved red scarf. Only the empty crock knew that. No one else had noticed or complimented her scarf anyway. *Boys* . . . She shook her head and worried again. Could they really succeed?

"Ma," Patrick said, reading her thoughts. "You're forgettin' I'm a man." He tilted his head toward his brother, who had stayed silent throughout the family meeting. "And little Jackie here can almost tie his shoes now."

"Get off, ya," Jack said, smiling broadly. He stood up to show his full height, which nearly matched his brother's. Conor chuckled and Biddy grinned, wiping at her tears. *They're good boys,* she thought. *Good . . . young men,* she corrected herself, not liking the feel of the word.

The following evening, Conor and Biddy watched the train for Galway disappear out of the cavernous Knightsbridge Station, a place none of the Gossetts had been before. Patrick and Jack were on a crowded third-class coach where the ticket seller said they would be lucky to find a seat. When she'd told Mr. Young of the trip in the kitchen that morning, he pulled out a few coins from his pocket for the boys to get a tea basket to share. She was grateful, though, having never been on a train, she had no idea what her sons would find in the basket. What she did know was that her boys got hungry, and she tucked four scones and hard cheese into their sacks.

To Biddy's quiet amazement, Conor came home early the next evening and every evening after, putting his "pub coins" in the crock to rebuild Biddy's savings. She gave him a pat each time she heard the clink of the metal hitting the inside of the pot. The crock was building steam again for uncertain future needs. Conor was trying to be a good father and husband, and she wanted him to know she appreciated it. Their togetherness was comforting and kept them both sane as they waited. Ten days later their sons returned. The Gossett family was never the same.

— • —

January 1882

Biddy stood in her kitchen, packing her well-worn wicker basket with the root vegetables, fresh parsley, and leeks she had gathered from her small garden out back. The vegetables were for the Youngs' dinner that night. Miss Frances would pay her for them, something that usually brought a smile to her face.

She shifted the basket from one arm to the other as she walked toward RockView, thinking of the hard, uncertain life of her father, Finn. She pictured him in front of the two-room cottage in rural Cork where she grew up, with its welcoming red door, its paint peeling, standing open to their tidy home and neatly swept dirt floor. He was tipping back in his chair even as her mother, Aine, warned him that it would break and put him in the dirt. "Ya might well deserve it," Biddy could hear her say.

"Biddy, darlin'," he said to her, "your mother and I have been married since we were eighteen yar. I'm close to seventy now!" Biddy nodded at the memory. Her father wore age as a badge of honor. "We survived An Gorta Mór. Took most we'd known all our lives. We lived through it. Me mother, too, God knows how. Lived on a broth of grass and dandelions. Brighter days ahead, Biddy, but don't neglect the dandelions." Biddy smiled thinking about the dandelion tea she'd learned to make for her family when they weren't feeling well.

Her sons hadn't been able to bring Norah home. The night

they returned from Galway, Biddy and Conor had sat at the table with them to hear their news. "We tried our best, Ma," Jack said. "We came back to the prison day after day."

"Fuckin' Brits treated us like shite." Patrick's anger had frightened Biddy. It still frightened her.

"They wouldn't even tell us if she was there," Jack said.

"They're Brits!" Patrick said. "It's like we're scum to them." A silence settled among all four of the Gossetts. "We failed," Pat said.

Biddy put her basket down, wiped her tears, and blew her nose with her kerchief, then breathed in the chilly moist air to help her get hold of her thoughts. *Crying won't make the soup,* she told herself. She gathered her vegetables and continued on her way.

That afternoon, George Fenn arrived at the Youngs' house breathless, having rushed up the front stairs. "Norah's been transferred to Kilmainham Gaol right here in Dublin," he blurted out to Biddy and Elfie, who had met him at the door. He wanted it to be good news, but each of them knew it wasn't. George lightly touched Biddy's arm. "At least she is closer to home, Biddy," he said. Kilmainham was a dreaded place. It was the prison where rebels and well-known political enemies were sent. Firing squads were held in the yard, and the reports of rifle shots bounced off the stone walls and echoed in the streets.

"My Norah shouldn't be there!" Biddy said angrily. The effort of keeping her feelings to herself was too much. "She's not well known to anyone but ourselves, and she is no more guilty of being a rebel than any other person who went to that rally." By now they all knew Miss Elfie had been at the protest in Knock that night. Unlike Norah, she had come home safely. Miss Elfie was British. Biddy lowered her eyes to gather herself.

"You are right to be angry, Biddy," she heard Miss Elfie say gently. "She shouldn't be there."

"I am hoping to find a friendly ear in the local British government at Dublin Castle to work with me on her release," Mr. Fenn said. Biddy nodded her thanks and returned to her work without speaking to anyone in the house for the rest of the day.

That evening, Biddy took the news home, and her boys flared with anger. "Jesus, Mum, this is horrible. They'll kill her there for sure." Biddy and Conor were terrified, too.

"Mr. Fenn is working to get her out," Biddy said, trying to sound confident. "I pray for that."

"Go on praying, Ma," Patrick told her. "It won't do a damn thing for her. There is no God!"

Every day, Biddy watched Pat and Jack's anger move them further from the family. Biddy stood at the door watching her sons tramping their way toward the pub. One night, she caught a neighbor shaking her broom at the young men's backs.

"Mrs. Finney!" Biddy reprimanded.

The woman turned to face her. "You know they're meetin' up with the Flaherty boys, don't you? They're bad company, carryin' knives and guns maybe. Spoilin' to fight. No-goods, they are." Biddy resented Mrs. Finney for gossiping about her family, and gave her a cold stare. Mrs. Finney turned away and went back inside without a word. Biddy had also heard rumors of arms being cached and sieges planned and wouldn't have been surprised if the Flahertys were involved. *Oh God,* thought Biddy. *Has the world gone mad?*

She continued to place her hopes in men like Mr. Fenn and Mr. Parnell. What other choice did she have? Whenever she had the chance, she told her boys about the Anglo-Irish gentlemen trying to bring change to Ireland. Jack and Pat just shook their heads. They'd seen firsthand how the system was rigged against them. "It isn't going to change just because a few of your Irish Brits want it to. You know what they did to Liam Reilly just for speaking his mind in public. Slapped our chum in prison and threw away the keys. He's a goner, too. Do you really think the Queen of England is going to suddenly up and change her mind and let the Irish rule the Irish? They're not listening, Ma. Not to your precious Mr. Fenn and not to us. Not yet, anyway. Wait 'til they see what the Irish can do."

Their talk frightened and infuriated Biddy. She couldn't stand the thought of her sons being sent to prison for fighting the British or, worse, being killed. But all she could say was, "Don't ever think your sister is a goner. We will get her back."

CHAPTER 31

FRANCES'S NIGHT OUT

April
Frances

Frances put a pin through her hat and took a final look in the long bedroom mirror. Pleased with what she saw, she picked up her gloves, bag, and shawl and left the room. "No tic by my eye tonight," she said. Her father had meant to accompany her to the art lecture that evening. She was sorry he wasn't feeling well, but the freedom of an evening out by herself put a lightness in her step that almost made her giddy. In the entryway below, Biddy waited. Frances called down to her, "Is my cab waiting?"

Biddy looked out the window toward the street. "Yes, Miss Frances. He's here," she said, adding when Frances made it to the main floor, "You look very fine tonight."

Frances gave Biddy a short, playful curtsy and grinned.

"Thank you, Biddy. I am looking forward to the evening and seeing my friends. I want to look my best."

"Shall I ask your father if he's feeling better?" Biddy asked.

"Biddy, I am no longer so young that I require a chaperone," Frances said to the frowning housekeeper. "Besides, I sent word to Mr. Laird, and he has agreed to drive me there and back. I'm quite safe and all is proper." Looking at the mirror by the door, she released the hat pin, placed her fingers lightly on the brim of her hat, and moved it to a jaunty angle toward her right eye. Pleased with herself, she walked out the door.

Halfway down the porch stairs, she had an awakening and turned around.

"Forget something, Miss Frances?" asked Biddy.

Frances walked back up and touched Biddy's shoulder with her gloved hand. "Yes, I did forget something important, Biddy. Thank you for being so generous to me when you have so much on your mind. I know every day must be difficult for you, and you have been steadfast for our family and the school."

Biddy dropped her head to her chest and took a deep breath. "Thank you, Miss Frances. Kind of you. We're holdin' hope for our Norah."

"As are we. You are brave, Biddy. I hope I would be as brave." Dropping her hand from Biddy's shoulder, Frances said, "See you in the morning, Biddy" and turned to meet her carriage at the bottom of the stairs.

Mr. Laird stood by the carriage door as Frances approached. "Evening, miss," he said, his arms at his side. The horse snorted with impatience, waving his head as if trying to release the reins. "There, boy," Mr. Laird said, gently patting the horse's rear end. "He's just glad to see you again, miss. He's fond o' all the members of the Young family." Frances smiled, then looked at her watch. Five sharp. Both she and the cab were right on time. Mr. Laird held the cab door open with one hand while offering the other to Frances.

Inside, she was surprised to see a small, simply dressed woman sitting opposite her. "Mrs. Laird!"

"Evening, Miss Young," the woman greeted, in her soft lilting voice. She pointed to the front of the cab. "The mister thought I should come along to make it proper, since your father couldna come tonight."

"Oh, I see." Frances did her best not to sound or look annoyed that they seemed to think she would not honor the rules on her own. "How kind of you. And of Mr. Laird, for looking after my best interests. I feel protected and safe in your company."

As Frances smoothed out her skirt and settled inside, another carriage rounded the corner and drew up across from them. *George,* she supposed grumpily. *Elfie might have mentioned he was coming tonight.* She watched Biddy open the front door as if expecting his arrival. *I suppose she's hoping for news of Norah,* Frances thought. *More likely it's just another visit with Elfie, smoking cigars and drinking whiskey with Father. I hope Biddy isn't too disappointed.*

Frances had accepted George as a frequent fixture in their home, but that didn't mean she felt they should have surprise visitors bounding in and out at will. Even as she thought it, she knew her annoyance was petty.

She watched George jump down from his carriage with a show of boyish energy. Removing his hat, he offered her a brief wave as her cab moved forward. Frances did wonder what she might be missing at home. She waved back at George but did not tell Mr. Laird to stop. She was going to enjoy a few hours with no one to care for but herself.

In the meantime, she readied herself for polite small talk with Mrs. Laird. Frances put on a smile that quickly turned genuine as she faced her companion. The woman had already gone to her knitting, showing no interest in her fellow passenger, who watched her until she fell asleep from the jostling of the cab along the country road.

Frances rested against the seat and let out a pleased sigh. She would arrive at her destination early, as was her custom. She and her friends wanted good seats, up front. The excitement and controversy the French impressionists stirred in the art world was certain to draw a sizable crowd.

For the occasion, Frances had worn her new suit. It was an extravagance, but her seamstress had convinced her the suit would work well for her summer travels too. The gray fine-wool jacket nipped in at the waist, flattering her slender figure. Its broad lapels made her waist seem even smaller. Frances fingered the silver brooch on her jacket. It had been her mother's and Frances had coveted it.

Still struggling with the expense, she told herself that dressing well was important for a headmistress. *And if by chance it brings me a glance from a gentleman, I won't mind.* She smiled at the thought. The latter would be welcome, but she did not expect it. Not just because she was no longer of a "prime marriageable age." Her social circle had become greatly limited by her work. She also suspected there were few available candidates willing to treat her as a *co-equal*, a term she had picked up from Lily's letters about her women's suffrage luncheons. *If my independence scares men, so be it. Yet one never knows,* she reminded herself, thinking of Elfie and George.

As the cab jostled on the uneven road, she leaned back against the leather seat, causing a light aroma of cigar to rise. She rather liked it. Her father enjoyed the occasional "social smoke," as he called it. His social smokes were more frequent these days, coinciding with George's visits. She wasn't sure she approved of their new smoking club. Elfie had waved off Frances's concern. "A man smoking is a fact of life. If our students haven't been exposed to that in their own homes, then it becomes our responsibility. Besides, it's Father's house too." Frances still felt chagrined by the scolding. Elfie was right. *Just as long as Father doesn't start wearing Eliza's smoking jacket* she thought, stifling a laugh.

Her sister was still doing her share in the school, and the students adored her. Still, Elfie was clearly distracted. *All of her free time seems to be spent seeing George, writing to George, or keeping track of his daughter,* she thought, feeling more irritable than she cared to. Elizabeth Fenn's participation in the social scene in London seemed to have sent Elfie atwitter. Frances found her sister's enthusiasm for things beyond their home and school worrisome. Elfie was acting like a proud mother to the young woman. Frances sighed. *Lily could be right,* she thought. *I might be envious of Elfie.* A feeling of unease passed through her. *What will become of the school if Elfie marries George?* The question felt closer to the true cause of her agitation.

On top of it, Father is encouraging Elfie and George. Doesn't he realize Elfie might leave, just like Lily? Everyone and everything seemed to be changing. Age was catching up to her father. He moved more slowly, although he still managed to follow his routines and got out of the house on a regular basis. *Thank goodness at least for that.*

Frances gazed out the window to take a break from her unsettling thoughts. The agricultural lands and old estates in Harold's Cross were slowly shrinking as Dublin grew beyond its boundaries. The roads were still rough in places outside the city proper, however, keeping Frances busy holding the small bar on the side of the coach to keep her seat.

Father has never slipped easily into a jocular man's world, she thought. *He is an observer, more comfortable slightly apart from the crowd than at the center of it. He certainly comes to life when George is around. Around John Yeats, too.* Thomas Urry Young was not a man's man, and that made begrudging him a friendship with George even more of an unkindness. *At least George Fenn isn't another John Yeats, raucous and full of tall tales.* Neither of them was the kind of man she wanted, though she didn't fully know what that might be. Neither she nor Elfie nor Lily had chosen to become debutantes when they were of age. Even now the thought of the tradition made her roll her eyes. *It could be I've done myself a disservice,* she considered. The formal introduction to society was a way to meet eligible men, and so far, she had met very few.

The carriage slowed to a stop, and Mr. Laird called down to her. "Looks like there's a checkpoint ahead, miss. Nothing to worry about. I'll get you to your appointment on time."

Frances closed her eyes. Her thoughts shifted from taking stock of the changes in her life to worrying about political unrest in Ireland. That hadn't been her intention. *There isn't anything I can do about it anyway,* she thought, then stopped herself short. Biddy's Norah was in jail because of the British crackdown on the Irish, and Biddy was like family. Frances had reason after all to be grateful for George.

It was Elfie and their father who'd convinced George to intervene on Norah's behalf, so *they* were helping. The Youngs avoided speaking of Norah's situation in front of Biddy and, for the most part, the unfortunate event remained at arm's length from their lives. *George is helping Norah, and best for the rest of us to stay out of it,* she thought. The Anglo-Irish faced risks too. Some people were of the opinion that even outings like this lecture carried a shadow of risk. Hence their unplanned stop. The very idea annoyed Frances.

Once the cab reached the city proper, the streets became smoother, and Frances relaxed. Looking out at the bustling evening crowds, she wished she could find more time for both music and art. The last time she had been to a concert was to hear Mendelssohn's Scottish symphony with Lily, James, Elfie, and her father. *Oh, my, that was nine years ago?* The school was consuming making her summer travel very important. She could hardly count the occasional afternoon tea recital by

Maggie Barrett, and she didn't. Dublin was beginning to draw a variety of musical talent, helping to lift the "cultural backwater" label hung on Dublin by its snobby continental neighbors. *Would a "cultural backwater" host a lecture on the French impressionists?* she thought. *Hardly!*

Since the school had started, Thomas and Elfie had spent their summers traveling to the north, south, and west of Ireland for her father to record the Irish landscape and people in soft watercolors. *And now my sister has George's attention in her life,* she thought. Travel with their father carried advantages Frances had not considered before. Somehow, Elfie had managed to use the time when their father was occupied with his art to her advantage. *Traveling with a father who is an artist and a dreamer could actually be a plus,* she thought, and then shuddered. *Though not for me.*

She looked forward to the trips to the Continent with her students over school breaks. This summer they would travel to Italy. Their itinerary would include operas by Rossini and Verdi, walks through ruins in Rome, garden-fresh tomato-based pasta dishes, warm weather, and, for herself, a glass or two of red wine. A delicious combination. What could feel more of another world for someone who lived in provincial—not "backwater"—Dublin?

The horse's hooves clopped again on the cobbled road, bringing her attention back to the evening at hand. She was meeting Olive and Louise, childhood school friends. Both were married, and Frances was pleased they'd wanted to attend the lecture with her. In fact, to her surprise, they both jumped at the opportunity. "What courage it must take the artists to fight the Paris Salon," Olive had said. She described the salon as a "tide of snobbery, wealth, and influence," which Frances supposed it was; mostly she wondered how her married friends with children had the time and energy to remain so well informed. Olive had looked at her somewhat puzzled.

"Frances, we have nannies and cooks. Did you think we did it all ourselves?" *Of course they do,* Frances chided herself. *Mother had Biddy. We still have Biddy!* Why had she thought otherwise? It seemed a husband and children did not have to be so constraining after all.

The carriage came to a full stop outside the three-story Royal Hibernian Academy, its façade adorned with plaster heads of Palladio, Michelangelo, and Raphael, representing the academy's areas of interest—architecture, sculpture, and painting. Frances stepped to the ground without waiting for the assistance of Mr. Laird. Uncertain thoughts banished, she felt a sophisticated, slim woman cutting an energetic figure who might draw attention and even envy. *I am a not a spinster yet!* she thought with a smile. Before Mr. Laird could insist on escorting her inside, she walked up to a couple whom she knew to be acquaintances of her father's. "I'm in good hands now, Mr. Laird, thank you," she called up to him, hoping to show the appreciation she should feel. *Women's independence can't come fast enough,* she thought.

Once inside, the trio walked through the exhibition room before the natural light—meant to enhance the works of the watercolors displayed opposite the oil paintings, which included some of her father's—had faded. Arriving to the larger salon, she saw Louise wave to her, and Frances extracted herself from the couple. Her friends had found seats near the front of the room. Making her way toward them, Frances glanced around, hoping to catch the eye of anyone else she knew. She rather liked being noticed. When she reached them, Olive leaned over and kissed her cheek. "I adore your suit, Frances," she whispered. "If that doesn't draw a suitor's eye . . ."

"Perhaps it will," Frances whispered back.

She felt suddenly disappointed her father hadn't joined her. He attracted men who had studied under him at the academy, and she thought, *While the purpose of a chaperone is to protect, I want to attract!* With Lily in Canada and Elfie well on her way to making a life with George, she would be the daughter left alone to care for her father. The very thought made her anxious, but she banished it.

At the front of the room, the speaker advanced to the podium, adjusted the pince-nez on the bridge of his thin nose, and began his talk. He spoke rapidly, and his French accent was heavy. Frances had to be attentive to catch his meaning. *Why doesn't he just speak in French?* she thought, frustrated that she might be missing something vital. Staying with him required absolute concentration, and Frances had hoped for a relaxing evening.

When he finished his talk, he asked for questions from the floor. Frances raised her hand. She was not the first called on, but eventually the lecturer said, "And what is the lovely lady's question?"

Flattered, Frances rose and projected in her best schoolteacher voice: "Can you tell us how it is they are called impressionists?"

The lecturer smiled at her. "Ah, madame, of course," he said and then rattled on about the haughty dismissal of Claude Monet's *Sunset* as "hardly worth looking at, just an impression," bringing polite laughter to the room.

Having spoken up, Frances was glad to be back out of the spotlight. *Maybe I am more like Father than I realized,* she thought. Had she been too bold, calling attention to herself by standing to pose her question? *Nonsense,* she answered herself. *Anyone who criticizes me for using my brain and being curious isn't worth my worry.* Victorian norms for women were limiting, and that made it more exhilarating to do the unexpected. She glanced surreptitiously around the room. Louise had mentioned Giles Morgan might be at the lecture. He was a few years older than Frances and had been a widower for over a year. "He'll be snatched up soon," Louise whispered to

Frances, causing her to blush at being caught. "I'm going to host a dinner party. You and Giles are invited."

After the final question was answered, followed by another round of applause, Frances and her friends stood up to leave. Through the crowd Frances spied Giles waiting near the back of the salon. He wasn't waiting for her, was he? Louise could be rather clever at setting up "unplanned" meetings. Frances blushed again. Sure enough, Louise made a point of introducing them to each on their way out. Frances couldn't help but notice that Giles Morgan had an appealing touch of gray at his temples. *I'll admit he's quite handsome,* she thought. He smiled politely at her and, rather than complimenting her on her appearance, he complimented her on her question for the lecturer. Frances was charmed.

CHAPTER 32

NEVER THE RIGHT TIME

Elfie

Elfie could not find the right moment for her and George to announce their engagement. The routines of the school and a highly chaperoned life seemed to keep them more apart than together. Two weeks had passed since George held Elfie's hands in the garden, looked in her eyes, and said in a determined and loving voice, "I want to marry you sooner than later, Elfie."

"Yes!" she'd said quickly. They glanced at her father, who stood several feet behind them making a pretense of studying a shrub. Elfie giggled. George had told her his intentions rather than asked for her hand, but she was determined not to lose this second opportunity to misunderstanding. "Of course, Mr. Fenn," she whispered. "I want to marry you, too."

George had wanted to announce their engagement that evening. Elfie wasn't ready to share the good news with anyone yet. More specifically, she wasn't ready to tell Frances.

She'd had just enough time to ask George to wait before her father joined them, putting an end to their discussion. Elfie feared her sister's reaction and the dynamic it would create—her stomach still tightened just thinking about it. The parson's homily last Sunday on being a crucible of love and loyalty had added to her hesitation. *That's me,* she'd thought. *Except I'm split right down the middle between my love and loyalty for my fiancé and for my sister.*

She'd written immediately to Lily about George's proposal, her excitement about becoming Mrs. Fenn, and her worry about Frances. *I am quite anxious of her reaction, Lily. I must think clearly before sharing my happiness with her.* Elfie went to bed listening to the wind kicking in and the house creaking in protest, knowing full well they were not the reason she lay awake.

George continued to return often to RockView for evening meals, full of good humor and opinions on the world but respectfully silent on the subject of their engagement—so silent that Elfie eventually started to worry she'd made the whole thing up. She became determined to find the time and space for a proper conversation with George without interruption. *And soon,* she scolded herself.

It was George who offered the solution. "Thomas," he said before he left RockView one night, "I'd like to show Elfie where I take my morning constitutional in Mount Pleasant Square."

"Splendid idea," Thomas said. "I enjoy strolling beneath the canopy of the old trees in that park as well. It's been a long time. The winding paths, the benches by the River Swan. Yes, a splendid idea, George!"

Elfie alerted Frances of their departure. "We will be back before dinner," she assured her. Frances, who was becoming used to her sister leaving the school in the middle of the day when George was around, nodded and offered Elfie a wan smile.

In the cab, Thomas sat in the center of the seat across from his daughter, giving George no choice but to sit beside Elfie, who then looked out the window and tried not to blush. Lily had shared with her sisters that once their father got to know James, he became relaxed in his chaperone duties, visibly present and yet not overtly interfering. *He's being a little more than "not interfering,"* Elfie thought. Her father had closed his eyes as soon as the carriage took off, pretending to rest, allowing George and Elfie's shoulders to touch during the jiggly ride without comment. George turned his eyes in her direction and suppressed a smile. This time Elfie could not hide her happy embarrassment.

At the park, the jarvey and George helped Elfie and Thomas down from the carriage. The street was lined with tiers of Georgian homes that gave the area a sense of security and stability—a feeling, Thomas observed, that was much harder to find inside the city of Dublin these days. George paid the man to return for them within the half hour.

They all stood for a moment, buttoning the tops of their warm coats against the cool April temperatures, and Elfie resecured her hat with a pin. Thomas walked behind the couple at a distance—claiming, and probably honestly so, that he was unable to keep George's brisk pace.

"I hope you understand, Thomas," George called back to his friend. "I want to be ready to enjoy Biddy's fine meal." A brisk walk before or after dinner was part of George's regular health regime. Elfie had purchased special walking shoes with flexible soles and strong leather laces in anticipation of joining his exercise walks with some comfort once they were married. She was very grateful for them now as she worked to keep up with George. What she hadn't considered was her skirt, which pressed annoyingly against her shins with her swift pace, slowing her down. *How ridiculous,* she thought, pulling at the material that had caught on the tops of her boots as she walked, *and hardly ladylike.* She made a note to have her most practical skirt hemmed up to her ankles so it would not impede her gait. *What will Frances think?* She giggled at the thought.

When the two of them had gained some distance on Thomas, Elfie said, breathlessly, "George, I need your help."

"Do you want me to slow down?"

"Well, a little, but that's not what I mean. I want to explain why I haven't been ready to announce our news to the family."

George stopped and waited for Elfie to catch her breath.

"George," she said once they started walking again, though more slowly this time, "I am hesitant to pull the rug out from under Frances"—Elfie spoke haltingly as the winding path moved them away from the street and into the park—"and from under the stability of the school with our engagement news. . . . We started the school as a team . . ." She looked over her shoulder and saw her father still well behind them.

"Elfie, the school is a grand success," George said. "And like any business, it can be reorganized."

"Yes," Elfie replied. "It is a success, thanks to a lot of hard work on *both* our parts. George . . . ," she said cautiously, "you do understand that I want to help Frances develop a plan for the school after our marriage."

"Of course I do!" George replied. "You and your sister have a business together, and my dear, I do understand the challenges of a family business. I've had to deal with enough of them."

Elfie smiled with relief, but to make herself clear she added, "Until I find a replacement or decide to continue teaching, I am uncertain what to tell Frances."

George picked up the pace, saying nothing until they were out of sight of her father. Elfie was certain then that he hadn't considered that she might want to continue teaching.

"I am traveling so much," he said at last, "that the current arrangement can work for now. But not forever, Elfie."

They passed another couple strolling in the opposite direction. George tipped his hat and Elfie was glad for her gloves, which hid her lack of a wedding ring. "As for telling your sister about our plans to marry . . . ," George continued, "my dear Elfie, do you think our Frances is blind? She probably wonders why you have not yet confided in her. I know your father wonders the same thing."

Elfie was not so sure. "George, she depends on me. I really don't want to cause a row. You have never seen Frances when she feels betrayed. I don't think I could bear it after how hard we've worked."

George turned to her with a broad smile. "Elfie, you are the boldest woman I have ever known. I want you to remember that. You started a business with your sister, you attended a political protest unchaperoned and at night, and, I will add, you rejected my initial proposal of marriage. Secondly, you are not betraying Frances. You are marrying me. I have confidence you will find the right words."

Elfie dropped her head and stopped abruptly. She nearly started crying, she was so concerned about all the changes her marriage would bring to her family. George stood quietly beside her and waited.

Elfie breathed deeply and looked up at the man who loved her and believed in her, but who did not fully understand what her leaving the school and RockView would mean for her sister. "You are right, George," she said. "I will tell Frances. No," she corrected herself. "I will not tell her. I will confide in her. That's what sisters do."

Thomas came into view, announcing his presence with a wave followed by a show of swinging his walking stick like a young boy. Elfie pulled her handkerchief from her sleeve and dabbed her eyes while George laughed at his antics and waved back.

"I'm ready," she whispered. "I will talk with Frances

tomorrow after you leave for England." The decision made, Elfie was suddenly filled with happiness and relief. She *was* ready to move forward and would help her sister make sure the school remained on steady footing. Elfie walked to her father, kissed him on the cheek, then turned to George and grinned, certain that from that moment on, her life would never be the same.

— ♦ —

Frances

Frances couldn't help noticing her sister's mind had been wandering more than usual, but the morning after her walk in the park with George and their father, she had been unusually quiet. That evening, Frances caught Elfie once again staring wistfully into the classroom from the hallway and decided to speak to her to get whatever needed to be said out on the table.

Frances waited until the girls closed their books and put away papers and inkwells in their desks. A few desk lids banged closed, and polite murmurs of "I'm sorry, Miss Frances," added to the general end-of-class clatter before the room emptied. The girls were going out in the garden for an afternoon break. This was as good a time as any to speak with her sister. Frances stepped into the hall behind Elfie and put her hand on her shoulder. "We need to have a talk, don't you think?"

Elfie's face flushed.

Below them, lighthearted voices moved down the stairs punctuated by an excited squeal that told the sisters someone was sliding down the banister. "No broken bones, I hope!" Frances called out, breaking the tension between them, and they both smiled.

Elfie spoke first. "Frances, I am sorry to have had my head

in the clouds lately. I have wanted to tell you my news, and yet I have felt conflicted, not knowing what your reaction or the consequences would be."

Frances looked at her sister thoughtfully. "Go on . . . ," she said.

"George and I plan to be married next summer," Elfie said in a rush. "There," she said, reaching for Frances's hand. "I have said it. I have wanted to shout it. I have dearly wanted to share my happiness with you. I haven't even told Father yet, though I assume he suspects. After all, George must have asked him permission during our visit to Sligo, before he first proposed. Oh, that seems so long ago!" Elfie paused to gather herself. "I have been so worried that I would hurt you or the school. Frances, I want you to be happy for me, but I know this means dislocation any way we do it. I love you, Frances, and admire you, and all I want is your blessing and Father's, and of course your happiness, too."

Though she had long since guessed Elfie's news, Frances was struck dumb. Her sister embraced her, and over Elfie's shoulder Frances said, "I am not surprised, just a little knocked off my pins." Frances disentangled herself so she could look Elfie in the eyes. "I am happy for you, for you *and* George."

"Dear Frances!" Elfie exclaimed. "I have been so worried." She took Frances's hands in hers. "The only question left is the school. Can I remain part of the Misses Young School for Girls as well as your life and Father's by living nearby, or should we find someone to take my place?"

Frances held her breath, covering her uncertainty with a smile as she sought the right words. "Of course!" she said, sounding more enthusiastic than she felt. "I see no reason why we cannot continue to make the school work with you living nearby, if that's what you want. You and George, I mean. The change will naturally require flexibility from all of us. What do you think about our advertising for a helper who can lighten the workload for both of us as soon as possible? You will be busy planning a wedding, after all. And . . . if it comes to it, I hope you will help me to find someone to take your place." The last sentence was the hardest for Frances to say. She did not want to lose her sister altogether. Nor did she want to learn to work with someone new. *Life is full of obstacles we'd rather not deal with,* she admonished herself. *Not all change is bad.* They embraced again and Frances asked, attempting to be cheerful, "How soon does George return to RockView? We must plan a celebration. But first I want to hear all about his proposal. Both of them!"

CHAPTER 33

PROMISES

London, Ontario, Canada
Lily

Eight years ago, April had arrived with wintery snow every day until the middle of the month, giving Lily her first experience with cabin fever. She'd been convinced they'd made a terrible mistake in coming to Canada. James had been just as convinced the late winter was an aberration and urged his bride to be patient.

He'd been right. *James is often right,* she thought, both admiring of and feeling irritated by that particular attribute. The following springs had brought warmth and hope for her garden plans. This spring was no different. From where she stood at the top of the lawn, she could see the branches of both the maple and cherry trees already bursting with promise.

Her mother had taught her children the importance of measured confidence. "Too much pride is unbecoming. We do not succeed alone," she'd counseled. After all the years of work she'd put into the garden, Lily couldn't help herself. She was very proud of what she—and Jim—had accomplished. Sculpted paths, beds ready for planting, three "rooms" hidden around a hedge or turn of the path, and a reflecting pool! Each feature followed the curving lines that nature provided. In the greenhouse, petunia seeds, ordered from England two months earlier, would soon be sprouting under Jim's care. Lily imagined ruffled petals of violet and purple filling in the edges of the beds. *The garden will be absolutely perfect for our June party,* she thought. This year would be their fourth annual "Welcome to Summer" event. It would have been their fifth, but an unseasonable June of cold, rain, and sleet the previous year had forced them to cancel. Lily and James had eaten canapés and drunk champagne by the fire for weeks. *I feel good luck in my bones,* she told herself. *This year we will have a perfect day. Why not hope for the best?*

She reached into her coat pocket to go over her lists of plans and guests and pulled out instead her most recent letter from Elfie, which she'd wanted to read again. Lily grinned broadly. She still could hardly believe it. George had proposed and Elfie had accepted! *Good for Elfie,* she thought, and then wondered if that were "suffragette" of her. She was thrilled for her sister and worried for Frances. Lily walked down to the bench that faced the river and read the letter.

Elfie had invited all of them (the children too!) to both the engagement party in June and their wedding the following summer. "George wants us to be wed this summer or possibly after Christmas," Elfie had written, "but I believe he will agree to wait until next summer so that you all can join us. And even if we do wed before then, why not come home next summer to meet your new brother-in-law and stay for a few months?"

Lily and James had already discussed the possibility. James would find a doctor to take over his practice for at least a month so the family could travel to Ireland and even visit some of Europe. What he'd actually said was "I'll do my best," but Lily knew he would succeed. She felt selfish hoping Elfie and George would wait to hold their nuptials until the following summer so she could be there. Her sister's engagement party in June was too soon for them. Lily was disappointed to miss it, especially as it was being held at Stephen's Green Club. *Imagine being inside Dublin's Anglo-Irish men's club,* she thought with a chuckle. Her "literary club" would be thrilled.

George was a member, of course. "George assures me that the club and private dining hall are elegant enough for ladies," her sister had written, "and that politics will not be the favored topic at our celebration!"

Lily would write to Elfie tonight that they hoped to attend the wedding and that they would raise a toast at their garden party to Elfie and George's future happiness. She quite liked the idea of giving a transoceanic flair to her sister's nuptials. *Elfie will be pleased, too.* Lily did worry for Frances, though. *Will she feel left behind? Burdened with caring for Father? I do know what that is like. Maybe Father will live with Elfie and George,* she considered. *Oh dear, then Frances truly would be alone. How will they work the school when Elfie is married? Is Frances the reason George and Elfie set their wedding so far ahead, to help our sister and the school? I must write soon and ask these questions carefully.* Lily wasn't even certain if Frances knew about the engagement yet. When Elfie had written the letter, she was still gathering her courage to tell their sister her news.

Lily sighed and put the letter back in her pocket. She would learn answers to all her questions in time; meanwhile, she needed to focus on the task at hand. Lily now pulled out her lists for the garden party. She had already started adding names to last year's list. There were new social friends and acquaintances from the suffrage movement, new medical faculty associates from the university. Then, of course, their six new neighbors. Lily recalled her first few lonely years in Canada. *It takes time and effort to make your place in the world*, she thought. Friends, especially, could take longer than hoped for. And now she was surrounded by them!

Lily checked her food and drinks list:

- *canapés—4 each—Marian and her daughter, make last minute*
- *Mother's Favorites—Marian and Lily to make the day before*

Her mother, Sarah, had believed "the trick to a good party is to do enough ahead to make it look easy, put your guests at ease, and spoil them with good food and drink." Lily added the word "double," scratched it out, and wrote "triple the ingredients."

- *French champagne and single-malt scotch—James to order*

She almost put a check by that because her husband had already met with the local liquor merchant, but instead she wrote a question mark. Had he ordered enough?

- *Fruit punch—Lily*

She spent a few more minutes writing notes before turning to the next page: her supply list. It was growing along with the invitation list. When she finished making her additions, her eyes were tired. She enjoyed making lists, but the truth was she already knew most of what was needed.

What she wasn't confident about was the addition of Marian's husband, Logan. This would be his first year working at the party. Marian had told Lily she needn't worry about her husband. "He knows how to pour. Does it for himself every night. I'd call the man well practiced," she'd said playfully. "The portion served might be his only challenge. He likes a full cup."

Lily had run Marian's endorsement by James, who laughed. "As an Irish gentleman, I threw out the dram a long time ago. It barely wets the glass. He will be a fine server in my book." Lily was not so sure. She opened her eyes, found her planning list, and added, *show Marian appropriate amounts of liquor for Logan's party training.*

Logan's dubious pouring abilities aside, Lily was happy. She not only had come to think of Canada as home but also was still in love with her husband (she suspected that was not true of all the couples she knew), *and* they had three children who were thriving. Unlike her mother's, Lily's childbirth had been kind to her, and she was in good health. She was especially grateful for her children's well-being when James told her of the illnesses and injuries he saw in his practice.

Lily stood up and followed the path through the lower garden. A breeze came up from the river and lifted the hem of her skirt. *The children will be so excited about visiting Ireland!* she thought, reflecting again on Elfie's news. Lily could hardly wait to tell them. *It will be nice to get there before the students arrive so we can stay in the house and have a real reunion.* The image of them arriving at her family home, her father meeting his grandchildren, and her sisters playing the role of doting aunts made her smile. Lily wanted to meet Elfie's George and, if there was time, visit their home in Sligo. The sun went behind a cloud, and Lily shook away her daydream. *Don't get ahead of yourself, Lily,* she thought. *The trip isn't a certainty, yet.* But as with her party, and most things in life, she hoped for the best.

— • —

May
James

The warming weather increasingly pulled James's thoughts beyond the house and garden. After all his years in Canada, he still looked forward to the ride through the countryside to the surgery. The month of May brought him past young wheat fields pushing toward the sun and gnarled elderly oaks with fresh green growth that reminded him of Ireland.

He'd been surprised to find he enjoyed helping Lily with her plans for the garden party. The activity was entirely different from his doctor duties, and with his wife full of anticipation, her mood was infectious. Even their children wanted to participate, though James noticed their efforts were more often a hindrance than a help to Lily. In his practice, he saw another side of life, especially how quickly a good life could turn into a hard one. One moment a family was in a place of stability and happiness, the next one of tragedy and loss. All it took was an accident or a heart attack or stroke. Fortunately, the surgery mostly dealt with lacerations, broken bones, hangovers, ladies' problems, rashes, and colds. Still, coming home to Lily and the children and his busy home was reassuring, restoring. His family was healthy and happy, and he was grateful.

— ◆ —

Lily

Jim drove Lily in the trap and dropped her off at the Ullman Press while he went on to run other errands in town. As she entered the print shop, a mix of arresting odors brought Lily's finger to her nose. She should have been better prepared. Ullman Press made their garden party invitations every year.

Was it the ink? Lily detected a jumble of scents. *Maybe camphor and linseed oil? Most certainly a strong solvent like kerosene,* she thought. Whatever they were, they all combined with the wood scents from the paper and almost sent her out the door again. The invitations for their wedding had been selected in an elegant, *odorless* stationers in Dublin. She shook her head to clear her thoughts and chose to ignore the smell. Life in Canada was often about different experiences.

The printer waved his hand at her. "In just a minute," he called. He bent over his press, giving the large handle a quarter turn. Seemingly satisfied, he turned and came to her, wiping his hands on what at some point had been a white canvas work apron, now showing signs of long duty in an inky environment. The wiping gesture seemed of little use to Lily. *His hands couldn't possibly be made clean by that,* she thought behind her smile. He came to the counter, friendly as always. "Glad to see you, Mrs. Niven."

She was touched he remembered her name from only seeing her once a year. "It's nice to see you again, Mr. Ullman," she replied and then described to him what she wanted. He pulled out a sample box of crisp, clean paper, separated into whites, creams, and grays, for her to make her selection. She chose the cream-colored linen, with the assurance that the envelopes would be made from the same paper. She handed over the text she had carefully written out just the way she wanted it placed on the page. The printer brought over a board that held the typefaces she could choose from. This is where Lily paused each year. She looked through his offerings, wondering if she should use a different font from that of her past invitations, but her preference was always the same—the one that looked like beautiful handwriting. "Let's use that one," she said, pointing to it.

"I will send you a sample in two days for your approval," Mr. Ullman said. "And I hope you don't mind my saying this," he added before she turned to leave. "I see you and Dr. Niven at Sunday services. Everyone knows your husband because he is a doctor, and of course you won't recognize me in my Sunday best." He pointed to his ink-stained arms and the smudges on his face. "My wife scrubs me head to foot on Saturday night so once a week I emerge in church like a newborn babe, ready to receive the spirit."

Lily shared a laugh with him and said, "Please say hello next time, Mr. Ullman. We have our three children with us, and we all love newborn babies, as does Dr. Niven." They had both started to laugh again when a loud, hacking cough came through from the back of the shop. Lily frowned and picked up her handbag from the counter. "Mr. Ullman," she said, stopping in the doorway, "send whoever is coughing back there to see my husband. It sounds very serious."

"Thank you, Mrs. Niven, I should do that. That's my wife, Greta, my Saturday-night scrubber. She has been poorly but insists on coming in."

Lily paused as they listened to another deep spasm of coughing.

"I'll bring Greta to see Dr. Niven soon," the printer assured her.

Lily nodded and closed the door. *My heavens,* she thought.

The invitations were delivered to the Niven home two weeks later, arriving in spotless, handsome blue boxes. Lily was thrilled. She sat at her desk to hand address each one herself. It took a few evenings because her hand would cramp and she had to stop to rest before the next session. Lily looked at each one, admiring the finished product, then felt satisfied to check that task off her list. Jim, and Sean, an occasional helper for the Nivens, hand delivered the invitations on May thirteenth, exactly six weeks before the party on Saturday, June twenty-fourth. Lily had them organized in batches by neighborhood so everyone would receive them at the same time. She didn't want anyone to hear of the party from others and feel left out. Acceptances came in quickly. During the last weeks of May, there were messages arriving almost every day. Each one was a source of excitement for her as she wrote "yes" by the name on her guest list. In the evening, she would sit with James and read to him the growing list of friends who were due to gather in just a few weeks.

Lily floated through the following weeks, returning to town to speak with shopkeepers about the types of flowers they expected to arrive in June for her table bouquets, stopping at the seamstress for her dress fittings, checking the markets for unusual fruits to add to her menu, and generally enjoying each step in her preparations. She even stopped at Ullman's to thank him for the invitations and to check on Mrs. Ullman, but the shop had been unexpectedly closed. *Perhaps they are away on a holiday,* she thought. Lily meant to ask her husband about Mrs. Ullman's health when he came home that night, but with so much on her mind, she forgot.

CHAPTER 34

MRS. ULLMAN'S SYMPTOMS RETURN

June 1882
James

A week before the party, James opened the door to find Lily in the living room, lying on the sofa with her eyes closed and the house quiet. She gave him a weak smile in response to his greeting, saying she was too tired to dine with him that night. "It's not a wonder you're tired," he said. "All those details and plans to keep in mind!" He felt her forehead. Her skin felt warm but not hot beneath the back of his hand. "Are you feeling all right?" he asked, expecting her to deny anything but temporary exhaustion. But she shook her head and said irritably, "No, James, I'm not. I don't feel at all well."

"Then let's get you to bed," he said, using his practical bedside manner. "Marian can bring you some tea."

The next evening James was surprised to see Marian's son still waiting in the wagon outside the house to take his mother home. "Mrs. Niven is still up in her room," Marian said as she greeted James at the door. "I have dinner for you and the children on the table and more in the kitchen for Mrs. Niven when she's hungry. She hasn't eaten all day," she added before leaving. James peeked in on his wife, who was sleeping peacefully, then called the children to dinner. "Marian has made something delicious for us this evening. Hurry up and clean those hands. I'm quite hungry!"

Since the windy nights and damp days of early May had left London, entire weeks had passed without James hearing so much as a cough in the surgery. So he was concerned but not worried when he learned Lily had remained in bed the next day.

"I've got just the thing to make her feel better, Mr. Niven," Marian announced. He raised his eyebrows, and Marian laughed. "I'm not talking about potions passed down from my great-grannies! Teas and broth, sir. I'll bring them tomorrow."

James laughed too. With rest and Marian's careful tending, his wife would improve soon.

But then Mrs. Ullman's symptoms returned. James recommended continued rest and plenty of fluids for Mrs. Ullman and told Mr. Ullman not to hurry his wife back to work until she felt strong enough. James went straight home to check on Lily rather than return to the surgery. Mrs. Ullman's symptoms were similar enough to Lily's that he wanted to tend to her care himself. James was not certain what was wrong with either of them.

Marian, of course, looked surprised to see him home early. "I thought you could use a break," he said. Lily slept through their evening meal again. After a dinner of warmed-up soup and Marian's fresh-baked bread, James entertained the children with a story from his own childhood about leprechauns and fairies.

Once they were in bed, he checked on Lily again. The bowl of broth Marian had brought up to her earlier was half-empty on the bedside table. A good sign. Lily was asleep, so he sat down in his chair to review her case like any doctor would. His wife had not been to town for nearly a week. Jim had been doing her errands while she remained at home working on party preparations with Marian and enjoying time with Knox. Lily and Mrs. Ullman had nearly the same symptoms, and Lily had gone to the Ullmans' print shop when Mrs. Ullman was sick, but with so much time passed since then, it seemed highly unlikely the two women were suffering from the same illness. He also knew that Mrs. Ullman had felt well enough to go on a business trip to Toronto with her husband but had a relapse after she returned home. He didn't know nearly enough to help either Mrs. Ullman or Lily get better quickly.

James poured Lily a fresh glass of water, placed it by her bed, then took the tray of cold broth with him downstairs to the kitchen. He would sleep on the sofa again.

In the morning, James found Lily awake and resting beneath the covers with her head propped up on pillows, her upper body wrapped in her quilted peach-colored silk bed coat. The fabric's reflection made her own color appear better.

"I brought you a fresh pot of tea," he said, removing the cozy and pouring her a cup. She didn't move to take it, so he placed it on the bedside table. "If you're in doubt, Marian made it, not me."

He liked seeing his wife smile, however briefly. She closed her eyes and took a breath, bringing on a coughing fit he hadn't heard from her before. "No, no, James," she said when he came over to her. "I'm sure it's just a cold, but you don't want to catch it, do you?"

"No, I do not," he said, smiling. "But you seem to have forgotten that I am the doctor in this family." James kissed her forehead. He was relieved it felt cool to the touch.

"How is life in your world?" she asked, blowing her nose on the handkerchief James handed her, "and how are my children? I am feeling out of touch sitting here wrapped in blankets. I have work to do."

"Don't worry, my love. Marian, Jim, and I have your lists well in hand, and you will be up soon. But not too soon," he added.

"As for your children," he said, picking up the paper he had placed on the dresser when he came in, "Lucie has sent you a drawing she made last night." James held the picture so Lily could look at it. "It's of Count eating your roses."

"Oh no!" she said, half coughing and laughing.

"Your garden is still beautiful, and we are tying up Count. If you look closely at the picture, you can see that Lucie has taken his reins," he continued, "and is trying to minimize the damage. It seems she has made herself the heroine saving your roses." Lily smiled again, and James propped the picture up on her desk, placing a book behind it so she could enjoy it from bed. "Hugh wants you to see his small wooden boat with a fine sail he made from one of Marian's old kitchen towels. He and Jim built the boat out in the barn. They named it after you. The boys plan to christen it tomorrow after school. No champagne, just cookies for the *Lily*'s launch tomorrow on the reflecting pond. If you're feeling up to it, you can watch the festivities from the window. Let's hope it floats! And little Knox, of course, is absolutely fine. He just wants his mama."

Before he left the room, he reminded her of what she already knew. "Marian will be in the house with Knox. Hugh and Lucie are going to school soon, and your job is to rest and get well. You have this silver bell"—he pointed to it on the bedside table—"to call for Marian if you need anything." He bent close to kiss her and whispered, "*You* and our children are my world. Get well, my love." He pulled the bed quilts up to her shoulders and tucked them in around her.

"Thank you, James. The achiness seems to come and go, but I am improving. No fever last night," she said. "I will be throwing the covers off soon." He could see she was willing herself to be better. "James," she said, "the children, this new life . . . we have accomplished so much together." She closed her eyes, but her lips held a smile.

Lily drifted off and color rose in her cheeks. Her temperature was going up again. James took one of the small clean linen cloths Marian had stacked next to a bowl of water, dipped it and wrung it out, then gently placed the cool compress on his wife's brow. He replaced the compress with another and then another, until the fever broke and Lily was sleeping peacefully.

James let his mind rest as he rode into town, the rhythm of the horse under him soothing his thoughts, the greening of the countryside reminding him that life continues, the morning air refreshing his face and lungs. Count slowed from a trot to a walk when the hard dirt road turned to cobblestone. James saw the Closed sign in the window of the printer's shop and guessed that Mr. Ullman was upstairs taking care of his wife. James would stop to see them on his way home.

His day at the surgery was launched before he could hang up his hat; the small waiting room was already full. His assistant told him in a hushed voice that there were two families with fever, nausea, and respiratory problems needing visits at home. Cattermole had already made a visit to one of the families and would be going out soon to see the next one. James caught him in the hall between patients and got a quick report. "Both children and the mother had high fevers, vomiting, and coughing and struggled to breathe. One of the children seemed delirious," Cattermole said. "And I'm not liking the sound of all that coughing in the waiting room. I don't want to jump to any conclusions, but if we don't get on top of this, we might be seeing the start of an epidemic."

James told his partner that Lily had been in bed with a fever, and the two men stood quietly. Cattermole put his hand on James's shoulder, "Your wife is young and healthy, James." James nodded but said nothing.

At noon, he took a break. He was making himself a cup of tea when Jim, their gardener, burst into the office. "It's Miss Lily," he said.

James entered the house and took the stairs to the second floor two at a time. In the bedroom, Marian was sitting beside Lily, applying fresh compresses to her brow, but she immediately got up and gave James her place. "Just ring the bell if you need me, Dr. Niven."

James nodded and regained his calm doctor's demeanor before speaking to Lily. He lifted her head gently and looked down her throat and into her nose. Her passageways were swollen and partially closed. "My sweet Lily," he said. "Fortunately, I have just the thing to help you feel better." He called down the stairs to Marian to bring boiling water and a towel and opened his medical bag, pulling out a small stash of precious crushed eucalyptus leaves sent by a colleague from the Trinity College medical school. Several minutes later Marian appeared with a steaming kettle and a bowl. He watched impatiently as she switched the bowls on the bedside table and poured the steaming water from the kettle. She slipped the towel from her shoulder and handed it to him. James sat at his wife's side, creating a tent with the towel over her face to catch the steam rising from the bowl.

Within a few minutes, Lily pushed the tent away, looked at him impatiently, and asked for Lucie, Knox, and Hugh. James relaxed. Her fever had broken and she was breathing easily. Her recovery might be longer and slower than he'd originally thought, but she would survive. "Your children are outside playing right now," he told her. "When you're a little more rested, I'll bring them to you. They're anxious to see you, too." He expected his wife to argue with him, but she had already fallen back asleep.

James stood in the hall outside their bedroom. He heard the children playing outside on the lawn. Through the window in the stairwell, he could see them and the last of the early lilacs blooming in the garden. The scent of Lily's lilacs and a romp with his children would cheer him up. *Children are resilient,* he thought.

He had a footrace with Hugh, admired Lucie's newest drawing for her mother, and helped Knox look for bugs until Jim arrived from the barn leading James's horse. James did not want to leave Lily unattended for long, but there were patients waiting. He still hadn't checked on Mrs. Ullman.

He asked Jim to sit outside Lily's room to reassure her if she awoke and to fetch James again if necessary. Marian, he knew, would continue to care for Lily and watch over the children. He was fortunate to have Jim and Marian as a trusted part of their family. They understood that his duties to the community required him to return to work.

Jim followed James to the bottom of the stairs, where he hesitated. He seemed uncertain, lacking his usual ease. "I have never been on the second floor of your house, Dr. Niven. I don't feel I belong there."

"Of course, Jim. I didn't think." James looked up to the top of stairs, then back at Jim. "You would be doing a great service for me and for my wife," he said, "if you could." Jim nodded, and James put his hand on the man's shoulder in gratitude. He left Jim sitting outside the open door of Lily's bedroom, looking uncomfortable in the fine Windsor chair James had pulled from the bedroom. His hands and face were freshly washed, but mud still caked his mucking boots. "I'm just glad you're here," James said.

James had just stepped out of the house when Lucie ran to him, clasping her arms around his waist, her serious young face turned up toward him. "How is Mama?" she asked. "Marian said she needs to stay in bed longer."

James held his daughter's shoulders tenderly. "Mama is going to be fine," he told her. "You, Hugh, and Knox need to be especially helpful and good, using soft voices in the house so she can rest and recover. This evening the four of us will spend time together."

Lucie suddenly seemed older than her eight years, both emotionally and physically. James guessed his daughter would mature early and would need her mother's guidance in that passage. He walked over to the boys, giving each of them a hug and a kiss on the forehead before he left. "Oh no!" they both shouted. Their eyes went wide and they pointed behind James, who quickly turned around to see Count Lisburn at the top of the lawn once again nibbling away at the grass and Lily's pink Duchesse de Brabant roses. James hurried over to gather the reins and gently admonish the horse. "Thanks for the alert, boys!" he called to his sons.

James was exhausted by the time he came home that evening. All he wanted to do was sit in his chair and sip a whiskey. Instead, he headed to the stairs, where he saw Marian on the landing above him. "Oh, Mr. Niven! Thank goodness." In the bedroom, James found Lily awake, but her mind was not clear. Marian told him that Mrs. Niven had started talking to her father and sisters and telling them to come quick.

"Delirium," he said. "This may be the last symptom before this illness goes away," he explained, hoping he was right. He had found Mrs. Ullman sitting in her kitchen when he stopped on his way home to check on her. She seemed weak but was clearly on the mend, eating a bowl of soup her husband had made for her. "It's not too bad," she teased. "I've had worse."

Mr. Ullman told him privately that his wife had been delirious last night. "And this morning she is better! Crazy things she was saying," he said, "and she doesn't remember a thing of it. Just as well, eh?"

James asked Marian if she wouldn't mind making Lily another pot of tea before she went home. He handed her another packet of herbs from his bag and gave instructions to brew it as a tea. "To open up her breathing," he explained.

Lily drank little of it when the brew arrived, then shook her head as if to say, "Take it away." She slept fitfully through the night.

James fell asleep in the Windsor chair he'd brought back in the room. It was uncomfortable rest, and he awoke regularly to a stiff neck and aching body before reaching to his wife to check her pulse and breathing. Her vital signs were erratic, an indication that her body was struggling to fight the infection. "Thank God you're a strong woman," he whispered to her. James leaned back in the chair and waited.

He awoke at dawn. His back ached to lie prone on the bed beside his wife. He longed to take his accustomed place, but not at the expense of making her more uncomfortable. He stood and rubbed the kinks from his neck and back, then reached over to check on his sleeping wife. In the half light, he kissed her forehead, then quickly stood up, fully awake now. Reaching over her, he placed both hands on the bed next to each of her thin shoulders and looked straight down into her face. "Lily," he said firmly. He shook the bed. "Lily!" James placed his head to her breast, then fell back in the chair. "Lily," he whispered.

— ♦ —

Ireland
June 10, 1882
Biddy

At eight thirty in the morning, Biddy was standing at the kitchen sink, washing the last of the breakfast dishes, when a chill swept over her. The plate in her hand slipped, shattering into unmendable pieces on the floor. "Dear God in heaven," she said, and crossed herself twice.

CHAPTER 35

THE ENGAGEMENT PARTY

Dublin, Ireland

Upstairs in their bedrooms, the Youngs were getting ready for Elfie's engagement party. Thomas had long since dressed and was sitting in his chair, waiting until he heard his daughters open their doors. He thought it would be nice for the three of them to walk out together. He wished Sarah could be there to share in their youngest girl's engagement. She'd been twenty-two, eight years younger than Elfie was now, when he first met and fell in love with her. Their families allowed them to "keep company" after meetings at their Swedenborgian church, which eventually led to slow walks down country lanes, never taking the most direct path, ending at her home, where her father waited at the door for the safe return of his daughter.

Elfie is at a good time in her life, love's first blush, he thought, tenderly. *Hold on to the good times, my dear.*

Frances had chosen what to wear weeks earlier. A black skirt with a white blouse would not compete in any way with Elfie's dress, though the skirt she removed from the wardrobe was anything but simple. She had reason to stand out, which is why she was pairing the outfit with her mother's small diamond earrings and the citrine fob from her aunt Zadie. From the wardrobe, Frances retrieved her ivory satin blouse and put it on. The blouse opened at the neck, with draped lapels falling to each side in soft folds, framing the exposed skin on her neck in a modest *v*. Next, she buttoned the long, black watermarked taffeta skirt around her waist. A long diagonal ruffle fell from the right side of the waistband down to the hem, which skimmed the floor with an inch to spare. Slipping on her black kid shoes, she examined herself in the mirror. The shoes peeped out from beneath the skirt hem, showing off small grosgrain bows at each toe speckled with gold. *If there is an eligible man at the party, he won't help but notice me,* she told herself. "You may have missed your chance, Mr. Giles Morgan."

Elfie sat before her dressing-table mirror, putting on her mother's jewelry. She wanted to feel her presence at her side that night. The signet ring from Lily and James was already on her pinky finger. "Oh, Lily! I wish you and your family were here," she said, clasping her ringed hand to her breast. Elfie opened the second layer of her jewelry box and removed the tortoiseshell comb bearing her initials, ASY, in gold script. The comb was George's engagement gift to her from London. Replacing it with her brush, she swept up her hair the way George liked it, exposing her ears and neck, and secured her hair with the comb. With her index finger, she softly touched her slightly rouged lips, then turned her head side to side, admiring the whole effect. "Mother, your pearl drop earrings look so lovely with my hair up and away from my face," she said, smiling widely. "I feel . . . elegant." She blushed. It was a word she normally reserved for her sisters. Closing her thin gold bracelet around her wrist, she was done with the adornments. Frances had taken her to Madame Violette, who had chosen a celadon green velvet for her. "The color compliments your hazel eyes, does it not," the woman had said more than asked. Elfie didn't disagree. Her mother used to say she had magic eyes, and the dress looked beautiful on her. "Tonight, everything feels like magic!" she exclaimed to her image in the mirror.

Biddy and Mary had agreed to spend the evening with the girls, and George, who was busy in town, arranged for a carriage to come fetch them at six o'clock. All was in hand.

The carriage arrived at the house promptly at five thirty. Biddy and Mary saw them off, waving from the porch, the girls crowded around them blowing kisses to Miss Elfie and giggling in their excitement. Thomas, Frances, and Elfie chatted nervously, followed by long spells of quiet as the carriage approached the city, making its way to Stephen's Green Club. Outside the club, Thomas escorted Elfie and Frances to the Ladies door, then returned to the main entrance (for men only). Elfie's pulse raced. Frances winked at her. "Well, here goes, Elfie," she said. "We finally made it in the club!" They shared a laugh, and the door opened to admit them inside. Once the sisters stepped into the well-lit vestibule, their wraps were taken from them by a butler. "I will escort you to the dining room. Mr. Fenn has arranged for the celebration," he said upon his return. Sharing smiles, they followed the butler down the hall toward an open door where light streamed out onto the deep-red carpeting.

"Welcome, my dear ladies," George greeted them when

they stepped inside the room. Elfie's heart skipped when George took her hand and kissed it. He gave Frances a kiss on the cheek and whispered, "I hope you enjoy the evening, Frannie." A blush instantly heated her cheeks. It was not an innocent blush but one that came from her hackles rising. Her childhood family name was rarely used, and she felt it had to be earned. Composing herself, she followed George and Elfie, glancing discreetly around the room for a friend. *Drop the petty thoughts, Frances,* she scolded herself, then nearly stopped walking when she caught sight of Giles Morgan.

All of Louise's previous planning to get them together for dinner had been for naught, as Giles had been in England since they'd met at the lecture. Somehow, here he was, deep in conversation with her father. Frances quickly returned her attention to George and Elfie, who led her straight to Elizabeth. "How wonderful to see you, Elizabeth!" Frances said. "I've so enjoyed our exchange of letters, but it's even better to see you in person. I've envied Elfie that."

Before the two women could get into a conversation, Elfie excused herself to Elizabeth and hooked her arm into her sister's to introduce her to two of George's closest friends. Frances had to force herself not to look back for Giles Morgan. *He should come to me, shouldn't he? If he's interested,* she thought. Within minutes, her friends Olive and Louise appeared at her side with their husbands, and Elfie introduced everyone. Louise soon put her arm around Frances's waist and causally glided her away from the group over to where Giles and her father stood.

"Mrs. Davies," Thomas said to Louise, stepping back to include the two women. "It's been a long time since you've come to visit us at RockView. How are your mother and father? Mr. Morgan, you and I must continue this important subject over lunch one day. Will you excuse me? Mrs. Davies and I have some catching up to do." Frances was amazed at her father's sensitivity and smooth departure. She turned to Giles. "You must tell me what the fascinating subject is."

It seemed like only minutes before George called for the group's attention. "Does everyone have a drink to their liking? I would like to propose a toast." Elfie looked up at him with deep affection. "Thank you all for coming tonight to celebrate with Elfie and me and the Young family. My daughter, Elizabeth, represents the Fenn clan, having traveled here from London. She was a student at the Misses Young School for six good years, so she quite properly feels part of both families! The rest of you are important friends we want to share our happiness with. To Miss Elfie, you have my love and affection. I feel so fortunate to have found you." He bent and gave Elfie a kiss on both cheeks and finally the lips.

She lifted her glass and touched his, turning to the audience. "I can be such a talker, but I find I am quite speechless tonight. Thank you, George. Thank you, all, so very much for being here. This is the happiest moment of my life." The ring of fine crystal goblets meeting filled the room, along with a chorus of "Cheers."

Thomas cleared his throat and lifted his glass to the couple to make his toast. "This will be quick, I promise," he said to the room. "Godspeed, my children. Enjoy every moment." Everyone clapped, took a sip, and at George and Elfie's invitation began to move to their seats for dinner.

Place cards had been set, with Elfie's attention to her sister's welfare made clear. Giles helped Frances into her chair before sitting down at his place beside her. The two fell quickly into conversation regarding their mutual interest in the Zoological Society of Ireland's recent magazine series on Charles Darwin's theories of evolution. Giles said he was aghast that there were still skeptics questioning the ideas of survival of the fittest and natural selection. To which Frances related a recent trip to the zoo with the girls from the school that still astounded her. "Our guide spoke to them in the aviary, where he pointed out the finches and told Darwin's Galapagos story. Martha Emmons—who is only ten years old, mind you—piped up with 'I wonder if natural selection will favor the Irish. My brother says they do all the hard work.' Fortunately, our guide seemed more amused than shocked. I think she was quite sincere. It does show that children are more aware of the forces around them than we would think."

Giles, impressed with her candor, was delighted. "I believe our children's lives will certainly be marked by Ireland's evolution, or the lack of it, Miss Young," he said. "We have a lot to learn from them."

The meal was served, and Frances leaned toward him. "Please call me Frances," she said.

When dessert was served, Frances noticed the butler approaching George, who then excused himself to Elfie and left the room. Frances was relieved when he returned a few minutes later and might have thought no further about it had George not offered an explanation. As the evening drew to a close, he stood up to thank Elfie and their friends and family for joining in the celebration. He begged for their indulgence for his brief absence earlier. "I learned that Charles Parnell was in the main dining room tonight. We met years ago, when my daughter was a girl, and I wanted to say hello. Well, not only did I have the opportunity to greet the famous man, he introduced me to his dining companion, Michael Davitt, a leader in land reform and founder of the Land League!" George couldn't contain his excitement at his discovery. "I'm sure you are aware these men are making a bold move to couple Home Rule with agrarian reform. To think such an important thing could be happening right in this building, tonight. I admire their courage, and I hope they will be successful."

The guests were quiet in response to the unexpected

announcement. Frances was mortified and thought, *What is the man thinking, bringing politics to my sister's engagement party?* Elfie smiled at George. Frances couldn't be certain there was sincerity behind it.

Suddenly, Giles stood up next to her and raised his glass. "Here is to a better, more peaceful future for Ireland," he said. The words "Hear, hear!" slowly, then enthusiastically spread around the room, and the tension was broken. Frances placed her hand on Giles's arm and whispered, "Thank you." She felt nearly overcome with gratitude.

Later, in the dining room and hallway, guests bid one another good night. Giles thanked Elfie and George for the evening, then returned to Frances. He bowed and thanked her for the conversation, said a warm "Good night," then left to retrieve his cloak. Frances watched his retreat, hoping for a backward glance, but there was not one.

Sensing someone beside her, she turned and saw her father. He placed his hand lightly on her back and smiled. The two of them retraced their steps, meeting their driver at the street and climbing into the carriage. After a few words, they remained silent on the ride home, holding their own counsel. Frances held the citrine fob on the long gold chain around her neck in her right hand and turned it compulsively. However irritated she'd been with George, he seemed to truly care for her sister. *He is loyal,* she thought, *and sincere. Elfie is lucky to have someone she can count on, someone who cares for her so much, someone who turns to catch her eye when he has to leave her.*

Sitting opposite his daughter, Thomas was in his own world. He had enjoyed the wine and the company that night, not to mention the political excitement of Parnell's and Davitt's presence in the house. He had suspected there might be something between Frances and Giles Morgan, but it seemed not. *I wonder what happened?*

— ◆ —

Elfie arrived at RockView in a separate carriage with George after they left Elizabeth at a hotel. Inside the foyer, the couple found Frances and Thomas waiting for them. Biddy and Mary were there too, their heads bowed and leaning into each other. Elfie saw her father, looking white as a sheet, staring at a telegram. Frances was at his side, her hand on his shoulder. "Father?" Elfie asked.

It was Frances who answered her. "Oh, Elfie!" she said, weeping. "Our sister is gone."

CHAPTER 36

CHROME HILL

London, Ontario, Canada
August
James

Bedtime rituals took longer now. Lucie came into the boys' room, and James listened to his children's random, sometimes anxious thoughts and precious silly stories before they said their prayers. Lily was always there. "Please, God, take care of Mother," each of her children prayed. Always, he would kiss the boys good night, pull their covers close to their little faces, and turn out the light, then walk Lucie to her room, where he would kiss her good night and tuck in the covers, something she hadn't wanted since she was a very little girl. Alone, he would retire to the drawing room.

James sat in his chair as he had for the past month and stared at the unlit fireplace, sipping a watered-down glass of whiskey until he was sleepy enough to go to bed.

At some point, he glanced toward Lily's chair, but seeing the emptiness, his eyes moved to the settee. His mother's bright choice of fabric jumped at him. *Never mind that her daughter-in-law might have had ideas of her own on how to decorate our house,* he thought bitterly. Lily hadn't really minded. She'd appreciated Eliza's dramatic, if unsolicited, gift, seeing it as intended: an offer of style and excitement from a good heart. "Eliza is not my mother," Lily explained, "and that makes it easier to accept. Besides, your mother has shown me how to be bolder in both thought and deed." James shook his head at the memory. The two women were so different. Lily's kind nature had made the relationship work. His willful mother was still very much alive. . . . *Mother loved Lily too,* he scolded himself. *Why not? Lily was lovable.*

In Eliza's condolence letter, she had encouraged James to do his best for the children. *Why would she assume I would do anything less?* he thought, feeling the bitterness slip back in. *Because she failed so miserably with me?* He finished his glass and stood up to pour himself another. Considering another possibility, his temper softened. Had she finally understood the impact of her pathetic behavior toward her son when his father died? James drew a deep breath and sighed. That time in his childhood could not be remade, but he could and would do better than his mother had. He put the bottle of whiskey down and turned out the lights. Without thinking, he sat down on the settee in the dark instead of retiring to the bedroom.

James thought back to his father's death. *I was three years older than Lucie at the time,* he thought, *and I still feel his loss.* He had been given the news by his headmaster. Walking alone from his classroom along the long hallway and down the stairs to the office, his mind had searched for a reason for Dr. Westfield's summons. What rule could he have broken? Had he written in a book? Tucked in his bedsheets poorly? He knocked on the heavy oak door. Dr. Westfield opened it himself, inviting James inside. The man was stooped with age and his hair was white, but he carried a stern authority. Dr. Westfield told him of his father's death without preamble, and James stared at floor, looking up only when the headmaster reminded him that he was twelve years old. "Old enough to be the man of the house now," the man said firmly. "Your family needs you at home, James. When things are settled, come back to St. Ready's. We will welcome your return."

At Chrome Hill, Fiona, their housekeeper, had met him at the door. Behind her were three men: his father's solicitor, Alexander Foxworth; the Reverend Samuel Kind; and Dr. Simpson, their family doctor. Simpson moved forward to shake his hand, but James stood frozen on the porch. The doctor stepped through the doorway and put his hand on James's shoulder instead. Together they walked through the door and into the library. The two other men followed. This was the room where his father sat in the evenings before and after dinner. It smelled of leather, moldy books, and his father's cigars. James remembered that he had cried then. He had never been in the room without his father's invitation, but he allowed the doctor to lead him to his father's overstuffed leather chair by the fireplace and, feeling small, sat on its front edge. Reverend Kind sat next to him in the chair where his mother sat whenever she joined his father after dinner. When James was home from boarding school, he would sometimes be invited in to sit in front of the fire, adding a piece of wood at his father's direction and poking it with the iron rod by the hearth to watch the sparks fly up the chimney. The best times were when his father would choose a book from the shelves to read out loud to him.

The other two men had settled on the stiff couch on the opposite side of the room, watching him. James didn't know what they expected of him. "My father?" he whispered, and suddenly they seemed to speak to him all at once.

"Your father is with God now. You must take solace in that."

"A freak accident with the carriage."

"He did not suffer long."

Their words were meant to soothe. Instead, they made him angry. If he was a man now, he needed to know the truth. His father always told him the truth was best, and now he understood. He wanted to know exactly what occurred. He didn't want to imagine something that wasn't true. "But how did he die?" he asked them. The men fell silent and looked at each other. "Dr. Simpson," James said, looking directly at the man as he had seen his father do when addressing those who worked for him. "I need to know about my father, and someone must tell me if my mother is all right. Where is she?" He felt in control of himself. *As a man should,* he thought.

James had been assured that his mother was fine, "taken to her bed with a sedative from the doctor." The men told him what they knew of the accident. His father had chosen to ride on top with his coachman on the way to work. A wheel broke, and the carriage had toppled. Both men had died.

The doctor got up and took a seat on the arm of the chair where James sat with his toes just touching the floor. He put his arm around James and pulled him close. "This is a shock for you, for all of us."

The Reverend Kind followed with "Your father was a wonderful man, James. We know from experience, my dear boy, that time and faith help us heal. You will remember your father, and your life will mend and go on." The words were gentle but not helpful to James. He felt alone. With reassurances they would handle all the "details" and visit often, the three men said their farewells and left Chrome Hill.

It was Fiona who had brought him to see his mother. She was asleep, the sedative doing its work. James stood beside her bed wondering how their lives had changed so quickly. On her best of days, his mother was emotional, controlling, and given to drama. He feared for the two of them without his father's leveling hand.

The following months were dark in his memory; it was a long time ago. James remembered that he and his mother had lived a ghostly life in the mansion for too long. He missed his father. His mother was inconsolable. She lay in bed for weeks, clutching his hand when he visited her, refusing to let him out of her sight, until the doctor appeared, soothing her with another sedative. Fiona later told James, "'Twas like she was livin' outside in the damp chill of Northern Ireland, wishin' for death from the cold. You, poor child. You were trapped by all of it."

The loss of Lily felt unbearable. For the first time, James had some sympathy for his mother. He would always be grateful for Dr. Simpson's visits to his mother after his father's death. James had come to understand that the doctor had also helped with his return to St. Ready's. Eliza, under the influence of the opiates the doctor prescribed and feeling stronger with a man to rely upon, had relaxed her grip on her son and let him return to school.

That dear doctor, thought James, pulling up the distant memory.

He had been too young at that time to see how the drugs his mother took put her in danger of remaining forever somber, introverted, and addicted. As a doctor, he was chilled to think she might have been lost forever. Once again Dr. Simpson had rescued them. Over time, he encouraged Eliza to find new reasons to live and carefully withdrew the opiates.

Still, over the next eight years of his childhood, James remained a strong focus of his mother's life and controlling hand. Only once he left for college did she begin to use her energy to improve the lives and education of the people employed in the family's chemical dye business. He had almost felt sorry for them. James knew his mother's intelligence. Once focused, she was a force to be reckoned with.

James had suppressed these dark memories. His desire to make a life for his family away from his mother's well-meaning control had driven him to Canada. James never wanted his own children to feel or experience what he had. His role was now to provide comfort and as much normalcy as possible for Lucie, Hugh, and Knox.

He would set a better example. His children needed him. Lucie was so young, but she would see herself as a mother to her younger brothers. If he wasn't careful, she might feel she needed to care for him, too. *Exactly what drove Lily from Ireland,* he thought. "I promise you, Lily," James whispered, "I will not let that happen."

CHAPTER 37

FULL OF THE UNEXPECTED

Dublin, Ireland
November

Five months after Lily's death, the Youngs exchanged their black mourning clothes for half-mourning apparel: George and Thomas wore a black band on an arm of their coats. The sisters pinned a jet brooch on their lilac or brown clothes. Biddy and Mary, who had found it difficult to wash the grease from their black aprons without ruining the material, were happy to put them aside for black handkerchiefs pinned to their usual white aprons. The sadness of Lily's passing remained, but the family agreed she would have been the first to trade her mourning black for something more hopeful.

Elfie had refused to begin making lists for her wedding while dressed in black. She and George were to be married the coming August, and while it was only November, she was eager to begin the planning. *Lily, of all people, would understand,* she thought. She hoped James would too. He had sent his regrets for not attending the wedding in a brief letter updating the Youngs on the welfare of his children. "I am saddened Lucie, Hugh, Knox, and I will not be attending Elfie and George's upcoming nuptials as hoped," he had written. There had been no explanation given, leaving Elfie wondering if he felt next August too soon for a family celebration.

"I should think quite the contrary," Frances had said, not bothering to hide her irritation. "What better way to honor Lily's memory than to spend time with her family in Ireland? Besides, a change of scenery would be good for James and healthy and healing for the children." All three of the Youngs were disappointed with James's decision, but agreed to leave it to Eliza to change her son's mind, as they had no doubt she would try to do.

Since the engagement party last summer, the Youngs had settled into a new pattern that included George. He not only continued to visit with Elfie and engage in long discussions with Thomas but also made time to sit in the kitchen with Biddy and Mary, sharing news he thought they would be interested to know.

Frances's resistance to George was softening. "He has had some positive effect on our lives," she told a smiling Elfie.

"I'm so happy you feel it too, Frances!" Elfie said. "I feel George has brought a renewed spirit to RockView." Frances wasn't certain she would go that far—she still hadn't found a teacher to replace her sister or a helper to tide them over—but didn't spoil the moment by saying so.

George tested the changing atmosphere by suggesting a dinner party for the publisher and editors of the *Nation* and their wives. "I may only be an investor in the paper, but I have no interest in being a silent one. They need to get to know the families who read the *Nation*, and what better family to begin with than the intelligent and thoughtful Young family," he announced.

Thomas thought it a fine idea. Elfie looked to Frances, who shrugged her approval. George's ideas involving the Youngs no longer distressed her. Once they were married, Mr. and Mrs. Fenn could hold dinner parties in their own home, and she could be the guest.

In truth, Frances enjoyed having a reason to bring life back to RockView and volunteered to help Elfie plan for the evening. Thomas sent out for cigars and whiskey for the men, to which his daughters responded by ordering a bouquet of flowers as a kind of oversized nosegay to separate the seating in the drawing room after dinner.

The night of the dinner, George surprised everyone by arriving to RockView early. He brought flowers for Elfie, wine for Thomas, and a worn Moroccan-red leather-bound edition of *Jane Eyre* by Charlotte Brontë for his sister-in-law-to-be. "Frances, I thought you might enjoy this." He held the book out to her with both hands. "I found this exquisite book in a shop a few days ago. I am sure you have read it, but I hope you will enjoy having this special edition. It includes beautiful etchings of Jane, Rochester, and Thornfield Hall."

Frances had read *Jane Eyre*. Several times. Her own copy was well worn and familiar in her hands, but she felt the sincerity of the gesture. "Thank you, George," she said, genuinely touched. "This is very thoughtful of you." They nodded to one another, and Elfie thought they looked like two retiring gladiators acknowledging a draw. *At last,* she thought. No more needed to be said. The war was over, and peace was made, at least for now.

"Now," George said. "If you'll all indulge me, please follow me to the kitchen. Bring the wine, Thomas. We'll need it." Half frowning, half smiling at the air of suspense George had conjured, the Youngs followed him into the steamy realm where Biddy and Mary were preparing dinner.

Biddy turned from the stove to look up at the four of them. "To what do we owe this honor?" she asked.

In his excitement, George skipped the buildup he had planned and announced in a rush, "Mrs. Biddy Gossett, Norah will be released from prison tomorrow!"

There was a stunned silence, followed by gasps and hugs among the Youngs. Biddy burst into tears. After one very long year and a half, she had nearly lost hope of seeing her daughter again. Elfie, Frances, and Mary applauded, thrilled by the unexpected news, and Thomas opened the wine, pouring a glass for each of them. Through Biddy's tears, they toasted the happy occasion. Biddy hugged Mary, dampening her cousin's shoulder, then sat at the table, feeling too overwhelmed to stand any longer.

"George," Elfie asked, "what changed? How did you manage to free Norah?"

"I cannot take all the credit, my dear," he replied. "Biddy, I want you and Conor and Norah to know there are some very fine men in this world—friends of mine, actually, from my Cambridge days—who understood the injustice and did all they could to secure Norah's freedom." George sat across from Biddy. "Norah will be watched by a probation authority," he said gently. "She will have to mind her behavior, be careful with the people she chooses to be seen with, and find a place to work, but she will be out." Biddy nodded her head to show she understood, but she could not stop crying.

"Biddy," Mary said, "If the Youngs don't mind, I can finish cooking and serve dinner on me own tonight."

"Another fine idea," Thomas said.

Mary took her cousin's hand and gently helped her up from her seat. "Go tell Conor and the boys. This is your night for a tipple with your family at home, not working here in this kitchen. Go on." Biddy nodded and wiped her nose with her kerchief. She looked dazed, as if she barely heard Mary's words. With help from Thomas, who quietly slipped into her hand enough money for a carriage ride home, Biddy pulled on her coat, took up her basket, and walked out the back door. Her Norah was coming home.

— ♦ —

Two hours later, Mary patted her cheeks with cold water, put on a fresh apron and cap, and served the Youngs, Mr. Fenn, and their guests a fine meal of pork roast with baked apple slices and mashed turnip and parsnips, a favorite of Thomas's. Mary glowed with uncharacteristic smiles and enthusiasm as she moved about the room, causing Thomas to share a wink with his smiling daughters. The conversation about culture and travel that filled the dining room changed to humanist philosophy and the Brits' latest affronts in Ireland once the group retired to the drawing room. Frances and Elfie were pleasantly surprised to find the women as well informed and interested in the subjects as their husbands. Despite the flower arrangements, conversation flowed pleasantly across the room.

"What a delightful evening," Frances whispered to Elfie, who smiled in agreement. "Have you noticed how diplomatically the wives disagree with their husbands?"

"We should invite them back to give lessons to our girls!" Elfie said.

Later than anyone had planned, the evening came to an end. Frances had sent Mary home an hour ago, with Mary promising to arrive early to finish the cleanup. "I expect Biddy will want to be with Conor and the boys at the gaol in the morning, Miss Frances," she explained.

Once the guests had departed, George said his goodnights to Thomas and Frances. In a rare moment alone, he held Elfie's hands tightly as they stood in the foyer, reluctant to release them. His flat in Kingstown wasn't far. He might have found a reason to stay longer, but it was already after ten o'clock, and they'd had a heady evening of wine, whiskey, and discussion. Elfie glanced upstairs to be sure there were no watchful eyes from the girls' floor, then, standing on her toes, she kissed George, first on his cheek, and then directly on his lips. It was on her request that they had waited so long to be intimate; she felt only right then to be the one to be bold now.

George wrapped his arms around her, pressing her against him as their kiss deepened and lingered. "I love you dearly, Elfie," he whispered in her ear.

He loosened his embrace, but she did not move. "I love you dearly, George," she whispered back.

George led her by the hand outside to the porch, where he kissed her hands and held them to his face, ignoring the coachman watching from the street. Not feeling the least cold in the chilly night air, Elfie watched until George climbed into the coach and closed the door before turning back into the house. She turned the heavy lock on the door, put out the light in the hall, and went upstairs feeling happy and hopeful about her future and very relieved for the Gossetts. Norah was going home. George had seen to that. Her wonderful George. *Father is so very right,* she thought. *Life is full of the unexpected.*

Once in her room, Elfie quickly settled in bed, pulling the warm comforter under her chin. Her thoughts were full of her husband-to-be and their kiss. She giggled, feeling deliriously happy, until the conversations earlier that night worked themselves to the front of her mind. Elfie had been especially disturbed to hear about the violent measures proposed by the Fenians and the subsequent resistance from the Anglo-Irish and British. If she believed the newspapermen, tensions were high in many of Ireland's cities, with no way to stop the terrorists' plans as their groups were loosely organized. *That can't be right,* Elfie thought. *George and his cronies found a way to save Norah, and that had seemed impossible! We were only just celebrating her release a few hours ago.* Elfie sighed. *Why is it,* she wondered, *that good news is so often followed by bad?* Her thoughts moved to Biddy and her family, falling asleep relieved and happy tonight, and then her body remembered the kiss she'd shared with George. Elfie smiled, a dreamy, happy smile. She reached for the pillow next to her and wrapped her arms around it, longing for the day she would be sleeping with George's arms wrapped around her.

Elfie was the first one up in the morning. She quickly dressed and quietly walked downstairs to make herself a cup of tea. Mary would be arriving soon. Elfie hoped Biddy and Conor would stop by on the way to pick up Norah so she could wish them well, but she didn't imagine they would. *They may well have been up through the night talking,* she imagined, *and are sleeping in this morning.* Then she corrected herself. Conor did not strike her as the kind of man—no matter what the situation—who would miss a good night's sleep, certainly not to talk with his wife. A delicious smile grew across her lips as she thought of the nights she and George would share. She took a deep breath and let it out quickly. *When the time is right,* she told herself.

Elfie poured her tea and had pulled her chair up to the kitchen table when both Biddy and Mary came bustling in, talking a streak. They were breathless with the news of a tannery fire and explosion during the night. Elfie held her teacup midair. "Tannery fire?" she said.

"Oh yes!" Mary exclaimed.

"I'm surprised you didn't hear the explosion even way up here," Biddy added.

"I certainly heard it," Mary said. "I'd been home just over an hour when it happened. Like a roll of distant thunder."

Elfie stood up, nearly dropping her cup on the table. "An

explosion?" she asked. "At the tannery George passes on the way to Kingstown? What time last night did you say?"

Biddy and Mary grew quiet. "I'm not certain, Miss Elfie," Biddy said. "But there's no news of anyone hurt." Biddy and Mary exchanged glances. "Mary, wake Miss Frances and Mr. Young before seeing to the girls," Biddy said. "I'll take care of the breakfast. I'm sure Mr. Fenn is all right, Miss Elfie, or we'd have heard."

"Biddy," Elfie said, keeping her voice steady, "you need to be with your family to meet Norah."

"Don't you worry about that, Miss Elfie. Conor and the boys are already waiting outside for her. There's no telling what time she'll be let out today. I'll be joining them soon, sure enough." Biddy poured Elfie a fresh cup of tea, stirring in a spoonful of sugar for the shock. "We'd have heard something, Miss Elfie," she said again, though she wasn't at all certain that was true. Biddy waited in the kitchen until Mr. Young and Miss Frances came in to sit with Miss Elfie before she slipped outside to pick up the newspaper. The *Nation* was a weekly and wasn't expected, but the *Post* was waiting for her on the back stoop. She picked up the paper and scanned the pages. There was nothing about the tannery explosion that she could see. Biddy felt a tremendous relief.

She had turned to go back inside with the paper when she heard a carriage stop by the front of the house. She frowned, wondering who would bother the Youngs so early in the morning. Two men dressed in black and wearing somber expressions stepped out of the cab and walked up to the front door of RockView. Biddy waited with her hand pressed against her mouth, listening as the knocker rapped against the door a second time before Mr. Young appeared to let the men inside. She could hardly take in the truth of what it all meant. There was nothing to do but return to the kitchen where she would be needed.

CHAPTER 38

CLARA MOORE

London, Ontario, Canada
February 1883
James

James made his way along the long entry hall of the University of Western Ontario, his steps echoing through the emptiness. Classes were over, the students gone for the day. Murals along the walls depicted classical figures representing the institution's areas of study: art, divinity, and medicine. Local medical training pleased him. The province needed more doctors, and he could use assistants and, someday, a replacement. The population seemed to be increasing without end.

Learning there would soon be a university in their city had been a source of great excitement for James and Lily. When Western at last opened its doors two years ago, James and Lily were among the first to visit. Without her at his side, walking the same hallways was a painful exercise. She was the outgoing one, cheerfully greeting the instructors and professors, extending a dinner invitation to the dean and his wife. Her intelligence and curiosity brought an energy to his life that had left with her. Why had he bothered to come today?

A shaft of light from an open door caught his eye and he walked toward it. On the other side of the door stood a tall, slim, well-dressed young woman at the front of a large room. She was being introduced by the dean to a group of the people standing around her. Her eyes lifted and she turned her head toward James, beckoning him inside with a wave of her hand. James felt a familiar flickering of interest.

As he stepped forward, a young man burst in from James's left side, thrusting a hand forward to shake his. "Good afternoon, Dr. Niven, sir," he said. "We are so glad you could join us today for the celebration. I am Oliver Monroe, student ambassador. I'm in my first year of medical studies. I was told to look for you." The young man's face beamed. If Monroe noticed he did not have James's full attention, it did not stop him from continuing with his declarations. "I have very much wanted to meet you, sir, and visit your practice."

James averted his eyes from the woman and smiled at the young man. "Yes, yes, of course, Monroe," he said, patting the young man on his shoulder.

"I hope we can speak after the tour, Dr. Niven. My duties are currently with Miss Moore." The young man glanced back at the woman, and James took his chance to move in her direction, forcing himself to stop at an appropriate distance.

She smiled. *A beautiful smile,* James thought.

"Dr. Niven," the dean said, reaching out to shake his hand. "We are pleased you could join us today. This is Miss Clara Moore, vice provost of Western."

"Good evening, Dr. Niven," Miss Moore said. "We were

hoping you would come. The university's medical school is eager to engage our students in community practices like yours."

James, distracted by her proximity and foreknowledge of him, nearly stated how impressed he was at her position at the university. He had never heard of a woman vice provost, or a woman of any advanced station at a university. Lily and her suffragettes would have scolded him for the assumption. *Clara Moore must be an exceptional woman,* he thought. "Pleased to meet you, Miss Moore," he said. She held his gaze and raised her eyebrows. James was flustered. Had he said something wrong? "Yes, of course," he answered, understanding at last. "I would be glad to speak with you about the possibility of engaging your students in our practice, Miss Moore."

The dean excused himself to the visitors, leaving Clara Moore in charge, with Oliver Monroe by her side. She lifted her hand gracefully and called for the attention of the assembled guests. "We are all here now, so let me begin our tour of the new teaching facilities we celebrate today, and afterward we will return to this room to toast the future of Western." James followed along, only realizing as the tour drew to a close that he'd been smiling the entire time.

The room where they'd started and now returned to held platters of canapés and poured glasses of wine and champagne. Miss Moore was immediately surrounded by the other visitors. James picked up a glass of champagne from the buffet and made his way into the circle where Miss Moore was speaking to a local barrister. She was charming the man, and he looked like he was enjoying it. James was impressed and amused at how skillfully she fluffed up the old boy to fund the expansion into his field. James knew him. Four months earlier he had removed the man's angry appendix. One of the problems with being a doctor was that you forevermore saw your patients in human terms, minus the degrees and finery. Miss

Moore seemed to have the ability to make the degrees and finery of others work for her. *Clever,* he thought, *like Lily.*

There was a lull in the conversation, and without thinking, James told Miss Moore he would be happy to provide real-life opportunities for the university's medical students. It was a generous offer, one he should have discussed with his partner first, but the words had tumbled out. "Your young ambassador, Oliver Monroe, has already asked if he could visit my practice," he said by way of explanation. "They will be helpful for us, too, as the number of patients we serve is growing rapidly."

Miss Moore seemed pleased. "That is a very generous offer, Dr. Niven," she said. "Perhaps we could find a time to discuss it further?" James saw her cheeks blush and he paused, unable to read the moment. "It would be my pleasure, Miss Moore," he answered.

James left the building with his mood pleasantly lifted. He hoped Cattermole would be accepting of his spur-of-the-moment invitation to have medical students underfoot. Once again, James was reminded how fast life could pivot. For the first time since Lily's death, he felt he was looking forward, not backward.

An invitation to meet with Miss Moore and the dean of the medical school arrived two days later.

With Cattermole's wary blessing—"Don't want too many eager young men following us around, old man"—the decision was made to accommodate two students to assist them in the surgery and to go along on house calls. "On a trial basis only," he said, to which James, and later the dean and Miss Moore, heartily agreed.

At the end of their meeting, Miss Moore rose from her chair and escorted James to the door. He felt a slight electric current pass through him, resulting in a disconnection between his brain and tongue. He had no question now about his attraction to her, and he was almost certain she felt the same. With her hand on the doorknob, she turned and said demurely, "Out of this office and off these grounds you may call me Clara."

There was no uncertainty now of her meaning, but James hesitated. He was a recent widower still in love with his wife. Then there had been George Fenn's death following so closely after Lily's. That news had further upset him. He often considered how close Elfie had come to having the happy life she sought. *How terribly sad life can be,* he thought. *How terribly sad I've been.* James opened his mouth to thank Miss Moore and be on his way when he thought of something Lily used to say: "Look for the opportunities."

"If I am not being too forward, Miss Moore," James said, regaining control, "I hope we have the opportunity to meet again soon."

"I would like that very much," Clara answered, returning his steady gaze.

— ◆ —

Three months later, James proposed, and to his delight Clara accepted. All he needed to do now was find a way to tell the children.

CHAPTER 39

THE SUBJECT OF LUCIE

May 1884
James

James stared out the window from the warmth of his bed. He had not slept solidly for weeks. His new wife, snoring softly beside him, seemed to have no such problem. He had not expected home life to be the same as with Lily, but he never imagined encountering difficulties that would keep him up at night. *Clara and Lucie are both strong personalities,* he thought. *As was Lily.* Marian had noticed it too. Last week, when he had stepped outside once again to remove himself from the tension within the house, she had walked over to him while keeping an eye on the boys playing in the garden.

"Your Lucie knows her mind," she'd said.

"She is very much like her mother," James agreed.

"And maybe like Mrs. Clara?" Marian suggested.

He smiled thinking of it now. A strong mind was a quality

he admired in all three of them. But nearly a year had passed since he remarried, and neither Clara nor Lucie had yet to make much effort toward creating a harmonious relationship. James frowned. Lily had known her own mind, and yet she and Lucie had hardly exchanged a cross word. James pushed his fist into his pillow and lay his head in the pocket.

Lily would have told him that if he wanted to sleep, he should focus on the good in his life. He found that advice easier said than done. *There's Clara, of course,* he thought. He appreciated her efforts to guide the children and the household. But there was the rub. Her determination often created more discord than ease in the house, especially with his daughter. Lucie had grown sullen from the moment Clara moved into their home. *She hasn't really given Clara a chance,* James thought, *which seems most unfair.* More than once he'd had to caution his daughter for replying to her stepmother in a mumble. Most recently, Lucie had chosen to sit as far away from the rest of the family as she dared without giving James a reason to scold her. She rarely smiled now, even with her brothers. What had happened to the darling Lucie he knew? James sighed, quietly so as not to wake his wife. His opportunities to observe his family were limited. He did not arrive home until evening and left very early in the morning. The one observation he had made, as both a doctor and her father, was that his young daughter's journey into womanhood had arrived early. That could be part of the problem. In any case, Clara hadn't expressed concern over Lucie's physical changes. Or was it that she chose not to notice? *Or it could be,* he told himself, *I'm worrying about nothing of consequence and our familial situation is better in hand than I realize.* James grimaced and shook his head. He rolled onto his back and scrunched the pillow again with his fist.

The disconcerting thoughts that plagued him during the night nearly always disappeared by the time he reached work the next day. James was a busy man. His days were full—a steady stream of setting bones, sewing up lacerations, inspecting rashes in hidden and not-so-hidden places, depressing coated tongues, and staring down angry throats in kitchens and bedrooms around the community as well as in his examining room at the surgery. When he was at work, he was almost able to forget his concerns about Lucie, until the day a letter arrived at his office from his children's teacher, Miss Levering. The letter did not specify which child she wished to discuss, only that she wished to speak with him at his convenience but sooner than later. *Hugh?* he wondered. He was a smart lad but rambunctious, and could cause disruptions without meaning to. Still, it was hard to dismiss the possibility that Lucie's moodiness extended beyond their home. *No,* he thought, shaking his head. He couldn't imagine Lucie being rude to Miss Levering. The real question was whether he should mention the meeting to Clara. She might be hurt that the teacher had not included her. *Don't overthink this, James,* he cautioned himself. *Best to find out who and what the problem is and then talk with Clara.* He made arrangements to leave the office for an hour that afternoon and sent a reply to Miss Levering that he would meet her directly after school that day.

As he and Count made their way to the schoolhouse, James considered the problem waiting for him there. In his haste to avoid the mistakes his mother had made when his father died, had he sent Hugh and Lucie back to school too soon? Would they have been better off at home a little longer with their little brother and Marian? He had a feeling he was about to learn the answer.

James tied Count to the hitching post outside the school and made his way up the steps. Lily had taken care of the children's educational communication. He'd never even set foot in the school until that day, and he felt slightly nervous. Through the open door he saw Miss Levering sitting behind her desk.

A shaft of afternoon light caught her thick blond hair, woven into two full braids and wrapped neatly around her head. Her white blouse appeared overly starched and stood away from her body, almost like armor, stiff. *Must be scratchy,* he thought.

Miss Levering glanced up and waved him in, greeting him with a friendly smile. James took the small wooden chair she offered on the opposite side of her very deep desk. Its highly polished surface was like a chasm, keeping a cool distance between them. *She's been taught to do this,* he thought, *to protect herself from unwanted advances.* Even so, he sensed they were both uncomfortable.

"Good afternoon, Miss Levering," he began. "Your note said you wanted to meet with me. Well, I am here and curious about what you wish to discuss."

Miss Levering smiled and took back the lead. "Thank you for coming, Dr. Niven," she said softly but firmly. "As I am sure you know, both your children are good, happy students. Lucie has always been a bright, joyous child and a delight in class." She hesitated as James nodded his agreement and then got right to the point. "I am sorry to report that in the past month Lucie has not been herself. She sits out of games in the school-yard and resists entering classroom discussions. This behavior is most unusual for her. Of course, I felt I had to reach out to you to see if you knew what was bothering her. Her normal pattern is to be in the middle of everything, waving her hand to be called on and first to kick the ball."

James shifted uncomfortably on the hard seat of his short-legged perch. How much did he want to say? How much should he say? His family life was no one's concern but his own, and he wasn't used to talking about his private business with any-one other than his wife.

After a long pause, Miss Levering looked directly at him and answered her own question. "Of course the loss of her mother would affect her, Dr. Niven. I know that can be very hard on girls in particular . . . and of course I have met your new wife, but as you've known Lucie all her life, I thought I should ask you if you have noticed any changes in Lucie's behavior at home."

James was taken aback by her straightforwardness. He had noticed changes in her behavior, but he wasn't about to confess to Miss Levering the details of his family life. What if she chose to share it with someone else in the community? The current emotional landscape of his home was complicated and evolving, but that was for his family to figure out. How to articulate that rather obvious fact to Miss Levering without insulting her was the challenge.

Miss Levering didn't strike him as a gossipy busybody type who might like to stir up trouble with a whisper here and there. Still, it was a matter of propriety, wasn't it? He rose from his chair. "Thank you for sharing your concerns about my daughter's behavior," he told her, using his kindest but most authoritative doctor tone of voice. "My wife and I are aware Lucie has a lot to adjust to, and I am, of course, concerned to know that she is not enjoying school as she always has loved it. Thank you for caring about her welfare." He turned to leave.

Miss Levering stood and smiled stiffly. Her arm shot out across the desk to shake his hand. James reciprocated. "Thank you, Dr. Niven," she said, still grasping his hand. "I look forward to hearing from you soon. The summer break is coming in another month, and I think we would both like to see Lucie end her school year on a positive note. I also want to reassure you that you can trust I hold our discussions in the strictest confidence. As a teacher I have your children's best interests at heart, as I know you do too."

James nodded. "Thank you again," he said. He walked out the door feeling Miss Levering's eyes on him. He tried to keep his best posture as he descended the stairs, but in truth he felt like a scolded schoolboy. That old guilt crept back in, whispering, *Is this on you, James?* He sighed. What *was* his role in Lucie's behavior? Miss Levering had made it imperative that he squarely face the causes of his daughter's problems and think about her welfare. His promises to Lily sat uncomfortably in his heart and mind.

He rode at a slow pace back to his office to finish out the day, wondering how to approach Clara on the subject of Lucie. He must handle the news of meeting with Miss Levering carefully. *Clara will likely put up her guard if I suggest that Lucie is not happy,* he thought, *but if I don't speak to her, she could—and quite reasonably so—be upset that she is being treated as an outsider in her own family.* Lucie was their child now.

By the time he'd reached the surgery, he'd decided on a partial plan. It was the same plan he had come up with earlier that day. He needed more information before talking to his wife. He would take Lucie to school the next day to see what he could find out from her. *And no more sitting in my chair at home and letting the rest of the household go on with their business,* he admonished himself, *however much I need the rest.* His practice *was* very busy. Having an eager young wife taxed his energies too. James was almost fifty-two and beginning to feel the years. Still, the liveliness Clara brought to his life made him happy. In many ways, Clara made him feel like a young man again. But he had other responsibilities, and he loved them dearly. *I must pay more attention to the children,* he thought. *But will Clara feel I'm ignoring her?* The very fact that the question occurred to him took him back to the beginning of his problem: *Are these the normal troubles a man has when he remarries with children, or is something else the matter?* James remained perched on his horse, letting himself imagine what it would feel like to turn Count around and race out of town to ride in the forests with abandon. In many ways, being a doctor was much easier for him than being a husband and father. *Fewer emotional variables for me,* he thought. *But also less joy.* Only after he dismounted and entered the surgery did he realize that he had been riding in the rain. He shook off his oilskin coat in the vestibule outside his office and hung it on a hook.

He had a soggy ride home and upon entering the house looked about, but Lucie was nowhere to be seen. *In her room,* he thought, *and likely with the door shut and locked.* That was another new habit of hers that he worried about. He heard giggling come from the parlor, where he spied a blanket hanging unevenly over a table and a small bench sticking out on one side. Hugh and Knox were making a campout in the house because of the dreary weather. Certain he'd find chaos but also happiness under that table, James walked over and lifted a corner of the blanket. Hugh was under the table, and Knox looked happily pinned under the bench. They had treasures in bundles clutched to them, like pirates on the run. "Hello, Papa," Hugh said. "Do you want to come in and join us?" James smiled at the idea of his fitting under the table with Hugh, Knox, and their booty.

"Hmmm . . . ," he said, "I'm not sure I'd fit." Knox wiggled out from under the bench and popped up on the outside of the blanket tent.

"Me neither," he said. "Hello, Papa. Hugh refuses to give me enough space in his den." From under the table Hugh said, "Knox can make his own fort!"

"I'm not going to make a fort. I am tired of this," Knox replied. "I'm going to finish the puzzle." James patted Knox on the shoulder and the boy smiled weakly, then headed to the gaming table where a wooden jigsaw puzzle lay mostly in piles and pieces.

Knox was a quiet boy who would rather retreat than fight, whereas Hugh was energetic, loud, and very much the older brother. The puzzle Knox had chosen was of Canada, with each province delineated. James watched Knox work to put the pieces together. "Good boy, Knox," James said, "You may be our cartographer and Hugh our explorer. He would be lost without you." To which Hugh replied from his blanket den, "Ha!"

James greeted Clara, who was reading in her chair, one James had bought especially for her. Lucie had claimed Lily's chair before Clara's arrival. He kissed Clara on the forehead and asked if she had seen Lucie. Her response was curt, and she kept her eyes focused on her book. "You will find your daughter upstairs."

Your daughter, he thought, feeling the chill. *What happened now?*

He walked up the stairs to Lucie's room and knocked on the door, which he was pleased to discover was unlocked. He found his daughter lying on her bed, staring at the small watercolor painting on the wall. "How are you this evening, Miss Lucie?" he asked, leaning down to give her a kiss on the top of her head. He scooted her over so he could sit by her on the bed.

She peered up at him, and he saw tears on her cheeks. "Clara does not want me here," she said.

"Of course she does," he replied. He felt Lucie not wanting Clara here was closer to the truth, but she had kept her tongue, and James appreciated his daughter's restraint.

"If I lived with Mother's family . . . ," she began.

"Now, Lucie," James said firmly. "We've talked about this." James was no longer shocked about Lucie's suggestion that she move to Ireland. She had brought up the idea soon after Clara became part of their family, and continued to privately speak of it to him as a solution to her disagreements with her stepmother, which were happening with increasing frequency.

Lucie looked down at her knees. "I would miss you and Hugh and Knox terribly," she said.

"And we would miss you, Lucie," he told her. "*All* of us."

"I'm just so unhappy, Father." Lucie started to cry. He

pulled his daughter close to him to embrace her, something he didn't do often enough. She didn't sink into his arms as she once had but sat stiff and determined and stared at the floor. Her resistance to his offer of comfort irritated him.

"Lucie," he said, "I believe we must go down for dinner now."

Lucie shook her head and sniffled. "I'm not hungry, Father." Clara had given him no clue about what had transpired between them, and he considered letting Lucie stay in her room to avoid any further unhappiness. But he didn't want to give in to Lucie's growing willfulness. "We will talk later about what's making you so unhappy," he told her, "*after* we all have dinner. I would also like you to ride to school with me tomorrow morning. How about that?" Lucie blew her nose and wiped her tears. When she gave him a small smile, he felt relieved.

Lucie followed James downstairs without further argument. "Help the boys wash up and bring them to dinner, there's a good girl," he said. His voice was firm but not unkind, and his daughter seemed willing enough to do as he asked. Perhaps all she needed was more direction from him. *Another "perhaps,"* James thought. *Lily would know what to do. But then, these problems wouldn't exist if Lily were here.* He felt guilty about the admission. James continued to miss her, and especially at times like this. He had never imagined he would be able to love two women at the same time. Lucie was on her way to womanhood; soon he would have three women in his life. That was going to be an emotional stretch for James.

Following her brothers into the dining room, Lucie placed her hands on their shoulders, steering them to their seats. Hugh looked up and made faces to make his sister laugh. Lucie half-smiled and put her hand on his head, patting his hair gently. "Hughie, you are so silly." Once the boys were seated, Lucie rounded the table to take her chair across from Hugh and Knox. She sat with her back stiff and eyes downcast. James and

Clara took their places at either end of the table, and James smiled at his family. He reached out to make a circle. Lucie glanced at him, and when he raised an eyebrow she put her arms on the table, closing her eyes before Clara clasped her hand. "Let us pray," James said. "Thank you, God, for this food. Bless it to the use of our bodies. Amen."

"Amen," Clara said crisply. "The food will be getting cold." She held out her hand for her husband to begin the passing of plates in front of him so she could serve the meal. Besides Hugh telling them about his adventures in the fort, there was little conversation at the table, and what there was felt awkward. Clara kept her eyes focused on Lucie as if expecting something from her. *An apology,* thought James. He agreed. His daughter should be respectful and take responsibility for when she was not. Lucie kept her eyes focused on her plate. James suspected he was only just beginning to understand the rift between his wife and daughter. Whatever the reasons behind it, the rift was growing and needed his attention. His loyalties and diplomacy were about to be tested. Once again, he wished he could seek Lily's advice. She would tell him to act with both love and logic, not one without the other. Neither of the females in his life were currently acting logically or lovingly. It was up to him to provide both. The strain was not healthy for Lucie or Clara, and he wasn't certain how it might be affecting Hugh and Knox. It was certainly affecting him, and not for the better.

The five of them had been living this strange dance in his home ever since Clara had moved in last summer as his wife. He could see it clearly now, as if in pantomime, full of silent gestures and facial expressions. He had dismissed Lucie's requests to go to Ireland and attend the Misses Young School as a dramatic reaction, responding with a pat or two on the shoulder followed by "Lucie, I know you don't really want to leave home." But perhaps she really did want to leave. Too many evenings had ended with Lucie shedding tears and retreating to a corner of the room or her bedroom, Clara regarding James in frustration but holding her place as a parent by staying put, and Hugh and Knox crawling into their latest fortress, whispering to one another. He had remained stubbornly blind to the upset in his home in hopes of a gradual change and adjustment. *Well,* he thought, *my eyes are open now.* He frowned, feeling a deep sadness at what he saw but having not a clue about what to do about it.

Clara entered the bedroom later that evening as James stood before a long mirror removing his tie. She threw herself on the bed and spoke with an edge that had become all too familiar of late. "School will be over in three weeks, and Lucie and I will be together all day, every day. In case you haven't noticed, we are already in near-constant combat, James. At first, I hoped we only needed time to get to know each other and find our places, but we've been a family for nearly a year, and I feel as if there's a war building between Lucie and me. I am exhausted. Your daughter dislikes me. Intensely."

James was shocked by her candor but not surprised by the subject matter. Clara was direct about many things, but rarely about his children. She had an ability to get her way without saying much. Hugh and Knox responded well to her silent, gentle authority, but with Lucie she seemed to have the opposite effect. Clara's frankness that night was both upsetting and, he had to admit, refreshing. There was no hiding from the problem any longer. At least now they could discuss the issue openly. "Clara: Lucie, Hugh, and Knox are *our* children now, not just mine," he began—a poorly thought-out start that caused Clara to roll over on the bed so her back was to him.

"Miss Levering asked to see me today," he continued. "She told me that Lucie was withdrawing in class and on the play yard."

Clara sat up and faced James. "I am glad at least to hear the problem isn't just at home." She buried her face in her hands.

James wondered what she was feeling. Was she sad or just exasperated? He wasn't at all certain that the problem *hadn't* begun at home, but he wasn't about to say so. Not yet, anyway. He replied clinically, as a doctor, to give himself some distance from the expanding emotions in the room.

"Her behavior sounds like melancholia to me. I have seen it in older people but not so often in children. I also observe, as I imagine you do, that Lucie is coming to maturity early, and that process does affect moods." Clara frowned at him but nodded her head. "Of course, she misses her mother, and our marriage"—James paused, choosing his words carefully—"has not settled well with her." Clara didn't argue. She was a sensible woman. She had to know the truth of his words.

"Well, we have to do something, James," she said. "I cannot continue to live with this tension and disrespect, and I don't think it's fair to Lucie either, not to mention the boys and you."

James let out a sigh of defeat. "There is something I have been considering," he began. Clara looked up at him. "I am thinking," he started again, "that we should consider sending Lucie to school in Dublin with Lily's family." He waited for Clara to say something.

She moved over and sat on the edge of the bed next to James. "How soon?" she asked.

PART THREE

A NEW BEGINNING

CHAPTER 40

LUCIE ARRIVES

Dublin, Ireland
October

Lucie's father let go of her hand when they reached the top of the porch stairs. RockView was bigger, taller than she imagined, and she instinctively took a step back. "Go on, Lucie," her father said, pushing her gently in front of him. "Let them know we are here." She looked up at her father, then at the looming oak door. The lion-head knocker felt heavy in her hand, but she rapped it twice, heard it echo within like a distant thunderclap, and stepped back beside her father. A portly woman with a pleasant face and wearing a starched white cap and apron opened the door. Lucie had never seen anyone curtsy to her father before. "Welcome back, Dr. Niven," the woman said, smiling broadly. Behind her, an elderly man and two women hurried toward them. The man shook her father's hand, squeezed his shoulder, then leaned toward her. Grandfather Thomas.

He smiled so brightly, was so kindly, and looked nothing like his stern photograph back home. "Lucie, my dear!" he said and wrapped his arms around her. She held her breath until he broke the embrace. "Look at you," he exclaimed, holding her at arm's length. "My beautiful granddaughter. I am so very happy to meet you at last."

Aunt Frances and Aunt Elfie squeezed past him to stand beside her. "Hello, James! Hello, Lucie. Welcome to RockView," they said as one, then ushered her in to her new home. Lucie was too stunned to speak. Whatever she had imagined of RockView, it wasn't the large, cheerless house she stood in now. A painting of an old man in a burnished gold frame on the opposite wall seemed to watch her every move. "This is *our* grandfather Young," Aunt Elfie said. "Isn't he handsome?" Lucie glanced back at her father for reassurance. He raised his eyebrows and smiled, then turned to reply to something her grandfather said. Her aunts chattered at her as they all moved toward the dining room for lunch. "You must be exhausted from your travels, my dear. Oh my, you look so grown up! Lucie, you will soon have many new friends when your class-mates arrive. After you've rested, we will show you the places in Rathmines that your mother loved." The Youngs were kind and they were her family, but all Lucie could think was that she had made a terrible mistake. *Please, Father,* she thought. *Please don't leave me here.*

At the table her father fell into conversation with her grandfather while her aunts served the soup. "One of Biddy's specialties," Aunt Frances told Lucie, handing her a plate of soda bread. "Oh my, yes," Aunt Elfie agreed. "There is some-thing special about Irish cooking. Wait until you taste Biddy's scones!" Frances leaned toward Lucie. "Your aunt Elfie has a sweet tooth."

"Nothing wrong with a sweet tooth," her grandfather said from across the table, catching her eye.

Lucie blushed and glanced down at the bowl on her plate. "This looks like the soup Mother used to make for us," she said.

The table grew quiet. Lucie glanced up to see her family watching her. "Why yes, I believe it is, Lucie," her father said, breaking the spell. He brought a spoonful to his lips and swallowed. "It tastes just as delicious! I imagine Biddy would be willing to teach you to make it too. Like mother, like daughter."

"Just what I've been thinking," Aunt Elfie said, smiling.

Her father lifted his glass. "Thank you," he began, smiling at the Youngs, "for this warm homecoming for Lucie and me. I feel Lily is here, blessing us for gathering around your table and knowing her beloved daughter has come to live in her childhood home and in the care of the family she so loved."

The only thing Lucie felt was a slowly rising panic. Why had she been so certain this was where she wanted to be? She felt nothing of her mother here at RockView, nothing of the playfulness she had with her brothers or the familiarity of her own home. On the long voyage across the Atlantic, a fellow traveler, an older woman, had recognized Lucie's plight long before Lucie would. "My dear," the woman had said to her as the passengers took air on a calm and sunny afternoon, "you seem rather young to be going to school so far away from your family."

I do? Lucie wondered.

She looked to her father, who answered quickly for her. "My daughter will be living with family in Ireland," he explained. "Her aunts run an excellent boarding school for girls in their home just outside Dublin. We're very excited for her." Lucie had beamed beneath her father's supportive words.

But couldn't he see *now* that she was sorry she had come to Ireland? Didn't he understand that she did not want to live with strangers, no matter how much they wanted her to live with them? Lucie's face burned with the tears she worked to hold back. At nearly eleven, she was *not* too young. She had just changed her mind. Lucie tried to make the meal last as long as she could, hoping to come up with something that would convince her father to take her home.

While she still had half a piece of bread left to eat, her father folded his napkin and announced that he had to be on his way. "The train to Belfast leaves within the hour. Mother will not understand if I'm not on it!" He laughed and stood up from the table to walk over to his daughter. "Your grandmother Eliza can hardly wait to see you, Lucie," he said, giving her a kiss on the cheek.

"But, Father—" she began.

"We've already talked about this, Lucie," he said without letting her finish. "It's best for you to first settle into your new school and be with your classmates. We all concur. Even Mother. She has agreed to wait until next month to visit you. I'm sure you two will have a wonderful time together."

Weeks later, Lucie could not remember their final goodbye or if her father seemed sad or reluctant to leave her behind. There was a blank in her memory between his kiss on her cheek and the arrival of the rest of the Misses Young's girls the next day. If the Youngs noticed she was unhappy, they never said so.

Then one evening, her aunts called her into the drawing room before bedtime and told her about a girl in their very first class. "We overheard her planning to return home for good the first month of school," Aunt Elfie said.

"What happened to her?" Lucie asked.

"She graduated at the top of the class," Aunt Frances answered.

"She visits us whenever she has the chance," Aunt Elfie said. "And I visit her every summer." Lucie's aunts smiled. They reminded her so much of her own mother just then that she couldn't help but smile back. Lucie supposed she might get used to being at the school too, away from everything she knew and loved, but she had her doubts. She was pleased her aunts didn't seem to expect a response from her but suggested she return to the dormitory.

Late that night, while she was staring at the empty ceiling above her bed, her mother's face appeared to her. "Mama!" she whispered. Lucie tried to reach out to touch her, but exhaustion eased into her body and her eyes grew heavy. The last thing she remembered was feeling a comfort she had missed for far too long. For the first time since she arrived in Ireland, Lucie slept through the night.

Lucie's grandmother did not wait an entire month to visit her but showed up at the end of the second week of school with an invitation to stay two days with her at the Touths' in Dublin. "This way you can get to know your Niven relatives, too." Lucie caught the surprised glances among her aunts and grandfather just before Grandfather Thomas said that of course she must meet them.

"You'll want to pack appropriate clothes for our dinners and outings in the city," Eliza told her. Aunt Frances volunteered to help. "All of your clothes are appropriate, Lucie," she whispered on their way up the staircase. "Maybe leave behind the school pinafore," she added, making Lucie laugh.

When she returned to RockView that Sunday evening, she felt as if she had come home. Without her realizing it, during her short time there Lucie had become comfortable with the Youngs and the school, a part of things. Her grandmother was exciting to be around. She seemed to know all the best and most interesting places in Dublin, putting Lucie on her best behavior every minute of the day. Unlike the Youngs, though, Lucie decided her strong-minded grandmother was someone she liked to visit with but not someone she'd like to live with. On the carriage ride back to RockView, Grandmother Eliza had told her she had something wonderful planned for Visiting Day. "Of course we will also be together at Christmas," she said. "I'll make the arrangements with your aunts and grandfather." Lucie felt overwhelmed just thinking about the upcoming visits.

By November she had begun a friendship of sorts with the girl who slept in the bed next to hers. They helped each other braid their hair at night and sat next to each other in class. Maggie Barrett was what Lucie thought of as spoiled and what her mother would have called "strong headed." Maggie was full of her own ideas, some of them running contrary to Lucie's aunts'. She wasn't one bit shy about sharing her thoughts with Lucie and sometimes with everyone in the dormitory after lights-out. Lucie had long stopped talking to the other students about her life in Canada. They only stared at her blankly or asked her if she'd seen any Indians or, worse, why she pronounced so many words differently. "She's Canadian, not Anglo-Irish like us," Maggie would remind them, rolling her eyes. Lucie envied Maggie's boldness. Eventually, when Lucie was feeling particularly low, she imagined what Maggie would say about Clara if they ever met. She was still homesick, but it felt good to have something to giggle about.

CHAPTER 41

NOWHERE TO RUN

December 1885
Norah

Norah was angry and ready to run. She might have if her mother hadn't been right beside her and if she had some place to run to. After days of arguing with her ma and pa, she agreed to talk to Miss Frances Young about working at RockView, but she wasn't happy about it. "It's better work than you'll get anywhere else," her father had said. "And it will keep you out of jail."

"Better work, but doing what?" Norah had asked. She still didn't know, and she was almost at RockView. *Nothing but spoiled Anglo brats in there,* Norah thought, not for the first time.

"They're wain. Children," Biddy said, as if reading her mind, "but you'll refer to them as 'young ladies.' It is a job in a safe place. You need to earn your keep and stay out of the pubs—and jail, for that matter."

Norah rolled her eyes. *So I've heard,* she thought.

Norah followed her mother into the house through the kitchen door. Someone already had the woodstove burning, and her mother put on the kettle. Last night's dough had risen high in a bowl sitting on the table; the linen towel covering it looked like a huge bubble about to burst. With an expert hand her mother lifted the towel, punched the dough down for a final time, then placed it near the stove to rise again before she made the morning biscuits. "Sit down, Norah, and hang your coat on the hook by the door. Mine too." She shed her coat and handed it to Norah. "You can help Mary when she finishes warming the dining room, which should be soon."

Norah stared blankly.

"To set the table for the girls' breakfast," her mother said impatiently. "Miss Frances will be down for tea and will want to interview you and show you the house."

No further words were spoken until Mary came in, her face registering surprise at seeing Norah. "What have we here?" she asked, smiling.

"Norah has come to see about a job with the school, Mary. At Miss Frances's suggestion." Norah thought her ma sounded defensive.

The kitchen door swung open, and one of the Misses Young walked through. *Miss Frances Young,* Norah judged. She had been a girl when she'd last seen any of the Youngs. The woman was handsome but appeared rigid, like she had a stick in her spine. *This will never work,* Norah thought uneasily.

Biddy introduced Norah to the woman. Without thinking, Norah did a little curtsy, which made her blush with embarrassment and her mother smile.

"Norah," Miss Young said. "May I call you Norah? Let's take our cups of tea and go where we can talk." Norah glanced at her mother, wondering if she should mention setting the table first. Miss Young answered for her. "Your mother and Mary have plenty to keep them busy here while we get to know one another."

"Yes, Miss Young," she answered politely, carefully holding the cup and saucer Mary handed her. She followed the woman's quick pace through the butler's pantry, into the dining room, and across an open space by the stairs to the drawing room. *What's the hurry?* she thought, trying not to spill her tea. *I guess they need to move so quick to get through so many rooms to reach their destination.*

Norah felt better once her teacup was on the table and she was settled on a chair across from Miss Young. She glanced around her. It was a nice room, almost exactly as she had imagined from her brothers' description: framed paintings on the walls, furniture made with rounded edges, and a gleaming piano in the corner. The fire in the small grate had warmed the room, but only one lamp glowed through the morning gloom. Norah thought how pretty everything must look when the sun came up higher.

"Norah, I know you have had a very difficult few years," Miss Young said matter-of-factly. "Your mother is a beloved member of our family, and we feel as if you are family here too. My sister having, by chance, observed the night in Knock when your friend Gavin . . . Well, that must have been a painful experience for you. We want to be of help to you."

Norah was surprised by the woman's willingness to associate herself and her sister with a protest, let alone a violent one. *What would the Youngs be doing at such a thing? And one of the sisters, at that?* Norah wondered if Miss Elfie might be simpleminded. Her ma had never said as much.

"I didn't know about your sister being there, Miss Young," Norah said, gathering herself.

"You may call me Miss Frances and my sister Miss Elfie.

You will meet her later this morning. We would like to see if working with us and our students will be a good thing for you and for us. Does that sound like something you are willing to try?"

"Yes, ma'am . . . Miss Frances," Norah replied, though she still wasn't certain exactly what they wanted her to do. "Better be careful, sister," her brothers had warned her. "Brits feel it's their right to take advantage." Their ma had told them to hush, but Norah suspected her brothers were right.

"Tell me about yourself, Norah. Have you worked with children? These girls are quite well educated and though they are young, they have had many experiences that others their age might not."

I know for sure they haven't had experiences most Irish girls have had, Norah thought smugly. But then Norah had experiences other Irish girls her age had not.

"I know your . . . young ladies have a life different from mine, but I have a great ma . . . as you know . . . and my gran in Cork. They set me a good example. I help the mothers with their wains on our street, so I know how to be with them. Children, I mean."

Miss Frances nodded slowly. "Your mother helped to care for my sisters and me when we were children. Did you know that? She was quite young at the time." Norah said she did. The woman grew quiet and smiled. "Well," she said at last, "follow me. I will introduce you to our young ladies upstairs, and then you can join us all for the morning meal, always a treat. Your mother is an excellent cook, as you know." Norah couldn't help but smile. She liked hearing an Anglo complimenting her mother.

Standing inside the dormitory, Norah wasn't sure what to make of all the fuss in front of her. Mary was overseeing nine girls who were talking and giggling while pulling on layers of clean, starched clothes and jostling for space at the mirror.

One of the girls was sitting on the edge of a bed, pulling a brush through the long straight brown hair of another girl. Norah remembered how her own ma used to brush the tangles out of her wavy red hair when she was wee. *They're like sisters,* she thought, feeling slightly envious for the first time since she arrived, *but not like any clan I've ever seen.*

Norah followed the girls downstairs, where Miss Frances ushered them into the dining room and she was told to go to the kitchen where Miss Elfie was waiting for her. The round, nicely dressed woman greeted her as if they were old friends, offering her another cup of tea and one of her mother's scones, then chatting on about the school and never asking Norah a question. Twenty minutes later Norah headed home feeling slightly stunned. At some point, without discussing the matter with her further, her mother and the Misses Young had agreed that Norah would start work at the school in the new year. She still wasn't certain what she was expected to do at RockView or the school, but she felt curiously lighter than she had in a long while, and that was something in her favor.

CHAPTER 42

A CHOICE IS MADE

Patrick

Patrick sat hunched over in the loft on the lone spindly wood chair in the bedroom he shared with his brother, worried he was no closer to getting to America than he'd been last year. He'd outgrown everything around him, even the chair; his knees were almost up to his chest. This was the chair he'd learned to tie his shoes on at age five and propped against the door to keep his ma out when he practiced rolling smokes at age ten. Ma had insisted they bring it with them to the loft Da had built for them so Norah could have her own room when he and Jack started sprouting curlies. He was too old to be living at home, but he was saving his money. Trying, at least. Pat cranked his stiff neck back and forth and glanced at his brother sprawled out on the bed they shared. "Jesus Christ, Jack," he whispered. "We got to get the hell outta here, make a life for ourselves. I'm almost twenty-five, and you're not a mama's baby anymore. It's time to go."

Jack rolled over on his side and looked at Pat. "What'd you wake me for? I was dreamin' 'bout Erin. You always did have a terrible sense of timin'." He sat up and stretched. "So, what's troublin' you? I don't smell nice, or you don't want to sleep with me anymore?"

Pat laughed. "You never were a sweet rose with your soakin' nappies. Now you're as sour and yeasty as a stout barrel gone bad. Hardly an improvement."

"Breakfast will be ready soon," their mother called from below.

Pat stuck his head past the heavy quilt and into the loft doorway. "It's our day off, Ma."

"Seriously Jack," Patrick whispered, leaning back inside their room, "you need to start plannin' how to bring your smelly arse with me to America. Stinky as you are, I'd miss you."

Jack shrugged. "Too early in the morning to go to America. Besides, I told you, I got my eye on Erin." He sat up and moved to the side of the bed, pulling on his pants and shirt before standing up. "Besides, 'it's our day off, Ma,'" he said, parroting his brother. Like Pat's, Jack's head at his full height was only inches from the rafters, and he instinctively lowered it. "I can come up with better ways to spend it than worrying about America. Starting with breakfast."

Pat watched his brother brush past him and climb down the ladder but didn't follow. Instead, he sprawled out on the bed, glad of the warmth his brother had left behind. When he rolled over, he ran his finger over the faded, awkward scratches Jack had long ago scraped in the wall with a nail: JCG, John Conor Gossett. Ma had given Jack hell for it, but there it was and always would be.

"Well, not me," he said, thinking of the small tobacco tin beneath the mattress. He'd found the scratched and dented tin by a dustbin as a boy and kept it. The box no longer held his childhood treasures; it held his freedom—four pounds. Enough to get him to America. He checked on it each night and each morning, so he resisted checking it again.

Pat was ready to be out of the house for good. He felt sorry for his parents. All three of the Gossett offspring were like powder kegs waiting for a match. He and Jack had built too much resentment toward the Brits during Norah's time in prison to let go of it, and Norah had returned ready to knit herself right into her brothers' resentment. She had lost her job at the pub for mouthing off to some dumb-ass Brits, who had no business being there as far as he and any self-respecting Irishman knew. *Now Ma wants her workin' at the Youngs' Anglo school. Holy Christ, what next? What are we Gossetts—Irish or British?*

Ma seemed sure of herself about Norah taking the job. Pat could not let go of his anger over the powerlessness of the Irish in in their own country. George Fenn had pulled levers at Dublin Castle for Norah, levers the Irish could never hope to touch. Pat was thankful his sister was out, but the system that held her still hung over all of them. The truth of it sat like an ugly scar across the entire family. A wound that had yet to be fully healed and was carried not just by the Gossetts but by every Catholic in Ireland. His own country was smothering him, and the British were slowly cutting off his air. No vote, no civil rights, no land, no life.

"To hell with it," he shouted at the bedroom ceiling. "I'm leavin', gettin' out!"

— • —

Biddy

Biddy closed her eyes and counted to ten. Whenever she heard Pat talk about leaving for America, her insides tightened so she could hardly breathe. She opened her eyes in time to catch her youngest son putting on his boots and heading out the door. "You just sat down to eat. Where are you going now?"

Jack turned around with a grin, cocking his head in that way that never failed to warm her heart. *And doesn't he know it, too?* she thought, shaking her head.

"To walk with Erin on her way to work."

"It wouldn't hurt you to clear your bowl from the table first, would it."

"Ma!" he protested and disappeared before she could take another moment of his time.

Norah was already at the dishes and warning Patrick he'd better get down to the kitchen before she fed his food to the alley cats. Biddy busied herself by pouring another cup of tea while she waited for Patrick. She had some motherly sense to offer. When he didn't appear, she said to Norah loud enough for her son to hear: "At least Jack has the right idea. Having a good woman at his side will help him prosper here."

"Ma," Norah said, over her shoulder, "how do you know Jack's Erin is a good woman? No one's met her but Jack."

"Norah!" Biddy scolded. "We don't know that she's not a good girl. That's not the point."

"We know the point you're making, Ma," Patrick said, suddenly behind her. "You don't want me to go to America."

"The Donnell girl has eyes for you," Biddy said. "Her mum tells me so when we meet in the market, and you know it, too." Biddy turned around to face her eldest, but he was already sitting on the bench by the door getting ready to leave. She frowned and shook her head.

"Ma," Patrick said gently. "I'm going out to look for more work. I'm a man. I need money." He finished tying his boots and grabbed his jacket, then walked over to her. Biddy could feel the full height of her eldest, and the strength of him in the hand he lay on her shoulder. Patrick had grown into a man; she couldn't deny it. He could make up his own mind about his future, but she was his mother and still had influence. At least she hoped she did. "We'll see you for supper, then?" she asked. Pat kissed her on the head and left the house without answering her.

Biddy fixed a stew for dinner, Pat's favorite. To her pleasure, he not only came home in time for the meal but also had dragged his brother with him. She didn't ask if Patrick had found extra work. He would have said so, and she didn't want to get Conor stirred up about why Patrick wanted the extra money. Both her boys smelled liked the pub, something she chose to ignore.

"Well, this is nice, isn't it?" she said when her family was seated. Their bowls were filled and the bread she'd baked was torn and already being dipped into the thick broth. "All five of us sitting at the table at the same time. When was the last time that happened?" Conor patted her on the back and kissed her cheek. Her children said nothing, but Biddy knew. It was right after Norah came home from the gaol. Their family unity hadn't lasted long. Once she was safe at home, the strain they'd felt when she'd been imprisoned only grew, threatening to split them apart. It was as if they couldn't all stand to be in one room with each other anymore. Biddy was so happy they were all together again, she couldn't stop from chittering like a bird, talking about the day she'd had and the gossip she'd heard from their neighbors. "Oh! I nearly forgot. I saw Mrs. Ryan's new grandbaby today. A little girl. Ah, she's a sweet one. Conor, one day soon we'll have to get ourselves a bigger table for all those grandbabies we'll have." Biddy had gone too far.

She knew it as soon as the words were out of her mouth, but it was too late to take them back.

"Ma!" Patrick shouted. "I am not signing up to have babies with Lizzy Donnell or anyone else. The only way for someone like me to get ahead in Ireland is to die a martyr and leave the ladies weeping over my coffin. *Snap*, you are gone. Who'll take care of those babies when they've put me underground, Ma?"

Now it was Patrick who had gone too far, and Biddy couldn't hide the hurt she felt. "I'm sorry, Ma," he said in a gentler voice. "I'm sorry! It's just . . . that life's not for me. I'll have better luck of making something of myself in America."

"Stop it, Pat," Conor growled. "You break your mother's heart with this talk of leaving, and you annoy the bejesus out of me too." He pushed his chair back and left the table, taking a sopping piece of bread with him. "I'm just going to sit over here and make my peace with the sad details of my footballers," he said, settling in the rocker in the corner of the room. He made a show of opening that morning's newspaper and smacking it with the back of his hand. "The Dubs lost again. And to Wicklow!"

Pat's reply dripped with sarcasm. "Oh, Da, that's really important."

Conor's face went red. "God damn it, that *is* important, and I have to listen to you whining about your ma wanting grandbabies! You have no idea what's waitin' for you on the other side of the sea. It may not be as pretty as you make it out to be."

"Go on, Da," said Patrick. "We all know if Jack and I left, you'd have extra jingle in your pocket for pub stops to down a few and talk about your precious Dubs."

"Don't bring me in to this," Jack said, taking another spoonful of stew.

"I don't have to bring you, you're already there!" Pat said. "You just haven't faced up to it yet. Da doesn't care anyway. To hell with independence or anything real important like a better life for your sons. Nah, you got the Dubs."

Conor slammed the paper down and glared at Patrick. "Get out of here, you little prick!" he shouted.

Pat pivoted without a word and slammed the door behind him as he left. Biddy burst into tears.

CHAPTER 43

NOT ONLY A NIVEN— ALSO A YOUNG

Lucie

Lucie thought her classmates made little difference to her new life, until the Christmas holiday arrived and she realized she was going to be alone with the Youngs for the next four weeks.

To her surprise and relief, as soon as she and her aunts waved goodbye to Maggie, the last girl to depart, Aunt Elfie offered to have Lucie's bed brought up to her room so Lucie would not have to stay in the empty dormitory by herself. Sleeping in her aunt's room might feel strange and uncomfortable, but it would be better than being all alone on the second floor of the old house. "Yes, thank you," she said, quickly.

After their evening meal that night, Lucie had gathered her courage to ask about something else that had been worrying her. Normally she would join the girls upstairs after dinner, but now it would just be her by herself until her aunt came to bed. "Aunt Elfie? Aunt Frances?" she asked, "May I sit with you in the drawing room before I go to bed?" For reasons she didn't understand, her aunts and grandfather looked at each other and laughed.

"Now why didn't we think of that?" her grandfather exclaimed. From that night onward, evenings with the Youngs became something she looked forward to. Aunt Frances brought her up to her bedroom library and told her to choose any books she'd like to read, and Grandfather Thomas taught her to play chess. Her favorite nights were when Aunt Elfie would play the piano as they stood around her and sang. At nine o'clock she would follow her aunt to their room on the third floor, and when they were both in bed and the room was dark her aunt would say, "Good night, Lucie," and she would say, "Good night, Aunt Elfie." She was not home, but she was beginning to feel like part of this new family.

During the day, Lucie was rescued from boredom or loneliness while her aunts were busy making social calls and preparing for the return of school by Biddy and Mary, who let her help in the kitchen the way Marian had. One morning, Lucie woke before the sun. Unable to fall back asleep, she dressed as quietly as she could so as not to wake her aunt and waited at the top of the stairs until she heard noises in the kitchen.

"Good morning, miss!" Mary said when Lucie peeked her head around the kitchen door. Biddy nodded her greeting and pulled a big bowl from the cupboard. "As long as you're up early," she said, "I think it's time to try your hand at making my famous scones."

"Me?" Lucie exclaimed. Marian had often let her help in the kitchen at home, but Lucie never made anything like scones by herself. Mary tied an apron around Lucie's neck and waist and suggested she roll up her sleeves to keep them from being covered with flour. "And later there's plenty of hot water to clean yourself up before breakfast," she added pointedly, then left the kitchen to get on with her chores.

The Youngs made every effort to make the holidays cheerful, but it was hard for them to compete with the fun of cooking with Biddy and Mary or with Lucie's memories from Canada. As the days grew closer to Christmas, RockView seemed to become more calm, orderly, and gentle, if that were possible. Her grandfather took quiet walks or disappeared into his room to paint. Her aunts wrote letters and embroidered landscapes and bouquets of flowers. They taught her to make pomander balls and how to cross-stitch ("Your mother didn't much take to embroidery either"). In the evenings, her favorite songs, "In the Gloaming" and "Won't You Buy My Pretty Flowers," were set aside and replaced with church hymns. There were no snowball fights at RockView, no spinning jump ropes or Hugh and Knox laughing and spilling their cocoa. The Youngs gave her warm milk to sip before bed. She wondered if her brothers were having as much fun around the holidays without her. Since she had left Canada, she had received many letters from her father, with her brothers squeezing in a sentence or two at the bottom of the thin paper to let her know they missed her.

Three days before Christmas, her aunts instructed her to put on her warmest coat, scarf, hat, boots, and gloves and surprised her with a carriage ride into Dublin. "We are going to meet your grandmother Eliza at a tearoom she has selected," Aunt Elfie explained as they neared the city center. "She has come to Dublin to do her Christmas shopping and have a visit with us." The city was big and exciting compared to London, Ontario. Shops large and small were lined up one against the other, with windows glowing and bells ringing out the arrival of customers whose shoulders and hats were dusted white from the light falling snow.

Their carriage stopped in front of a well-lit tearoom with tall windows facing the street. Eliza was waiting for them at a table laden with sweets and finger sandwiches. After greetings all around, Aunt Elfie picked up a scone, sat back, and whispered to Lucie, "Not light as a feather like the ones you and Biddy make." Lucie blushed and tried not to grin too proudly.

"Their seed cake is scrumptious!" Grandmother Eliza declared, placing one on Lucie's plate. Lucie didn't mind at all. To her everything on the table looked scrumptious.

Following tea, the four of them walked to her Aunt Frances's favorite bookstore, Hodges Figgis. "Oh my," Lucie said when they stepped inside. "I've never been in such a grand shop. At home we order books from Toronto or Montreal for special occasions, but usually we borrow books from the lending library where our family has a subscription membership."

Grandmother Eliza looked annoyed. "How many times did I tell James Canada was an uncivilized place? I am so glad you are here with us now to experience the finer things, my dear."

"Lucie," Aunt Frances said, putting her arm around her niece's shoulder, "this shop has a fine selection."

"Figgis does have a good selection," Eliza agreed. "Though not as comprehensive as one can find in London, England."

Aunt Frances gave Aunt Elfie a look but said nothing. Lifting her hand to direct Lucie's gaze, she said, "Look at these shelves full of books. They go all the way up to the ceiling. See the ladder that rolls along the top? They use that to reach a book on the highest shelves."

Lucie thought it would be wonderful to work at Hodges Figgis just to climb the ladder and push herself across the rows.

After a few minutes, Lucie was left to peruse the shelves while the ladies examined and chatted about the books on display. Lucie would have liked to buy a book for the Youngs, but she'd already spent the money her father had left her on other Christmas gifts. She'd almost finished cross-stitching a flower on the corner of a linen handkerchief for each of her aunts, and the letter "T" on the one for her grandfather. She had made one for Grandmother Eliza that Aunt Elfie had wrapped in a piece of silk and Lucie had tied in a ribbon. To both keep hidden and carry the gift, Aunt Frances placed it in her mother's beaded reticule before they left that morning. Lucie had already mailed handkerchiefs, stitched with their own initials, to her father and brothers. At her aunts' encouragement, she had sent a handkerchief to Clara, too, one with a small lace edging but no added cross-stitching.

Lucie presented her gift to Eliza as they parted, and Eliza gave them a book each and one for Thomas. Eliza would be on the evening train for Lisburn. "Goodbye, my darlings, and Happy Christmas," Eliza said as she climbed into her carriage. "Lucie, I'm looking forward to your stay with me at Chrome Hill for New Year's," she said by way of invitation—at least it was the first Lucie had heard of it.

"Apparently you'll be visiting your father's boyhood home soon," Aunt Elfie said, sounding more bemused than surprised. Lucie wondered what staying at the home of her flamboyant grandmother would be like. Frances said as the carriage pulled away, "that generous woman has the energy of a fast-running colt."

Inside the drawing room, Lucie and Aunt Elfie unwrapped the box of Christmas ornaments Biddy had brought down from the attic for them, checking to see if any were broken or needed new ribbon to hang from the tree's branches. "Ah!" her aunt exclaimed, holding a paper-wrapped ornament carefully in her hand. "Now this one, I think . . . yes!" She gently dropped the paper back into the box and held up a miniature pair of leather ice skates dangling from a piece of fading purple ribbon. "These were your mother's favorite when she was your age. She tied the ribbon on them as a decoration for our Christmas trees. I cannot recall where they came from or when she got them, but I've never seen anything like them in the shops, have you, Frances?"

"I think your mother would like you to have them. Don't you, Father?"

Lucie looked up to see her aunt Frances and grandfather at the entrance to the drawing room, watching them.

"I believe she would," her grandfather said quietly, touching the corner of his eye. "I believe we all would." Lucie stood and hugged them. She walked back to Elfie and hugged her, too.

"Would it be all right if I kept them by my bed? Just until the tree arrives." Her parents had given each of their children a pair of real ice skates the Christmas before her mother died. Her mother had read *Hans Brinker, or The Silver Skates* to them. It had been their last Christmas together. But Lucie had left her skates behind. "It doesn't get cold enough in Dublin for ice skates," her father had told her. "You won't need them there." She hadn't been very good at skating anyway. *I bet Hugh and Knox have figured them out by now,* she thought, wistfully. With the Youngs' approval, she brought the tiny skates to Aunt Elfie's bedroom after dinner. Seeing them at her bedside that night made her feel closer to the distant, interrupted life she had once thought she'd have forever.

Christmas Eve morning, Biddy's sons, Patrick and Jack, knocked on the kitchen door while Lucie was sipping her milky tea. Mary hurried to open it and Lucie watched the two handsome young men wrestle in a bushy pine tree that filled the doorway. "Now, it doesn't belong in the kitchen," Biddy scolded them gently. "Dearie," she said, handing her wooden spoon to Lucie, "would you mind giving a stir or two more and then moving your grandfather's porridge off the hot part of the stove while I show my boys where to put the tree?"

Lucie made a few slow stirs in the pot, watching out of the corner of her eye as Patrick and Jack and their cargo moved through the kitchen. They both smiled as they passed her. She tried to guess how old they were. *Older than I am,* she told herself. The pot safely off the heat, she followed Biddy, the men, and the tree through the butler's pantry and dining room, across the entry hall, and into the drawing room. In heavy Irish accents, Patrick and Jack called out directions and warnings to each other as they jostled the tree upright and found just the right spot by the window. Lucie had to concentrate to make out what they were saying and stifled a laugh when she did. Patrick and Jack weren't so different from her own brothers. Biddy stood a few feet away, watching her sons with a proud expression. From his chair, her grandfather offered a few instructions here and there, finally nodding his satisfaction. The tree in place, he stood up and reached in his pocket. "Well done," he said, offering them each a coin. Lucie couldn't see their value, but they caught the light like silver so they might have been shillings!

Patrick took off his cap and Jack picked his up from the floor. They both held them to their chests before addressing her grandfather. "Thank you, sir. Goodbye and Happy Christmas to you." Shoving their coins deep in their pockets, they put their hats back on and followed their mother out by way of the kitchen.

After their noon meal, Lucie joined her grandfather on a walk through the nearby park. She liked this place. "I know this path," she said, "the way it curves here and then you find a bench..." Her grandfather waited for her to finish her thought. "It's like Mother's garden."

"Remarkable," he said softly, taking her hand. "Thank you, Lucie. Thank you, for telling me."

In the early evening, the four of them gathered to decorate the tree. "Lucie, come here," her grandfather said. "You look old enough to help with tying the candles onto the branches."

Lucie grinned, excited to help. "Place them where they won't burn the branch above," she said, parroting her father's instructions. Grandfather Thomas took the high branches and she did low. When they finished, he struck a long match and lit his candles, then lit another and handed it to Lucie. In her mind's eye, she saw Hugh lighting the candles and Knox sitting on the floor watching the magic unfold. With the candles done, Aunt Frances turned down the gas lamps and the four of them sat quietly, staring at the Christmas tree. "We do the same thing," she said, excitedly, "at my . . . other home."

Aunt Frances turned the lights back up after a few minutes. She poured a dab of sherry into Lucie's glass of lemonade before filling a glass for herself and for Elfie. Grandfather took care of himself with "a wee dram of whiskey to ward off the chill," making her aunts laugh.

"Doesn't look so wee to me, Father," Aunt Elfie said. He pretended to look shocked, winked at Lucie, and poured a tiny bit more in his warm milk before settling down with the rest of them at a game table covered with intricate wooden puzzle pieces. "It makes a German Christmas street scene," Aunt Frances explained. "This is our third Christmas putting the puzzle together, but it doesn't seem to have gotten any easier."

"We have plenty of time to get a good start on it before church tonight," Aunt Elfie said.

"I'll put the pieces of the horse carriage together," Grandfather volunteered. Her aunts exchanged glances and smiled, but said nothing.

At nine o'clock, Aunt Frances disappeared. Lucie had already been told that to help them stay up late for the midnight church service, they would dine late and drink plenty of strong tea, but she felt another surge of excitement when thirty minutes later her aunt reappeared ringing a silver bell and announcing it was time for supper. Lucie was led into the dining room on her grandfather's arm. The room looked festive with red napkins and blazing candles lighting the table. On the table were loin of lamb, winter squash, and broad beans. Biddy, with Mary's help, had prepared the meal ahead so they could be at home with family, and Frances had followed their instructions to serve the meal hot.

"I've never been to a Christmas Eve service," Lucie told her family as her grandfather carved the lamb.

"It's magical," Aunt Elfie said.

"Not at all," Aunt Frances corrected. "It's . . . spiritual."

"It's long," her grandfather said. "Better drink more tea, if you know what's good for you."

With full stomachs the women cleared the dishes and Grandfather Thomas checked to make sure all the candles on the tree were snuffed out. They met in the entryway to bundle up for the short walk to the church, holding hands as they crossed the street just before the eleven o'clock service at Holy Trinity Church. Lucie breathed quickly as they walked, trying to identify what she was feeling. An hour later, they emerged on Christmas Day and walked back looking at the stars shining above. Inside the house, Lucie expected to go to bed. She had never been up so late and was very sleepy. But the Young family had their own traditions and insisted she participate in every part of them. As soon as her grandfather hung up his coat and hat, he began to sing "Jingle Bells," then slipped his arm in hers and swung her in a circle around the entryway before leading her to the drawing room. There they relit the tree, enjoyed a fluffy English trifle in front of the fire, and placed a few more pieces in the puzzle before saying good night.

"Now you have experienced the complete Young family Christmas Eve celebration," her grandfather said. "We hope you enjoyed it."

"I have," Lucie said honestly. Following her new family up to bed, she at last had words to put to what she had been feeling all day. She was more than a Niven; she was also a Young. Like her mother.

CHAPTER 44

TO AMERICA

February 1886
Patrick

The Gossett home had become thick with long silences punctuated by gestures and grunts from the men and sighs and eye rolls from Norah. Only Patrick's mother could find something to say, occasionally filling the air with news and questions, hoping for a response that rarely came. Fortunately, the Gossetts were not often home at the same time, and Pat came home later and later at night. It wasn't just his family that was unhappy. Emotions were frayed wherever he went. News of revolutionary activity and British reprisals was everywhere, keeping Irish Dublin anxious, on edge.

Patrick continued to make his deliveries but now paid nervous attention to his surroundings, watching every detail. The rumors of revolt grew, and he saw danger for himself down every street. Challenges, real or imagined, took on the impact of a personal insult. Someone who got in his way while he drove the wagon was a "brainless son of a bitch." The barkeep who silently watched Pat lift and stack the barrels he'd ordered before telling Pat he hadn't put them in the right spot was a "pissing idiot." He barely managed to keep the thought to himself but kicked at a feral cat racing past him as he walked back to the wagon.

At home he spat out his irritations to his mother whenever she woke to heat the dinner he had missed. Each time, she would remind him they had a lot to be thankful for. "George Fenn's connections worked, God rest his soul, and we need to be grateful to him for your sister's freedom. Not all Anglos and Brits are bad."

There was no getting through to her. No getting her to see his choice was a half-lived life, violence, or America. He didn't want to leave Ireland without her blessing, or at least her understanding. One night as he lay in bed, he heard her stirring in the kitchen when she should have been asleep. Quietly, he climbed down from the loft and called out to her. "Ma, you OK?" They were among the first gentle words he'd spoken to her in a long while. He found her standing at the stove, warming her hands, but she stopped to pour him a cup of the tea she'd brewed and placed it at the table.

"Got a few things to sort out," she answered. "I know you do too, Pat."

"Ma," he said, taking the tea. "You are right, Ma. I know it isn't people like the Youngs or your special Mr. Fenn who are doing us wrong. But, Ma, what George Fenn did is proof that we have no power. The system can be bought but *only* by the Anglos and British, the bastards. Don't forget that, Ma." He took a sip of the hot tea and waited for her to let him know she at last understood. His mother turned her back to him and faced the stove. He heard her sigh and watched her body shudder, but when she spoke, her words were calm and clear. "Pat, maybe you *should* leave. It may be the best for all of us."

Pat was stunned.

"I love you, son," she said, "but I am at the end of my thread." Pat thought that might be as close to a blessing as he was going to get from her.

He wasn't ready to go yet. He had managed to save nearly five pounds with the help of Mr. Young's tip, a small fortune. He'd need at least three more pounds for his brother to join him, and even then there wouldn't be enough left for food. Above all, he needed a plan before he could sail to America, including convincing his brother to go with him. Until then, he had his daily routine to keep him sane.

Loading the barrels of Guinness on his wagon and following his delivery routes took him to different pubs throughout the week. These "locals" were social hubs for the Irish. There they found food, drink, and unfiltered public opinion from their own neighborhood and class. Pat caught the grumblings and sometimes a good smutty joke from the regulars at each pub. He took breaks along his route, taking a stool to listen as he refueled with a day-old kidney pie or soda bread with a slab of butter and cheese. Anglo-Irish men in the Trinity area did not patronize these pubs. They had their private gentlemen's clubs.

At Clancy's Inn, "Drinkin' Dan" was working his crowd when Pat arrived, and he hung back for a minute to listen. "Halloran," Dan called out, "did ya hear the Brits are tightening the screws in the wee hours now to try to control the bloody clashes erupting here and about? Word has it the costs are high on all sides."

Halloran smiled and straightened up from leaning on the bar. "Yes, Dan," he answered. "We've all heard. The part to make ya cry is we've got buckets and buckets of young Irish lads to pour into the fight, and fight they will. They see no hope in their lives, so why not?" Halloran turned to the man resting his head in his hands next to him. "Whadaya say, Flaherty? Ya look ya have a bad tooth, pained, as I talk."

Flaherty didn't move, but he spoke loudly. "Me sons are out there. They tell me the Brits are pissin' themselves, they are so scared. They have muskets and men, but there are more of us. They march around in columns and our boys hide in bushes and jump them."

Halloran took the floor again. "Our boys have the jump, but they are not well armed. Pitchforks won't do it." He pounded down his mug for a refill. "Makes me thirsty to think of it. Fill my cup, man. Our ragtag militias are brave and a wee daft, but they grab the Brits by the balls often enough to keep 'um nervous."

Dan poured him his drink. "Sure," he said with a loud sigh. "The boys are brave, but these're losin' routs. They pull up their courage and charge like knights in bedtime stories, racing like fools into musket fire at castles and forts held by the British, even public buildings! Brave. But sad. I hear they're falling like toy soldiers."

Flaherty slammed his mug on the bar and glared at Dan. "Ya don't know what you're talking about!" he said. Another patron down the bar, someone Pat didn't recognize, shook his fist, making Pat wonder if there was going to be a fight. "Maybe so, Danny boy," the man growled, "but I say why the hell shouldn't we take 'um back? They stole the castles and forts from the Irish!"

"Hear, hear," Flaherty said, calming down.

Halloran put cash on the bar and offered a round. Dan smiled and poured. *Useless,* Patrick thought angrily. *We're in a losing fight.* He slipped his cap back on his head. *We're pitiful. Outmanned and outgunned. Powerless.* He stood and walked out the door, his temper rising with his blood. He wished he had a bag of hops to smack with his fist. "I'll not spill my blood in this misery," he told his horse as he took his seat on the cart. His back was tired and his neck was killing him. His shoulders had climbed up to his ears from lifting barrels and worrying. The skies had clouded over, but he consoled himself that his workday was almost over.

His own local, the Trump & Whistle, was on the way home, and by the time he arrived, the wind was driving the rain sideways. Patrick stepped inside to dry off and have a pint. Going home was to be delayed as long as possible. Seamus, the bartender, was a friend from early school days and a willing ear. Patrick trusted Seamus. He knew Norah's story inside and out, as Pat and Jack had recounted it at the pub many times in vivid detail, exchanging roles in what had become a practiced storytelling.

Patrick slid on a stool by the bar. "Good to see you," he said wearily. Seamus drew him a pint and leaned in for a chat. The pub was quiet, with most of the working blokes home for dinner and the women either feeding or trying to corral their straying children before coming out for a foaming mug to start the night.

"I am dead serious," Patrick told Seamus, picking up their ongoing conversation without explanation. "I am going to America. Tomorrow I'm taking on a second shift at the brewery."

Seamus frowned. "A night shift? You're already earning extra money doing odd jobs around here. When are you plannin' to sleep?"

Patrick ignored the question. "You haveta come, Seamus. Jack has thrown his lot with me," he added confidently.

"I thought he was sweet on Erin," Seamus said.

"Ah, there's a new one each week," Patrick answered. "'Course, Ma and Da are brokenhearted, but they're also sick of the pressure at home. Ma even told me she wants me to go."

Seamus raised his eyebrows. "She didn't mean it, Pat," he said softly.

"But you know I mean it when I say I'm sick of being called to fight a losing cause!" Patrick replied.

"I do, Pat, I do. The local Fenians are calling on us to stand up for ourselves. They call it patriotism, but a revolt against the Brits is too risky. It will get us killed, and that's about all."

Pat leaned back, trying to think of what more he could say. Once again his friend had agreed with him about Ireland but stopped short of saying he'd join him in America. Seamus had shown some interest in his sister, so he started there. "Did you know Norah has agreed to join the Youngs' school where Ma works? She'll be siding with the Brits before we know it."

Seamus laughed. "Your ma has worked there for years and I don't see she's turned against us."

"Maybe," Patrick said. "With Norah I think it's already happening. She rarely comes to the pub anymore, does she?" Seamus nodded as if he'd noticed the same thing, and Patrick went on. "Sure enough, she is home in her room writing in a little book and carries it next to her breast so no one can find it lying about and read it. We're all wondering what could be in there. Wouldn't you like to get your hands on that book?"

His friend cocked his head to the side and a boyish smile played across his lips. "At least to be the one to be lucky enough to remove it from its hiding place," he said.

Patrick laughed, taking no offense at Seamus's joking about his sister. "Whatever she is recording in there," he said seriously, "she seems to be more at peace than I am, Seamus. I'm in a tug-of-war, for my life and my soul. It is eating me up. It can't be disloyal or cowardly to leave if there's no point in staying to fight. I want my life. I want a future. Here, I see no future. Even if it is not my own blood that's spilled on the streets, I can't bear to watch it. I know I'm repeating myself with you; I just don't see a way to go forward here. Come with us, Seamus. We will make a way for ourselves in America."

"I'll miss you, Patrick," Seamus answered him. "And I'll think no less of you. I may be sorry, but leavin' Ireland? It's not right for me." Changing the subject, he asked, "You see Willy Kelly out there when you came in?"

Pat shook his head. He wasn't done convincing Seamus, but he knew to stop pushing him right then. "Not here," he said. "Earlier today when I was delivering at a local close to the docks. Looked like he was waiting for something." Willy had been leaning against the outside wall and cleaning his dirty fingernails with the point of his sharp knife. Pat was familiar with that knife. When Willy wasn't using it, he kept it close and ready, sheathed on his bad leg as if that made the leg stronger. As long as Pat had known him, Willy walked with a limp—an accident he'd had as a child. He wasn't too intelligent, but everyone who knew of Willy knew his skill with that knife and was careful not to get on his bad side. Pat used to think of him as a blowhard, more bluster than action. If that had once been true, it wasn't any longer. Pat stayed clear of the man, not just for his knife. Willy had a nasty temper.

"He's a thug," Seamus told Pat. "The sight of him turns my stomach." He looked Pat in the eye. "You know he's got an eye for your sister, don't you?"

"And you know Norah won't give him the time of day," Pat said with a laugh, but he suspected it was the man's dented pride that had escalated his insults toward Norah. Seamus seemed to know it too. "Might be better she's with the Anglos than on the street near the likes of Willy," he said.

Pat nodded, conceding the point. The Brits were one thing, but Willy was something worse.

There were many poor lads who'd grown up in the poorhouse. But they hadn't all turned out like Willy. He had a nose for trouble at an early age and a quick pickpocket hand. He'd always been small. Pat's own ma had called him a runt. She'd seen how Willy made up for his size by ruling the other street urchins with a mix of bravado and fear and had warned her sons to stay away from him. Pat was pretty sure some of those street boys were still with Willy. They had to know he cheated them, but there was always a price if you wanted to belong.

Behind Pat, the door to the Trump & Whistle swung open and Seamus, who had been leaning on the bar, stood up. Pat turned his head to see Willy Kelly slowly walk into the room. His limp was more noticeable, likely from the cold weather outside. In back of him, his collection of brutes trailed in.

"Beat a British bastard silly and liberated his wallet like the true patriot I am," Willy announced. He held up a fat, wet billfold plump with cash for all to see. "Drinks on England!" he shouted.

Patrick exploded with anger. "What were you thinking, Willy? You just made life harder for everyone in this room by attacking a Brit. They'll be all over us 'til they find who did it."

"Trust me," Willy growled, "he'll never identify anyone." He laughed at his own sick joke.

"So he's dead?" Pat asked. "That's your idea of patriotism?"

Willy stepped toward him. The limp seemed to have disappeared. At that proximity, Patrick could smell Willy's ripe body, and he wrinkled his nose in disgust. Willy spit in Patrick's face.

"Who are you to say I killed him, brother of a whore? I never said anyone was dead and you never heard it."

Patrick wiped the dark spittle from his cheek. "Insulting my sister is a weak defense, Willy. Tell us, then, are you a patriot or just a lousy shit?" Willy lunged, but Patrick was too quick and too sober, and Willy landed face down on the floor.

Seamus moved from behind the bar, put his foot on Willy's back, and told him to leave with his grimy friends or he would call for the constable. Patrick held himself against the bar, fighting the urge to give the man a good thrashing. Willy grabbed the wallet that had fallen to the floor with him and cleared out, throwing a look at Patrick when he reached the door. "This," he said, "is not over. I will find you, Gossett." Willy drew his finger across his neck. "When you least expect me."

Seamus poured a round on the pub to settle things down. Patrick calmed himself with a third stout, knowing he should never have even looked at Willy. He waited at the bar until the local crowd began to piss and moan over the same issues they chewed on every night—armed rebellion for dignity and freedom—and he couldn't stand to listen anymore.

Patrick made his way home in the driving rain, keeping to the main streets where there were more people. It was bucketing rain and people were rushing for cover. He wanted more light. Willy's kind liked dark alleyways. He believed Willy would kill him if he got the chance. If Patrick had had any lingering doubts about America, they disappeared that night. Willy's threat had been the final straw. Patrick had to leave Ireland before Willy hurt him so badly he wouldn't be able to travel anywhere, let alone America. *Why did I come after the likes of Willy Kelly?* He had to do it, he told himself. He had no choice. The man was a disgrace to Ireland and Irishmen. With such high stakes for the people who were offering their lives for independence, his thievery and assaults appalled Patrick.

He stopped walking. There was more to it than that. No one else in the pub had stood up to Willy. No one else felt they had to confront a dangerous man. And then he understood. No one else felt guilty for planning to leave Ireland to the likes of a Willy Kelly. Patrick started home again. Whatever his reasons had been, his choice was made.

Pat arrived home without incident. He shook off his wet coat and hung it on his peg by the door and felt strangely calm.

All his anger and fear seemed to have been washed away by the rain. He had the serenity of having made a decision. Jack had to have *some* money saved up. Seamus would lend them the rest; he was almost sure of it. They were going to America.

Norah was making a pot of tea and Ma and Da were reading quietly in their warm kitchen. Jack was nowhere to be seen, and Patrick guessed he was braving the rain to the local. The scene was so peaceful he hated to break the spell. Pouring him a cup, Norah asked, "Where ya been? Dinner's cold."

Patrick took the tea and turned to his parents. There was no need putting off what he'd been telling them all along. "Ma, Da, I am booking passage to America. Next month, earlier if I can."

His parents looked up at him with little surprise. He had said the words often enough. Tonight there was strength behind them. "Will you go with Jack?" his father asked.

"That's what we planned. But Da, with or without Jack, I'm going."

Patrick told them of his confrontation with Willy Kelly. Norah blushed with shame and grumbled "the lousy bastard." Patrick had intended to also tell them about Willy's threat to kill him. Now it seemed like a jinx to mention it. They knew enough to have guessed it themselves. His family had heard enough hard news for one evening. And he had made enough hard decisions for one night. There would be plenty of difficult choices ahead, and there was nothing more he could do to prepare for them. He would face the coming uncertainties as best he could. He had to move on. Alone or with Jack, the time had come.

CHAPTER 45

WHO AM I?

June 1887

A crisp breeze came off Dublin Bay, making the trees dance and the surface of the River Dodder ripple beneath the soft afternoon light. Norah lifted the hem of her skirt and waded in. From her grassy spot on the bank, Lucie laughed at her friend's bravery. "How cold is it?" she called out.

Norah waved her skirt like a cancan dancer. "Bloody cold, and the bottom is slippery." She tucked her skirt into her belt, then reached a hand toward Lucie. "Here." Lucie shed her shoes and stockings and walked down to the water's edge, where she stopped warily atop a large flat stone that wobbled ever so slightly beneath her. "Take my hand, Lucie. It feels so free to have the water run across your feet. I've a mind to do a jig right here."

"No!" Lucie said. "You'll fall in!"

"Best take my hand then."

With Norah's help, Lucie stepped into the water, lifting her hem only enough to keep it dry and staying near the bank's edge where the current was less strong. She let out a yelp at the cold. "Oh, Norah, what a sight we are! Bare ankles and legs. 'Such shocking behavior for well-bred young women,'" she said, imitating her Aunt Frances.

Norah snorted. "Speak for yourself, Miss Lucie. You are well bred. I am a cook's daughter."

"The stuff is coming up between my toes!" Lucie squealed. "My brothers played in the creeks back home, not I. They would be surprised I would even *think* of standing here!"

"Mine wouldn't," Norah replied quietly. "You must miss them. Your brothers, I mean."

"I do," Lucie said. "I'll miss you too this summer, unless you come to Sligo with us. We will have so much fun together."

Miss Elfie had issued Norah an invitation to join her and Lucie and Mr. Young for their trip to the west coast and Mr. Fenn's home in Sligo, which was now Elizabeth's. Norah was uncomfortable with the idea. Miss Elfie's generosity had crossed a social line. She had invited Norah as a guest, not as a tutor or a servant. One misstep or misunderstanding from someone outside the Fenns or Youngs, and she could end up not belonging anywhere.

"That's enough for me," Lucie said, laughing. She grabbed Norah's hand and together they stepped on the grassy bank to sit in the sun and dry their pale calves and feet with large cotton scarves they then spread out to dry well away from the fine spray of the fast-running river.

"Lucie, I don't think you met or even saw me brothers, Patrick and Jack," Norah said, then corrected herself: "*my* brothers." Glancing skyward, she said, "Yes, Miss Frances," before continuing. "Probably not, as they left for America in a big hurry. They're gone and so very far away. We can't imagine their lives but we try. When we get a letter from them, we practically wear out the thin paper reading and re-reading it."

"I saw them once," Lucie answered, "at RockView. Your brothers are very handsome!" Norah looked at her curiously, surprised Lucie would think any Irishman handsome. "They brought our Christmas tree into the house my first year here," Lucie explained. "Of course, your mother and Mary speak of them. I know what it's like crossing that big ocean. It's lonely, especially when you know you can't go back anytime soon and you are not sure what is waiting for you on the other end." Lucie saw that Norah was watching the river now, her mind elsewhere. "I'm sorry. I've already told you all that," Lucie said. "We are talking about your brothers."

Norah kept her eyes focused on the rushing current. "I might have gone with them," she said wistfully, "if I'd been brave enough. Instead, I went to work for your aunts, which took some courage, let me tell you. I had no idea what they expected of me."

"I didn't know that about you," Lucie said. "I was scared, too, when I first came."

"I like being part of your aunts' school *now*, and I am determined to take advantage of my time there." Norah sighed. "That water is in a big hurry. My brothers couldn't leave this country fast enough either."

Norah turned to Lucie and put her arm around her shoulders. "Your grandfather was clever to have us write about our lives and thoughts in journals," she said in a lighter tone. "I used to be afraid to talk about the darker parts of my life. I *never* thought I would put them on paper. The interesting part of it all is, I am no longer ashamed. I have given my story to the past. It is history, over and done. I can move forward. The big question remains—what does moving forward mean for me as an Irishwoman?"

Lucie opened her mouth as if to speak, then closed it.

Norah laughed and lay back on the bank. "That's all right, Lucie. I don't have an answer yet either. Let's talk about something else."

Lucie stood up, stretching her arms overhead, hands clasped. "Did you know Elizabeth Fenn went to the Misses Young School? She was in the first class. I could have gone with Aunt Frances to Spain this summer instead, but I decided I would rather be with Aunt Elfie and Grandfather."

Norah blinked. Sometimes Lucie's excitement felt overwhelming to her.

"I'm with them every day," Lucie rambled on, "but that's school. I feel I should be with them in Sligo. Grandfather is getting old, and Aunt Elfie lost her Mr. Fenn. Aunt Elfie still talks about him as if he is part of her family, so that sort of makes him my family too. But I haven't met Elizabeth or her little Henry, or even Elizabeth's brother, Philip, yet. Aunt Elfie is so fond of them. She's a different person right before and after her trips to the Fenn home. Happier. Though I find it all a little sad."

Lucie sat on the bank again and took a breath. "I know how it feels to lose someone you love. Oh, please come with us. Aunt Elfie says the house sits on Sligo Bay. At night we can listen to the waves, and during the day we can explore the grounds, which Aunt Elfie says are wild but beautiful. We would have so much fun there. Are you considering it? You don't have to work. You will be just part of the family."

Norah didn't answer right away, mostly because she wasn't certain she could make Lucie understand. "You and I have shared some of our deepest troubles," she began, "but Lucie, we live in different worlds with different expectations of us. Every day when I arrive at RockView, I wonder, how far into your world should I go? I feel safe at your aunts' school because I understand how I fit in. But that's not the same as living with your family at RockView, is it? I talked about Sligo with Ma and Da last night. Seamus was there, and even he thought the trip would be . . . awkward."

Lucie looked puzzled. "I never thought of it that way for you."

"Why would you?" Norah asked. "You are from away, but you are family to the Youngs. You came to another world, but it is more your world than mine. I am grateful for the opportunity your family has given me, and I want to take advantage of what they have offered, but I don't want to get too comfortable in a place I cannot stay. My life will not be lived like yours or the Fenns'. My life is with the Gossetts and people like us. Ma says I can work at RockView again this summer. Same as last year when you were away with your grandmother up north. Oh, come on now," she said, seeing Lucie's frown. "You will have a grand time, and I will look forward to seeing you when you return."

Lucie was quiet for several minutes, and Norah went back to watching the river, letting the girl work out her own thoughts. "I just wanted you to come," Lucie finally said, "because I like being with you. I never think of you as different. To me, you're just Norah."

Norah straightened her back but kept her eyes on the river. "My brothers were so angry at me when I went to work at RockView. They told me I was becoming soft in the head and too much like the Brits. They couldn't see that Mr. Young would become like a grandpa to me or that the care and attention your aunts give to me is sincere. To my brothers that seemed impossible. To be honest, I once thought so too. Even now, when I walk away from RockView in the evening, I know I am still just the same old Norah. But I also feel I am changing, so I ask myself, 'Norah, who are you these days?'"

"Who *are* you?" Lucie asked.

"Let's start our walk home," Norah said. She stood up and circled her hips, making her long skirt fly out from her ankles both to help dry out her clothes and to lighten her mood. "What I mean is, I am not you. I get afraid I am getting too fancy in my thinking. I'm Irish, and that means I'm Catholic, end of story."

Lucie stopped in her tracks. "What does *that* mean?"

"Your aunties taught us in class that the British rule people all over the globe in their la-di-da empire. What they don't say—and maybe that's because they don't see it—is there are black people, brown people, and Irish Catholics in the empire, and the British look down on the whole bunch of us."

"My family doesn't look down on you or Biddy or Mary or any of your family," Lucie protested.

Norah nodded, keeping her doubts to herself. "The church has done no favors for us, either," she said bringing the conversation back to safer ground. "Nuns whipped both my brothers and me in school, and some girls we know who got in a family way were treated like criminals. What kind of religion is that?" Norah had tightened her grip on Lucie as she spoke and now let go of her hand. "Poor Lucie, that was more of an answer than you were looking for. I've been doing a lot of thinking, and it all spilled out."

"Then why be Catholic?"

Norah had never thought to question being a Catholic. "I think if you're Irish, you're just born Catholic. It isn't necessarily a belief for every Irish man and woman," Norah said. "It's more of a culture. Or maybe a tradition," she added. "I'm not even sure it's something you can choose. Ma would tell you something different, but that's how I see it."

As they drew closer to RockView, they slowed their pace, and Norah tried to explain again. "Lucie, there's the British and the Anglo-Irish world, and then there's the Irish Catholic world. They are separate. It's only because Ma was working for your family that I was offered something my brothers didn't get. That's been hard to live with, Lucie.

"If I get more educated and have more experience with the Anglo-Irish, maybe I could be a guest in places like the Fenn home. But will I feel dishonest? Will I be fooling people? Sometimes even now I feel like an actress when I'm at RockView, changing my speech and manners to play the part of . . . I don't know who. An Anglo-Irish? An Irish Catholic–Anglo-Irish? Is there even such a thing? Am I becoming a new Norah or a Norah in disguise?" She stopped walking. "That's what I mean when I ask myself who I am."

"That does seem . . . confusing," Lucie said.

Norah laughed. "Let's keep walking."

"I have not thought much about who I am, Norah. I didn't think I belonged with my family in Canada anymore with Clara there, and I wasn't sure how I'd feel with the Youngs, but I know now that I belong with them. I feel it." Lucie frowned. "That's not the same thing, is it?"

Norah didn't answer.

"I'm sorry your brothers are so far away," Lucie said. "Mine don't write much. Have your brothers sent you a photograph or picture postcard from New York?"

Norah doubted Patrick and Jack had the money to spend on a postcard, let alone a photograph of themselves, but she could imagine them standing in front of one of those tall buildings to have their picture taken like big, important men. "That would be fun, to have that to remind me of them and believe they are all right. I wonder what a photograph costs?"

Lucie, who Norah was certain never had to think about the cost of anything, said, "Father sends me pictures and I almost wear them out. I try to memorize their faces; I only remember Hugh and Knox as little boys."

Norah wanted to have a photograph of her brothers one day.

By the time they reached Lucie's home and said their good-byes, Norah had made her decision. She would stay home that summer. When Patrick and Jack left, the tension and frustration that had once filled the Gossetts' home was replaced by emptiness and sorrow. She thought she understood why Lucie had chosen Sligo over Spain.

"Norah," Lucie called out.

Norah turned to see the girl hurrying to catch up with her.

"You are my friend," Lucie said. "To me you are my friend, no matter what you do or how you speak." She grabbed Norah's arm and gave her a kiss on the cheek. Norah laughed and they turned from each other, going their separate ways once more.

CHAPTER 46

CODES AND WAYS

April 1888
Thomas

The trees were just beginning to leaf out along the meandering Dodder. Among its many scenic curves, Thomas chose a spot for his class where the river ran past the ruins of the old, crumbled fort walls of Rathmines. While waiting for Norah to join them, Thomas instructed Lucie, Victoria, and Annabelle to each find a vantage point that took in the bucolic scene. The girls sketched quietly, but their fourth classmate never appeared. Thomas was more curious than worried. Norah occasionally missed a class, and always for a good reason. His art lessons weren't part of the school's curriculum but something he had started offering long ago at the behest of his daughters and a few eager students. He had required his students to attend every class. He just assumed they would.

When enough time had passed, Thomas pulled out his

watch from his pocket vest, flipped it open, and summoned the girls' attention. His students repositioned themselves on the sit-upons they had brought and turned their focus from their sketchpads to their teacher. "By now," he began, stopping to clear his throat, "you will have sketched shapes and dimensions. It's time to add detail and think about color. Think how that will add to your work. Look carefully again at your subject; note the color suggestions and gradations you can use in the watercolor you will create later. Keep in mind our talk about how depth and perspective can be emphasized through the use of dark and light colors. You will use paint, brush, and water to bring your creation to life."

After a few questions and Thomas's suggestions, the girls went back to their sketchbooks. This wasn't their first watercolor session, but it was the first taking place out of the classroom. A new and unexpected environment could be both exciting and paralyzing, and he wanted his students to feel reassured by the familiar instructions. "Very good," he said, pleased by their focus. He sat down again, adjusting himself on his precious collapsible stool. The girls sat closer to the ground, but Thomas stayed a foot or so up from the damp earth that caused his arthritis to bark at him—not to mention that getting up gracefully had become increasingly difficult.

He glanced over the eroded rock and earthworks, the last remains of the once-protective rath. Patchy stones here and there indicated where a stout wall once stood, a bold defense for those on the other side. *I feel a bit patchy these days myself,* he thought. *Time marches for all of us. Even for the girls. They aren't truly girls anymore. They're young women now. Lucie must be at least fourteen.* They reminded him of others he had watched move so remarkably from girlhood to adulthood: his wife, Sarah; his daughters, Frances, Elfie, and Lily; and now Lucie and Norah. Each meant so much to him. Some were gone. All were changed. He was too. How long had the moss and lichen been working to break down the rath? Seven hundred years or more, he guessed. *What remnants of my life will stand over time?* Jonathan Swift's line "May you live all the days of your life" came to mind. Thomas certainly had tried.

His thoughts cast precariously beyond his immediate circle. In this tempestuous political climate that had caused Lily and others to leave and made Ireland two "countries," Irish and Anglo-Irish, he wondered: what, if any, impact was his life having?

His family, his daughters' school, and his community of students and fellow artists were the places where his life mattered. That was his sphere. He looked again at the young ladies sitting cross-legged on the ground (an unmanageable position for him), their pads on their knees or laps, squinting at their subjects to record as much detail as possible. The world beyond—social change, politics, and nationalism—was just that: beyond him. He was happy to turn all that turmoil over to the younger ones.

He thought about those subjects, talked about them, but was not ready to stand on the hustings or man the barricades. Not Thomas. *I suppose this means I must make the best of myself a benefit to my family, friends, and colleagues.* The thought brought him a measure of peace. He turned his gaze upward to the almost cloudless sky. An osprey flew overhead, its graceful brown wings and gray breast catching the light.

Like the rath, the memory of his life would erode and fade. What rune, marking, would be left for the future? It was moments like this when he missed Lily the most. He would have carried this conversation forward with her. Her sudden death had sent Lucie into his life. An unexpected gift. He turned toward his granddaughter, intent on her sketch, blond curls highlighted by the weak sun, and once again felt a deep connection to her. He hoped she would carry his love for her wherever life took her, as he did. She was his next generation, the one that would remember her family in Ireland.

Thomas checked his pocket watch—*has it been forty minutes already?*—then signaled to the girls to pack up. "Time to make our way home," he said brightly. He felt a certain lightness as he surveyed the scene. That little conversation with himself had pulled together some important threads for him. Perhaps he had more purpose and direction than he had thought. His art and his teaching, what he was doing that very day, might be his best gifts to the next generations.

As the girls gathered their materials, he heard them whispering. Did he hear Norah's name? The hearing was fading too. *Eyes, ears—what's next?* Annabelle and Victoria chattered away quite openly. Something about Norah becoming less friendly. "Why didn't she come today, Mr. Young?" Victoria asked.

Lucie was quick to stand up for Norah. "She is much older than we are and has other things to do."

She might have, Thomas considered. He recalled his own state when Lily and James left for Canada. *Would that grief ever end? Not really. Norah is likely still grieving her brothers,* he concluded. The diaspora continued to drain Ireland of its youth and, consequently, the hopes of those left behind. Once again, he told himself there was nothing he could do to change that. *It could be something else altogether,* he thought. *Women have many moods, not all of them logical to my mind.* He would ask Frances to check with Biddy and possibly even Norah herself.

— ◆ —

Frances

Frances had not noticed a change in Norah's behavior. But as she thought more of it, perhaps there was less warmth, less hugging, and fewer soft smiles from the girl. "I will speak to Norah directly, Father, and check in with Biddy too, of course. Thank you for telling me."

"Apparently, she left early from her work today. I would think you should know something about that, Frances," Thomas said as he walked to the door leading to the entryway. "Whatever the case, she didn't come to the sketching class."

Frances frowned at the rebuff from her father. "I would think so too," she said. She put the ledger in its drawer, pushed back her chair, and followed her father out of the drawing room. "I'd better check on that."

Frances found Elfie in the classroom, writing instructions for the next day's lesson on the blackboard, and asked if she had seen Norah. "Not since she told me she was leaving early today."

Frances was annoyed. "That's information I should be informed of, don't you think?"

"I assumed she had," her sister said without looking up.

Frances breathed through her nose. *I wish you had thought to make sure she had,* she thought. Elfie had never quite come out of her grieving for George. Not only for George, Frances knew, but also for her life as a wife and mother. Frances had expected to take up the slack with the school for the first year after George died; now it had been nearly six. It wasn't that Elfie shirked her responsibilities at the school. She wasn't putting as much of herself into any part of it anymore, or into much of anything or anyone, as far as Frances knew. Her father continued to counsel patience and understanding. "Think of our queen," he'd say. Frances wasn't worried about Queen Victoria. She was worried about Elfie. She missed her sweet, lively sister.

In the kitchen, Frances found Biddy and Mary in full swing, making shepherd's pie with Sunday's leftover lamb. Neither had noticed her yet. Biddy was at the stove with her back to

Frances, and Mary was working hard with the ricer to make the potatoes light and fluffy. "Ya taught me well, Bid!" Mary said. "I told me husband about your addin' the egg to make the potatoes puff up like a white cloud sittin' on our meat pie, and you know what he said? 'Leave it to the Brits to want ta eat a cloud instead of a nice mashed potato!'" Biddy smiled as she filled pans with the lamb and vegetables, then Mary added the potato cloud that would brown and crisp on top.

Frances enjoyed listening to their teasing and laughter. *They're like sisters helping to make light of their work and their lives,* she thought, like she and Elfie had done before George died. The lighter side of her relationship with her sister was coming back. Slowly. There was still a sadness in Elfie, less spark.

Biddy shifted her ample body as she opened the oven door and with strong arms lifted the pies one by one and slid them inside.

The oven shut, Biddy turned and saw Frances. "Miss Frances! What can I do for you?"

Frances smiled. "How about some tea?" she asked, sitting down at the long kitchen table. She waited until Biddy poured her a cup before continuing. "I am wondering about Norah. The girls have been asking. They say she's been keeping to herself lately. Is everything all right?"

"Oh, Miss Frances, it's a long while since the boys left us, but their absence is a sorrow we Gossetts carry in our hearts every day."

"I suppose that might be it," Frances said. Biddy moved about, cleaning the kitchen, and said no more. Frances watched her thoughtfully and realized Biddy hadn't looked at her once since she sat down, and Mary, who had excused herself to take the trash out to the back porch when Frances mentioned Norah, hadn't returned from the short task. *There's something more going on,* she thought. Frances knew Biddy well enough not to push. Instead, she asked Biddy to have a cup of tea with her. "You look like you could use one, and I could use the company."

Biddy nodded, wiped her hands on a dish towel, and sat down across from Frances with her freshly poured tea. "At first, we were relieved the boys were safe," Biddy said without preamble.

Safe from what? Frances wondered but didn't ask, as Biddy didn't often open up to her about her family life.

"As time has gone by, we're no longer sure that's true. Now we're always wonderin' how they are, Patrick and Jack. Not many good evenings at our house these days. Norah goes to her room and shuts the door to avoid quarrels with her da. The only change o' luck in this story is Seamus, Patrick's friend. He's made a habit of visiting us since my sons left. Those nights Norah stays in the kitchen. Seamus fancies himself Norah's protector."

Frances nearly gasped at learning Norah needed a protector. She heard the back door open and saw Mary slip quietly into the kitchen, but Biddy either didn't notice or didn't care and continued talking.

"Well, we can all see Seamus clearly wishes for more than that. But Norah has a mind of her own. Truth is, I'm glad he's 'round. It's that ruffian Willy Kelly we're worried about. A bad sort, miss. Before our Pat left us, he had a run-in with Willy at the Trump & Whistle. That's where Seamus works as barkeep. Pat told us Willy was insulting Norah to his face. I can tell you Pat didn't let that pass, but now we all hold fear that Willy will find a way to settle the score. Thank God Pat and Jack managed to give 'um the slip. It's him who's the reason they left so quickly." Biddy frowned and sipped her tea. She let out a long sigh and wiped her eyes with the back of her hands. "They made it to Galway," she said, "and are long gone to America. But Willy is still here, and so is Norah."

Frances stared into her still-full cup, speechless. Biddy stood, took the cup out of her hands, emptied the tepid liquid into the sink, and refilled the cup with a hot brew. *No wonder Norah is acting strangely,* Frances thought. She knew Patrick and Jack had gone to America but had assumed it was something they wanted—an exciting adventure, not an escape for their lives. Frances understood so little of the Gossetts' world and could only imagine the circumstances they lived with.

Biddy removed her own cup from the table to wash it, then opened the oven to check on dinner, letting a waft of warmth and savory aroma escape. Still Frances said nothing, and Biddy plunked herself down on the high stool by the worktable. They were alone in the room again. Frances had no idea when Mary had left. "I shouldn't have told you so much about me troubles, miss. But you asked about Norah. It's a lot on us and has been for some time. We don't speak much of it. We are all feeling unsettled, Norah especially.

"She feels guilt, you see. Long ago Willy followed her about and she let him do it, mainly to defy Conor and me. She was a handful when she was younger, not like she is now. We only learned recently that when she came home from the gaol, Willy tried to get her attention." Biddy sighed and shook her head. "She laughed at him. And being who he is, he pitched a fit; told her she'd be sorry, that he'd make sure of it. Norah said she hadn't thought much of his threat at the time, but now with her brothers away. . ." Biddy sighed again. "Fear and regret are heavy stones to carry about. Seamus tries to make the situation lighter for her and jokes that if they dodge him long enough Willy will be locked up. I don't want to frighten you, Miss Frances, but Willy and his gang have a long list of crimes they've done. He'll get caught one day. Seamus even said he might be killed by his own kind. He cheats them."

Frances shook her head, trying to take it all in, "Biddy, is Willy the reason Norah left early today?"

"Willy Kelly won't be bothering you or the girls here!" Biddy said quickly. "That man hangs about in the shadows of his local and the wharf. You don't have to worry about that."

"I'm not, Biddy," Frances said firmly. "I am worried about Norah. She told Elfie she was leaving, but she didn't ask my permission as well, and she really should have."

Biddy looked at her shoes. "I don't like it that she didn't follow your rules, Miss Frances. I think Norah is stirred up and Seamus is a source of comfort to her. Today is Seamus's early-off evening as barkeep. I suppose she could have gone to see him. Sometimes they meet for a pub dinner to avoid the scratchy evenings at our house. Maybe she went home early to primp a bit? I would say they have an eye for one another . . ." Biddy looked a bit sheepish. "Of course she should have asked, there is no excuse for just leaving . . ."

Frances stared at her full teacup, perplexed by the overlapping, disturbing pieces of news and wondering what it meant for the school and for Norah. She was taken aback by Biddy's harrowing story, but she preferred to be constructive rather than petulant. "Is there anything we can do to help or protect Norah?" she said, straightening her back to appear confident and decisive. "We are so fond of her. She is such an important member of our school. The girls love her and look up to her. We want her safe and at her best."

Biddy stood up and adjusted her apron, smoothing the wrinkles over her ample stomach. "Miss Frances," she said, "I do not know what to ask for."

"Would living here at the school be safer?" Frances suggested. "Is the constable where you live aware of this threat? Perhaps Father should have a talk with him."

"Oh, Miss Frances, that is generous of you, but don't get tangled up in our mess. I've said too much and shouldn't have. You have your school and your family to think of. I'll speak with Norah. The Gossetts will get through this. Livin' 'round people in the Liberties, we know the codes and have ways to get by, solve problems. It is just a bad time, and we have seen them before."

Frances felt so moved, she walked over to Biddy to embrace her. Biddy backed away, saying, "Don't ruin your dress by hugging me. I'm a messy Irish cook covered with shepherd's pie. Thank you for your kind thoughts. I will tell you if there is a way you can help Norah. For now we have to handle this as Irish. Now, I've taken too much of your time, and you'll be wanting to get the girls ready for their dinner. You've been kind to let me unburden myself."

Frances left the kitchen thinking about "codes" and "ways" and handling things "as Irish." *What does that mean?* she wondered. She had a lot to tell her sister and father.

CHAPTER 47

WILLY'S REVENGE

Norah had initially agreed to meet Seamus after sketching class at the local near the canal, their favorite spot. But she stopped at his work to tell him she had changed her mind and was going home first. She didn't tell him the reason—to change into her new jumper to look especially nice for him.

Miss Elfie hadn't seemed to mind her leaving, but Seamus didn't like her being out alone and told her so. "Just wait here 'til I can walk you home. Willy's been coming around, and I don't want you running into him."

"It's still the afternoon, Seamus," she said. "He's like a cockroach. He doesn't come out until after dark." She smiled as she walked out the door. Keeping her independence and primping for Seamus both made her very happy.

As Norah approached the corner of Clanbrassil and Canal, she saw a figure standing behind a lamppost that looked like Seamus. *It can't be,* she reasoned. *I've only just left him.* Unless he found someone to watch the bar for him so he could walk her home. *That'd be just like him,* she thought, feeling both giddy and slightly irritated that he didn't think she could take care of herself. She squinted to get a better view of the man. In the fading afternoon light, it was hard to say who it was. When she thought about it further, it didn't make sense that Seamus would be ahead of her already. *He'd come up behind me.* Thoughts of Willy, combined with the stench from the canal, made her uncomfortable. She crossed the road.

As she reached the other side, a cloth sack came down over her head and rough hands pinned her arms behind her. Before she could scream, her captor shoved the sack deep into her mouth. "Keep your trap shut," he whispered, "or I put a knife in you." A muscular body lifted her up and another two hands sank into her armpits, dragging her onto a splintery wood floor. Norah lifted her leg to kick at her captor, but her boot only sliced air. "Hold her down!" she heard. She had no doubts now. Her captor was Willy Kelly.

Strong arms forced her face onto the floor. *I am going to die,* she thought as Willy and another man came heavily into the wagon beside her. They fell across her hard so she couldn't move. "Let's go!" Willy called. The wagon lurched beneath them and began bumping its way along the rough cobbled streets. The odors of the men, mixed with the smells of cabbage and onions cooking in nearby homes, nauseated her. Her heart raced with fear. *Where are they taking me?*

The wagon stopped and Norah was dragged into what felt like a stone cave or tunnel . . . *or alley,* she thought, hopefully. Someone might hear her or see her! Her hope was brief. She was shoved against a wall and fell to the floor, hitting her head on something hard on the way down.

When she came to, she heard Willy and his men rolling dice, challenging one another with ugly oaths and thieves' argot. The sounds were accompanied by the heady smell of cheap ale. She lay still against the cold, damp wall and prayed the men would drink themselves into a stupor so she might have a chance for escape. Time drifted as she went in and out of consciousness.

She woke when big hands lifted her off the floor and propped her in a chair, where her head covering was removed. Willy sat across from her, gloating, a knife in his hand that flashed in the dim light. "I am trying to decide where to carve my first mark on you, whore," he said. He spat on the floor, then grinned, showing yellowed teeth with ugly gaps where his tongue slipped through like an old crone's. His face was swollen and gruesome as if he'd only just been on the losing end of a fight. Norah's stomach churned. She was terrified. Willy stood up and approached her, waving the knife in front of her face. His men laughed nervously.

One spoke up. "Willy, don't go too far," he said. "We got lucky with that dead British bloke."

"Shut up!" said Willy. "She's been asking for this."

— • —

Norah had not been wrong about Seamus. As soon as she had turned to leave the pub, he grabbed the stock boy in the back, told him to mind the pub, and ran after Norah. *She's too cocky for her own good,* he worried, *thinking she can survive anything after her time in the gaol.* He spotted her down the street from the Trump & Whistle and hung back, wondering if he should let her think she was alone. Seamus was so intent on watching Norah, he didn't notice the two men coming up behind him.

The next thing he knew, he was waking up, bound and gagged, in a ditch near St. Steven's Green. He looked up to see two well-dressed fellows staring at him. *Swaggers from Trinity College,* he guessed. "What the hell is he doing sleeping here?" one of them said. "Maybe he fell in," the other answered, laughing a silly, drunken laugh. The young men angled them-selves to the left of Seamus and relieved themselves. "Better!" "Yes, much," he heard them say. Seamus was afraid they were going to turn around and leave, but soon their clumsy fingers were on him, releasing his hands and feet and finally the gag that had been tied tightly around his mouth.

Seamus got up slowly and crawled back onto the road. "Bit of bad luck. Thanks, gents," he explained while checking for his money. Of course, it was gone.

Feeling the effects of his beating by Willy's thugs, Seamus limped his way back to the Trump & Whistle, where he planned to find men to help him locate Willy and his den. Inside the pub, he made a beeline to a grimy fellow who hung out with Willy. "Willy's up to no good," Seamus heard him say to the stock boy who had just poured him a whiskey. Seamus grabbed the man and spun him around, spilling his drink. "Where is he?" he demanded, "Where is Willy? Has he got Norah?"

The man wouldn't look him in the eyes. "Willy's gone mad, Seamus," he said. "I want no part of it."

"No part of what? Has he got Norah?!" Seamus let Willy's thug go. "Take me there. Now."

"He'll kill me on the spot," the man said. "But I'll tell you where they are."

"Is she dead?" Seamus asked, full of fear.

"Not when I left."

Seamus grabbed two of Patrick's friends sitting in the pub, Fritz and Liam. They were big men, but unarmed. Seamus found a confiscated truncheon behind the bar and told them to grab what they could find along the way. It wasn't far. Half a mile down the road, they turned onto a stone path to the landing by the River Liffey and soon found the damp, moldy storage cellar Willy called home. The door was old and thick, with large straps of metal to hold the heavy wood together. It was ajar, apparently from the hasty exit of the man now in the pub, and those inside were unaware of the breach.

Seamus, Fritz, and Liam slipped in. They could hear Willy ordering Norah to remove pieces of her clothes one by one, followed by a cry of pain from Norah. Seamus raced toward them. He hit Willy squarely on the back of the head with the truncheon, then turned to see a man slipping out the door. Fritz and Liam gave chase, quickly returning with the man, who they tied up next to Willy. Norah was weeping, trying to cover herself and her wounds. Willy had sliced her skin with each piece of clothing he forced her to remove. Seamus gave her his coat to cover her bare arms and carefully helped her put on her stockings and boots. With his arms holding her up, he walked Norah to her house while Fritz and Liam waited for the police.

— • —

Willy was found dead in his cell within days. At Trump & Whistle a mug was held high and Seamus offered the best blessing that could be made: "The lousy bastard got what he gave. His own kind hated him and finished him off. Justice has been served." A murmured sense of relief passed through the crowd, and someone capped it off with "The devil take him!" Seamus poured them all another round.

CHAPTER 48

HEALING

May 1888 to May 1889
Norah

Willy's knife left thick, ugly scars Norah would carry for life. For weeks she had to pull her clothes slowly over her wounds. If she'd lived alone, she wouldn't have bothered, but long sleeves and long stockings hid the marked parts of her body from her family and from friends who stopped by to lend support. For herself, she was learning to accept the disfigurement. It was the trauma of the assault that challenged her. The gaol had left a different mark. There, each conscious minute had been charged with fear and uncertainty, keeping her both alert and exhausted. Her kidnap and assault had taken place on a beautiful day as she walked home. Norah pulled her brush gently across her bruised scalp and caught her worried expression in the mirror. Would she ever shake off the memory of what had followed and regain her confidence? She relaxed her jaw and shoulders and finished her slow morning routine, twisting her long hair and securing it with a comb before taking one last look in the mirror. *So, there it is, Norah. Move on, girl.*

Seamus would be in the kitchen waiting for her before he went to work, as he had been every morning. *He's always been there,* she realized. He and her brothers had hung out together in the lane by the Gossett house since they were young lads. After Pat and Jack left for America, Seamus had nearly become a fixture in the Gossett kitchen, taking on the unspoken role of Norah's protector—not that she'd asked for one. She wished now that she had been more appreciative of his offer. *You're too proud, Norah,* she reminded herself each morning. *Look where that landed you.*

"Norah," her mother greeted her when she stepped out of her room. "Look who's here to see you."

"Good morning, Seamus," Norah said.

Seamus stood up and pulled out a chair for her at the kitchen table. The assistance was no longer necessary. She was perfectly capable of sitting on a chair herself, but she thanked him anyway. As her mother kept reminding her, Norah owed him quite a bit. They all did.

"It was Seamus who helped you escape from Willy's den and Seamus who stopped him from doing you further harm," Biddy told her almost daily, as if Norah needed reminding. "He's like one of ours." Seamus had become something much more than her brothers' friend to all of them, first to Norah and then to her parents.

The first time he complimented the evening meal, her ma pointed to her da and said, "A thank-you now and again might not hurt ya." He slapped her bum and she yelped. "So, there's an overdue 'thank-you,' my dear Miss Biddy," he said, "for keepin' me fat and happy." Her ma smoothed her skirt and flirted back: "Be ashamed, Conor Gossett..."

Seamus kept her da happy talking about his beloved Gaelic

football and bloody boxing matches, and not just the ones between blokes in a public ring. They both listened for rumors of a local street fight where the men would crowd around shouting encouragement. "Your da is quick to throw a coin in the ring," Seamus whispered to her once. "Pretty sure Ma knows, Seamus," she told him. "Doesn't mean I want her to hear it from me," he said with a chuckle. In a street fight the last man standing got the coin sweep, and probably a broken nose too. Neither Biddy nor Norah took to any of it, but they accepted that football and boxing were baked into the Irish male culture.

Norah lived tight inside the house as her wounds healed. Other than Seamus, Lucie was the only friend to visit her. Even Thomas Young, who dropped off Lucie at the Gossetts' in the afternoons and picked her up a half hour later, did not come inside. "Grandfather says he doesn't want to interfere with our time," Lucie explained, "but he asks how you are on our way home. He's been worried about you. We all have." Lucie brought Norah books from the Youngs' library and watercolors and cards from the students. The books made Norah happiest. When she wasn't too tired after cleaning up the evening meal, she would bring a book out to read at the kitchen table while her ma knit and her da read his precious sports news sheet, holding the paper as far away as his arms could reach, noisily batting its thin sheets with a hand and talking to himself about the players, game scores, and betting odds. There was a comfort in being quietly occupied together, and when Seamus joined them, the Gossett home felt nearly perfect. The prickliness between them over the last few years had disappeared at last.

"*The Wild Irish Girl*," Seamus said one evening, surprising her by reading the cover of the book she held in her hand. "Now that sounds like a book I'd be interested in," he teased. "Why don't you read it to me?" He sat himself down on the other end of the kitchen table and leaned toward her, making her laugh.

"Why don't *you* read it to *me*?" she replied, then frowned. Norah had no idea if Seamus could read more than a bar tab and didn't want to embarrass him.

"Only if you'll help me with the hard parts," he answered and moved his chair next to hers. From then on, Seamus settled himself beside her at the table while they took turns reading aloud to one another. She found the sharing lightened the time. Seamus was a fair reader, better than she'd expected, and he was quick to learn. They were in their own bubble as they concentrated on the words before them and helped one another with pronunciation and meaning. While he was with her, her worries about what lay beyond the front door disappeared.

Other than Thomas, Norah had never felt comfortable in conversation with a man outside the Gossett family, especially one who was interested in and listened to her thoughts and ideas and who also believed in her. One evening, Seamus unexpectedly popped up from his chair after dinner, grabbed the dish towel, and helped Norah with the tidy-up at the sink. "So when is Miss Norah planning to rejoin the world?" he asked.

Without thinking, Norah hit the soapy water with the back of her hand and gave a surprised Seamus a drenching. "Whoa," he said, lifting his hands, palms forward, in defense. "Just a question."

"And what makes you think it's your business to ask me that?" she asked, more sharply than she'd meant to. She surveyed the wet mess she had made of his clothes and smiled sheepishly.

Seamus stood back, brushing his wet clothes with his hands. "Well, maybe we could discuss that if you would step out for a walk with me so I can dry off in the evening air from my unexpected Thursday-night bath?"

Biddy looked up from her knitting with a soft smile of approval. If her father had an opinion, he kept it buried along with his nose in the paper. It seemed only Norah was hesitant. The sun would not set for another hour or so, but she was nervous even being outside during the day. "Willy's gone, Norah," Seamus said. "I promise. I won't leave your side."

After that first walk, it became their custom to step out in the evenings when Seamus came around. Each time they walked hand in hand, she felt a little more ready to return to the Misses Young School and rejoin the world. The Youngs had been very generous with her taking her time but she knew, without their saying so, they hoped she would come back soon.

Norah and Seamus returned later and later until Norah was no longer afraid of being outside or in the dark, and they'd arrive home after her parents had gone to sleep and she would invite him to her room. They sat close together on her bed without the light on, trying to avoid making the bed squeak. He would kiss her and hold her close, moving his hands from her back toward her breasts and whispering in her ear that she was "the prettiest colleen in all of Ireland," which made her giggle. She didn't hold him back from her body but leaned naturally into him for a long kiss, feeling a desire for much more. But she always pulled herself away to hold them off from the inevitable. That would have to wait.

"Are ya sure you are a good Catholic girl, Norah?" he teased her more than once, to which she always responded, "No, Seamus, I am not, and never was. I told you, I don't want a wee babe in my life just now. That's not being Catholic. That's being practical."

"I can be practical, Miss Norah," Seamus answered her one night, "but you should know I have strong intentions of making lots of wee babies with you, so you might as well let me know now if you have those intentions too. When you're ready," he added, seeming less sure of his declaration in the silence that followed. "Norah?" he asked after another pause. "Well, do you?"

"I do, Seamus," she answered at last. "Of course I do!"

CHAPTER 49

DOING IT RIGHT
BY THE CHURCH

August 1889
Norah

Biddy insisted Norah and Seamus "do it right by the church." Seamus said he was more than fine with that. "I don't want to give any man cause to doubt we are betrothed. In fact, say the word and we can make it a church wedding," he added. Norah knew he was only half teasing but wasn't going to explain reasons to wait again. She did agree to a church ceremony so they would be formally promised to wed, but only to please her mother. "No reason to make this a difficult time by stamping my feet unnecessarily," she said. "If it makes you happy, Ma, you'll get no argument from me."

One week after Seamus proposed, he invited Norah on a picnic and proposed again, this time with a ring. "Norah, I can't wait another minute. I'm feeling like a wee lad at Christmas," he said. Letting go of her hand, he pulled a small satchel from his pocket and gently opened Norah's fingers, placing the soft leather bag in her palm. Sitting back on the ground, she opened the satchel excitedly. It was a claddagh ring meant for betrothal and marriage. Norah's was made mostly of silver, which meant Seamus had paid a dear price for it. Seamus removed the ring and slipped it on her left finger. The picnic could wait.

— ◆ —

Lucie

Lucie had never attended a promise ceremony. "I imagine it will be very similar to your father's wedding to Clara," Aunt Elfie said. "Norah and Seamus will pledge their love and loyalty, the ceremony will be held in a church but in front of a priest instead of a pastor, and their family and good friends will be their witnesses. It should be lovely." She sighed and looked out the carriage window. "After the ceremony, you must feel almost as if you are truly married," she said to no one in particular. Lucie watched Aunt Elfie turn her focus to the passing landscape. She didn't seem particularly happy or even sad to Lucie. Only distracted, as she mostly seemed to be when she wasn't teaching, as if her mind preferred to be somewhere other than where her body was.

"You and George had one of the nicest engagement parties I've attended," Grandfather told Elfie. "I remember thinking at the time, 'Why, it's as if they're already married.'" He patted her hand.

"I hope Mary and her daughter are all right with the girls in the other carriages," Frances said, changing the subject.

"We probably should have shared the burden rather than all four of us ride together."

"We're a family attending a family ceremony, or as close as," Elfie said, sounding defiant. "Mary and Bridget and the girls are fine."

"I know they are as excited as I am!" Lucie said. "Imagine promising your love to a handsome and kind man and he promises to love you back forever. It's so romantic," she said with a sigh. "It almost feels like a fairy tale!"

"Lucie," Aunt Frances said, "love isn't a fairy tale."

"Oh, I know," Lucie answered. "Did you see Norah's ring? It looks like Mother's wedding ring."

"It does," Aunt Elfie agreed, turning to look at her. Lucie was glad to see her aunt smiling.

"Get ready, ladies," Grandfather Thomas said. "We're nearly at St. Mary's."

—　•　—

Norah

Norah and Seamus stood before the priest, smiling at each other. The gray-haired man held out his hand, and Seamus placed Norah's ring on his palm. "I am told the claddagh originally came from Galway, where Seamus's family has roots, and has since spread throughout Ireland. I can see why," he said. "The claddagh is not one ring, but three. Entwined we see two silver hands clasped over the center hearts. No explanation needed there, I trust," he said, receiving approving smiles and nods from the guests. The priest opened the claddagh and held it up so all could see its three rings. "These rings stand for faith, loyalty, and love, which Seamus and Norah are pledging today. Not only to each other but also God." Norah smiled and breathed through her nose. She was OK with pledging to God but not to the social and political power of the church as an institution. Closing her eyes, she said to herself, *Not now, Norah . . .*

Lowering the rings, the priest asked Norah to put her finger in one end ring and Seamus to put his in the other. The priest put his own finger in the center circle, then asked the couple to repeat after him a pledge to one another and to God. Norah couldn't see, but she felt her mother smiling behind her. Their vows complete, the priest blessed the couple with holy water and collapsed the rings into one. He handed the closed claddagh to Seamus, who slipped it on Norah's ring finger with the tips of the heart pointing toward Norah's fingertips, indicating she was engaged. When they wed, the ring would be turned so that the tips faced in toward her hand and heart. The couple kissed and their guests clapped, and some of the girls giggled even as Mary and Bridget shushed them. Norah was happy. She saw Thomas smiling broadly at her, Elfie catching a tear with her handkerchief, and Frances slipping her hand into Elfie's and squeezing tight. Best of all, her mother's face was alight with joy. Norah watched her put her hand on that of her husband, who was fidgeting, probably wanting to get to the pub for the "afters."

— ◆ —

Thomas

Thomas had become sentimental while watching Norah and Seamus. *Makes me think of my wedding day,* he thought, *and Lily's.* His eldest had insisted on a gold claddagh ring for her wedding. *Funny how life has so many full circles and common touch points,* he thought. *Weddings, funerals, christenings, all stored as memories in deep places and, when recalled, poignant to savor.* Thomas fingered the old coin he had brought in his vest pocket to give to Norah and Seamus. The family had discussed waiting to give their gift when the couple was formally wed. Thomas offered to take care of a gift for the promise ceremony. "Something small and appropriate," he assured them. Thomas had his own plan and would choose his moment to present it.

After the service, he noticed Elfie and Frances still holding hands, which was not their custom, as they and Lucie chatted with the girls and with Biddy and Mary's family. He should have joined them, but his desire to nose around the inside of the pro-cathedral won out over expectation, and he broke away from the congratulators to explore. St. Mary's was a symbol of Irish Catholic emancipation. He wondered if Norah had chosen it for that reason. *More likely this is the Gossetts' church,* he decided. But he liked the symbolism. *Norah isn't one to do something she doesn't want to do.* He smiled, hoping Seamus was up for the task of living with an independent woman.

Thomas took a slow turn around the huge catafalque where Daniel O'Connell's remains had lain in state in 1847 before his burial in Glasnevin Cemetery. Putting on his glasses, Thomas leaned in to read the shiny brass plaque. "Daniel O'Connell, The Liberator, 1775-1847." The man had inspired Thomas in his youth—nothing like the way O'Connell had changed the lives of the Irish, but he had inspired Thomas to liberate from his own family and move to Ireland. Thomas had been only seventeen years old when the penal laws were at last lifted off the backs of the Irish back in 1829. O'Connell had been the first Irish Catholic to serve in the British Parliament and had celebrated Mass in this church to mark the day when Irish Catholics were finally allowed to publicly celebrate their faith and elect members of Parliament. Thomas remembered the hope at the time—not of most of the English, but of the Irish and those who quietly and not so quietly supported the Irish. Progress had been made. But progress seemed to come with a price, and all these years later the Irish were still fighting for fair treatment, if not to rule themselves. Thomas chided himself. The most he had done to rule himself was move from England to Ireland. And since his daughters had become women, he wasn't sure he still even was still in control of his life.

Elfie beckoned him to rejoin the party as she moved out of the church. He must be thoughtful of her, he reminded himself. His own rambling thoughts had taken him back to his time of melancholia over Lily's departure from Ireland after her wedding and then again to when she had died. *Attending Norah's betrothal must be a very difficult moment for Elfie,* he thought. Thomas still felt shocked by the sheer randomness of death. One moment Elfie and George were looking forward to spending the rest of their lives together, and then after a fine evening at RockView, he disappeared from her life entirely. Thomas stepped up to Elfie and offered her his arm to cross the street for the reception. Frances walked behind them with Lucie.

In front of them Conor was playing the pied piper, waving his hand over his head outside the church, inviting everyone to cross the way to the Confession Box Pub for a toast to the young couple's happiness. Thomas breathed in the pleasant aroma of ale as they neared the pub. He caught sight of Mary's daughter walking beside the church with the girls toward the waiting carriage. Not that he'd been asked, but Thomas had been doubtful about putting Bridget in charge of the girls while her mother attended the after celebration. He had continued to think of Bridget as Mary's miracle child until he had unexpectedly met her in the kitchen last month. Bridget had a formidable presence and a quick smile. She was only fourteen years old, but then so had Biddy been when she was helping to care for his own daughters. *Younger than that, even,* thought Thomas. "My daughter is very responsible, with plenty of experience caring for children," Mary had assured him. His daughters were right to hire Bridget, of course; a pub was no place for their students. He didn't think it was a place for Lucie either, but as usual, he had been overruled.

Thomas intended to stay close to his granddaughter. At fifteen she was a blossoming young woman. Her womanly figure was hard to miss even if you weren't looking for it, and he was sure men were. Had he worried as much about his own daughters? He still did, to a point. What he did remember was the feeling of relief when Lucie had not returned to Canada after finishing her studies with the school. The idea of her disappearing like Lily was almost too much for him. Frances had continued tutoring her in more advanced studies, and Lucie had stepped in to help with the girls when Norah was unable to work. *This has to be quite an experience for Lucie,* he thought, smiling at the Irish crowd as they entered the pub. Everyone inside was either talking loudly or laughing, and all were celebrating with a pint or two, and at midday. Frances and Elfie had formed a sort of barrier around Lucie, but from what he could see, his granddaughter seemed mostly at ease in the boisterous room. *After all that time she spent at the Gossetts' over the past year, she might well be*—certainly more than her aunts, who hadn't ever set foot in their home or a pub, for all he knew. Thomas wanted to laugh. He felt very good about Lucie and Norah's friendship, and if that had happened through their shared writing and lessons with him, Thomas was happy to take the credit. He stepped up to the bar for a pint of Guinness and relaxed his attention, a little.

With his free hand, Thomas dug his finger into his vest pocket once again, feeling the warmth of his body's heat on the old coin and its smooth, worn surface. He was looking forward to presenting it to the betrothed couple. For him the coin repre-sented good luck because he'd been holding it in his palm after a friendly wager on the annual County Cork steeplechase—a timed race, ride your own route, from landmark to landmark. Betting was something he rarely did, and he was astounded when he won. What else could he attribute his winnings to but luck? Seamus and Norah could hold it or sell it; he didn't need to know. John Yeats had never told him its value, if any, so Thomas had looked in a book of old coins. To his amazement, he seemed to be in possession of a colonial coin pressed during the reign of Henry VIII in the sixteenth century. After some cleaning with a messy paste Biddy made for him of salt, flour, and vinegar, the image of the harp, Ireland's ancient symbol, emerged. He had never shown the coin, clean or dirty, to any-one else in the family. Frances would have scolded him for wa-gering, and Elfie might have insisted he donate it to her Irish history society. But he knew Biddy, whose Conor seemed to bet on every Gaelic football game, would take pleasure in shar-ing the conspiracy with him. The coin was his alone to bestow when he wished, to whom he wished, and that pleased him. Norah's betrothal seemed like just the right reason to pass the luck along.

CHAPTER 50

DEB SEASON

March to May 1891

Unbeknownst to Lucie, her grandmother Eliza's familial alarm bells had gone off during her visit to Dublin when Lucie mentioned she was considering returning to Canada in time to celebrate her twentieth birthday. Eliza was horrified. She wanted her granddaughter to remain in Ireland and stated so clearly in the letter she wrote to the Youngs as soon as she returned home.

> *I've lost my son to Canada. I don't intend to lose my granddaughter, too. It's time Lucie be properly introduced to Dublin society. I can't think of a better way to keep her here than for her to marry a young gentleman of means and culture in Ireland. I met my Richard during my debutante season, and there is*

*every reason to expect Lucie will find romance
during hers.*

Frances stopped reading aloud to note the reactions of her father and sister.

"How . . . unexpected," Elfie said.

"Indeed," Frances agreed.

"I know you two make most of the decisions around here," Thomas said, jumping in before his daughters could put a quick end to any further discussion, "but as her grandfather, I think we should at least consider Eliza's idea." His daughters looked at him with surprise.

"Really? I don't recall you or Mother suggesting your daughters become debutantes," Elfie pointed out.

"Not that any of us wanted to," Frances said.

Elfie frowned. "I believe most of our students have been debutantes, and a few have married into the aristocracy," she said.

"Well, yes," Frances admitted. "Our school combines the traditional idea of readying the girls to marry into a higher class—if that is what their parents choose—with a more progressive idea of teaching the girls to think for themselves. Our girls learn not just about the world but also how to express their curiosity and how to support their own opinions." Frances paused. "Eliza makes a point, though," she said thoughtfully. "We lost Lily to Canada, never to see her again."

After further discussion that brought them no closer to a decision, the Youngs invited Lucie to join them in the drawing room. They would let her decide.

"Our parents never thought much of working at making social connections," Elfie told her. "Your grandmother—our mother, Sarah—was a passionate egalitarian who did not believe in striving for social status. You either had it or you didn't; that was that. Isn't that the truth, Father?"

"Yes . . . ," he said, and Elfie and Frances turned to him, their eyebrows raised. "You are correct that we didn't feel a formal introduction into society necessary. Your mother was not a debutante and she led a good life; we had a good life together, if I say so myself. But, my dears, to be honest, with the three of you so close in age, there was the cost and the time involved to consider."

His daughters continued to stare at him as if he were speaking another language.

"It would hardly have been fair to let one of you become a debutante and not the other two, now, would it?" Thomas said defensively. He turned from their increasingly judgmental expressions to focus on his granddaughter. "Lucie, neither money nor time is an issue now. If you decide you would like to be formally introduced to society in Ireland, you have not only our support but also your grandmother Eliza's, and, I should think, your father's. I understand the process can be hard work at times but also quite enjoyable."

"Though unnecessary," Frances said. "When Elfie and I set up our school, Lucie, it was, in part, to teach young ladies to move easily and comfortably within any society, including the aristocracy. In that, we do disagree with our mother's opinion on the question of established social status. A young lady moving upward in class and standing often has more to do with the financial success of her family than the young lady's own happiness. Frankly, we hoped that as women our students would have the confidence to take their place in thought and discussion and not sit back and let the men be the be only voice in society. You have greatly succeeded in that area."

Lucie, who had yet to say a word, thanked her aunts and grandfather for presenting her with the opportunity and for their thoughts on the matter. She stood up to leave. "I will think about it," she told them. "They may not even want me," she added, not knowing exactly who "they" were but understanding from her friends Bea and Sophia that not just anyone could be a debutante. One had to be accepted first.

"Of course they'll want you!" Elfie said. "Without a doubt," Frances assured her. Thomas chuckled at his daughters' sudden turnaround.

Lucie climbed the stairs, and upon reaching her room, she flopped on her bed. Bea and Sophia had already shared with her some of the social protocols and festivities of a debutante season. "Parties, new dresses, a ball gown, and so many social gatherings. Aren't you planning on being a debutante? You'd better hurry. We already have our handbooks, and there is a lot to prepare for." When Lucie had demurred, they argued it was the best way to meet eligible and respectable young men. "And for them to meet you! You don't want to be an old maid, do you?" Bea warned.

Lucie wasn't particularly interested in marriage yet. She'd met hardly any boys her age, let alone gotten to know them. That part she was interested in. Lucie wished she could ask Norah her opinion. She hardly saw her friend outside of the school since she'd become a married woman. Lucie missed their friendship. *Of course, Norah didn't ask me what I thought about her getting promised to Seamus,* she considered. She hadn't expected her to. Norah was a grown-up.

Lucie smiled. That's exactly what she wanted to be. Becoming a debutante was a brilliant opportunity to take a giant step away from the girls' school, RockView, her aunts, and her grandfather and into the world. She was ready.

— ◆ —

Frances and Elfie

Eliza arrived in April to set Lucie's debut in motion. After a week of visiting the "right people" and paving the way for Lucie's acceptance, she came to RockView to personally go over instructions with Elfie and Frances. "I have already sent the necessary letters and informed James he will be traveling to Ireland to be Lucie's escort at the ball," she said as soon they sat down for tea in the drawing room. "I hadn't planned it, but what a clever way to get James to visit me!"

The sisters smiled and nodded, thinking of Lily.

"I do apologize for such a brief visit," Eliza said. "I want you to leave all expenses to me. James will argue it's his right, but we will settle that later. The rest is on your shoulders." Frances and Elfie exchanged glances. With Eliza, it was better just to listen and to say as little as possible, but the woman had caught their questioning looks and answered them. "As a debutante, Lucie needs to be available to attend daytime teas and luncheons, which means appropriate outfits need to be ordered, as well as engraved calling cards."

"That's it?" Elfie asked, feeling relieved. "I think we can manage that, don't you, Frances?"

Before Frances could answer, Eliza exclaimed, "My heavens, no! There's much, much more. Now that Lucie has been accepted by the debut committee, she will receive a debutante's etiquette handbook, which I will send to her. No, you don't have to thank me; she's my granddaughter, after all! Lucie must begin studying the book immediately. The season begins early fall." The sisters didn't dare look at each other but smiled and nodded again. "You must too, of course. Otherwise, how will you know how to help her?"

"How will we know how to help her with etiquette?" Frances asked. "Eliza, you are aware we run a school for young ladies."

"This is *debutante* etiquette," Eliza explained. "It's very specific and important to Lucie's reputation and standing in society."

A week after Eliza returned home, the *Handbook of Etiquette for Debutantes* arrived at RockView. Eliza had made it clear in her conversations with the Youngs, and repeated in a note sent with the book, her wish for them to begin Lucie's preparation immediately, starting with dancing lessons and curtsy practice.

> *Lucie must be put in touch with the full range*
> *of our culture's teachings for young women.*
> *Mrs. Pomeroy has graciously agreed to include*
> *Lucie in her debutante dance classes. I will*
> *visit on occasion to check in on her progress.*

Elfie read the note to Frances and Thomas. Frances shook her head in annoyance. "Just how backward does she think we are?"

"I admit I am disappointed she does not want *me* to give Lucie dancing lessons," Thomas joked, bringing a smile to his daughters' faces.

Throughout April and May, and with plans to continue through June, July, and even August if necessary, Lucie and the Youngs worked their way through the chapters in the heavy handbook on weekends and every evening in between. One late May evening after Sunday supper, Elfie stood, agitated, in front of the fireplace, holding Eliza's big book open to that evening's lesson. "How to curtsy," she read. She rolled her eyes and stepped toward the window to take in the evening sky. Unable to distract herself, she turned and said pensively to Frances, "Honestly, a lesson on how to curtsy? It's not as if Ireland's debutantes will be presented to Queen Victoria. Will they?"

"I have no idea," Frances admitted. "I think Eliza would have mentioned it several times if they were."

Lucie was still upstairs, but Elfie walked to the door and shut it so as not to be overheard. "The procedure for becoming a debutante is so rigid, so British, so formal. Why do the British love rules and codes of honor? Establishing acceptable behavior and order?" Lifting the tome, she said, "Here we have over one hundred pages of rules and careful illustrations for introducing eligible young women to society as perfect ladies."

"What are you saying, Elfie?" Frances asked. "We knew what we were in for as soon as that brick was delivered to our front door."

Elfie sighed. "The reality of going through all this"—she lifted the book again for emphasis—"makes me even more aware that I am no longer solely British. Etiquette has its place, but this feels out of date."

"The expectations are rather high," Frances agreed. "I would make a terrible aristocrat's wife." Elfie didn't laugh, which meant something deeper than etiquette rules were bothering her.

"What about the Irish?" Elfie asked.

"What about the Irish, Elfie?"

"Someone like Norah would never be accepted as a debutante. No young Irishwoman would."

Frances sat quietly, trying to catch up with her sister's thinking. "Well, first," Frances said slowly, "*we* weren't interested in becoming debutantes, and I suspect someone with confidence as hard won as Norah's would not be interested in becoming a debutante either, but we'd have to ask her."

Elfie huffed. "That's not what I mean and you know it. Why does everything have to be British or Irish?"

"I don't know, Elfie. I can't say I like it either," Frances answered honestly. "The debutante is a British tradition. As you just said, we no longer think of ourselves as only British; we are Anglo-Irish. We're a blend, and even though we are not Gaelic or Catholic, we love this country and feel loyal to it; it is our home. In some ways we are in no-man's-land as Anglo-Irish. That has made us resistant to this custom. Ten years ago,

I would never have said this, even to myself, but I recognize the duality we struggle with."

Elfie brightened. "Well said, Frances! I think we should share our feelings about being Anglo-Irish in Ireland with Lucie so she understands what she is getting into with this British tradition."

Frances stretched her spine and rubbed one hand on the back of her neck to release tension. "Elfie, I think we need to let Lucie enjoy this time. She is a smart young woman and a keen observer. And she's having fun. It seems unfair to burden her with our issues. Soon enough she will be part of the adult world, where she will struggle with larger problems."

Elfie turned her head away and was silent. Frances walked over to her sister and put her hand on her shoulder. She was pleased to see Elfie exhibiting some of the passion she had carried before George Fenn died. That was nearly ten years ago. Whatever Frances felt about the debutante tradition, she was thrilled it had brought her sister's spirit front and center again.

Frances gathered her thoughts before proceeding carefully. "What you say is correct, but at Lucie's age we had little idea there were difficult differences in our society. We were only just becoming aware that we were not Irish! Fortunately for us, we lived in a family that did not think of itself as superior to the Irish around us, like Biddy and Mary. Lucie sees that same thing every day in this house. She will learn about the social and political complexities over time, or perhaps she already knows more than we think she does from her friendship with Norah."

Elfie reached across to her shoulder and put her hand on her sister's. "We did think we were Irish, didn't we?" she said, smiling. "Biddy must have thought we were soft in the head."

The door to the drawing room opened and their conversation stopped.

Thomas and Lucie walked in arm in arm, unaware of the

nature of the conversation they had interrupted. Their father must have sensed tension in the room, because he made a comical plié and said, "I heard tonight was curtsy night. Lucie invited me to watch."

They all laughed, and Elfie said, "Right you are, Father." She opened the handbook to the marked page and began the lesson. "Now, to do a proper curtsy, it says here . . ."

CHAPTER 51

NEW TERRITORY

August 1891
Norah

Norah knew of Lucie's debut in society; she would have had to be blind and deaf not to. Even the girls spoke with giggles and excitement about it between their classes. But she said nothing about it to her friend unless Lucie herself brought it up, and with Norah working at the school only three days a week and studying to become a teacher in between, they rarely saw each other now, so there hadn't been much said at all. She was surprised but very pleased when Lucie asked if they could spend some time together on a Thursday after classes were over. As they walked away from RockView toward their favorite spot on the River Dodder, Norah linked her arm in Lucie's while her friend talked nonstop about her new social life.

"I feel I'm in a whole new territory, Norah. There is so much happening at once. The luncheons, the dance lessons, the recitals. I'm not sure I would have agreed to become a debutante if I'd understood all that is expected of me, and always with a smile. I nearly nodded off at the last social tea—oh, Norah, there are so many of them!—I was exhausted."

"And also having fun?" Norah managed to ask.

"I am most definitely having fun," Lucie said, with a grin. "You should see all the new dresses I have. I'd love to show you. They make me feel . . ."

"Like an aristocrat?" Norah said.

"I was going to say beautiful," Lucie answered.

The two walked the rest of the way in silence until they reached the bank where they spread out the blanket Lucie had brought and sat down.

"I'm sorry, Lucie. Of course you feel beautiful, and I'm glad you're having fun. It's just all so . . ."

"British," Lucie said for her.

"It's hard to imagine. Or more, I don't like what I'm imagining: 'No Irish allowed.'"

Lucie nodded. "My aunts said something similar."

"It's OK, Lucie. Our friendship has grown because of our differences. The world is not the judge of it, we are."

"I hope you know I'm not trying or wanting to be an aristocrat! Everyone seems expected to grow up within strongly defined lines. I want to experience something beyond my lines. To see what's out there. Except not everything I want to know is explained in that handbook they sent me. And I don't think my aunts have much experience in those areas."

Norah was intrigued. "Such as?"

"Men," Lucie said, causing them both to laugh so hard, they fell into each other.

"All right, then," Norah said, composing herself. "Let's stand up. First, be sure those lads keep their hands away from . . ." She pointed to the parts of her own body where she said no one but Seamus had business being. "I've known a hand to take advantage of being close by, especially when dancing. I've also been known to slap a face or two, but I don't suppose your debutante committee would approve." Norah held Lucie in a dancing position and showed her how to politely but firmly put an errant hand back in place. "Be proud of and protect yourself, Lucie, and you will be wanted by all of them."

Lucie grinned. The thought of being attractive to men thrilled her. "But what if a man tries to kiss me?"

"Now, that depends on whether or not you want to kiss him, doesn't it! Is that allowed in your book?"

"Just on the hand," Lucie admitted.

"Don't you worry, Lucie. There are some things in life that come naturally to a woman and a man. But if one of those gents tries to place his unwanted lips on yours and you can't step away, just turn your head and he'll end up kissing your ear."

— ◆ —

Lucie

Four months later, Lucie, James, Eliza, and Hugh Niven made their entrance to St. Patrick's Hall in Dublin Castle beside Thomas, Elfie, and Frances Young. A disappointed Knox had been left at home in Canada, as his father decided he was too young to make the trip. The debutante curtsies and bows to the gathered "society" took some time, but at last the orchestra struck up. Lucie beamed as her father escorted her to the dance floor for the first dance. They had practiced their dancing every night since James and Hugh arrived from Canada, but that night in her father's arms, Lucie felt the happiest she had been since she was a child. "Lucie, you truly take my breath away," he said as he waltzed her around the room. "I can hardly believe the woman my daughter has become. The other men in this room are jealous of me right now." Lucie blushed and forced herself to keep her head up rather than look down. "I mean it," her father said. "You are an appealing young woman, just as your mother was. I still miss her, you know. I always will. And we all miss you, my very grown-up daughter."

"I miss you very much too, Father," Lucie said. "But I'm having trouble concentrating on my dancing right now. Can we talk later?"

James smiled, pleased his daughter was still as candid as ever.

"Just one more thing," he said. "I know that I am in a contest with my mother and the Youngs, each of us hoping you will marry on our side of the Atlantic so we can share in your life." Lucie's eyes widened. Before she could respond, her father kissed her on the cheek. "Enjoy yourself; that's not for tonight," he said, sounding apologetic. "Those decisions are for later."

The ball flew by, giving Lucie no time to rest. She saw her brother Hugh twirling on the dance floor with Bea, laughing and playful. Lucie's dance card had filled up quickly, but not before she'd made Hugh sign his name for two of them. The evening felt like a fantasy to Lucie. She caught her grandmother smiling at her in approval and more than once glimpsed her aunts watching as she moved about the room in a flowing white silk ball gown cut to show her shoulders and her decolletage, where Eliza's locket hung gracefully on a gold chain. Her grandmother had received it on her wedding day, long ago, from her husband, Richard. She told Lucie that she had hoped to leave it to Lily.

Her father danced with Elfie and Frances at least twice, and three times, that she saw, with his mother. Lucie marveled at how comfortable she was with whomever she danced with. All the preparation was worth it. She felt like a young woman ready to meet the world. And not just because of the handbook. Lucie hoped her aunts knew they had done a good job with her, given her the best of themselves—their curiosity, poise, knowledge of how to dress and present oneself—as well as a good education. She wanted to embody their generosity and resiliency too.

Thomas was seventy-nine years old, and though not frail, he had decided not to chance the dance floor. "I had the fun and honor of practicing with you at home," he'd told Lucie before they arrived. "I hope you'll excuse me tonight." Lucie laughed, recalling her grandfather humming the music as he gracefully swooped her around the drawing room with the "one, two, three, one, two three" Viennese waltz steps. She did wonder what was in her grandmother's mind as she sat next to Thomas. Both of them were moving their fingers from side to side as if counting the rhythms of the waltz. But her grandmother appeared misty-eyed, as if she was thinking of another time. Was her memory of dancing with her husband and of the locket that was now Lucie's?

Lucie let go of Hugh's shoulder to finger the necklace. Would she meet someone who would make her feel misty-eyed when they were apart? She hadn't so far.

"You all right?" Hugh asked.

"Oh, just thinking," she said, "about what a very good dancer my brother is!"

"Thank you for saying so, Lucie," he said, looking genuinely relieved. "Knox said I looked like a dancing chicken when he saw me practicing at home with Clara. She's not so bad, you know," he added when he saw Lucie's eyebrows furrow. "She's just not Mother. Or you!" he said, grinning.

Lucie grinned back. She didn't want to think of her home in Canada that night. She just wanted to enjoy her last night as a debutante, dressed in her beautiful gown while dancing in the arms of handsome young gentlemen.

— ◆ —

In the days that followed, her family, both the Youngs and the Nivens, seemed to be bracing themselves for her decision about what she would do next. Would she go to Canada or stay in Ireland? The lingering glow of the ball and the time she was spending with her father and Hugh seemed to have erased any ability to make such an important decision. She almost wished she *had* fallen in love during the debutante season so the decision about whether to stay or leave would be made for her.

The day her father and Hugh left for home, she nearly burst into tears. She had no doubts she would miss her aunts and grandfather just as much if she moved back to Canada. "I don't know what to do," she told Norah. Once again they had found some time to spend together and had chosen the banks of the Dodder. "There's no easy choice. I love my family on both sides of the Atlantic. And you, Norah, who are a sister to me."

"As you are to me," Norah said. "Whatever your decision, Lucie, you are a lucky girl to have so much family to love. But if you choose Canada, I expect to receive at least one of those photograph postcards you go on about."

"Agreed," Lucie said. "And we send each other at least one letter a month."

"Agreed," Norah said.

In the silence that followed, both women realized Lucie's decision had been made. She would return to Canada, and in less than three years. The friends held hands, silently watching the waters of the Dodder slipping out to sea until it was time for them to each return home.

PART FOUR

THE LEAVING

CHAPTER 52

FRANCES

June 1, 1894

Frances awoke with a feeling of unease. She dressed quickly and sat by the window to look out on the garden. The view was calming, and this morning her mind was filled with disturbing, unwanted thoughts. Lucie was leaving soon. In a week, she and Elfie would accompany their niece on the train to Queenstown Harbor in County Cork. There, Lucie would board a steamship that would carry her to Quebec, where her father would meet her. James, not Eliza, had purchased her ticket. Frances suspected Eliza was making a point by not doing so. Regardless, Frances was pleased her niece would be traveling in comfort and not, as Elfie had pointed out, a few decks below with the continuing flood of Irish emigrants traveling in steerage.

Frances agreed with her sister on at least one point: Lucie was fortunate. She was leaving Ireland because she had chosen her path; this time the journey had not been forced on her by unfortunate circumstances.

Frances had never left her home for longer than one or two months. Others had left, but she had stayed. The school had sensitized her to the difficulties of these separations for both parents and children. She'd been surprised when she developed profound affection for many of the girls, and when they finished their studies, the farewells held a very real poignancy. Even today, they brought forth long-buried feelings from Lily's departure over twenty years ago. Now Lucie.

Down the hall she heard the familiar rumblings of her father dressing. She would wait until he was ready before she went downstairs for a cup of tea. He'd retired from the academy more than ten years ago, and though he still had more strength than most at eighty-two years of age, his bearing had become stooped over the past year. She remembered how he balked long ago when his bedroom had been moved up another flight of stairs. "I think climbing the stairs to the third floor two or three times a day has been good for him," Frances had told Elfie. But she could not ignore that he was less engaged in life at RockView since Lucie's announcement. Frances assumed he was trying to insulate himself from the sadness they all were feeling. He spent more time alone in his room rather than entering activities or being with his granddaughter. Once, over morning tea, Frances had asked him what he was working on in his room. His response came with unexpected energy. "Most recently, I am reading Jeremiah. Searching for some spiritual medicine, knowing there is no balm in Gilead."

She was grateful her father had turned to God this time rather than to melancholy as he had done so long ago, when Lily left. *Aren't we all searching for something?* she thought. "I admire you, Father," she'd told him. "You have always been my teacher. Let me know if you find a cure."

"A spiritual cure, if we are lucky enough to find it," her

father said, "can be better than a physician's, and better than what's in this newspaper." He had turned his attention back to the *Post*, and Frances had left the kitchen.

All this thinking makes me glum, thought Frances, taking a final glance out her bedroom window. *What I need is a strong cup of black tea.* That got her going. She knocked on her father's bedroom door to ask if he wanted to head downstairs or have tea brought up to him. Just as he mumbled an answer, Elfie's door opened. "I'm happy to assist Father this morning if you want to get on with your day," she told Frances. "I haven't heard the second boot drop, so I assume he'll be awhile." Frances smiled her thanks and descended the stairs. Before she came to the kitchen, an idea hit. *We will have family breakfasts, all together, while Lucie is still here. I'll ask Biddy to set the table for us in the dining room. With school out we can have long, leisurely chats when we are fresh from sleep. It will lift everyone's spirits.* Without testing the idea on Elfie, Lucie, or Thomas, she told Biddy and Mary of the change. She had no doubts about whether her family would approve or be surprised by the new routine. They were well accustomed to her decisiveness, always followed swiftly by an action plan. Frances felt pleased with herself. She liked action, but she hadn't fooled herself into thinking that the breakfasts were anything other than a way to deal with her own tender feelings.

That afternoon, Frances walked up to the parish house, hoping to catch Reverend Barnes. He was their fourth vicar at Holy Trinity Church since Reverend Dunne, who had attended her father's sixty-second birthday party all those many years ago. The new vicar, as he was still referred to even though he had been at the church two full years, was in his fifties and a widower, a fact not lost on the unattached women in the congregation. Yet it was Frances who had become his companion for evenings of music and theatre. Their friendship had begun when Frances asked the reverend about his use of metaphors from plays and operas in his sermons. "My late wife," he'd replied, "both of us, actually, were fond of plays and opera. We met at a play. It was our life, in many ways, beyond our work for the church."

Frances had been both touched by his openness with her, and intrigued. "I am always looking for stage performances that are appropriate for our students," she told him. "We want them to experience Dublin's culture while they are with us. Perhaps we could look at the coming season's offerings and take some in together as chaperones for my girls?"

Frances had brought with her the season's play listings to go over, but it was some perspective she badly needed. Reverend Barnes had his dedication to his spiritual life and the job of comforting and enlightening his flock. She had her family and the girls at the school but, after quiet introspection, realized she did not feel like a spiritual person. She tended to look to herself, even as she prayed, for strength and answers. She did not feel she was talking to God; she was talking to Frances, the best and wisest part of her. Today she needed someone else, someone outside her family. The reverend was the closest thing she had to a confidant.

Ernest Barnes was a tall, balding man, always appearing in his black suit and a starched white clerical collar that looked like an eggcup propping his head atop his wiry body. She saw him through the window, leaning back in his chair and holding a paper he was reading, pen in hand. He was working on his sermon. Seeing her walk up the path to the vicarage, he met her at the door before she had the chance to knock.

"To what do I owe the honor of this visit, Frances Young?" he asked. "I am at a perfect spot to take a break from my homily, which is straining its metaphor and needs a rest! Shall I make some tea?" He waved her in and suggested they sit in the parlor alcove, where they could enjoy the afternoon sun. Without saying anything more, they walked comfortably to his small kitchen, where Frances put cups, saucers, spoons, and sugar on a tray and he filled a small pitcher with milk while they waited for the kettle to boil. Ernest turned to her and said with sincerity, "It is nice to have company to share afternoon tea."

When they were seated in the alcove, Frances poured the tea. They sat quietly enjoying the sun's collected warmth in the small, windowed space. *This is what it is to have a true friendship with a man,* Frances thought. *A welcome place for private conversation and discovery. No need for the strain and drama of becoming the perfect match. Ernest and I fit where we fit and find our differences interesting.* The realization, as always, made her feel peaceful. There was a lot on her mind she wanted to share.

When she was ready, she opened her mouth to speak, and her thoughts came out in a tumble. "Ernest, I need your perspective as a friend. I am struggling and don't know where to turn. Father is aging and more physically vulnerable. As you know, it's been ten years since Elfie lost George. His family—his daughter, Elizabeth; Elizabeth's husband, Jonathan; and their little Henry—has become her family. She has an emotional base beyond us now. I am truly happy for her. But when I look at my own life, I see a spinster schoolmarm who has made bringing up Lucie and the success of the school the two centers of my world. Lucie's departure is very difficult for me. She embarks for Canada in two weeks, and I am feeling . . ." Frances paused. She felt childish admitting her true feelings, but then she had come this far . . . "I am feeling abandoned, hollowed. Rationally I want her to find her own life, but selfishly I wonder what I will do without her."

Ernest placed his hand on hers. She did not recoil from his touch but gently placed her hand on top of his. "Thank you, Ernest. I needed to say all that so I could hear it. So much has built up inside of me. It is nice to have it out."

"I could help you find solace in God's word, but I think

you might prefer another source," he said, making them both smile. "Many of life's challenges are captured in the plays we have shared. The outline of the story goes: Act one, you find love, fall in love, and in the process give your life to the object of your affection. Act two, you find, through living, the many flaws in yourself as well as in the one you love. Act three, you find you have no power to change the course of another's life or your own in most circumstances, and you realize your vulnerability began with act one. Act four, the finale. You grieve and come to whatever peace you can with your imperfections and the fact that loss is part of life. Nature makes the physical world we inhabit and offers this lesson, but we can be challenged to accept that we are part of these inevitable cycles."

Frances thought about her life in the framework of this four-act play. Ernest poured them another cup of tea, and they both stared out the window in silence. She had been right to unburden herself here. Ernest was wise and kind, and patient. "You are right, Ernest," she said at last. "I must work my way toward a place of acceptance, but my strong-mindedness sees acceptance as a form of weakness. I am still in act three, working on tolerating my vulnerability, and, frankly, the clothes don't fit. They are tight and uncomfortable. Oh, but I am in no hurry for act four to begin."

Ernest held her hand gently. "I believe it already has, Frances," he said. "When I lost Betsy, my faith was severely tested, and I still struggle with it. In fact, when a few months after her death our cat got out of the house and met his fate out near the rath one night, I realized how unhealed I was. The loss of the animal unhinged me. It was not merely the loss of a creature of which I'd become fond; it was the loss of another source of comfort and routine affection that I had come to rely on, and of my inability to control the situation. *How weak am I?* I thought. I am constantly tested. We all are. I am honored you told me about your struggle, and I hope we can help one another find strength as we absorb and make sense of these inevitable losses. Christ is a healer, but you must want to be healed from within."

Frances cocked her head, smiling. "Father recently said something similar to me." She put her teacup down and said, "I am unexpectedly surrounded with the wisdom of two biblical scholars! Your play metaphor is clever, and I think you already have your next homily ready to go."

She bid Ernest farewell and walked home, feeling the sadness she had been holding back but also that she was and would not be alone.

CHAPTER 53

NORAH

June 8, 1894

Norah found Lucie waiting for her on the front steps of RockView. The early afternoon sun shone on her back, which was curved over as if she'd gathered in a protective ball. Norah touched her friend's shoulder lightly, and Lucie's head popped up. "Oh, Norah, I'm a wreck. There is so much going on, I feel like hiding or crying."

"Come on, now," Norah said. "Let's take our walk to the river. You'll feel better soon enough." She reached for Lucie's hand and they took off toward their favorite spot.

When the women were well out of earshot of the house, Lucie began to speak. "Your mother and Mary have kindly taken on my packing-up to make sure I have everything I need for the transatlantic journey. I'm only allotted one trunk that will fit in my tiny stateroom."

Norah nodded as if she understood her dilemma. She had clear memories of her brothers leaving for America, each with only a single sack over their shoulder. She wasn't an Anglo, but she was sure Lucie could make do with her single trunk.

"All the rest," Lucie continued, "the clothes, hats, shoes, books—they are already packed in the two large steamer trunks Grandmother Eliza purchased for the trip. I'm not sure where they'll go. Somewhere belowdecks, I guess."

"So, you are worried about your luggage?" Norah asked.

"My lug . . .? Of course not!" Lucie looked at Norah and laughed. "Is that what you think of me after all this time? No. I don't think I can take another minute of all the emotions in the house. The way my aunts and grandfather look at me, their eyes so tender and sad and intense, as if they are memorizing my face."

"Oh dear," Norah said, understanding perfectly now. "Ma had that look before my brothers left."

"I have promised to write and visit when I can, but . . ." Lucie paused. "Nothing less than my staying in Ireland is going to make them feel better, is it? And then yesterday," Lucie said without waiting for Norah's answer, "your mother and Mary told me that all this packing reminded them of when they helped my mother and father prepare for Canada. Then later I saw Aunt Elfie burst into tears and leave the room when she saw the trunks."

Norah and Lucie walked the rest of the way in silence. They were both looking forward to slipping off their shoes and stockings and dangling their feet in the cold runoff pushing at the river's banks. There would be no wading that day. The water's flow was strong, and neither was game to risk slipping or falling. Life's currents were already pulling the two of them apart, and that was enough to deal with. No need to add wet clothes and a sore bum.

When they reached the familiar curve in the river, they carefully walked down the bank and Norah spread the blanket they had brought over a dry patch of grass.

"I remember when your mother and father left RockView," Norah told Lucie, who turned her head in surprise. "I was only seven years old, of course, but Ma would come home with stories about 'Miss Lily's move to the wilderness of Canada' and all the trunks she and Mary were packing for her. 'I never thought Thomas Young would allow his daughter to move to the wilderness,'" Norah said, mimicking her mother's voice. "'Miss Frances even said there were bears over there!'"

Lucie laughed and sat down on the blanket next to Norah. "London, Ontario, is hardly the wilderness!" she said. "I never saw one, but I suppose there are bears. Not where we live, of course. Poor Biddy and Mary and the Youngs, being so fearful over nothing." Lucie laughed again and leaned over to unlace her boots. Norah was already wiggling her toes in the water.

"Well, not nothing. They were likely frightened about other things they couldn't quite say." Norah felt sympathetic, but the problems Lucie was wrestling with were of a different sort than her own. Hers were about forgiving and trying to forget the nearly overwhelming hurts and difficulties in her life. Each time she thought she had managed to let one go, another came sneaking back in, shaking her awake in a cold sweat in the middle of the night. She'd be happy to go to Canada—with Seamus—if it put an end to her troubles. "None of it is easy," Norah said. "Our worries take their toll."

"Oh, I agree," Lucie said. "I am very worried about what I'm going to do with my life in Canada."

From the day they met, Lucie had looked to Norah for answers or ideas for life questions that were difficult, if not impossible, to discuss with her aunts or grandfather. Norah's wisdom was in no small part derived from hard lessons. Norah had confronted situations, most of them from the luck of birth and social class, that Lucie would never encounter. "Ma always said, 'Norah, girl, you are stubborn and have to learn by getting burned.' She was right."

"Are you saying I made the wrong decision?" Lucie asked.

Norah closed her eyes and shook her head. "You know the answer to that," she said.

Then she gave Lucie a hug and said, "So, you are all packed up . . . and you are not worried about your luggage . . ." She smiled slyly at her friend. "That leaves the tough part, saying goodbye." She pulled Lucie closer to her side, to reassure her, as they walked down the grassy slope. "Of course you're distraught."

Lucie bowed her head, fighting back tears, and looked up at Norah wiping her own tears. "The hardest will be Grandfather. There is little chance I will see him again. He has been both a father and a grandfather to me, and my leaving is very difficult for both of us. It will require courage that I fear may fail me."

"Let's talk about our plans," Lucie said suddenly. "It is too hard for me to think about Grandfather."

"All right," Norah answered. She kicked her feet in the water and sighed. "Ah, this feels good! My toes aside, I can say I am happily bound and tied to Seamus and our life together. Married life is a big part of my future, which you know. Someday we both hope there will be babies, christenings, and holidays with my family and friends, which you also know. But first, I plan to finish my teaching certificate. I'd rather not scrub floors for a living."

Lucie looked horrified. "Norah, you will never be a scrubwoman! You are too smart for that," she said.

Norah was taken aback. *Has she forgotten that I married a barman?* She felt an old impatience stir up in her. *That my father is a bricklayer and my mother started as a scrubwoman before becoming a maid and finally a cook and housekeeper?* Norah shook her head. "I'd think you know by now that being smart has nothing to do with how people earn their living," she said quietly.

"Of course I do, Norah," Lucie answered, sounding a little hurt. "But you're going to be a wonderful teacher."

Norah nodded and gathered herself before speaking again. "Your turn," she said. "You must have some idea of what you'll do when you get to Canada."

Lucie pulled a letter from her pocket and opened it. "It's from Father. He says Clara and her friends are looking forward to introducing me to society."

"Again!?" Norah said. "How many societies do you need to meet?"

"I hope not again!" Lucie said, laughing. "Once was plenty. Father thinks Clara means something less formal, like dinners and picnics and attending events at the university where she used to work. It feels as if I am about to take a huge jump into a world I don't really know anymore."

Norah waited as Lucie closed her eyes and took a deep breath through her nose, and then another. When she opened her eyes again, she was smiling. "There is one thing I am excited about," Lucie said. "Father wrote that he bought me a beautiful chestnut colt he found on a neighboring farm. I'm going to name him Thomas."

Norah laughed and said she hoped Lucie's grandfather would feel honored with the news. "I know we talked about it, but let's make a pact. We write each other once a month," she said. "Our friendship has done so much for me, much more than going to the church for confessional. Here I get to sit with you and with my toes in the river and say what I think, which is far more helpful than sitting in a dark box and whispering through a screen to an old man who smells like whiskey at nine in the morning."

Lucie grimaced, then smiled. She placed her hand, palm up, in front of Norah. Norah then placed her hand, palm down, on top of Lucie's and they squeezed tight. "Pact made!" they said, grinning happily at each other.

The women brushed the grass from their feet and ankles and pulled on their stockings and boots to begin the return trip to 14 Belgrave Road. Too soon, they reached the bottom of RockView's steps. Norah put her arms around Lucie and hugged her. "None of us know the future, Lucie. We can only hold hope for the best, whatever it is. I will come to see you on the fifteenth and before then, too, if I can get away. Seamus is so enamored of my company, he got me a job working with him at the Trump & Whistle this summer! Now, don't worry—Mother told me when your carriage to the station is coming. I'll be there."

They parted with a long hug and a few tears, wiped away by damp kisses. "Try to enjoy your last week at RockView," Norah said. She turned and strode purposefully toward home, not daring to look back.

CHAPTER 54

ELFIE

June 14, 1894
Midmorning

Elfie slipped her folded nightgown and dressing gown into a muslin bag and placed it flat into the small leather valise on the end of her bed. She was packing for her overnight stay in Queenstown with Lucie and Frances. The carriage that would take them to the train station would arrive tomorrow at ten o'clock in the morning. After a last night together in Queenstown, she and her sister would see Lucie off, then wait on the quay to watch her ship sail out of Cork Harbor. Elfie could hardly imagine that Lucie was leaving them. The return train trip to Dublin would be heavy and quiet.

Lucie's arrival turned out to be a deliverance, she thought, tucking her toiletry bag into an end of the valise. They had lost Lily, then George, and quite unexpectedly Lucie walked into their lives. *She has rescued us,* Elfie told herself, *and I believe we have rescued her.*

Lucie was not quite eleven years old when she arrived, and suddenly the Youngs had a deeper purpose, each of them taking on the job of helping her grow into the strong, independent young woman about to take her voyage back home. *It's a kind of miracle that she came to us, I could say,* Elfie told herself. *I do say! We have been so fortunate to have her in our lives.* Elfie sighed. *Now Lucie's journey had come full circle and it's time for us to let her go.* Her face screwed up and she pressed her knuckle to her nose, determined not to cry. She was weary of crying, even wearier of losing the ones she loved. Elfie breathed through her nose until she felt stronger.

She packed and then unpacked a shirtwaist, put it back on its hanger, and hooked that over the doorknob. She would pack the shirtwaist tomorrow at the last minute. Fewer wrinkles. *Maybe an extra pair of black stockings and two more handkerchiefs.* Elfie was certain she would cry again before Lucie left them. She removed the items from her armoire and tucked them in her travel case.

Elfie's fondest wish was that she and Frances would visit their niece in Canada. *I am quite sad that Father cannot manage an ocean voyage. That makes this leaving an even more significant ending for him, of course.* After tomorrow, her father was not likely to see Lucie again. Elfie had nothing to complain about, but that did not lessen the poignancy of this moment for the whole Young family.

Her father had turned to the Bible for solace almost as soon as Lucie told them she would be leaving. And now Frances was doing the same thing. She couldn't recall seeing her sister read the Bible before. At church she was never without her book of prayer, but Elfie long suspected the book was more for appearances than for solace, as she rarely opened it. *I wonder why it is that spirituality has not come easily for Frances?* Elfie smiled, thinking of the new vicar and what a good development he was in her sister's life. "God works in mysterious ways," she said, "whatever those ways may be!" She might have giggled at her own witticism had it not been so very clear that Lucie's imminent departure had unearthed both tender longings and regrets in Frances. It had for all of them.

Elfie paused her packing and moved to her desk. She had made a decision. She would write a letter to give Lucie to read after the ship sailed. Her father had created a small annotated book of his watercolors for Lucie to take with her, paintings that would remind her of her home and surroundings in Rathmines. *Her home in Ireland,* Elfie corrected herself, and then corrected herself again. *RockView is her home, and we are her family.* That is what she would put in her letter. *Oh dear.* Elfie sniffed. She removed a lace handkerchief from her sleeve to dab her eyes and nose. *The tears come so easily.*

She opened her desk drawer and selected a piece of soft blue paper and its matching envelope, a gift of writing paper from a friend on her last birthday. Lucie loved blue, the color of her eyes. She would appreciate Elfie's choice. Elfie placed the inkwell carefully to the right of the desk and found her blotting paper, a sheet long ago taken from her watercolor notebook. The paper was soft and thirsty, ready to absorb the extra ink that might collect from a pause of the pen. She lifted the blotter and admired the patterns left by her earlier letters, words crisscrossing the surface, many reversed and all unintelligible. She thought of the letters she had written to George and the love they carried, of the notes to his grandson, Henry, when the boy was young, about imaginary characters she conjured for their ongoing storytelling. It was all there, a jumble of sketchy impressions and ink trails left from lives lived and stories told. *There's been so much to convey,* Elfie thought. *I favor the written word, there to read and reread. The spoken word too easily disappears into the air,* poof. She held the pen over the inkwell, wondering where to begin her letter. Elfie sighed. Knowing at last where to start, she dipped the pen in its well and set it to paper once more.

> *June 14, 1894*
> *Our Dear Lucie, You are embarking on a new*
> *adventure in your young life and we will have*
> *to, as your father has, enjoy it from afar . . .*

CHAPTER 55

THOMAS

Midafternoon

Thomas thought a pint or two with John Yeats on a regular basis might raise his spirits after Lucie had departed. He'd already sent a note to Yeats asking him to let Thomas know whenever he was in town so Thomas could meet him at his favorite pub near Trinity College. Yeats was a skilled distraction. His knowledge and observations of current life and politics were astute, laced with obscenities, impolitic, and controversial. The man had the ability to create a carnival.

What was coming next was hard to accept. Thomas's world was shrinking again. To stave off the familiar melancholy, he made himself dress and go out of the house every day, even if it was just across the street to the park. He even attempted some pencil sketches that might lead to a new painting, but his concentration was poor. At the urging of Reverend Barnes, Thomas had found some solace in the Bible, surprising both himself and his daughters, it seemed. For the past few months, the book had resided at his bedside along with his diary. He wrote little on its lined pages, more often reading the names of those he'd lost before falling asleep. His wife, Sarah, who died at forty-six years old; his children who never left childhood, Lucy, Elizabeth, Samuel, Thomas Jr., Sarah, and Henry; and then Lily (whose given name was Rebecca Jane), not even as old as her mother had been when she passed away. *I have lived too long,* he thought.

Now his granddaughter, Lucie, was about to disappear from his life. Tomorrow morning when the carriage to the train station pulled away from RockView would be their final goodbye.

Once Lucie began packing, he was certain everyone in the household was thinking the same thing. Years ago, they had seen trunks stacked in the front hall, never dreaming that Lily would not return. Now history was repeating itself, and there was a tension he and Biddy shared. She had confided in him that since she had seen her boys off, she prayed every day she would see them again. He decided then to start praying, too.

His thoughts were interrupted by Biddy knocking on his door to bring him his afternoon tea.

"Do you have the time to sit for a few minutes?" he asked her. Biddy studied him for the meaning of the unexpected sit-down, but she pulled the chair from beside his desk and took her seat, arranging her skirts modestly. "Biddy," he said, "you and Conor dealt with Patrick and Jack's departure. . ." Thomas paused, unsure how best to continue.

Biddy reached out and placed her hand on his arm. In all the time they had known each other, she had rarely touched him. "I really don't know what to say, Mr. Young," she said. "Life seems to give us these troubles. It is not easy, I'll grant you. It was a sad and bitter pill to see my boys go away. Still sits in me craw." Biddy sat back and folded her arms, appearing thoughtful. "I've come to believe how we take their leavin' tells us about ourselves. I so, so regret my boys' last memory of me was bawlin' away standin' in the street." She shook her head, and this time Thomas patted Biddy's arm. "Why couldn't I see anything but my own sorrow?" she said.

"I think I understand, Biddy," Thomas said. "I know that Lucie returning to her father and brothers is best for her, but I can hardly bear the loss. I feel old and selfish. I almost wish I were not alive to have to withstand it."

Biddy clucked and *tsked*, shaking her head and looking down into her lap before lifting her eyes to meet his. Thomas recognized the mix of compassion and a motherly admonition that was about to come his way. "You are a good man, Mr. Young," she said. "And Lucie knows it." She rose from her seat and left the room, leaving him chuckling at the brief lecture and in admiration of Biddy's wisdom.

In a short time, he wrote Lucie a note asking her to meet him that night in the foyer at eleven o'clock, well after her aunts had gone to bed. He had already presented his granddaughter with two gifts to remember them by. One was a small book of his sketches and watercolors he had made for her—Elfie's idea—begun soon after Lucie informed them that she would be returning to Canada. The second was two small pieces of Sarah's jewelry, a ring and a locket, which he wanted Lucie to have to remember the grandmother she had never known. His third gift to her required more than a satin bow; it needed a shared adventure. Instead of taking his usual walk, Thomas pulled a shawl over his shoulders to take a nap before dinner. He would need the rest.

At the appointed hour, Thomas walked down the stairs, pleased to see Lucie already waiting for him. Per his instructions, she was wearing a warm jacket, walking boots, and a hat she was adjusting in front of the mirror. Thomas saw two images at once: the nervous almost-eleven-year-old girl who had arrived nine years ago and a statuesque young woman tilting her hat to a stylish angle. Lucie and Lily. His heart pounded in his chest with both love and grief. The images turned at the creak of his footsteps on the stairs and smiled. At that moment love pushed sadness aside.

"Good evening, Grandfather," Lucie said, her voice hushed and conspiratorial. "Though it is almost morning! Packed and ready to go," she said, pointing to her three large trunks. "I cannot imagine what adventure you have planned. Is it pirate treasure? I promise to do the digging if it is."

Thomas gave her a salute. "Something better, I hope. I may be wrong," he whispered, "but I believe we are breaking every rule Frances has set for us. That's part of what makes it so much fun," he added with a wink.

Thomas led her to the kitchen door at the back of the house. "Less noisy," he explained. They smiled at one another as the door clicked quietly closed. Thomas lit the lantern he had earlier placed on the back porch for them. The glow illuminated their excited faces. Thomas put his finger to his lips and they descended the stairs, then took the path to the meadow near the rath where the sky opened and felt as wide as the ocean. Luck had it that no fog had rolled in to obscure the heavens. The sky was alive with brilliant points of distant light, stars, planets, and constellations speaking a language impossible to fathom. It was hard to stretch the mind that far.

Lucie, her head tilted back, stood in wonder and asked, "Do you know the names of the constellations we are looking at?"

Thomas pointed out Orion's Belt as they stared up into the night sky. He eventually had to turn away but said, "Lucie, keep looking for me. I have to give my neck a break!" They sat close together on the folding stools Thomas had brought from the porch, sharing thoughts provoked by the darkness and scale of the endless, timeless universe. Thomas had placed their chairs with the old rock wall behind them for back support, which helped him resume the leaning and looking. "Each time I view this miracle, it reminds me of something I understand even though the sky remains a mystery. I know from observing this piece of sky at many times of year that no matter what we or any of the creatures on earth are doing, nature carries on in her own systems and rhythms. As human beings we have self-centered perspectives because this celestial universe"—he paused and swept his hand across the sky—"is beyond our understanding. I keep thinking that what I need are more cosmic thoughts. How's that for a big idea?"

Lucie laughed and he looked at her.

"I will miss you terribly, Lucie. But I do realize the plan for our lives is not in our hands. Something beyond us is in charge. We choose our paths but fate intervenes with detours." Shaking off those heavy thoughts, Thomas took out of his leather satchel a narrow box tied up in a bow and handed it to Lucie. She opened it and exclaimed, "Oh, Grandfather. A spyglass!"

"I want you to go off on your sea voyage and back to Canada with this lens to follow the night sky," Thomas explained. "The crew on the ship will know a great deal more than I do about it; they are trained to use celestial navigation for guiding the ship. But for now, I can show you something of how to use it." He held the small telescope to his eye and expanded the brass barrel to its full length. "Then you move it in and out until you can focus on a star." He handed the spyglass to Lucie.

While she was giving it a try, Thomas said, "I have one more present for you, Lucie, when you're ready." He waited for Lucie's attention, then reached into his bag again and pulled out an old leather-bound copy of Ptolemy's *Planetary Hypotheses*. Inside the book he had written an inscription for her, a reminder of their secret late-night expedition and their shared explorations of great minds through the years.

He opened the cover and tilted it toward the lantern's

light. "To my granddaughter," he read out loud. "A young woman who knows her True North. June 14, 1894. May the night skies forever unite us. Your loving grandfather, Thomas Urry Young." Lucie looked at him with love and appreciation, and Thomas reached into his pocket for a handkerchief.

CHAPTER 56

LUCIE

June 16

Lucie woke early the next morning, put on her travel costume, and stowed last-minute items in her travel bag before heading down to breakfast. She wrapped Ptolemy's *Planetary Hypotheses* carefully in a piece of linen to protect its worn leather cover and did the same with the box containing the spyglass, placing them both next to her grandfather's small book of paintings and her grandmother's jewelry. They were treasures she would keep close to her.

Lucie had presented her grandfather with a small braided lock of her hair mounted under glass and encircled in a two-inch gold frame. It was meant to attach to his watch chain next to the fob he used to draw it from his pocket. He would see it every day and think of her. The braid, she'd explained, was a metaphor for what wove them all together, the past into the present and future. He said he would always keep it beside him.

Lucie said a last goodbye to her room. She peeked upstairs to see if her grandfather had managed to wake early after all. Hearing and seeing nothing of him, she made her way down the staircase, placed her travel bag on the bench near the front door, and walked to the kitchen, where Biddy and Mary were making her a special farewell breakfast. Lucie didn't think she could eat a thing, but didn't dare say so. Everyone had tried to remain lighthearted over the past few days, carefully keeping emotions in check. "Do you have your valise down yet, Miss Lucie?" Mary asked. "The carriage will come by nine and they don't like to be kept waiting."

Lucie nodded and sipped her tea. Despite her anxious stomach, she enjoyed the poached egg dish with a rich cream sauce Biddy had made for her. The smells of the kitchen were so sweet and comforting. Lucie hoped she would never forget them. Biddy and Mary each gave her a small parcel of "things you love from our kitchen, including the recipes for Biddy's scones and Mary's cake." Biddy had added a handsomely wrapped bar of Hudson's soap with the slogan "Arrest all dirt" to make them all laugh. "If you get to America, maybe you'll find my boys? Make sure they are eating well enough without their Ma's cooking?" Lucie told her a visit to the United States, especially New York, was something she hoped to do soon, and she promised to look up Patrick and Jack when she did. "I will miss your cooking too!" she said and thanked them again for being so good to her and told Mary to remember her to Bridget.

"Now, your aunts have already been down and eaten and then gone back upstairs for their 'last minutes,'" Biddy told her. "Your grandfather hasn't shown up yet." She appeared puzzled and apologetic, as if she were letting Lucie down personally.

"I hadn't expected him to, Biddy. We said our goodbyes very late last night," Lucie explained.

"Well then, he'll be needing a bit of a sleep-in this mornin'," she said.

After breakfast, Lucie went to the front hall to gather her coat and hat and gloves and, even though it was June, a scarf to go around her neck until they settled on the train. Carriages were breezy.

The carriage arrived early, and a young, muscular driver bounded up the steps to get Lucie's trunk, carried it down the steps on his back, and secured it to the outside of the carriage, then returned up the stairs to bring down the three valises to where his passengers would sit inside the carriage. Lucie watched the last of her things disappear from the house, yet she felt she was missing something. It wasn't the larger trunks; they had been sent ahead to be stowed in the hold of the ship. She had her Canadian passport and money for the trip, though she would need little. All seemed to be in order. Her passage had been booked two months earlier and fully paid for by her father. She worried about tipping. Her grandmother Eliza had suggested she watch others to learn what was appropriate. "A young lady doesn't want to appear overly generous, so be discreet. If that wasn't covered in the handbook, then it should have been." Lucie's eyes grew wide just thinking about doing such a thing. Handing people money was a new, independent activity she must learn to master.

Lucie looked up to see her aunts walking down the stairs with their father in front of them. This is what she had been missing. Her family. When her grandfather reached the foyer, he gave her another long embrace. They winked and smiled over their escapade last night, and he showed her the small piece with the braid that he had already attached to his watch chain.

Lucie walked toward the carriage with her aunts, who settled themselves inside and told her not to take much longer. Her grandfather waited with Biddy and Mary. The women stood on the steps with handkerchiefs in their hands, alternately waving them and wiping noses or eyes. Lucie had lifted her arm to wave goodbye when she spied Norah running down the road and ran toward her friend. Norah said breathlessly, "Seamus was so sorry not to be able to come. He had a big delivery this morning and couldn't get anyone to shake out and meet the wagon so early." She reached deep in her skirt pocket and whispered in Lucie's ear, "Seamus and I want you to have this to remember us by." Norah pulled out her hand and opened her fist. "Your grandfather thought it was valuable, but we learned from the antique coin man that's not so. No matter, it is still good luck. We have been very happy. We want you to be too." Norah placed the coin into her friend's hand. "Oh, I will miss you terribly, Lucie. We both will." Lucie looked at the old coin, pressed it against her cheek, and slipped it in the slender waist pocket Madame Violette had insisted on adding to all her travel clothes. "Thank you, Norah. You will be right here with me."

Lucie walked back to the carriage and stepped inside feeling sad, excited, nervous, and brave. Her aunts were sitting next to each other, facing straight ahead—most likely, Lucie thought, to avoid another bout of tears. Lucie turned in her seat to wave her last farewell. Norah had joined her mother on the steps. The last thing Lucie saw of RockView was its large oak door and four of the people she loved best framed by the rear window of the carriage as it moved away.

One day later Lucie was on the deck of the ship, waving again to her aunts on the dock. From her high perch on the promenade deck, they looked very small. She hoped they saw her. The ship's horn blasted one last time and pulled out into the harbor toward the open sea. She had done it. She was leaving Ireland and there was no turning back.

Feeling alone as never before, Lucie made her way out of the wind and into the warm salon where tea was being served. The tea table was crowded, so she took a chair to wait for an opening. Lucie turned her chair toward the window and watched the dark water separating her from the home and people she loved. The previous evening, Aunt Elfie had knocked on her hotel room door to give her a letter. Her aunt's voice had been a whisper as she kissed her cheek: "Not now, dear. Open it when you are at sea." Lucie decided she would read the letter that night.

She made herself wait until she was ready to go to sleep. Opening her valise, she carefully pulled out the blue envelope and settled onto her bed. Without bothering with her letter opener, Lucie slipped a finger beneath the red wax and tugged gently until the seal broke.

My dear Lucie, . . .

Lucie read the letter twice through, returning several times to a single passage that made her feel strongest and more certain of who she was.

> *Take comfort as you travel in knowing the*
> *vast, salty ocean with its many currents,*
> *harbors, coves, storms, and winds is at this*
> *very moment, every moment, touching and*
> *connecting the two countries you belong to.*
> *You will always have a home at RockView.*
> *Importantly, wherever you are, you carry with*
> *you the deepest meaning of home: a place of*
> *safety, nurture, and unconditional love.*

As she read, a warmth rushed through her. She was not alone. Her mother, Thomas, Frances, Elfie, and Norah were with her. She knew then they would always be there.

— ♦ —

Over the next twenty-six years, letters between Norah, Frances, Elfie, Thomas, and Lucie traveled frequently across the same ocean route to be read and reread, then bundled and saved to be savored time and again. Some bore a personal or family signet on the wax seal, but all carried news of daily life, of secrets and uncertainties, of joys and sorrows, arriving into the hands and hearts of their loved ones as precious and private as whispers across a sea.

AUTHOR'S NOTE

As I close a book and savor its conclusion, I often wish I could know what happened to the characters I am leaving. I relish epilogues, author's notes that tie things up in the context of personal, cultural, and political history.

Because I have chosen the novel form, I have the challenge of representing the real members of my family and their fictional cohorts. Lucie, Thomas, Lily, James, Eliza, Frances, Elfie, Hugh, and Knox are members of my family, forebears of whom I only knew my grandmother Lucie. What I have is the stories I was told and fragments of their lives in photos, portraits, letters, and diaries. In *Whispers* I have reimagined these family members' thoughts and actions while mixing in fictional characters to add dimension to the story. If I have succeeded, they will all live on in our imagination.

LUCIE MARY

Lucie Mary Niven returned safely in June 1894 to London, Ontario, where she was welcomed by her father, brothers, and friends. Her brothers, Hugh and Knox, were young men now, eighteen and sixteen years old. Lucie helped her father in his surgery. They were a busy household, occupied and independent as they settled into life, glad to be together again. Lucie kept up her correspondence with her aunts and grandfather, faithful to her promises to keep them part of her life. She visited her Irish family in 1897 and did see her grandfather Thomas again. She also visited her father's mother, Eliza Boomer Niven, in Lisburn at her home, Chrome Hill. Eliza died in 1900 and Thomas in 1901, just after his ninetieth birthday.

LUCIE MARY AND SHEPHERD IVORY FRANZ

Lucie made friends easily and kept them for a lifetime. As a result, she had a social life that took her into Canada's society in London, Montreal, Toronto, and beyond. In 1901 her friend Edna Gartshore took Lucie along to Boston, where Edna was visiting her fiancé, Alex Cleghorn, who was teaching at Harvard Medical School. He, in turn, brought along a young assistant in the medical school, Shepherd Ivory Franz, a psychologist. A lifelong love and friendship began that evening.

The following year, on June 18, 1902, Shepherd and Lucie, twenty-seven, were married in London, Ontario, at St. Paul's Cathedral. Her brother Hugh was their best man. Knox was also present. Both young men would eventually join Princess Patricia's Canadian Light Infantry stationed in Edmonton, Alberta. Their units would eventually be called to serve in World War I. Lucie and Shepherd started their married life in Hanover, New Hampshire, where he taught at the Dartmouth Medical School.

Before settling in Hanover, they honeymooned in Dublin, where they visited the aunts, reinforcing a tie that remained important to Lucie all her life.

Marriage did not diminish Lucie. She was a strong partner to her husband, who encouraged her to be herself and develop her own world of interests. The Franzes' first child, Theodora Niven, was born July 16, 1905. By that time Lucie and Shepherd had moved to a suburb of Boston, where he became superintendent of McLean Hospital. Much of the early psychological research was done in "insane asylums," where subjects could be observed over a long period of time in many situations. Lucie was very proud of Shepherd's early research on the function of different parts of the human brain and how they related to physical and psychological abilities. Psychologists from around the world visited, and she thrived on knowing them as people as well as academics and enjoyed her role as hostess and tour guide. Like her mother, Lily, she enjoyed entertaining and did it well.

Elfie came to visit in the spring of 1906 to meet her new great-grandniece. Her ship landed in New York, and she took the train to Boston, where Shepherd met her in his newly purchased automobile. Elfie wrote to Frances about Shepherd's new auto, which cost $500 according to Lucie, an exorbitant sum. It was an open touring car, the 1906 Ford Model N Runabout. Shep was very proud of his fine car and quite new to driving. Elfie admitted in her letter to Frances: "Shep is, I suppose, a good driver, but I was terrified. I did survive to write this letter to you and was glad to have Lucie's reassuring arms around me when we finally reached their home." It was her first ride in an automobile. Theodora, known as Doedy, was a bright, inquisitive child, and Elfie was devoted to her during her stay and well beyond.

When Elizabeth Knox, my mother, was born September 23, 1910, the growing Franz family had resettled themselves in Washington, DC, where Shepherd assumed the post of superintendent at St. Elizabeths Hospital.

1911: IRELAND

Lucie took her new baby, five-month-old Elizabeth, and five-year-old Theodora to Dublin in early 1911. It was Lucie's plan to have Elizabeth baptized in St. Patrick's Cathedral with her aunts in attendance. I can only imagine the discussion that must have preceded the decision to take that trip. Shepherd knew Lucie, her deep feelings for Frances and Elfie, and how much these children meant to them, so off Lucie went across the Atlantic with two young children. The christening was beautifully documented in a formal photo and must have meant a great deal to the aunts.

1915: WORLD WAR I

Patricia Wilderspin Franz, Lucie and Shepherd's third daughter, was born on July 12, 1915, in Washington, DC. The family was complete with three girls.

Letters continued to flow back and forth across the Atlantic, bringing perspectives on World War I, now a year in progress. Shepherd and Lucie, living in the capital, felt the tension of war and the different opinions toward it. President Woodrow Wilson was keeping the United States as a neutral and independent power to broker peace. The American public, along with many European immigrants, were of many minds. There were those who were adamant the country should enter the war, but pacifism had strong support from the Protestant church in America and the growing women's movement. Elfie wrote that in Ireland, Irish Catholic boys and men were enlisting. Many signed up to have a paying job or for the chance at overseas adventure, or what she feared would be misadventure. Some Anglo-Irish Protestants were also joining the fight, wishing to support the British, whom they continued to view as their protectors. The two groups were kept in separate regiments. Irish Catholic troops made up the Sixteenth Division, while the Thirty-Sixth was Anglo-Irish Protestant. Elfie considered the separation a shameful apartheid. As she and many others feared, the Irish Division was treated poorly by the British, adding more aguish to an already troubled society and further dividing the people of Ireland.

1916: THE EASTER RISING

In early 1916 final planning was in motion for the ill-fated Irish rebellion that became known as the Easter Rising. It was veiled in secrecy and scheduled for the twenty-fourth of April by the leadership of the Irish Republican Brotherhood and Cumann na mBan, the Irish women's paramilitary.

Most Anglo-Irish were unaware of the coming rebellion, so it would have been of no immediate concern in the Young home. Thomas was gone, the school had closed in 1901, and the aunts were rattling around in the big house, tending to their own business.

Frances and Elfie must have been startled to read newspaper accounts of the Rising that had taken place so close to them. How had they been unaware, as were many Anglo-Irish and Irish, of this rebellion? The rebels had done a good job of keeping their secret, but had been tragically overwhelmed by British troops. An estimated 1,800 Irish volunteers were seized at the General Post Office in Dublin and other major buildings. All this was within a few miles of the Youngs' home, yet they learned of it after the fact. The rebels had held out for five bloody days before accepting the futility of their cause and surrendering to the British. Irishmen fought on both sides, and some five hundred people were killed, mostly civilians tragically caught in the crossfire. The public executions that followed left wounds in the Irish soul and psyche that would never heal.

An intriguing historical discovery occurred while my husband and I were in Dublin in 2016 as Ireland was celebrating

the centennial of the 1916 Easter Rising. As we were walking in the Youngs' Rathmines neighborhood—Holy Trinity
Church, with its sky-blue door, still standing in the middle of
Belgrave Road—my husband spied a shiny new plaque that had
been placed on the house a few doors from where the Youngs
lived. It read:

Dublin City Council
Dr. Kathleen Lynn
1874–1955
Lived here from 1903–1955
Physician and feminist
Surgeon General, Irish Citizens Army
Co-Founder St. Ultan's Children's
Hospital
Commanded City Hall Garrison, 1916
Rising
Following the deaths of Sean Connolly
and Sean O'Reilly

This woman had lived at 9 Belgrave Road, and the Youngs
at 14! This happenstance finding brought the Rising alive for
us in the context of the Youngs.

At the time, history of the rebellion only recorded the
actions and leadership of the men involved. Lynn's bold role
was illuminated much later when a historian, Margaret Ó
hÓgartaigh, wrote Kathleen's biography, *Kathleen Lynn,
Irishwoman, Patriot, Doctor,* published in 2006. In Kathleen's
reminiscences of April 1916, during Holy Week before Easter,
she wrote, "On a moonless night, I went out with the car to St
Edna's [Irish-language school established by nationalist leader
Padraig Pearse] where the guys loaded it with ammunition and
put theatrical stuff on top of it. Hoping to get through [British

blockades] Willie Pearse [Padraig's brother] brought it in with me and landed it safely in Liberty Hall where there were many willing hands to unload it." (The explanations in brackets were added by Ó hÓgartaigh.)

Ammunition and gun running! It was also revealed that Kathleen's basement on Belgrave Road was used to store ammunition. No wonder their street was called "Revolutionary Road" by the underground. The aunts, unbeknownst to them, were living next to an ammunition dump!

How I wish I knew if the aunts had known Kathleen! Nonetheless, this discovery was remarkable and fired my imagination.

1920

This takes us to 1920, when our story begins, when Lucie received the telegram telling her of Elfie's death. They were all gone.

She left her girls with Shepherd, a nanny, and a house-keeper who took them for the summer months to the coast at Shady Side, Maryland, traveling there on the *Emma Giles*, a steam paddle wheeler. Shepherd joined them when he could. At the end of summer, the girls returned to their home at St. Elizabeths to start the fall semester in their District of Columbia schools.

MARCH 1921

Lucie closed the door on RockView for the last time and handed the keys to her solicitor's assistant in March 1921. A month earlier Lucie had received a letter from Shepherd wondering just when she planned to come home. The girls missed her and so did he. He was teaching physiology part time at George Washington University. His position at St. Elizabeths had changed when research shifted focus from the neurological and physiological to the psychoanalytic study introduced by Sigmund Freud. He was also busy with a six-month course at the Bureau of Veterans Affairs in neuropsychiatry. She needed to come home.

She missed her family, too. She had been in Dublin for almost a year, sorting papers, finding bank books, settling accounts, trying to decide what to have shipped to America and what to give away, and visiting with her many friends. It was like sifting through their lives, and frequent social distractions were most welcome. Frances, Alfreda, and Thomas had lots of room in their old house, and they had kept everything.

The day after Lucie received her husband's letter, she called a shipping firm. A team of workers arrived by the end of the week and began packing up the house. In the end, the things she had not cleaned out—letters, glasses, pencils, pens, prayer books, books, Bibles—in bedside tables were all left as is, the drawers full. She marked and piled the pieces she wanted sent: desks, dressers, tables, chairs, paintings, books, silver, dishes . . . There were so many memories in these objects, she could not leave them behind. They were her history.

I have the handwritten ship's manifest, listing each piece in the shipment, thankfully sparing us the contents of the drawers. Lucie was sure she would have time for the small things when she got home, or so she thought. Everything went to Washington, DC, where many of Thomas's paintings were hung, furniture was arranged, and coveted objects found places in their home. Drawers were eventually emptied into boxes and stored for later examination. It is in these dumped-in boxes that I found a collection of their lives, the material that inspired *Whispers*.

LUCIE, SHEPHERD, AND UCLA

Lucie's life took a fortunate turn in 1924, when Shepherd became a professor and the first department chair at the new psychology department at the University of California, Los Angeles. They moved across the country to California. The campus started in downtown Los Angeles, and the Franz family made their new home at 1857 Kingsley Ave. When UCLA outgrew the downtown campus and moved to Westwood, where it remains today, Lucie and Shepherd bought a large Spanish-style home on Levering Avenue in Westwood. It became well known as a campus social center for faculty, students, and academic visitors who flocked to Lucie's generous hospitality and Shepherd's warm welcome. The professor was famous, but Lucie was the magnet. Their open-door policy was in full force. Shepherd was a smoker and kept his desk in the living room, where he smoked and worked as my grandmother entertained around him.

Shepherd Ivory Franz's distinguished career held the beginnings of the blossoming field of neuropsychology. As head of the department at UCLA, he attracted talented faculty and students and built a solid reputation for his field. He died of ALS October 14, 1933. When a new psychology building was built at UCLA in 1950, with an inverted fountain out in front, it was named Franz Hall.

Many of the boxes shipped in 1921 were never opened and, when Lucie died, they went into her daughters' garages. The furniture, silver, dishes, and paintings are distributed among Lucie's grandchildren today, but few in the next generation know the story of this bounty of their personal history. I received my share and took everything that no one else wanted. My exploration began about eight years later, when I started opening boxes . . .

THOMAS, ELIZA, AND JAMES

Thomas died on March 20, 1901, less than two months after his ninetieth birthday celebration. He was buried beside his wife, Sarah, and their children in Mount Jerome cemetery, Dublin. Frances and Elfie are also buried there. Lucie's father, James Simpson Niven, died a revered member of the community in London, Ontario, in 1916.

Lucie came to live with us after my mother came out of the TB sanitarium. She died in 1949 while living with my parents, Betty and Yngve Ahlm; my brother, Shepherd; and me. The night before she died, unexpectedly from a heart attack, she cooked food for the family to eat while she was away, packed her bag, and planned to take the Southern Pacific "night owl" the following evening to San Francisco to visit friends. She would have loved this story because she liked a good ending. I can hear her saying, "I just caught the wrong train."

LUCIE'S LEGACY

Granny Lucie, your story has been told for you, placing you and yours in time and history. I hope the tale will give life to the many personal treasures you brought across the ocean to America that will continue to be disbursed in our family, as the generations multiply.

You were an authentic person who embraced each of us and took life as it came, with a light touch. Your gifts to us were many: you taught us to laugh at life and ourselves, read for pleasure, enjoy the communion of food and drink, and tell stories as a powerful part of family and friendship. You taught us by example the pattern for passing on a human legacy, stories told around the hearth and table, as old as time. We have these deep yet simple tools ingrained in us. As a result, we know how to keep the thread of past lives with us, through story and imagination. In the end we see our lives painted on a larger canvas, reaching back as we move forward.

Christina

FAMILY PHOTOS

Rebecca Jane "Lily" Young Niven   1849 –1882

Christening 1911   Elizabeth Knox Franz
Frances, Lucie, Alfreda & Theodora

Thomas Urry Young   1812 – 1902

Christmas 1858   Frances, Lily, Henry & Alfreda Young

Wedding 1873 — Lily Young & James Simpson Niven

Lucie Mary Niven 1874 – 1949

Lucie and Shepherd's honeymoon, 1902, visiting the aunts at Rock View

Shepherd and Lucie, newlyweds, in Rock View garden

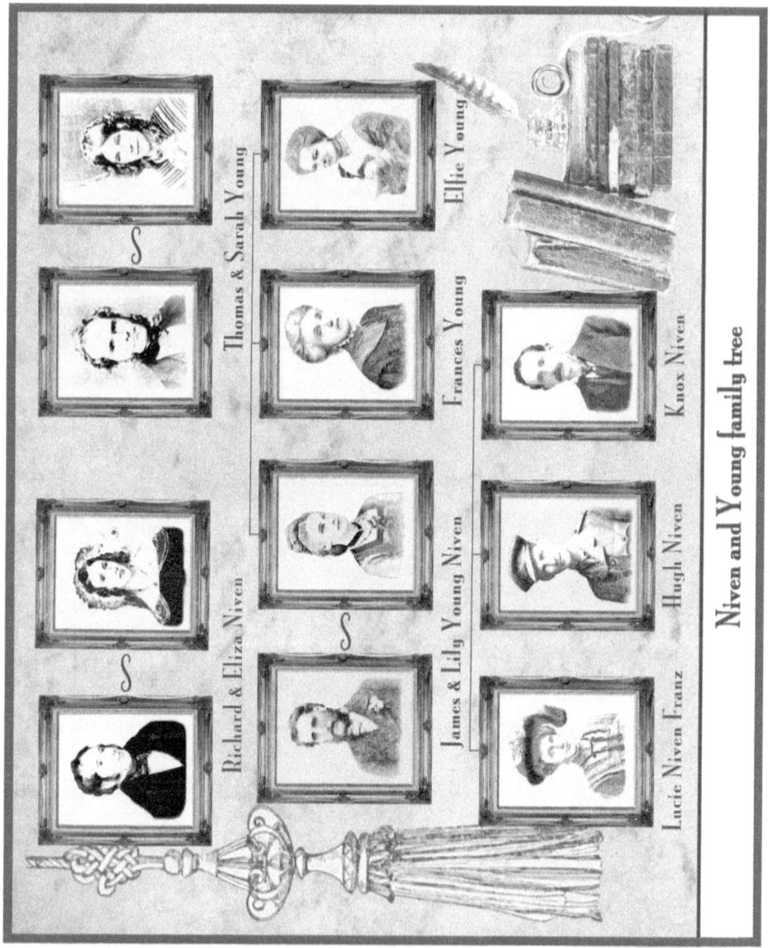

Thomas & Sarah Young
Elfie Young
Frances Young
Knox Niven
Richard & Eliza Niven
James & Lily Young Niven
Hugh Niven
Lucie Niven Franz
Niven and Young family tree

Lucie Niven married June 18, 1902
London, Ontario at St. Paul's Cathedral

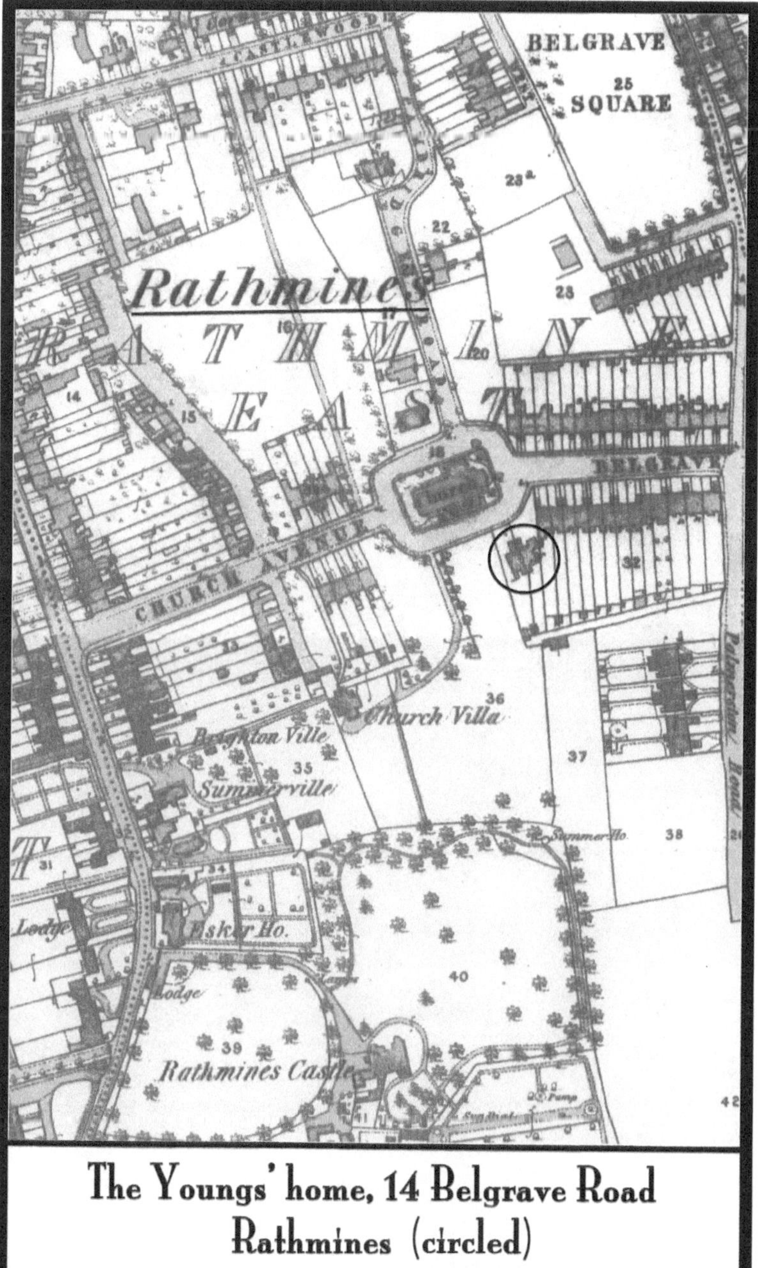

The Youngs' home, 14 Belgrave Road
Rathmines (circled)

HISTORICAL NOTES

Ireland's history as a colonial outpost of Great Britain began as early as 1169, when the Catholic Anglo-Normans (English-French) came across the Irish Sea to usurp power from the Irish and take command of their people and resources. Ireland was Britain's first colony. They did not want other invaders to take ownership of this strategic island. It would have been too easy to launch warfare on the British island using the numerous short crossings of the Irish Sea, ranging from twelve to fifty miles.

Colonization is an old human story and rarely ends well. This one has left a sad, destructive trail for centuries. History tells us no one likes occupation and domination by a foreign power. Irish history carries centuries of human stories of injustice passed, generation to generation, in legend, song, and myth, like a festering wound never healing, a constant reminder of powerlessness. Thus, the seeds of revolution were sown and had deep roots, like an ancient oak you pass each day, a living reminder of the past. It was only a question of when.

The invasion of Ireland was also a practical matter. England needed more land and subjects to provide tribute, to fill and feed their legions for constant campaigns to gain and defend turf. They saw this as their destiny, a logical and necessary means of taking their place as a world power. The Pope welcomed their conquest, hoping to regain control over corrupt Catholic monasteries created long ago, in the fifth century, by St. Patrick that had become remote, unruly, and unanswerable to Rome.

Ireland was historically fragmented by indigenous kingdoms and clans who were constantly at war for the same spoils sought by the invading Anglo-Normans: land, manpower, and treasure. Blood feuds and tribal antagonisms allowed the Anglo-Normans, over time, to split the Irish ranks and consolidate power. For three hundred years the struggles continued, and in 1537 many, but not all, Irish kings pledged allegiance to the invaders and King Henry VIII.

It was under the Irish kings and the Norman Catholics that the Catholic Church gained enormous importance for the indigenous people. It was the unifying cultural factor for the Irish underclass, who had no means of control over the circumstances of their lives. The Irish had essentially become slaves in their own country.

By the 1600s Britain had converted to a Protestant nation. For the British to continue control over the Irish Catholics, who were most of the population, harsh penal laws were passed, and the occupying British, referred to as the "Anglo-Irish Ascendancy" or "Protestant Ascendancy," began the task of enforcing these laws. These laws limited Catholic ownership of land, access to education, voting, and the right to bear arms. By the end of the eighteenth century, Irish Catholic ownership of land was minuscule.

In the early years of the nineteenth century, some of the Anglo-Irish Ascendancy, with roots in Ireland since the time of the Normans, began to recognize the need for reform. The Catholic Emancipation Act of 1829, passed by the British Parliament, allowed a limited number of Irish Catholics to be elected to the British Parliament but also reduced the voting rights for Irish peasants. This continued oppression caused the Irish to clamor for land reform. Some, not all, Anglo-Irish sympathized with the Irish desire for land ownership in their own country.

The Great Famine, the tragedy of the An Gorta Mór, in the 1840s, brought on by a potato blight and compounded by British policies, resulted in extraordinary death tolls among the Irish Catholics, causing large numbers of Irish to emigrate for a better life. The Irish population plummeted by 2.7 million people over the next forty years, down from 6.5 million in 1841 to 3.8 million in 1881.

This was the historical backstory at play in the Irish landscape when my great-great-grandparents, Anglo-Irish Thomas and Sarah Young, teachers and newlyweds, arrived in Dublin in 1837, full of hope and energy to help educate the Irish, start a family, and build a life across the Irish Sea from their family home in Cheltenham, England.

In the late nineteenth and early twentieth centuries, nationalism was on the rise in Ireland and a strange-bedfellow relationship was slowly developing between the Anglo-Irish, who were involved in political and intellectual leadership, and the disenfranchised Irish. Fragmented groups of the Irish were organizing revolutionary cells using guerrilla tactics to destabilize the occupying British military and government. The Irish and sympathetic Anglo-Irish coalesced around the goal, if not the violent methods used by some Irish organizations, of more Irish control over their own lives and eventual Home Rule for Ireland.

The cry for independence was fraught with risk for the Anglo-Irish, who had a privileged life with British protection. Yet living in Ireland, the Youngs and their contemporaries saw, if at a distance, the injustices visited upon the Irish and experienced the stratified society that was sending the youth and promise of both Anglo and Irish families to distant lands for a better life.

Change was coming. The gathering momentum of human

suffering was not to be contained; the dam was breaching and promised messy business ahead.

How did Anglo-Irish, like Sarah and Thomas, respond to the changing world around them? How did it affect their lives and the lives of their families? Did they choose to be observers or participants in a society moving toward change? Our story explores these and many more age-old human questions.

ACKNOWLEDGMENTS

Without the guidance and skilled teaching ability of my great friend and editor Susan Lyn McCombs, this novel would never have seen the light of day—or certainly not in its final form. She pushed; questioned; made me do research, go deeper, write more, cut what I'd written; and helped me craft the story and my characters. I will be forever grateful to have had her as a working partner on *Whispers Across a Sea* and for her friendship.

And my neighbor, friend, photographer, and graphic designer extraordinaire Sunny Scott has listened on our walks, inspired me, and skillfully made the photos I inherited come to life again.

No one has believed in me or been a stronger champion during this journey than my husband, Chuck Holloway. His faith and encouragement kept me going, as did his belief in my successfully finishing *Whispers Across a Sea*.

ABOUT THE AUTHOR

Christina Holloway has not lived a quiet life. Two years after she was born in England, her family escaped the Blitz in London and moved to California to live with her grandmother Lucie. When Christina was a child, her imagination was fired by the colorful stories of her granny Lucie's life in late Victorian Ireland.

Christina later inherited Lucie's Irish treasures, including personal letters, photos, paintings, and, best of all, Lucie's grandfather's diary, items that collectively inspired Christina's debut historical novel, Whispers Across a Sea.

For fifty years, Christina has been a leader in environmental education and land conservation in the San Francisco Bay Area. Her passion for environmental activism began in April 1970, when she pushed her four-month-old son in a stroller in the first ever Earth Day march. Using her leadership and communication skills, she cofounded the Environmental

Volunteers and became the first co–executive director of the Trust for Hidden Villa. She served on the boards of the Peninsula Open Space Trust, Yosemite Association, and Yosemite Fund for over two decades. In 2009, she played a key role in the complex merger of the two Yosemite nonprofits to form the current Yosemite Conservancy. From 1979 to 1980, she served as president of the Junior League of Palo Alto.

Christina lives on the Stanford campus with her husband, a retired professor and founder of the Center for Entrepreneurial Studies at the Graduate School of Business. They have three children and seven grandchildren. For further information about Christina and her book, please visit www.christinahollowayauthor.com.